Praise for the novels of Stefanie London

"Funny and sweet, with great characters and a diva dog who completely stole my heart. I devoured this book in one sitting!"
—Jennifer Probst, *New York Times* bestselling author, on *The Dachshund Wears Prada*

"London pairs…satisfying romance with a deep dive into dysfunctional family dynamics, the corrosive power of secrets, and the importance of communication. This is sure to win hearts."
—*Publishers Weekly* on *Pets of Park Avenue*

"This is the rom-com Carrie Bradshaw would have written if she were a dog person, and I'm obsessed!"
—Teri Wilson, *USA TODAY* bestselling author of *A Spot of Trouble*, on *The Dachshund Wears Prada*

"One of the year's most delightful rom-coms. Ms. London pens a sparkling confection of all the feels and I devoured it."
—Julia London, *New York Times* bestselling author, on *The Dachshund Wears Prada*

"London's likable characters resonate with hidden depths as she mines their hearts to deliver a fun, revealing story that will have readers rooting wholeheartedly for love—and dogs—to conquer all."
—*Shelf Awareness* on *Pets of Park Avenue*

SUSAN MALLERY

SYNITHIA WILLIAMS
STEFANIE LONDON

suddenly
this
summer

CANARY STREET PRESS

CANARY STREET PRESS™

Recycling programs for this product may not exist in your area.

ISBN-13: 978-1-335-00487-1

Suddenly This Summer

Copyright © 2023 by Harlequin Enterprises ULC

Say You'll Stay
First published in 2021. This edition published in 2023.
Copyright © 2021 by Susan Mallery, Inc.

This Time for Keeps
Copyright © 2023 by Synithia R. Williams

Best Man Next Door
Copyright © 2023 by Stefanie Little

For questions and comments about the quality of this book, please contact us at CustomerService@Harlequin.com.

Canary Street Press
22 Adelaide St. West, 41st Floor
Toronto, Ontario M5H 4E3, Canada
CanaryStPress.com

Printed in U.S.A.

CONTENTS

SAY YOU'LL STAY   7
Susan Mallery

THIS TIME FOR KEEPS   143
Synithia Williams

BEST MAN NEXT DOOR   253
Stefanie London

SAY YOU'LL STAY

Susan Mallery

Dear Reader,

I love a Christmas book. I really do. I love reading them and I really love writing them. Even so, you're probably wondering why I'm talking about that in what appears to be an anthology about, um, well, summer.

Say You'll Stay is a "prequel" to my holidaycentric Christmas books set in the amazing little town of Wishing Tree. To begin the series, I decided to do a "before" book, set in the summer. Winter certainly has its place, but let's be honest—everyone loves a summer romance. Plus, I knew if I started the book in July, I could take advantage of fun "Christmas in July" Wishing Tree activities. Trust me, you'll see what I mean on the very first page.

But the best part of the story is watching Shaye Harper figure out what home means. Because isn't that what we all want? A place to belong, a place where we know people care, a place to rest our weary heart. Shaye would tell you Wishing Tree isn't her final destination. She's only passing through. Except there's something a little wonderful about the town and the people, and there's something kind of amazing about having the man of your dreams look you in the eye and ask you to "say you'll stay."

Welcome to Wishing Tree and welcome to summer.

Happy reading,

Susan

CHAPTER ONE

SHAYE HARPER STARED at the crowd on the street. She'd grown up in a small town, so she was used to the quirks, but something very strange was happening here.

"I don't get it," she said aloud.

"It's a 5K run."

She turned toward the voice and saw a guy about her age smiling at her. As her head barely came to his shoulder, she would guess he was six feet tall. Cute, with big brown eyes, wavy brown hair and an easy smile.

"I understand the 5K part," she told him with a laugh. "It's the antlers that have me confused."

"It's Christmas in July. Every year on July 5, the three-week celebration launches with the 5K Reindeer Run."

"Christmas in July?"

"Yeah. We take our holidays very seriously here in Wishing Tree. Especially Christmas."

She glanced back at the participants, most dressed in shorts and T-shirts, all wearing reindeer-antler headbands. They ran or walked through the center of town. Crowds lined the route.

Now that she looked more closely, she could see the signs on several of the stores. They were very holiday-centric, with names like Jingle Coffee and Santa Baby Boutique.

"But it's July," she said. "Yesterday was the Fourth of July."

She would know: she'd spent a very lonely afternoon and evening by herself in a motel just outside of Spokane. Travel for one was not the thrill she'd hoped it would be.

The cute guy smiled again. This time she noticed he had dimples. She'd always been a sucker for a guy with dimples. Thank goodness she was just passing through, otherwise she would be tempted to flirt with him. Flirting often led to liking, and that led to trouble—at least, in her world. The only guys interested in her were disasters. Sad but true. Therefore, the only way to keep herself safe was to avoid men—especially men with yummy eyes and cute dimples.

"You're not from around here, are you?"

"No. I'm from a small town in Iowa." She looked at the last of the walkers, heading out of the town square. A square that was, oddly, round. "We have our traditions, but no one ever wears antlers."

"Christmas in July is a big thing for us," he said. "Like I said, it starts with the 5K, then we have the holiday bake-off, the tree-lighting at 10:00 p.m. on the fifteenth, the Sparklefest Ball, and finally the classic car show. That's on the twenty-fifth, the last day of the celebration. There's a big parade, too."

"With Santa?" she asked as the people around them started drifting away.

"Of course."

"Seriously? You have a Santa in a parade in July?"

"*Christmas* in July."

"Sure. Why not. But why is the tree-lighting on

the fifteenth? Why not tonight? And what tree do you light?"

"A Christmas tree, of course. It goes right there." He pointed. "In the middle of The Wreath."

"The what?"

"The Wreath. It's like our town square, only it's round. See all the businesses around it? They're in a circle." The smile and the dimples returned. "Come on. You have to admit, it's charming. I'm Lawson."

"Shaye. So you're a hometown boy?"

"Born and raised." He looked past her. "I've seen a lot of the world, and to me there's no place better than Wishing Tree."

There was something in his tone: the promise of a story. Not that she knew him well enough to ask what it was. She supposed everyone had past experiences to deal with. She certainly did.

"Are you here with your family?" he asked.

"No. I'm by myself. I was driving west on the highway when I saw the sign for Judy's Hand Pies, so I decided to stop." She paused, not sure if that made her sound odd. "I had them for the first time yesterday, and they were delicious." She smiled. "I guess I like pie."

"Me, too. Come on, let me buy you lunch at Judy's Hand Pies." He winked. "I happen to know the owner."

She laughed. "It's a small town, Lawson. I'm pretty sure you know a lot of people who live here."

"Not all of them. And we get a lot of tourists so there are plenty of new people to meet." He winked again. "Meeting new people can be a lot of fun."

She wanted to say that she wasn't exactly a tourist— she was just passing through on her way to somewhere else—but decided there was no point. She would have a quick lunch with him before getting back in her car and driving the remaining distance to her destination.

The crowds had thinned out since the last of the runners had passed by. She and Lawson walked the short distance to Judy's Hand Pies. The storefront was similar to the one she'd seen in Spokane. There were big windows with a mouthwatering display of hand pies and a small Help Wanted sign in the corner. When they stepped inside they were greeted by a pregnant woman, who looked at Lawson, then at her. Her brows rose as her expression shifted from welcoming to speculative.

"I didn't expect to see you here today," the woman said.

Lawson turned to Shaye. "This is my sister, Adien. Sis, this is Shaye. We met at the start of the 5K."

Adien mouthed *Quick work* before smiling at Shaye. "Nice to meet you. Welcome to Wishing Tree."

"Thank you." She looked at Lawson. "So your family owns Judy's Hand Pies?"

"What?" Adien laughed. "I wish, but no. I work here part-time." She patted her belly. "At least, I will for the next month. Then this one will make an appearance."

Shaye ignored the little stab of envy that pricked her heart. She'd always wanted a family, but so far she wasn't even close to having that happen. And given how she'd sworn off men, well, the whole falling-in-love-getting-married-and-having-a-baby plan was going to be a real challenge.

Adien pointed out the specials, then retrieved a small to-go box. "What'll you have?"

Shaye chose a chicken mushroom and a spinach feta, along with a fresh berry pie for dessert. Lawson picked two chicken sausage hand pies and a beef stroganoff. He also chose a berry pie, and they each took a can of soda. They had a brief argument about paying, which Adien settled by taking Lawson's money rather than Shaye's, then they grabbed plenty of napkins before heading to the seating area at the far side of The Wreath.

As it wasn't yet noon, there were plenty of empty picnic tables. They chose one in the shade. While it was still only in the midseventies, it would be getting hot later in the day. From what Shaye had heard on the local Spokane news, the start to summer in the Pacific Northwest had been a warm one.

They settled across from each other. Lawson passed out the food, while she split the napkins between them.

She took a bite of the chicken pie and had to hold in a moan.

He grinned. "As good as you remember?"

"Better. I thought the store in Spokane was the only one, but I guess they're a chain."

"Mostly in the western half of the country. Toby—he's the owner—started in Austin, using his grandmother's hand-pie recipe. She's the Judy in Judy's Hand Pies."

"How did he get from Austin to here?"

"He grew up here." Lawson's brown eyes crinkled with amusement. "You can take the boy out of Wishing Tree…"

"But you can't take Wishing Tree out of the boy. I get it."

Up close, Lawson was even better-looking than he had been at a distance. He was casually dressed in jeans and a T-shirt, but he had an air of confidence about him, as if he knew he could take care of himself in any situation. He was strong—she could see the outline of muscles in his shoulders, arms and chest—which could have been intimidating, but there was also something friendly and welcoming in the way he looked at her.

"Toby came back," Lawson added. "Last fall. Right about the time I came home."

"Where had you been?"

"All over. I did an eight-year stint in the army. Spent time in a lot of the US, then did tours through Germany and Afghanistan."

Her eyes widened. "Doing what?"

The smile returned. "I'm a car mechanic. Been crazy about cars since I was maybe three. I started working in a local repair shop here in town when I was fourteen. When I enlisted, they put me to work doing what I do best. If you have a Jeep or a Humvee break down, I'm your man."

"Sorry to disappoint. I drive a ten-year-old pickup."

"I can fix that, too."

His smile was infectious and nearly as yummy as the pies.

"My dad was a car guy," she said. "I loved hanging out with him, so I learned to help. We used to restore old cars together. Every spring he'd go find some old clunker, and we'd spend the summer making it right. It was fun."

Lawson's eyes lit up. "It is. One day I want that for my hobby. Just not now."

She finished her chicken mushroom and started on the spinach feta.

"So you got out of the army a year ago?" she asked.

"No." He raised a shoulder. "I was honorably discharged just about *two* years ago, but I didn't make it home until last fall."

"What were you doing for that year?" She paused. "Sorry. I'm asking too many questions. I'm kind of curious by nature."

"Curiosity is a good thing. It's how we learn." He smiled. "Let's just say that transitioning to civilian life isn't always easy. I knew I had some things to work through, and I didn't want to do that here. So I took a year to travel cross-country, working in gas stations and repair shops along the way. I got my head right, then came back."

He returned his attention to her. "And here I am. I work at the same auto-repair shop I did when I was fourteen. The owner's a good guy with two daughters who have no interest in the business. I'm taking online small-business-management classes and saving my money so I can buy him out in five years."

The flutter-inducing smile returned. "I've been saving since I was fifteen. Auto-repair shops are expensive."

"I can imagine."

She kept her tone light, but on the inside, she was openmouthed in shock and more impressed by a guy than she had been in probably forever. The men she knew tended to drift toward whatever easy money-making scheme they'd come up with—probably over one too many beers. They were opportunistic, thoughtless and likely to disappoint. Well, not her father, but he'd been the exception.

"You remind me of my dad," she blurted, then wondered if he would take that wrong. "I mean that in a good way. He was the best man I've ever known."

His steady gaze locked with hers. "That's a powerful compliment. Thank you."

"You're welcome."

LAWSON EASLEY KNEW he was in trouble. He'd assumed he was immune to a pretty face, but he'd been wrong. The second he saw Shaye, with her long red hair and freckles, he'd felt a kick in the gut that had about sent him to his knees. But that was nothing: appearances were superficial. The real problem was the more she talked, the more he liked her.

"Where is your father now?" he asked, picking up his berry pie.

She held in a sigh. "I lost him three years ago. He had a heart attack and died. It was really unexpected. It was just the three of us. Neither of my parents had any family, so we were tight. When we lost him, my mom and I were both in shock."

She tried to smile. "I moved back home to stay with her for a few months. I'd been going to college part-time, working the rest of the time to pay for it. My parents never had any money. My dad worked for the post office, and my mom had health problems, so she couldn't always hold down a job. They'd offered to take out a mortgage on the house to pay for school, but I wouldn't let them. They'd worked hard to pay off the house, and it was going to keep them safe during their retirement. I couldn't take that."

"I get it," he said. "All our lives, they take care of us, but then something shifts, and we start thinking about taking care of them."

She nodded. "It was exactly like that. Then he died, and I was so grateful my mom had the house, free and clear. He had a small life insurance policy, so she was going to be fine. I was just thinking of reapplying for college when she died, too."

She looked at him, her beautiful green eyes filling with tears that she quickly blinked away.

"She was sleeping late, which she sometimes did. It was no big deal, but then I got a feeling something was wrong. I went into her bedroom, and she'd died in the night."

Instinctively, he reached across the picnic table and took her hand in his. "I'm sorry. That must have been so hard on you. Losing them both like that."

"It was. They both went so fast, with no warning. I just… I fell apart. I didn't have any family, and I didn't know what to do with my life. My friends helped, but they were busy. It was a bad time."

She pulled back her hand and looked at him. "I have no idea why I just told you all that. You must think I'm very strange."

"I think you've been through a lot, and you're coming out the other side. Not everyone does. Be proud of the progress you've made."

She offered a smile that made his breath catch.

"I guess you'd know about dealing with the unexpected," she murmured.

He nodded slowly. "I've seen some things. I might have spent eight years working on vehicles, but I was close to the action in Afghanistan."

"I can't imagine what that was like. Where'd you get the courage to go?"

"Go where?"

"To enlist, knowing there was a war going on. Several. You had no way of being sure you'd come back."

"It's important to serve."

She smiled, and the whole world lit up again. "Just like that? You went because it was the right thing to do?"

He didn't understand her question but answered, "Yes."

"Wow."

"That's not wow-worthy."

She laughed. "It kind of is, but I'll let it go. Are you glad to be home?"

"I am. I'm ready for the next part of my life." He hesitated, then decided to confide in her. "I'm thinking of buying a house."

"Good for you."

"The down payment will eat into my savings, but I want to be settled. Right now I rent an apartment over my sister's garage. I like being close to Adien and her family, but I think it's time for a little separation."

"Is she your only sibling?"

"No. I'm one of five. I'm the middle kid, but the oldest boy. My two older sisters are still in town, but my younger sister and brother both wanted to see the world. My folks are still here. My mom has four grandchildren and one on the way, and she's still complaining she wants more."

"You're feeling pressure?"

He grinned. "Every now and then I have to deal with her tears as she tries to guilt me into fathering a few grandbabies."

"So far you've resisted?"

"I think I want to get married first. I'm traditional that way."

"Me, too."

They looked at each other, then smiled.

"Want to take a walk?" he asked. "I can show you around The Wreath. It should stay quiet. The 5K ends at String of Lights Park, where there's a whole barbecue set up for the participants and families. People won't make their way back into The Wreath for a couple more hours." He winked. "I can give you all kinds of insider information."

"I'd like that."

They tossed their trash and put their soda cans into the recycling bin. Lawson pointed to the first store on their left.

"Navidad Mexican Café. Everything's good. Seriously, their combo platters are the best, and my sisters and mom swear the margaritas are delicious."

Shaye grinned up at him. "You're not a margarita kind of guy?"

"Not my thing. Okay, next is Holiday Spirits. That's a bar. And they mean what the name says. Spirits."

"I don't get it."

"Hard liquor. No beer or wine. Howard, the owner, is very fussy about that. And while there's a food menu, he doesn't like when people order from it."

Shaye laughed. "Then, why does he offer it?"

"I have no idea." He pointed. "You know about Judy's Hand Pies, so there's no need to explain that."

They took a few more steps.

"We should go in here," he said.

"Yule Read Books? I love the name."

"It's a bookstore-slash-gift store. There's a lot of girl stuff like scented lotion and candles."

Her mouth twitched as if she were trying not to smile. "You don't enjoy scented lotion?"

"Not personally, but I like it on the women in my life."

Her eyebrows rose. "*Women* as in plural? More than one at a time? Lawson, you shock me."

He groaned. "I meant my sisters and my mom. They like to wear different scents, and it's nice. They always smell good."

"And the future Mrs. Lawson…"

"Easley," he offered. "As of now, she's being elusive, but I'm pretty sure she's going to smell good, too."

"Have you ever been married?"

"I was engaged once. She decided Wishing Tree wasn't for her, and I couldn't imagine living anywhere else."

They were standing nice and close. He liked that. Lawson thought briefly about kissing her. He already knew it would be a good kiss, the kind that not only got his blood pumping but actually meant something. Those were the kisses that mattered. He wasn't interested in a single night—not anymore. He wanted a relationship, and a first kiss often told him if that was going to happen. But it seemed a little soon, and he didn't want to rush things. Not when everything about Shaye felt so…right.

"Let's go check it out," she said, pointing to the bookstore. "I could use a good book and some scented lotion. You can help me pick out the right one."

"I can suggest several books," he teased.

She gave him a gentle push. "I meant the lotion."

"I knew that."

"I knew you knew."

They were both still laughing when they walked inside.

CHAPTER TWO

SHAYE LIKED THE store right away. There were big windows that let in lots of light, and the book displays just made her plain happy. There were at least a dozen people inside, mostly families or couples. The kids' book section had a fluffy rug on the floor and big stuffed animals that could be climbed on or leaned against.

Lawson put his hand on the small of her back and pointed to the gift section of the store. She was aware of the imprint of his hand—warm even through her blouse. The touch was oddly intimate, which surprised her, but not nearly as much as her instinct to step closer to him. A sure sign she liked him.

She briefly reminded herself of her last relationship. Calling it a disaster didn't come close to capturing the awfulness of what had happened. Worse, she'd simply gone along with the plan because she'd been sad and lonely and it had been better than spinning her wheels in her hometown. Although, when it came to Lawson, she was in little danger. She was, after all, simply passing through on her way to Seattle. It wasn't as if she were sticking around. She would enjoy a few more minutes with a kind, funny, handsome guy, then be on her way. Back on the highway, daydreaming about what could have been with Lawson would be a happy way to pass the time and the miles.

They walked over to a display of scented body lotion. She stared at the array of bottles.

"There are a lot of choices."

Lawson smiled. "What scents do you like?"

"Nothing too sweet. I don't want to smell like a sugar cookie or chocolate cake."

His brows rose. "I've never smelled chocolate-cake lotion. It doesn't sound very good."

She picked up a tester bottle and handed it to him. "You'll like this one."

He glanced at the label. "Vanilla?"

"Guys like that. I read it somewhere. Men like the smell of vanilla." She tried not to smile. "Personally I think it's about baking and their mothers, but I'm not a psychologist, so maybe not."

He put down the bottle. "Yeah, not that one."

They agreed on the appeal of coconut anything and that some of the floral scents were too overwhelming.

He picked up a bottle and sniffed but didn't hand it to her.

"What?" she asked with a laugh. "You obviously like it."

"I'm not willing to admit that."

She stepped close, took it from him and read the label. "*Vanilla Coconut.*" She grinned. "So Mom and sexy girls on the beach? That is a weird visual."

He winced. "Don't go there. I can't handle it. You've ruined vanilla for me forever."

"I think you'll recover."

They continued to sniff the various tester bottles. Lawson picked up one and held it to his nose. His lips curved into a smile.

"This one," he said, passing it to her.

She inhaled the scent and immediately felt herself relax. "Beachy, but not too sweet. I love it." She glanced at the label. "*Coconut Lime Verbena.* I need this in my life."

She looked at the display of bottles for sale. Lawson spotted it first and picked up two bottles, along with a bar of soap.

"Layering is important," he said, his voice teasing.

"You really do have sisters."

"Told you. But I held my own."

"Yeah, not if you know about layering."

He laughed. "Come on. We have one more stop in the store. I think you're going to like it."

He led her to a back corner where there was a small table displaying fudge. The sign claimed it was made locally.

Despite her big lunch, Shaye was suddenly hungry for chocolate. "I love fudge."

"Good. Theirs is really good. I don't know much about the candymaker. I know he's relatively new to the area, and he sells his work in different stores around town. I've tasted all the flavors. They're great. It's just a matter of what you like."

Shaye took in the beautiful display, the lotions Lawson held and the ambience of the store. It had been a perfect couple of hours. Maybe too perfect. Her good mood deflated as she wondered if she was witnessing a very polished performance.

She turned to him. "Is this a regular thing for you? A friendly lunch, then time here where we sample lotions and you ply me with fudge?"

His look of confusion was so genuine, she almost believed him. "What are you talking about?"

Before she could explain, something dark flashed in his eyes. "You think I'm playing you," he said, his tone hurt. "You think I do this all the time."

"It's effective, I'll give you that." She wanted to believe, but there had been too many guys who'd taken advantage of her in the past.

"You don't know me," he said.

"That's true."

His expression tightened. "Shaye, no. Just no. I don't do that, and this isn't an act. I've been back a year, and you're the first woman I've—" He pressed his lips together. "The last girl I brought in here was Cori, and I dated her in high school."

And just like that, her wariness and almost-mad faded. She stared into his eyes and saw nothing but honest concern and a little disappointment.

"I'm sorry," she said, immediately feeling foolish. "I shouldn't have judged you."

"Somebody hurt you."

"More than one somebody."

His dark gaze locked with hers. "Can I buy you some fudge?"

A simple question that shouldn't have been more than it was, but somehow Shaye sensed she was being tested. Not by Lawson so much as by herself. Was she going to assume all men were jerks, or was she willing to accept that there were still really nice guys in the world?

She smiled. "I'd like that."

They discussed the various flavors before she settled on one. "I'm going classic," she said, reaching for a square of the chocolate walnut.

"Always a good choice."

They started for the cash register. Partway there, a woman with a baby in her arms ran up to Shaye.

"I've lost Joey. I can't believe it. Would you hold Jessie, please?"

Before Shaye could answer, a baby was thrust into her arms, and the woman ran off yelling for Joey.

Shaye stared into the big, blue eyes of a really cute baby who didn't seem the least bit rattled by what had just happened.

"How could that mother do that? She doesn't know me." She shifted the baby, feeling awkward and not exactly sure how to hold her. She knew she was supposed to support her head and—

Lawson chuckled. "Okay, give her to me."

He set the lotion and fudge on a shelf and took the baby, holding her expertly and swaying back and forth.

"You're a beautiful girl, aren't you?" he said softly. "You're going to be a heartbreaker. That has to upset your daddy. Yes, it does."

The baby smiled and waved her little hands.

"So Adien has more kids than the one she's carrying," Shaye said.

"Two. The baby-to-be is her last, or so she says. I'm not convinced." He flashed her a smile. "Yeah, I do the uncle thing a lot. I like kids, and babies are easy. You tell them what to do, and they never talk back."

"They also never do what you say."

"A flaw in the plan, I'll admit."

The woman returned, a toddler in tow.

"Thanks," she said, taking the baby back from Lawson. "My husband is parking the car and getting the stroller. I thought I could manage, but this one is a runner."

Joey smiled winningly.

"You have a beautiful family," Shaye said.

"Thanks. I appreciate the help."

Keeping a firm grip on her son, she moved toward the exit. Shaye and Lawson walked over to pay for their items. They had a brief tussle over who would pay for what. In the end, Shaye convinced him to let her buy her own fudge, but he insisted on purchasing the lotion.

When they were outside the store, she looked at him.

"I can't believe that woman did that."

"What?" he asked.

"Handed over her baby to a total stranger. She doesn't know me. Why would she trust me not to take off?"

His smile was gentle. "It's Wishing Tree, Shaye. Bad things don't happen here."

"Bad things happen everywhere."

"Okay, sure, but this is a small town filled with good people. She knew her baby was safe with you."

She wanted to believe him. She wanted to know that there were happy places where there was no pain or heartache, only she knew that wasn't possible. Sometimes life was cruel, and sometimes people made stupid mistakes. There was no guarantee of a happy outcome in any given situation.

She felt her good mood shatter and her connection to Lawson break. Suddenly she was standing next to a guy she didn't really know, in a place she was never going to see again.

"I should get back on the road," she said.

"I thought you were in town through the weekend," he said, sounding disappointed.

She shook her head. "I'm on my way to Seattle. I just

saw the sign for Judy's Hand Pies and turned toward Wishing Tree. I was never staying."

His dark gaze locked with hers, and for a second she would have sworn that whatever she'd felt for that short period of time was back, more powerful than before. For a single heartbeat she wanted to say that of course she was staying and that he should ask her out so they could get to know each other. She wanted to offer her number and point out that Seattle wasn't that far, right? They could stay in touch. Only she didn't, because what was the point?

He handed her the small bag with the lotion. "I had a good time," he said quietly. "I enjoyed spending the afternoon with you."

"Me, too."

"If you're ever back this way, you can find me at Wishing Tree Auto Repair."

Despite her conflicted emotions, she laughed. "Is that really what it's called?"

"Yup, and when it's mine, I'm not changing the name."

"Why would you?"

He took a step back. "Bye, Shaye."

She thought maybe he would pull her close and hug her, or even kiss her, but he only waved and turned away, quickly disappearing into the growing crowd. She stood outside of Yule Read Books and wished... Well, she wasn't sure what she wished for, but something other than what she had.

The Wreath was filling with people. Couples and happy families. She thought she caught sight of the woman who had passed her the baby, but she wasn't sure. Shaye stood in the middle of all of it wondering how long it would be until she was able to feel like she belonged somewhere. Going back to Iowa wasn't an option, but moving on didn't seem right, either.

There was nothing waiting for her in Seattle—no friends, no job. She was chasing a memory first made when she was twelve years old. What did she expect to find when she got there?

Sadness settled on her. The deep, down-to-the-bone kind she'd felt when each of her parents had died. It joined the sense of being totally alone in the world. Her friends had drifted away when she'd spent months looking after her mom. There was no other family, and she was totally done with her idiot ex-boyfriend. When she drove out of Wishing Tree, there was literally no one in the world who knew her. No one would miss her or think about her or want her back. She was like a ghost.

Somewhere behind her a child laughed. The sound was so pure, so happy, she turned to see what was happening. A little girl, maybe five or six, had just bitten into a berry hand pie. The crust had crumbled, and there was filling everywhere: on her chin, her cheeks, her hands, and down the front of her dress. Her mom was laughing, too, saying something about making a mess.

It was a silly thing, just a moment in time the family probably wouldn't remember. But it struck Shaye as something hopeful. In a weird way, a sign.

There was nothing waiting for her in Seattle, no reason to get there today or tomorrow. Why not stay in Wishing Tree—just for Christmas in July? She could catch her breath, get her head together, come up with a plan for her future and then leave for the big city.

She didn't consider herself an impulsive person, but lately she'd been making a lot of snap decisions. She walked purposefully toward Judy's Hand Pies. The Help Wanted sign was still in the window. She brushed the front of her blouse, then stepped into the store.

A different woman stood behind the counter. She was older and a little stern-looking until she smiled.

"How can I help you?"

"I was wondering about the job."

The woman's expression instantly brightened. "Are you? That's great. Now, you know it's only part-time and just for the month, right? With all the activities with Christmas in July, we want to have a cart out in The Wreath. The hours are from eleven until three, Tuesday through Saturday. You load up the cart, roll it to your position, then sell pies until your four hours are up or until you sell out. Whichever comes first."

The pay for that few hours wouldn't be much, but it would help. Shaye had the money from the sale of her parents' house, plus her own savings. Only working a few hours a day would give her time to explore the town.

"You interested?" the woman asked.

"I am."

"Then let me get the boss down here."

She picked up a phone and pressed a couple of buttons. Seconds later she said, "I have someone here who wants to apply to work the cart. Uh-huh. Yes, I told her that."

She put down the phone and smiled. "Toby will be right with you."

Toby. Lawson had mentioned him. He was the owner and founder of the company. Suddenly nervous, she wiped her hands on her jeans, then turned when a tall, blond-haired man walked out into the front of the store. He smiled at Shaye.

"I'm Toby Newkirk."

"Shaye Harper."

He waved her in. "Come on back and we'll talk about the job."

Toby reiterated the hours and the short-term nature of the job.

"This is the store's first summer, so we're new to the food-cart scene," he said. "I have no idea if you'll be overwhelmed with customers or will have nothing to do." He smiled. "You'll be paid either way."

She laughed. "I appreciate I'm not on commission. And I am interested, but I have a weird question to ask."

His brows rose, but he didn't speak.

"I'm not from here. In fact I'm moving to Seattle, so this is kind of a pit stop for me. I like the town and think it would be fun to stay for the month, but I don't have anywhere to live and a hotel would be too expensive."

"You'd never find a hotel room," he told her. "Wishing Tree is a popular tourist destination. All the hotels, motels and cabins are booked months in advance."

Her heart sank. So much for staying through Christmas in July.

He took out his phone. "Just this morning my grandmother mentioned a friend of hers has a room for rent. If you'd be interested in that, I can find out if it's still available."

"That would be great," she said eagerly. "As long as the owner is okay with a month-long rental."

"I'll ask."

Thirty minutes later Shaye had filled out a job application and been given the contact information for the room rental. Kathy Vieira was expecting her. If she rented the room, Shaye was going to call Toby and tell him she was taking the job. If not, she would be on her way to Seattle. So either way, she had a plan.

Only as she walked to her truck, she knew what she really wanted was to stay. Not because she'd met a cute guy but because there was something about the town. She could do with a month of unexpected events and odd traditions. And if, in the meantime, she got to know Lawson better, well, that was just a bonus.

LAWSON FOCUSED ON the vegetables he was chopping. His days off were usually Sunday and Monday, and he often spent at least one of them helping his sister, when he could. She was eight months pregnant, with two little ones underfoot. Yesterday, the Fourth of July, had been an all-day event, with friends and family at the park. Everyone had stayed up late for fireworks. Both kids were tired today, and tired meant cranky. If he could help with a little meal prep, he was happy to do it.

At some point he was going to move out of the apartment above the garage and into something of his own. He was still debating buying a house. He wanted his own place, but he was cautious about making the commitment. In part because the down payment would eat into his savings, and he was still on track to buy the auto shop in four years and eight months.

His other worry about buying a house was the woman he hoped to one day have in his life. He wanted them to make the decision together. Choosing a house was an important time in a couple's life, and he felt there could be problems if he already had one she might not have picked herself.

Not that his future life partner was anything but a vague hope at this point. He was open to finding someone. He was looking forward to making a commitment, getting married and raising a family. The only problem seemed to be the lack of someone special. So far she didn't seem to exist.

Or if she did exist, she wasn't interested in sticking around.

"You're looking serious about something," Adien said, walking into the kitchen, her hand rubbing the small of her back.

"Nothing that matters."

"I doubt that. Tell me."

"I wish Shaye hadn't been just passing through."

"The girl from today? She seemed nice. So you liked her?"

He nodded, then scooped the diced cucumbers into the bowl. "I did. She was funny and nice and smart. But she didn't stay." He smiled at his sister. "Kidnapping is not a culturally acceptable way to get a date."

His sister laughed. "Was she kidnapworthy?"

"Maybe. I should have kissed her."

"Wow. You don't usually move that fast."

"I don't usually meet someone like her." He thought about how easily they'd talked all through lunch and how much fun they'd had at the bookstore. "I should have kissed her," he repeated, wishing he had. Wishing he'd said…

What? She'd wanted to leave. Maybe she hadn't felt what he had. Maybe he'd just been a way to pass the time.

"I know I should let it go," he said. "And I will. I just don't like regrets."

"You need to start dating."

"So you've said. I know nearly every age-appropriate woman in Wishing Tree, and none of them are for me."

"Go online."

"I prefer meeting someone in person."

"You're stubborn."

He grinned at her. "It's a family trait."

"Yes, I know." Her humor faded. "I'm sorry about Shaye."

"Me, too. But there's someone for everybody. I still believe that."

"I do, too. You're a great guy. I bet right this second, Shaye's feeling some regrets of her own."

Lawson hoped that was true, although regrets didn't make much difference when Shaye was a hundred and fifty miles away.

CHAPTER THREE

SHAYE LOOKED AT the directions Toby had given her. There was something odd about the street names. Half of them seemed to be trees while the other half were holiday-related. She was to take White Pine Street, cross West Mistletoe Way and turn on Jolly Drive.

"Crazy town," she muttered as she got into her truck. But crazy in a nice way. Maybe *quirky* was a better word.

She pulled out of the parking lot and drove along White Pine. When she got to Jolly Drive, she saw a block of stunning Victorian houses. Some were massive, but a few were more normal-sized. The biggest one had a sign out in front. *Wishing Tree Bed and Breakfast.* Two doors down was the house she was looking for. She parked in front, then grabbed her handbag and started for the front door.

As she approached, she took in the wide front porch, complete with a couple of wicker chairs and a swing. The planter beds were overflowing with blooming flowers and were decorated with little ceramic forest creatures.

The house was three stories, with big windows and plenty of detail in the white shutters and trim. The deep blue paint color was only a few shades darker than the sky.

She knocked on the front door. It opened almost immediately.

"You must be Shaye," the older woman said with a smile. "I'm Kathy. Come on in."

Kathy was probably in her late sixties with shoulder-length brown hair and a lean build. She had on a three-quarter-sleeve T-shirt over crop pants and bright fuchsia sandals. Her toenails were painted the same color.

Shaye had a brief impression of a beautiful, formal living room and a dining room with a period-appropriate chandelier before she was led into a completely modern kitchen. Kathy motioned to the bar stools at the island.

"Toby said you're looking for a room to rent," she said as she pulled a pitcher of what looked like lemonade out of the refrigerator.

"I am." Shaye explained about wanting to stay in town for Christmas in July, before heading to Seattle.

"It's a fun time," Kathy said, setting out two tall glasses, then pouring. "The real excitement is in the winter, of course, but we do a nice job in the summer months, and you don't have to worry about snow."

She sat down and smiled. "Now, let me tell you how I work things. I have a big house, and one of these days I'm going to sell it and move to the new retirement condos they're building, but not just yet."

She picked up her glass. "My Douglas and I lived here nearly forty years. We loved this house. It nearly broke us to buy it when it came up for sale, but we'd always wanted one of the Victorians. She was a poor, run-down girl when we got her, but as our finances improved, we did a little restoration, and this is what you see."

"The house is beautiful," Shaye said, thinking if she rented the room, she would get to live here. A far cry from her family's small 1950s rambler back in Iowa.

"Thank you. I rent out a room from time to time, mostly to have someone else in the house." Kathy's smile returned. "I don't expect you to keep me company other than to say hi if we pass in the hall. The room comes with a private bath and kitchen privileges."

Shaye looked at the gleaming stainless steel appliances. "It's an amazing kitchen. I'd be thrilled to use it."

"I'm in here a lot myself, but there's plenty of room for two. What else? Oh, you have a TV in your room, but you're welcome to come downstairs and use the one in the family room. Guests are fine, but no parties. And overnight visits aren't a problem."

Shaye shook her head. "I don't know anyone in town, so that won't be happening."

Technically she knew Lawson, but what were the odds they would run into each other again? Although he had told her where to find him, which was fun to think about, even if the thought of showing up at his place of work scared the crap out of her. She'd just never been that aggressive when it came to guys. Now if she had an excuse to go there... But she didn't.

And even if she did manage to run into him, the odds of things ever progressing to *overnight visits* seemed improbable. She was only staying in town for the month. Given her sad and humiliating romantic past, avoiding getting involved was really the smart decision.

Kathy named a very reasonable price for the room, then asked, "Would you like to see it?"

"I would. Thank you."

"I have to warn you, it's on the third floor. You have the whole area to yourself, but it's a bit of a climb."

They went upstairs. Shaye admired the hand-carved railing and the wainscoting at the landing.

"This is me," Kathy said, when they reached the second floor. "The master and two more bedrooms."

The third floor opened onto a pretty sitting area with a small sofa and a desk. Kathy pointed to one of the drawers.

"The password for the Wi-Fi is in there. I have one of those booster thingies so the signal is strong up here."

The west side of the third floor was storage. They turned the other way and entered a very large bedroom.

The room was bright, with windows on two walls. Nightstands flanked the queen-size bed. The walls were white, and the bedding was done in various shades of blue. There was a big dresser, with a TV sitting on top, and what looked like the original hardwood floors. Fluffy rugs were scattered about, but what really caught her attention was the small fireplace on the east wall. It was white marble with beautiful carving. Two plush chairs sat in front, each with an ottoman.

"It's beautiful," Shaye breathed, liking everything about the space, especially the welcoming feel.

"The bathroom is through there." Kathy grinned. "There's something I think you're going to like."

Shaye went through the open door and came to a stop in the glorious bathroom. The vanity counter was the same marble as the fireplace. There were two sinks, plenty of storage and a nice walk-in shower. And an incredible, huge, covetable claw-foot tub that sat in front of a stunning stained glass window.

"There's one just like it in the master," Kathy said, following her into the room. "It's heaven."

"I don't know what to say," Shaye admitted, over-whelmed by the beauty of her surroundings. "I've never stayed anywhere this nice. I don't think you're charging enough for the room."

Kathy laughed. "I'm glad you think that. So are you interested?"

"Yes. I love it."

Everything about the house was perfect, she thought. She could see herself here. Honestly, she had no idea why this was happening to her, but she was grateful.

"Then, let's go downstairs and take care of some paperwork."

It only took a few minutes to read over Kathy's rental agreement. Shaye signed the short-term lease and wrote a check for the payment, then took a house key in return.

"You're welcome to park in the driveway, next to my car," Kathy told her. "There's plenty of room." She paused. "Oh, wait. You said you were moving to Seattle, didn't you?"

"Yes."

"Then, your truck is probably filled with all your belongings. Would you like to store them in the garage until you're ready to move on?"

"That would be very nice. Thank you."

"I'll open it right now so you can sort what you want to take upstairs and what you want to keep in the garage." She led the way outside and unlocked the side door. "Please excuse the mess."

Shaye followed her inside the detached garage. When Kathy turned on the light, Shaye prepared herself for the usual garage clutter—boxes, lawn supplies, maybe some old furniture. What she wasn't expecting was to find a car—or at least all the pieces of a car—scattered around.

From what she could tell, the bodywork was finished, and the seats were covered in plastic and up against the back wall. The engine was strewn about in a few hundred pieces, and based on the condition, it hadn't been touched. But the rest of the vehicle was nearly finished.

She took in the lines, the shape of the back end and then spotted the familiar logo.

"It's a Mustang convertible," she said, pressing a hand to her chest. "A sixty-nine. No, a sixty-eight. She's going to be a beauty."

Kathy stared at her in surprise. "You know cars."

"I used to work on them with my dad." She circled around the chassis, thinking how much her father would have loved to work on this car. "Nothing this nice." She smiled. "They can be a little pricey for a hobby. But my dad always talked about how we'd fix one up someday. Are you doing the restoration?"

"Goodness, no. This was Douglas's project." Her expression turned wistful. "He was going to have it done in time for the classic car show a couple of years ago. There's a parade, and she was going to be one of the stars. But then he passed away, and here she sits. I should go talk to someone about fixing her up and selling her."

"Not before you get to ride in the parade," Shaye told her. "You have to do that." She looked at the pieces. "I think the bodywork is all done. The upholstery is finished." She continued to walk around the car. "Look, the dash is ready. From what I can tell, the engine needs to be rebuilt, and then the whole thing gets put back together and painted. It's not a lot of work."

She drew in a breath. "I could do it." She paused. "I know I could handle the engine. I've rebuilt them before. It's just a matter of cleaning it up and replacing a few parts, then putting it all back together. I might need some help with the assembly, but I'm sure I could ask around and find someone if I get into trouble."

Lawson came immediately to mind, but she ignored that. "My job with Judy's Hand Pies is only four hours a day. I'll have plenty of time."

Kathy smiled at her. "You don't have to convince me, Shaye. I'm more concerned I would be taking advantage of you. I'd want you to let me pay you."

"No, but you can pay for the parts, and the paint is going to be pricey. I'd really like to do this." She shrugged. "I lost my dad a while back. I'd like to do this for him. I think that would make him happy. I promise, if I get in over my head, I'll ask for help."

"All right. You do what you can. I have an account at a local auto-repair shop. Buy what you need, and have them charge it to me. If you change your mind about the rebuild and don't want to finish, it's perfectly fine. At this point, anything would help."

"Thank you."

Shaye looked at the car and felt a flicker of anticipation. She knew it was silly, but she couldn't escape the sense that if she got things right with the car, somehow she would get things right with herself. Once that was done, she would be free to start over and find a new life in Seattle.

SHAYE TOLD HERSELF there was no reason to be nervous. The fact that her landlord happened to have an account at Wishing Tree Auto Repair made sense, and the fact that Shaye needed to go there for parts was just a coincidence. She was a customer, nothing more. She was going to rebuild the Mustang's carburetor, and for that she needed a rebuild kit.

She'd spent a couple of hours the previous afternoon figuring out what was done on the car and what wasn't. Her initial assessment had turned out to be correct. The two big projects were going to be building the engine, followed by putting the car back together. The hard work had already been completed.

So at eight thirty in the morning, she found herself parking in front of the auto-parts store, trying not to hyperventilate. Anticipation and butterflies danced together in her stomach. She felt queasy and excited and worried all at the same time. Ridiculous emotions, considering she barely knew the guy, and so what if she was going to see him again? It wasn't as if she was stalking him. Besides, he'd said something about the auto repair side of things. She probably wasn't going to see him at all. She would go inside, buy what she needed and be gone before he ever knew she was there.

Only she didn't want to *not* see him. She'd liked him and had enjoyed his company. Last night, after getting herself settled in her beautiful room, she'd sat in front of the pretty fireplace and had replayed their time together. Hanging out with him again would be nice.

She got out of her truck and started for the store. She wasn't going to think about Lawson, she told herself. If she saw him, great. If she didn't, no big deal. She was in town for nearly a month, she reminded herself as she walked into the store. If she was still thinking about him in a couple of days, she would come back and ask if he was—

"Shaye?"

She came to a stop halfway down the aisle. Lawson stood not six feet away, looking really, really good. He had on jeans and work boots, along with a short-sleeved shirt with the company logo on the pocket. His dark eyes were wide with surprise and pleasure. The kind of pleasure that filled her with a happy little glow.

"What are you doing here?"

"I, uh…"

She really hadn't thought she would see him, so she hadn't planned what to say.

"I decided not to leave," she admitted, thinking the truth was always easier. "I was halfway to my truck when I realized there was nothing waiting for me in Seattle, and spending a few weeks here sounded like fun. I have a part-time job at Judy's Hand Pies. I'll be manning the food cart at lunchtime, and I've rented a room from a nice lady who lives in a beautiful Victorian house."

"Kathy Vieira," he said, his gaze never leaving hers. "She's good people. I'm glad you stayed. I wish you'd called me."

She grinned. "How would I have done that?"

"You're right. We didn't exchange numbers." He moved closer and pulled his phone out of his pocket. "Let's take care of that right now." He started typing. "Shaye…"

"Harper." She gave him her number, and he immediately texted back his contact info.

He tucked his phone away. "You're really here. I'm glad."

"It's just for the month."

"That's a whole lot longer than I had yesterday. I'm happy you came to see me."

She laughed. "Don't take this wrong, but I'm actually here to buy a kit to rebuild a carburetor. You're just the gift with purchase."

He grinned. "I can live with that. Are you having trouble with your car?"

"No. My little pickup is doing fine. Kathy has a car in her garage. I might get in over my head, but I offered to rebuild the engine and put it all back together."

His expression changed to that of a six-year-old boy on Christmas morning. "No way. She still has the Mustang? I would have thought she would have sold it after Douglas died."

"It's in her garage. The bodywork's all done, and you should see the amazing job someone did on the upholstery. All that's left is rebuilding the engine and putting her back together."

"Can I help? Putting her back together would be a dream."

"That would be great," Shaye told him. "I'm comfortable with the engine, but the assembly seems a little daunting."

They agreed they would be in touch to figure out when he would drop by to see how she was doing, then he helped her with the carburetor kit. All the while they talked, Shaye told herself she had to be careful. Liking Lawson was one thing, but being an idiot for a guy was another. She was only in town a few weeks. She could hang out with him, get to know him, but then she would be moving on. Expecting more than something casual would be foolish, and she'd sworn she was never going to be a fool for a guy ever again.

CHAPTER FOUR

LAWSON SPENT THE morning watching the clock. One of his service guys had a doctor's appointment, so he filled in, doing a couple of quick oil changes, then sat in on an interview for the new bookkeeper. Lately Vince had wanted him to participate in all the interviews—part of his on-the-job training for when he bought the business.

Most days Lawson loved his job. He liked the work, the other employees and the customers and looked forward to taking responsibility for it all. Just not today. Today he couldn't stop thinking about Shaye and the fact that she'd stayed.

Even as he told himself she was only in town for a few weeks, he couldn't stop wondering what had changed her mind. While he wanted to think it was him, he knew there were other factors. Still, he'd been given a shot, and he planned to make the most of the opportunity.

She'd said she was taking out the food cart at lunchtime. During Christmas in July, many vendors offered food in The Wreath, taking advantage of the influx of tourists. Lawson knew she would be plenty busy and wouldn't have much time to talk, so he decided to wait until near the end of her shift. That way he could walk her back to the store. As far as he was concerned, the more time he spent with her the better. He hadn't been this interested in a woman in a long time. Yes, she'd said she was leaving, but so far that hadn't happened.

About two fifteen, he walked over to The Wreath. There were several food carts set up around the perimeter of the big circle, but it only took him a second to spot her. She was talking to a woman with a couple of kids, pointing to the menu, as if explaining what was available.

He paused to enjoy the view. She'd pulled her long red hair back into a thick braid that fell to the middle of her back. She had a bright yellow Judy's Hand Pies polo shirt tucked into faded jeans and a small apron tied around her waist. She was petite but gorgeous. He gave himself about thirty seconds to admire her butt before heading over to her cart.

He got in line behind an older couple, then waited for her to notice him. She glanced up, saw him, smiled, then blushed slightly.

She was so pretty, he thought, doing his best not to grin like a fool. Big green eyes, a few freckles, and an easy smile. She was the total package, and he was going to do his best not to screw this up.

"I'm out of everything," she told him when it was his turn. "People love hand pies."

"Don't worry. I can grab something else. I just wanted to stop by and say hi." He pointed to the store. "I'll walk you back."

"Thanks."

"How was your first day?"

"Busy. I had no idea the cart would be so popular. I had a line the whole time. But it was fun."

She tucked the small point-of-sale device into her apron pocket while he unlocked the wheels on the cart.

Together they piled the box of napkins and bakery tissue onto the cart, then he folded up the table. They started for the store.

She looked around. "This is an interesting town. I'm looking forward to exploring the different stores in The Wreath."

"Did you try the fudge?"

She grinned at him. "I did, and it was addictive."

"Good. So I was thinking I could come by after work and check out the Mustang. If that works for you."

"Sure."

"Want to grab some dinner?"

She hesitated only a second before nodding. "That would be nice."

"I get off about five, so say five thirty. We'll come up with a game plan on the car, then go get something to eat. You like Mexican food?"

"I do."

"Then, we'll go there."

They reached the front of the store. Lawson held open the door. As she pushed the cart inside, he saw his sister behind the counter. Adien smiled at him but didn't say anything. He set the folding table inside.

"See you tonight," he said.

"You will."

Although he wanted to linger, he forced himself to leave. Hanging around when she had things to do wasn't cool. He would get some lunch, then get back to work. Tonight he would see Shaye. Over dinner, he would get to know her better. Assuming that went as well as he expected, he could start working on his plan to get her to stay in Wishing Tree.

SHAYE WASN'T SURE if she should dress for dinner or working on a car. She'd spent an hour sorting through all the parts and separating them by category. Then she'd watched a few videos on rebuilding the engine. Tomorrow she would tackle the hard work.

Around four thirty, she showered and put on a clean pair of jeans and a lightweight summer sweater. If she and Lawson ended up working on the car later, she could easily run upstairs and get changed. Once she was ready, she hesitated, not sure if she should wait for him downstairs or out in the garage. Finally she took her handbag and a book to the first floor, where she made herself comfortable on one of the sofas in the living room. A few minutes later, Kathy walked in.

"How are you doing, Shaye?" her landlord asked. "Getting settled?"

"Yes. I had fun at my shift with the food cart, and I'm getting to know your car. I'm going to start rebuilding the engine tomorrow. Um, Lawson Easley is going to help me."

Kathy's brows rose slightly. "Is he? That's excellent. The boy knows what he's doing. He's been in love with cars since he was little. There's no one I'd trust more."

She waved. "I'm off to play bridge. You have a nice evening."

"You, too."

When Kathy left, Shaye picked up her book, but she was too nervous to read. She hadn't been on a first date in a long time. Not that this was a date, exactly. It was more of a… Well, something.

Right at five thirty, there was a knock on the front door. Shaye opened it, then tried not to react when she saw Lawson standing there. By some quirk of fate, the man got better-looking every time she saw him. And when he smiled, which he was doing now, she felt flutters all over.

"Hungry?" he asked.

She laughed. "I am. Despite spending the middle part of my day selling hand pies, I forgot to get lunch."

"Then, we'd better get you fed. We can check out the car after dinner."

He waited while she closed and carefully locked the front door behind her, then he led the way down the front path.

"We're close enough to walk to The Wreath," he said. "This is a real nice part of town. The elementary school is only a few blocks to the south, so it's a family-friendly neighborhood."

She smiled at him. "Are any parts of Wishing Tree not family-friendly?"

His expression turned sheepish. "I guess not. We're more down-home than sophisticated around here."

"Sounds nice."

"I'm glad you think so. Did you meet any locals on your shift or just tourists?"

"A few residents came by to say hello, which was really fun. I met someone named Paisley. She seemed nice."

"She is. She works up at the resort. She manages their events. Weddings, parties, the big business conferences."

Paisley had said as much, then had offered to introduce her to a few of her friends, suggesting they all get a drink together.

"You know a lot about her," she said, her voice teasing. "Is there a Lawson–Paisley scandal I should know about?"

He laughed. "No. I've known her all my life, but we've never dated. In high school I was kind of a one-woman man."

"What happened to her?"

"We outgrew each other."

There was something in the way he said the words, as if there was more to tell. But before she could decide if she wanted to press him, they arrived in The Wreath.

Just like at lunch, the big, open area was filled with people. The handful of restaurants all had outdoor seating, and most of the tables were full. Children ran around, couples held hands, and music played from big speakers.

"This is nice," she said. "Friendly."

"Friendly is good."

She smiled. "Yes, it is."

He put his hand on the small of her back and pointed to Navidad Mexican Café. "Prepare to be amazed. Nearly everything is homemade. They make their own chips, and if you're not careful, you'll make a meal of them."

"Are the chips red and green?"

He looked at her. "How did you know?"

"Seriously?"

"Sure. What other color would they be?"

"I don't know. Chip-colored. Is this a Christmas in July thing or all year round?"

He held open the door so they could go inside. "They're red and green for the month, then at the holidays. The rest of the time they're, as you said, chip-colored."

"So I should feel special?"

"That's my goal."

She knew he was teasing, but his words still made her feel warm all over. He was saying and doing all the right things, which was hard to resist. Most of her was willing to believe he was exactly who he seemed to be, but a tiny sliver of her urged caution. She'd been charmed before, and every time the relationship had ended in disaster.

He gave his name to the hostess, and they were shown to an outdoor table tucked in a corner. A few tall plants in pots gave the illusion of privacy, while still allowing them a nice view of the square…or, rather, circle.

Once they were seated, their server came and took their drink orders.

"You'll want to try the margaritas," Lawson told her. "They're supposed to be the best."

"Sure. I'll try the house special."

"Beer for me," Lawson said. "We'd like some guacamole and chips, please."

When their server left, Shaye grinned.

"Still not a margarita kind of guy? You mentioned yesterday that they weren't your thing."

"They're not. I've tried them, though."

"So it's a taste thing and not because you don't think they're macho?"

A smile tugged at his lips. "I don't worry about having my manhood questioned."

She suspected that was true. Lawson was the kind of guy who wouldn't worry about that sort of thing.

She looked around. "This is nice. The weather is perfect."

"It gets cool when the sun goes down, but we're only

a couple of weeks after the summer solstice, so sunset isn't until nine."

"That's crazy."

"It is. Unfortunately, in the winter, it's dark around four in the afternoon. That's what it's like here in north country."

She laughed. "Is that what we call it?"

"Sometimes."

Their drinks arrived, along with the chips and guacamole. He picked up his beer and held out his glass. "Thank you for staying in Wishing Tree."

She touched her glass to his. "Thank you for inviting me to dinner."

She took a sip. The drink was perfect—not too sweet with a little bite from the tequila. "This is good."

"I'm glad." He reached for a chip, then waved it. "You have to admire the commitment to the color."

"They are seriously red and green." She took a red one and dipped it in the guacamole, then sighed. "That is so good."

"Told you."

"Yes, you did."

He sampled as well, then looked at her. "So what's waiting for you in Seattle?"

"Not a specific thing," she admitted, not sure how to explain. "Once I knew I couldn't stay in Iowa, I had to figure out where to move. My parents never had a lot of money, so a vacation that involved travel was rare. We drove out here one summer because my dad always wanted to see the Pacific Northwest. He'd done tons of research, and everything was planned out so perfectly." She smiled at the memories. "We had the best time.

When I was looking for where to go, Seattle seemed an obvious choice."

He nodded. "I get that. You'd feel connected to your folks. That makes sense."

"I'm not sure it does, but I appreciate the support."

They smiled at each other. Their server came by and told them about the specials. Shaye chose the taco plate with three kinds of tacos, while Lawson ordered a combo plate.

When they were alone again, he leaned toward her. "Why move now?"

A reasonable question. Why this month and not six months ago? As she wasn't a very good liar, her choices were limited. She could either not answer the question or tell him the truth.

Lawson lightly touched her hand. "Sorry. I'm getting too personal. You don't have to tell me."

"It's okay." She faked a smile. "Confession is good for the soul, right?" She drew in a breath. "After my mom died, I was kind of a wreck. I couldn't stop crying, I couldn't deal with managing her estate. I wasn't functional. And in the middle of that, I met a guy."

Lawson sipped his beer. "I already don't like him."

"You and me both. Anyway, at first he was great, helping me figure out what I needed to do. Things progressed. We were involved, but the relationship didn't seem to be going anywhere, which was about all I could handle then. One night about four months ago, he said he wanted to move to LA. He thought he could make it as an actor and did I want to come with him."

Lawson stared at her in surprise. "An actor?"

"Yes, well, I wasn't sure about that, either, but getting away to somewhere else seemed like a good idea.

I knew I wasn't happy where I was. So I agreed to go with him. I sold the house, sold most of the furniture, packed up my truck and prepared to move to LA."

"It's a long way from Seattle."

"It is." She grabbed another chip. "The night before we were leaving, I went to the local bar where we hung out. He was with his friends. He didn't see me walk in. They were teasing him about taking me with him, saying that he was being controlled by me."

"I doubt they were that polite."

"You're right. They weren't, but I won't repeat exactly what they said." She hadn't minded the teasing. It was Josh's response that had devastated her.

"He told them they had it all wrong. He was taking me with him not because he cared but so he could get laid any time he wanted. Once we got there and he found someone hot, he would dump me and get on with his LA life."

She still remembered standing in the bar, unable to believe what she'd heard. The words had landed like blows—a phrase she'd heard and read but had never experienced herself until that night.

She'd stood there feeling cheap and small and used while Josh had laughed with his friends. Then he'd seen her. The shock on his face had been comical, but not enough to in any way soften the blow.

"He tried to tell me he'd been kidding," she said softly. "He said he didn't mean it and of course he loved me." She managed a faint smile. "I chose not to believe him."

Lawson's jaw was set and a muscle twitched. She didn't know him very well, but she felt his fury and knew that if Josh had been anywhere nearby, Lawson would have taken him on. He would have stood up for her, protected her, because that was the kind of man he was.

"What happened after that?" he asked, his voice nearly a growl.

"I left. I walked out without saying anything. Got in my truck and drove away. Two blocks later, I realized I had nowhere to go. I didn't have a home, I'd quit my job. All I had was the money from the sale of the house and my savings and whatever was in my truck. I headed to the next town up the interstate and checked into a motel where I cried for two days." She sipped her margarita. "More about losing my folks and my bad decisions than about Josh."

"He doesn't deserve your tears."

"Thank you. That's what I think, too. On the second day, I started thinking about Seattle. I did a little research and decided to go west. And that's my sad, little past."

"He was a fool and a jerk."

"I know it's about him, but I'm still feeling a little burned."

He nodded. "How could you not feel that way? You trusted him, and he betrayed you. Plus your folks. That's a lot to get over."

She waited, but he didn't say anything else. "You're not going to tell me to give love another try?"

He smiled. "Nope. I'm going to tell you that you're about to eat the best tacos you've ever had, and later, we're going to take a look at Kathy's car. That's probably plenty for one evening."

"You're very smooth, Lawson. That scares me a little."

His smile faded. "I'm not playing. This isn't a game, not for me. I like you, Shaye, and I want to get to know you. I'm aware time isn't on my side, and now I'm fighting against a man who hurt you bad, but that's okay. I'm up to the challenge."

The bald honesty of his statement nearly knocked her off her chair. The men she knew never just put it out there. They played games and said they weren't all that interested in having a girlfriend. They tried to convince her that playing the field was a natural state for them, and her wanting more was because she was weak.

"I don't know what to say to that," she admitted.

He flashed her a sexy grin. "You don't have to say anything at all. I just wanted you to know."

CHAPTER FIVE

LAWSON WAS CAREFUL to keep the conversation light for the rest of the meal. He told funny stories about his deployment in Germany and the time he and his buddies went driving on the autobahn.

"We couldn't drive over a hundred and twenty," he said with a chuckle. "We tried, but there had been too many years of a speed limit ingrained into us. And we knew if something happened, we'd be in trouble back at the base."

"Still, that's pretty fast."

"Yeah, we had to borrow a car to go that fast. But it was fun."

Their server returned to check on them. Lawson glanced at his watch and was surprised they'd been sitting at the table nearly three hours. He paid the bill and added a generous tip, then escorted Shaye out of the restaurant.

The sun had slipped behind the mountains, leaving the sky all the colors of twilight.

"Give it an hour and there will be a lot of stars in the sky," he said, as they started toward Kathy's house.

"I looked out last night," she said. "The sky is different here than back in Iowa."

"We're out west. Everything is bigger."

"Even the sky?" she teased.

"You know it."

That made her laugh.

He liked this, he thought. He'd meant what he'd said earlier, about wanting to get to know her better. Her plan to leave in a few weeks wasn't helping, but he would do what he could. He was used to working under pressure.

"You ever think about finishing your degree?" he asked.

"I do. I was studying marketing. I was only able to take a couple of classes every semester before I left to be with my mom. So I'm probably about halfway through my sophomore year."

"It's a start. Seattle has a lot of good colleges close by. The University of Washington is the most well-known."

"And the hardest to get into." She smiled. "I'll have time to figure it out. I'll need to live in the state a year to establish residency. I couldn't afford out-of-state tuition."

He thought about mentioning North Cascades College, only twenty miles from Wishing Tree, but didn't say anything. Shaye wasn't staying, and he wasn't going to push.

They reached the house and walked into the garage. Shaye turned on the overhead lights, and Lawson moved close to the car.

"I see what you mean," he said, running his hands across the hood. "She's beautiful, and all the body-work is done."

He saw fenders and doors lying on the floor. The inside panels were removed and refinished, with the door handles and window cranks cleaned up and shiny. The engine was mounted on an engine stand, with the parts on a shop cart nearby.

"The cylinder bores need to be honed," she said, pointing. "At least one of the water plugs needs to be replaced."

"How can I help?" he asked.

She looked at him, her expression surprised. "That's it? You're not going to start telling me what to do?"

"Why would I do that? You have a plan, you say you can do it. Why wouldn't I trust you?"

"Because I'm a woman."

He grinned. "Shaye, I was in the military, working side by side with women mechanics. If you tell me you know how to do something, I'm going to believe you until you show me otherwise."

She tilted her head. "I'm not used to being trusted based on my word. Not about cars. Most guys want to be all in charge and tell me what to do, even if they're wrong."

"I'm not like that."

"I guess not. It's nice."

He smiled. "I'm glad you think so."

Their eyes locked, and tension filled the garage.

He wanted to kiss her. He wanted to do a whole lot more, but kissing would be a good start. His gut told him to take things slow—based on what Shaye had told him about her past, trust was going to be an issue, so he needed to make sure they had that first.

"Can I come by in a couple of days and help with the work?" he asked.

"Sure."

"Great." He stepped toward her, then bent down and

kissed her cheek. "I'll be in touch. Have a good night, Shaye."

Her eyes widened in surprise, but she only nodded. "Have a good night."

He walked out without looking back—which was about the hardest thing he'd done in a very long time.

"I'M A TEACHER at the local elementary school," Dena Somerville, a pretty brunette, said. "I had second grade last year, and I'm teaching third grade this fall. It's kind of nice because I'll have some of the same kids. I like that. There's continuity."

"How do you have the patience?" Shaye asked with a smile, grateful for the company during a rare slow moment on her shift. "I really like children, but twenty of them every day? I don't think I could do it."

"It's a skill," Paisley told her. "One I don't have, either."

"I love it," Dena told them. "Plus, we keep our classrooms small here. I only have fifteen students. So how are you settling into life in our little town?"

"I like it," Shaye said. "Everyone's very friendly. I'm getting to know the locals, and the tourists are always interesting." She grinned. "I was yelled at yesterday by a lady complaining there weren't enough vegan eating choices in town. I told her I could offer vegetarian pies, but not vegan."

Paisley waved her mushroom stroganoff pie. "There's no dairy in the filling."

"There's butter in the crust," Shaye pointed out. "To have it vegan, you'd have to use something else for the shortening."

"Would coconut oil work?" Dena asked. "I have no idea."

Paisley had become a regular at the food cart. She stayed to chat with Shaye when there wasn't a big line of customers. Today she'd brought another local, her friend Dena, who was a couple of years older.

"Most of the tourists have been very nice," Shaye added. "I don't want to give them a bad name."

Dena laughed. "You're not. I agree most of them are lovely. I own the Wishing Tree B and B, so sometimes I get to know them too well."

"But I thought you were a teacher."

"She's very busy," Paisley said, her voice teasing. "Dena puts us all to shame with her work ethic."

"That's not true," Dena protested. She turned to Shaye. "I inherited the B and B from my grandmother when she passed away. It's fully staffed, so there's not much for me to do. I work there in the summer, but during the school year, I don't get that involved in the day-to-day stuff."

"Her B and B, like the resort, is busy all year round," Paisley said. "We are a tourist destination, regardless of the season."

"I would guess Christmas is the busiest time."

"It is," Dena told her. "All the events draw a crowd."

"First snow is the worst," Paisley added. "The first snowfall is a huge deal here in town. There's a big celebration, and the tourists love it. The problem is no one knows when the first snow is going to happen, and when a couple books the wrong weekend, they get mad."

"But it's not your fault," Shaye said.

"You know that, and I know that, but they don't want to hear it's not going to snow."

Dena nodded. "Yeah, they can get really upset. But we deal."

"I'm sorry it's a problem for you," Shaye said with a smile. "But I do love the little idiosyncrasies of this town."

"We have many." Paisley laughed. "Okay, so next for you will be the tree-lighting. You have to go to that. It's really special." She paused, then sighed. "It's actually nicer to go with a date, but that's not happening for me these days. Stupid small-town demographics."

Dena nudged her. "You love the town."

"I don't like the lack of age-appropriate men. I know them all, and I've either dated them, or together we have the chemistry of a paper bag. I want some great sexy guy to walk up and kiss me."

"I don't know," Dena said, sounding doubtful. "I'm not sure how I'd react to a total stranger kissing me. I might accidentally use some of the moves my dad taught me when I first started dating."

Dena turned to Shaye. "He had two daughters, and he didn't want anyone taking advantage of us."

"He sounds like a great guy."

"He is."

Shaye thought about Lawson. He was the only *age-appropriate* man she knew in town, and she was plenty interested in him walking up and kissing her, but so far he'd only helped her with the Mustang.

"I'm giving up on men," Dena said with a sigh. "I've tried blind dates, double dates and a couple of different online-dating apps. I can't seem to find the right guy anywhere."

Paisley hugged her friend. "You have done more than

your share of trying. I don't get it. If I were a guy, I'd date you in a hot minute."

Dena laughed. "Thank you." She looked at her watch. "Okay, I have to get back to work."

"Me, too." Paisley wiped her hands on a napkin. "I have a meeting with a very emotionally delicate bride this afternoon. When she cries, the sound is so heartbreaking I find myself tearing up in sympathy. I don't know how she does it, but I'm really impressed by her abilities. No matter what it is, after the tears she gets her way."

"I'm not sure that's a positive characteristic," Shaye said cautiously.

"Only for her. For everyone else, it totally sucks."

They all laughed.

"We need to do something together," Dena said, hugging Shaye. "There's going to be a day of service coming up. Let's plan on getting together for that."

"That would be nice," Shaye said.

Paisley hugged her as well, then both women left. Shaye served a couple more customers. At three, she packed up the cart and wheeled it back to the store.

Paisley and Dena were really nice, she thought as she pushed the cart. So friendly and welcoming. She appreciated the overtures of friendship. She wasn't sure what a day of service was, but she could imagine and was happy to be included.

She went past the store, through a small alley that led to the back where she used the security pad to unlock the door. She pushed the cart into place, then began unloading the handful of pies she still had left.

Once they were on the warming shelves, she plugged in her point-of-sale device so it would upload the details of the sales. As she wasn't allowed to accept cash, there was no till to reconcile. Any tips she received were hers to keep.

She pulled out the shelves from the cart and carried them to the industrial dishwasher in the back room. After stacking them inside, she wiped down the cart, then resupplied it with bakery tissue and napkins so it was ready for the next day.

As she worked, she thought about what Paisley had said about the tree-lighting ceremony. Lawson had mentioned it the first day they'd met, when he'd listed all the Christmas in July activities. Maybe he would ask her to go with him.

Or not, she thought with a sigh. Most afternoons he swung by to buy a few pies and chat with her, and more often than not, he showed up to help her with the car, but he hadn't asked her out. Not since their dinner at Navidad Mexican Café. She had no idea why he wasn't suggesting something more datelike than working on the car. Not that she didn't enjoy his company, because she did. A lot. He was likable and knowledgeable and smart and funny. He always had great stories about his family or being in the military. He talked about the people he'd met and the places he'd been. The only subject he didn't touch on was his time in Afghanistan.

They were learning more about each other every day, but he wasn't asking her out, and she didn't know why. Yes, she was leaving at the end of the month, but until then they could—

She mentally paused, not sure what they could do. Get more seriously involved? Become lovers? That was a big step, especially with her plan to leave. Technically

Seattle wasn't *that* far, so maybe they could make a long-distance thing work. Or—

"How's it going?"

She turned and saw Toby standing in the doorway to the back room.

She smiled at her boss. "Good. I'm sorry to disappoint, but I didn't sell out today."

He grinned. "How many pies did you bring back?"

"Three."

He chuckled. "Okay, we'll live with the pain."

"Yes, try to get over it. I've increased the amount I take out by more than double what I had last week. I think word is spreading about how good the product is. Plus, it's kind of unique." She held up a hand. "I'm not dissing the other vendors. It's just you can get a hot dog anywhere, but a hand pie is more special."

"I like to think so." He leaned against the doorframe. "How are you enjoying the work?"

"It's fun. I like meeting the customers. Sometimes the little kids have such a hard time deciding what they want. It's like the most important decision they're making that day."

"You're doing a good job," he said.

"Thank you."

"I'm getting feedback from different people. They like how you handle yourself."

The unexpected compliment pleased her. "Thank you. That's nice to hear."

Toby studied her. "Adien is going to be heading out on maternity leave in a few weeks, and she's told me she won't be coming back to work. Not with three little ones at home. I'm going to have to replace her. I know you said you're only in town for the month, but if you were going to stay, I'd like to offer you a job here. You'd get a substantial pay raise, and the job would be full-time, with benefits."

The offer stunned her. "I don't know what to say," she admitted, suddenly feeling a little tightness in her chest. "I appreciate you thinking of me."

"You're good at what you do. It's a summer job for a few hours a day. A lot of people would simply go through the motions and not put any effort into it. You chose to get involved and work the program. I respect that."

"Thank you."

"What are your plans, Shaye? I don't mean leaving or not leaving, but what do you want to do with your life?"

The question surprised her. Almost no one had asked about her thoughts on the future—at least not since her parents had passed away. "I want to get a degree in marketing. I have about a year and a half of college. I want to finish that, then find a job in my chosen field."

"So not retail."

She smiled. "Not permanently."

He nodded. "Stick with your goals. Don't get distracted by life. My advice is worth what you paid for it, by the way. Think about the job offer. Adien's here through the month, so I'm not going to start looking for a replacement until after Christmas in July." The smile returned. "North Cascades College isn't that far from here. You might want to look at their curriculum."

"There's a college nearby?"

"A good one. You'd probably want to establish residency so you don't have to pay out-of-state tuition."

"Yes, I've already thought about that. It takes a year."

"The year is going to pass regardless of what you do.

I'll keep the job offer open until the end of the month. If you want to talk about it in more detail, feel free. I promise not to mistake interest for a firm yes."

"Thank you. You've given me a lot to think about."

"That was the goal."

He nodded at her, then left. Shaye stood in the back room of Judy's Hand Pies, her head spinning.

The job offer was unexpected, to say the least. As was the information on the nearby college. She'd never considered staying in Wishing Tree—her plan had always been to move on to Seattle. Only that was slightly less appealing than it had been. She didn't know anyone in Seattle. She didn't have a job lined up or a place to stay. She would be completely starting over.

Not that she was ready to commit to staying here, either. The town was great, and she was making friends, but it was still too soon to know where she belonged. She wanted to make a smart decision, a logical one, rather than choose something because she'd met a cute guy who made her heart beat faster and her knees weak.

"I have time," she whispered. Toby had said he wouldn't start looking for a replacement until after Christmas in July. So she could consider her options and think everything through. She knew whatever decision she made, it had to be based on what was right for her and not contingent on any man in her life. She'd learned that lesson already, and she wasn't about to make the same mistake twice.

CHAPTER SIX

LAWSON TOLD HIMSELF that despite how it felt, his plan wasn't going to kill him. He knew going slow, getting to know Shaye and letting her get to know him, made the most sense. Yes, every time they hung out, he was more and more attracted to her, but he wasn't interested in a superficial fling. He wanted the real thing, and he was hoping she did, too.

So he hung on to his self-control and stayed firmly in the friend zone. He joked with her, spoke freely about himself when asked and brought up what he hoped were unexpected and interesting topics for them to discuss while they worked on the Mustang.

"Of course I believe in God," she said one evening as they worked to reinstall the valves into the head using new valve seals. "And an afterlife."

"Is it Heaven?" he asked.

She smiled at him. "I'm going to shock you and say no."

"Hell?"

"I don't think the answer is that simple. Imagine trying to explain the concept of tomorrow to a puppy. Their sense of time and space is so different from ours that we simply can't do it."

"In this analogy, we're the puppy?"

"We are. I think whatever happens after we die is

so far beyond our comprehension that we were given a simple explanation that makes sense to us. We'll find out the truth when we get there."

"So there's a power much greater than ourselves, but not in the way we envision?"

"Yes. Most life-changing experiences are different than we imagine or than we've been told. Wouldn't God be even more like that?"

"I think that, too," he admitted. "Faith matters. It grounds us and sets us free at the same time. I appreciate what we're told, but you're right. We won't know until we get there."

He passed her the tools as she needed them, content to watch her do the work. She was careful and meticulous. Every now and then she asked him his opinion on what they should do next, but mostly she was confident in her abilities.

She'd pulled her long red hair back into a ponytail that sat high on her head, then had coiled it into some kind of a bun thing. She wore an old shop coat that was five sizes too big over a T-shirt and jeans. When he leaned close to tighten a bolt he could smell the scent of the lotion they'd bought together.

The whiff of scent had him thinking about where she'd put the lotion and how he would like to touch all those places, along with any others available to him. He'd start with his fingers, then follow with his tongue and they would—

He literally *and* mentally took a step back, telling himself to keep his mind on the work and off anything more physical. Wanting her was a given, but thinking about wanting her would only lead to trouble.

"Speaking of puppies," she said, "I had customers

today who had a new border collie puppy with them. She was so cute and full of energy. It was slow for a few minutes, so I got to play with her."

"Now you want a puppy."

"Sure. Doesn't everyone?"

"There are nondog people."

Her eyes widened. "I don't believe you. Have you seen puppies? How could you not want all of them?"

"They grow into dogs, and that's different."

"It is. I know it's the cuteness factor, but I can't help it. My heart is puppy-friendly."

He laughed. "Do you have plans to fulfill that need?"

"Eventually. When I get settled and have my life together." She wrinkled her nose. "I'd need a work situation where I was home a fair amount. I wouldn't want to get a puppy and then be gone all the time."

"I agree. My boss used to have a couple of big dogs that he would bring to the shop every day. We all enjoyed having them hang around. Now he has Burt, an aging miniature dachshund, who'd rather stay home and sleep."

"Burt?"

"I know, but the name suits him."

They went to work on the piston–connecting rod assembly, installing new bearings and rings. Once that was done, it was close to nine. Shaye glanced out the open garage door.

"The sun's set. It's getting late. I've kept you too long."

"You haven't kept me."

Her green eyes darkened. "You're not obligated to spend every evening helping me."

"Do I seem like I'm not having fun?"

"No, but…" She pressed her lips together. "I appreciate the help and enjoy the company."

"That's all I want to hear. The tree-lighting ceremony is in a couple of days. Would you like to go with me? It's an outdoor event, in The Wreath. People generally arrive a couple of hours early to eat dinner first. There's music and dancing, then the tree is lit."

She smiled. "I'd like that."

"Good. I'll bring the picnic, and I'll pick you up here."

"It's a date," she said, then held up her hand. "I mean that as an expression. I wasn't implying anything."

He stared into her eyes. "It's a date," he said quietly. "I mean that in every sense of the word."

Finally, she thought, her heart pounding hard in her chest.

"Oh." Her lips curved up in a happy smile. "Good. Then it's a date."

FOR THE FIRST time since Shaye had started her midday shift selling hand pies, the hours had crawled by. Every time she checked her watch, she was shocked to discover that only a few minutes had gone by. Watching city workers set up tables and chairs for that evening's events hadn't been much of a distraction. When her shift had finally ended, she'd raced home only to discover she had three long hours until Lawson picked her up.

She changed her sheets and ran the old ones through the washer and dryer. She used a facial mask that was supposed to make her skin glow, then put in hot rollers in an attempt to get sexy waves into her hair. She debated what to wear, changing her clothes three times before deciding on the original outfit, an apple-green sleeveless dress with a light sweater in case it got chilly.

She was ready a ridiculous forty minutes before he was due to arrive but couldn't stand to be in her room any longer so made her way downstairs. She found Kathy in the kitchen, cutting up fresh fruit.

"You look nice," her landlord said with a smile. "Going to the tree-lighting?"

"Yes, Lawson's taking me."

Kathy's expression turned mischievous. "I always liked that boy, although I suppose I should call him a man now. He was a good kid. The family's very nice. The two younger ones took off, but the older girls stayed. Oh, that's right. You know Adien. Isn't she pregnant?"

"Very," Shaye said, taking a seat at the island. "She's due in about six weeks, but she's getting bigger by the day. I don't know how she stands on her feet for so many hours at a time."

"She's young and healthy. But I'm sure she'll be glad when the baby comes."

Kathy sliced a peach and offered some to Shaye. "Fresh from the farmers market," she said. "They're delicious. I love this time of year. I'm buying more than I can eat, so at some point I'll start making jam. A silly hobby, but it's a tradition."

"I'd love to help, if you're open to that. I've never made jam."

"It's not difficult, and I'd love the help and the company." She sighed. "Douglas used to help me. Or rather he'd sit about where you are and offer advice. As if he knew how anything in a kitchen worked." She smiled.

"We were an old-fashioned couple. I cooked, he took care of the outside. But it worked for us."

"You were together a long time."

"We were. Forty-three years." Kathy laughed softly. "He would always say that forty-two of them were really good but we weren't talking about that one year."

"He sounds like a great guy."

"He was. I know I should be over him, but I still miss him. This old house gets big and lonely." She looked at Shaye. "So I appreciate the company."

"Me, too. Do you ever think about moving? You mentioned a condo before."

"I think about it. The condos are part of a new retirement community being built on the edge of town. They have stages of care." Kathy washed three more peaches. "I'd be interested in the independent living. I've gone by, and I have a brochure. Some days I'm ready to put down my deposit, and other days I'm convinced I'll never leave this house."

She looked around. "I'd want to sell it to a nice family who would appreciate what Douglas and I had here." Her gaze slid to Shaye. "So you and Lawson. How's that going?"

Shaye laughed. "Nice try, but no. We're not talking about that. I've known him less than two weeks. This is our second date. There will be no talk of us buying houses."

"You're right not to rush. It's just sometimes you know. I knew with Douglas. By our third date, I was already half in love with him, and after a month, he was the one. He proposed two months later, but our parents made us wait another year until we could get married. They wanted us to be sure."

She smiled at the memory.

Shaye had never felt that kind of certainty—not when it came to a man. It would be nice to be that secure in a relationship, she thought wistfully. As for the house, staying here permanently would be a dream. She could imagine a couple of kids and, of course, a dog. The house was built for a family and would be a wonderful place to make memories.

If she stayed...

No, she reminded herself. She hadn't decided she was staying. Yes, she liked the town and she was making friends, but she needed to be sure. There had already been too much heartbreak in her life without her messing up again.

Every time she was tempted to revise her plans, she reminded herself she wasn't going to be making decisions based on a guy. She had to know what was right for herself and herself alone. If only her mom was here. She would know exactly what to say to help Shaye make the right decision.

In a way, Kathy reminded her a little of her mom. She was kind and strong, with a sense of humor and an inner compass.

"You've had a very blessed life," Shaye said impulsively.

"I have. Oh, there have been sorrows, but all in all, I've been very lucky."

They chatted for another half an hour about nothing in particular, then the doorbell rang.

"That would be your young man," Kathy told her.

The old-fashioned phrase made Shaye smile. "It would be."

She walked to the front of the house and opened the

door. Lawson stood on the wide porch, a picnic basket in one hand.

"Hi," she said, taking in the dark jeans and the tailored gray shirt. He'd left the collar open and rolled up the sleeves to his elbows but was still dressed more datelike than she'd seen him before.

"Hi, yourself. You look beautiful."

He leaned in and lightly brushed his lips against her cheek. She felt tingles all the way down to her toes.

"You said there would be music," she said with a smile. "Christmas music or regular?"

He laughed. "It will be both. Regular until about a half hour before the tree-lighting, then it switches."

"I can't wait."

His dark gaze locked with hers. "Me, either."

She invited him in while she collected her sweater, handbag and the bottle of champagne she'd bought that afternoon and then had put in the refrigerator.

"Have fun," Kathy told her with a laugh. "I won't wait up."

"I'm ignoring that," Shaye told her, waving before she returned to the front of the house. She held up the champagne. "I thought tonight felt like a celebration."

"I like your style."

He tucked the bottle into the picnic basket, then put his hand on the small of her back as he escorted her outside. Once they were on the walkway, he took her hand in his, and they started toward The Wreath.

"How was your day?" he asked.

"Good. Still busy. The steady stream of tourists is impressive. I've never lived in a town with so many visitors. My hometown wasn't interesting enough to get people to come and stay."

"There are even more in the winter, and more things to do. We only have a few activities in July, but come Thanksgiving, all bets are off. There are all the outdoor sports along with the seasonal celebrations. Plus the daily Advent calendar. They set it up in The Wreath. On the first of December, there's a big party as the first box is opened. It's usually something fun like a sing-along or ice-skating. After that, the daily boxes are opened in the morning. They can say anything from *Go shovel someone's driveway* to *Bake cookies with someone you love*."

"I like the sound of that."

"There's always at least a couple of service projects."

"Paisley and Dena were telling me there's a day of service on Saturday. I'm going to be doing that with them."

He smiled at her. "You'll have fun."

"I'm looking forward to it."

He mentioned a few other holiday traditions in the town. Shaye enjoyed listening to him talk. Not just the sound of his voice but also what he said. There was a confidence in his tone and his words.

She hadn't known him long, but she had the sense she was getting to know him well. He wasn't the kind of man to use a woman for sex until something better came along.

Funny how the humiliation of thinking those words had faded. Now she was more interested in why she'd been so gullible and making sure she never was again, along with a big dose of gratitude that she'd found out the truth before she'd gone off to Los Angeles with a guy who didn't care about her.

They arrived at The Wreath. Shaye was surprised by

the transformation. When she'd left the space at three that afternoon, only a few tables and chairs had been set up. But four hours later, the big, open area had been filled with possibly hundreds of tables—some for two, some for eight or ten. There was a dance floor at the far end, close to the big Christmas tree that had been installed two days ago. That had been quite the production, involving a very large flatbed truck, several pulleys and nearly a dozen guys with ropes.

There was a line of people waiting to get inside The Wreath and student volunteers checked names against a list before handing over a card with a number on it.

"You have to make reservations?" Shaye asked. "To have a picnic?"

"There are a limited number of tables. A half hour before the lighting ceremony everyone who wants to come will be let in. But from now until nine thirty, it's by reservation only."

The line moved quickly. Shaye saw families and other couples, along with groups of friends of all ages. Some people had picnic baskets or takeout bags. Others were going to order from the nearby restaurants.

"This is a whole big thing," she said.

"It is. We take our traditions seriously in Wishing Tree."

"I like that."

He smiled at her. "Me, too."

When they reached the front of the line, Lawson gave his name and was handed a card. They made their way through the tables, studying the numbers on them, until they reached thirty-seven, a table for two away from the speakers and the DJ but with a nice view of the tree.

They were tucked in a relatively private area, with only other couples around them.

"So this isn't your first rodeo," she teased. "You're very smooth with your table selection."

Lawson didn't return her smile. "I haven't brought a date to the tree-lighting since I was in high school."

"You haven't?"

"I told you the first day I met you, this isn't a thing I do, Shaye. This is about you. I want you to believe me."

His gaze was steady as he spoke, his voice intense. He was willing her to trust him, and despite her past and recently broken heart, she wanted to. Everything she knew about Lawson told her he was honest and the kind of man she could trust. Even more than that, he'd have her back—something she'd never experienced in a romantic relationship before.

"I DO BELIEVE YOU," she whispered.

He took her hand and squeezed her fingers. "I'm glad. I arranged all this because I was thinking about spending the evening with you."

"Thank you."

They took their seats across from each other. Lawson had brought wine, which he promised to open later. He poured them each a glass of champagne, then they touched glasses.

"To a magical summer," she said. "Thank you for bringing me here tonight."

"I've been looking forward to it."

She smiled. "Me, too."

After they'd sipped their champagne, he began unpacking the picnic. First he handed her paper napkins and plates, then he set out the food.

"We'll start with melon prosciutto skewers with fresh basil and mozzarella," he said, putting a plastic container on the table. "Then we have a nice green salad with an herb vinaigrette. The entrée is a fresh corn-and-tomato fettuccine, and for dessert we have an assortment of cookies along with prosecco grapes." He grinned. "They are grapes soaked in vodka and prosecco, then rolled in sugar."

She stared at him, unable to fully grasp the menu. "I thought we'd have egg salad sandwiches and potato chips. How much did you make yourself?"

"My mom made the fettuccine, but I did the rest." He gave her a half proud, half embarrassed smile. "I like to cook. One of my friends in the army came from a family that owned a couple of Italian restaurants in Cleveland. He taught me a few things."

"And he cooks," she murmured, thinking Lawson simply got better and better. So what was the catch?

He opened the first container and served her a couple of the skewers. The salty goodness of the prosciutto went perfectly with the sweet melon and the cheese. As she chewed her first bite she realized that she'd been too nervous to eat lunch and was starving. Good thing he'd brought plenty.

"All right," she said, after she'd finished her second skewer. "Why aren't you married?"

He stared at her, his eyebrows raised. "Excuse me?"

She picked up her glass of champagne. "Come on, look at you. You're nice, you're funny, you have a plan for your life. You're good-looking, you can cook, you like dogs. Why aren't you married with a couple of kids?"

She expected him to laugh or distract her, but instead he exhaled slowly.

"I haven't found someone I can fall in love with."

The blunt, honest answer surprised her. "Not ever?"

"Not in a while. I had the serious girlfriend I told you about, in high school. We talked about getting married, but when that didn't work out, I took some time to think about what I wanted in my life. I dated a fair amount, but I never felt…sparks."

"You're not talking about passion, are you?"

"No. The other kind. I liked the women I went out with, but there wasn't anything special. No sense that any of them could be the one I wanted to spend the rest of my life with. I don't expect to hear angels singing, but an old-fashioned kick in the gut would be nice." He shook his head. "Maybe I'm a fool, but I want the woman I marry to leave me thunderstruck, at least once. I want sparks, and I haven't felt that."

He was perfect. Okay, not perfect-perfect, but so incredibly right about so many things. How was she supposed to not throw herself at him and beg him to feel sparks with her?

"Tell me more about the high school girlfriend," she said instead, because it seemed a much safer topic of conversation. "What was her name?"

"Cori. We were in love. Young, but we knew it was serious, and we had plans. I was going to join the army while she went to college. We were so sure we were going to make it."

"But you didn't."

"No." He shrugged. "About two years in, she told me that she liked living in a big city and that she didn't want to go back to Wishing Tree. Not ever. Not even for me."

Shaye knew that would have crushed him. "You, on the other hand, wanted to settle here."

He nodded. "It wasn't just about geography. I want to say she changed, but I'm sure it was both of us. The last time we saw each other, we didn't fight. We didn't anything. Whatever we'd had was gone."

"I'm sorry."

He smiled. "Thanks. I was sorry at the time, but looking back, I know we made the right decision."

"That's when you decided to figure out what you were looking for?"

"Uh-huh. Then I started dating." The smile returned, but this time it had a touch of sadness. "I figured I'd find someone in a matter of months. But I didn't."

"You're not giving up, though."

"No. I'll keep looking. I want to give my heart to someone special. Like I said, old-fashioned, but there we are."

Kathy had talked about things being old-fashioned, as well.

"Sometimes being traditional is a good thing," Shaye told him. "There's a continuity that can be comforting."

"So what about you? Before the jerk you told me about. Anyone special?"

"Not special enough."

"Are you giving up looking?"

She stared into his brown eyes. If he could be honest, then she could, as well. "No, I'm not."

THEY TALKED ALL through dinner. The meal was delicious, and the prosecco grapes were the perfect sweet ending to the meal. Shaye was very impressed with the thought and planning that had gone into everything.

As the evening progressed, The Wreath filled up. By seven, all the tables were filled. Their little section of the circle was quiet and surprisingly romantic.

When they'd finished eating, Lawson tugged her to her feet and drew her to the dance floor. His arms came round her, pulling her close. She went willingly, surprised at how well they fit together and how good she felt being so close to him. There was a sense of… she wasn't sure what. Belonging, maybe. She definitely felt safe, which was a wonderful sensation after being alone for so long.

Lawson was solid. He was physically strong and emotionally disciplined. He had a moral code she understood and respected. But he was also charming and way more open about his feelings than any other guy she'd ever known. She liked him. She liked him a lot, and while that should have scared her—for some reason it didn't. Not even a little.

CHAPTER SEVEN

THURSDAY AT THE end of her shift, Shaye got a text from Paisley.

Just confirming Saturday. It's our day of service. Rumor has it we'll be doing gardening around town. Dena and I would love you on our team. We meet in The Wreath at 8. See you then?

Shaye wasn't sure what all was involved with a day of service, but she was happy to hang out with her friends and help. There was just one problem.

I have to be at work at eleven, but I could join you until ten thirty.

Paisley sent back a smile emoji. Perfect. Can't wait.

Me, too. Looking forward to it. See you then.

She wheeled the cart back to the store and got it ready for the next day, then clocked out. As she started for home, she thought longingly about swinging by to see Lawson. Maybe they could hang out while he took his afternoon break or something.

He hadn't been over in the past couple of nights.

Adien and her husband had decided they needed some new baby furniture, and it had been delivered earlier in the week. The task of putting it all together was daunting, so Lawson was helping his brother-in-law.

While Shaye was still enjoying working on the car, she was willing to admit it wasn't as much fun without Lawson at her side. But he'd already asked her out for Saturday night, so she knew she would see him then.

But rather than bother him at work, she walked back to the beautiful Victorian house she'd grown to love. Her room was incredible—quiet and beautiful, with so many wonderful architectural touches. Now that she wasn't seeing Lawson every evening, she'd taken to having a bath when she finished with the car. The tub was a luxury she was definitely going to miss.

Kathy met her at the front door.

"It's gone," she said, a catch in her voice. "I'm being so silly, but there was something about watching them tow it away."

"The car?" Shaye asked, not sure what her landlord was talking about.

"Yes." Kathy sighed as she led the way to the kitchen. "Billy called this morning and said he had a cancellation and did I want them to bring it in early. You'd already told me it was ready to go, so I said yes. Now she's gone."

Shaye hid a smile. "She's getting painted. When she comes back, she's going to be so beautiful, you won't be able to speak. Trust me, it's worth it to have her all pretty again. Your car deserves a new paint job."

"You're right, of course. I want her all glowy for the parade. But it was so hard to see them take her away.

She's been with me for so long, and in some ways, having her close makes me feel Douglas isn't that far away."

Shaye's humor faded as she felt a stab of envy. She wanted that, she thought. A love that lasted years and warmed the heart even when the two parties were separated by space and time.

"You're very lucky," she said softly. "To have had Douglas in your life."

Kathy sniffed. "I am. All right. This is silly. It's just a car, and she'll back soon enough. I don't know why it hit me so much." She brought a tray of brownies to the island. "I made these this morning. I add chocolate chips because you can never have too much chocolate."

"You're spoiling me," Shaye said, reaching for one of the brownies. "Everything you make is so delicious."

Kathy smiled at her. "It's nice to have someone to bake for. I'm taking advantage of having you around."

"Feel free."

Kathy poured them each a glass of milk, then sat with Shaye at the big island.

"Saturday is our summer day of service. Do you know about this?"

Shaye had just taken a bite of the brownie and tried to not moan at the moist deliciousness. "Paisley told me about it a week or so ago, then texted me about it today. I'm meeting her and Dena Saturday morning."

"I'm glad you'll be going out with your friends," Kathy told her. "I would invite you to hang out with mine, but we're all too old for you."

"I don't believe that."

"You're sweet. Thank you." Kathy nibbled on her brownie. "Last year we painted several house porches and repaired front steps. This year we're sprucing up front yards. It's nice to help our neighbors who don't have the means to do that sort of thing." She smiled. "Someone always donates the needed supplies for our days of service. Our very own Secret Santa."

"The town seems to take care of its own."

"We're a close-knit group, and we want to take care of our neighbors. Was it like that where you grew up?"

"In spirit, yes, but the assistance wasn't as well organized. My parents never had a lot of money, so every now and then we were on the receiving end of some of the good works. When I was in elementary school, I desperately wanted to be in the orchestra. There was no way my parents could afford the instrument rental or the private lessons I would need. Someone paid for both."

Kathy smiled. "That's so nice."

Shaye laughed. "I was excited beyond words and couldn't wait to get started to learn to play the flute. Sadly, I had absolutely no talent, but I enjoyed playing for couple of years."

"It's nice when a community pulls together. It helps us have the strength to weather the bad times." Kathy finished her brownie. "All right, I've monopolized you long enough. You have things to do and people to see, and I'm playing bridge tonight. I'd best go get ready."

"Thanks again for the brownie."

"You're welcome."

Kathy left the kitchen. Shaye took the last bite of her treat, then rinsed her dishes and put them in the dishwasher. She was going to spend a quiet evening by herself. She'd finished as much of the engine rebuild as she could while it was out of the car. Once the Mustang was back in the garage, she would start the reassembly process and finish the engine work.

The parade wasn't that far away, she thought, climbing the stairs to her bedroom. The month was going by so quickly. Before she knew it, she would need to make a decision about herself and her future. There seemed to be fewer and fewer reasons to leave Wishing Tree. She had friends here, the promise of a job and a nearby college to complete her degree. Perhaps it was time to consider the fact that she may have already found what she was looking for.

SATURDAY MORNING DAWNED cool and overcast. Normally Shaye would be disappointed by such weather, but given that she was going to be outside gardening, she wasn't about to complain that it wouldn't be eighty by ten in the morning. After breakfast, she applied sunscreen, knowing she could still get burned with the clouds, and picked up the old straw hat Kathy had offered. Shaye had a brand-new pair of gardening gloves she'd sprung for, along with a couple of bottles of water. A few minutes before she was due to meet Dena and Paisley, she headed out for The Wreath.

She wasn't sure what to expect, but there were easily a hundred people waiting for the assignments. She found her friends and, more quickly than she would have thought, the three of them were walking along Noble Street, heading to the house they were going to work on.

The owner, a charming, elderly woman who had to be in her eighties, met them out front. Mrs. Marques was tiny and a little bent, but she had a smile that could light up a city block.

"You girls are sweet to help me," she said as she greeted them. "I don't get around as well as I used to, and this house is just too much for me. I'm buying one of those new condos in the retirement community they're building, but they won't be ready for a few more months. I pay a neighbor boy to mow the lawn, but he's never been one to enjoy gardening."

"That's why we're here," Paisley said, hugging the older woman. "We're going to spruce up your plant beds. We'll weed first, then put in some fresh color."

"You girls are so kind to help me out. Let me know when you get thirsty. I made some strawberry lemonade this morning, and it's delicious if I do say so myself."

Mrs. Marques went back into the house. Paisley and Dena had each brought plenty of gardening tools, along with mats to kneel on. The three of them got right to work, pulling weeds from the large flower bed in front of the porch.

"So, you're dating Lawson," Paisley said, about twenty minutes in. "You never said a word."

"Really? Lawson?" Dena sat back on her heels. "Why didn't I know this?"

"That's my question." Paisley's eyebrows rose inquisitively.

Shaye smiled at her. "I thought you knew. He came by when you were there at lunch a few days ago."

"I thought he was just buying hand pies. I didn't know there was an ulterior motive to his appearance. All right. Tell us everything."

"Yes, details please," Dena said with a laugh. "My dating life is a sad, barren desert, and I must live vicariously through you." She glanced at Paisley. "Maybe you could start seeing someone so I could have two friends who are falling for someone."

"I wish." Paisley dug into the earth and pulled out a

weed by the root. "But there is no one I'm interested in. I've either already dated them, watched them break the heart of a friend or figured out they're terribly flawed."

"You dated Lawson?" Shaye asked, wondering why he hadn't mentioned that. He'd made it sound like he hadn't gotten involved with anyone since he'd been back.

"What?" Paisley shook her head. "No, we've never gone out. I was speaking generally. Let's see. In high school, he had a serious girlfriend."

"Cori," Dena and Paisley said together.

"They were a thing," Dena added. "I was a couple of grades ahead, and even I remember them being serious. Everyone thought they were going to get married. She went off to college, and he joined the army, and then I guess at some point they broke up."

"That's what I remember, too." Paisley yanked out another weed. "And since he's been back, Lawson's been kind of—I don't know—not interested in anyone. You're the first woman I've heard he's gone out with."

Shaye felt good having his story confirmed. "We met my first day in town," she told them. "I arrived just when the reindeer 5K was starting. The antlers were confusing."

"Yes, we are a weird little town," Dena said, adding weeds to the growing pile. "But I wouldn't change a thing."

"Me, either," Paisley added. "So that was it? You talked, then what? He bought you lunch, and you were smitten?"

Shaye smiled. "Something like that."

"Wow. I'm happy for you and wildly jealous at the

same time. I want to meet a great guy. Lawson always seemed so… What's the word?"

"*Solid*," Shaye said.

"That's it." Dena laughed. "He's the kind of man you instinctively trust."

"And he just seems the type to be good in bed." Paisley grinned. "He just seems the type."

Shaye focused on the weeds in front of her. "I wouldn't know."

"Oh, but you will, and then we'll want to hear all about it." She paused. "Okay, maybe not details but, you know, a few broad strokes describing the event. I'm with Dena. This time we're going to have to live vicariously."

Shaye very much enjoyed being with Lawson, but she was in no way ready to take things to *that* level. It was too soon.

"Sorry to disappoint," she said, careful to keep her tone light. "But that's not going to be happening anytime soon. I like Lawson a lot, but it's only been a few weeks."

"You're smart," Dena told her. "Of course you want to take things slow and get to know him. Plus the falling-in-love stage is always so magical. Good for you, Shaye."

Falling in love? No. That wasn't happening. She didn't want to fall in love. If she did, she would be putting too much on the line. While her last boyfriend had battered her pride and left her feeling like an idiot, he hadn't broken her heart. She'd been more interested in leaving town with him because she needed to start over than because she couldn't imagine living without him. She'd liked him and had hoped they had a future, but it hadn't been love.

She wasn't ready to fall in love. Her heart was still healing from the death of her parents. Giving it over to a guy was just too big a risk. Sure, someday she wanted that. Someone she could be with for the rest of her life, but not now.

Right then the sun broke through the clouds, but instead of feeling the warmth of the moment, Shaye suddenly felt cold and afraid. All this time she'd thought she'd known what she was doing with Lawson. She'd been happy and had always felt safe with him. But now she was less sure of everything.

What *were* they doing? Dating, obviously, but to what end? A good time or something more? She knew she liked him, but was she ready to take on more than that? Did she have it in her? And if he wanted more than she was willing to give, where did that leave them? And where did it leave her as far as her decision to stay or to go?

SHAYE DID HER best to shake off her feeling of unease and just enjoy the morning. The new flowers were delivered around ten, and she and her friends made quick work of putting them in the ground. By the time Shaye had to leave for her shift with the food cart, Mrs. Marques's front yard looked significantly more cheerful than it had when they'd arrived.

Their grateful hostess gave her a package of cookies she'd made herself and thanked her several times.

"I know we're helping other people," Dena said as she and Paisley walked Shaye to the sidewalk, "but I have to admit part of the payoff is how good I feel after doing work like that."

"Me, too." Paisley laughed. "It's a true win-win.

When we're done here, I'm going to go home and get ready for the massage I booked for this afternoon."

"Smart," Shaye said. "I'll think of you as I'm working."

"But after work, you'll be getting ready for your date. That makes me jealous, so another win-win," Paisley said, her voice teasing.

"I will be," Shaye said, trying to sound more enthused than she felt. All her concerns had left her feeling uneasy about Lawson, and she didn't know how to set things right.

Shaye said goodbye and started home. On her way, she saw a couple of teams working on different front yards. Across the street, a few houses before her destination, she saw Lawson with a group of boys who looked to be maybe twelve or thirteen.

Their project had been more extensive. She could see a full yard-waste bin filled with dug up plants and bushes. The boys were busy replacing them with healthy-looking plants. Lawson worked alongside of them, obviously in control, but still laughing and joking with the kids.

He hadn't seen her, so she walked past them before turning to watch a little more. Lawson directed the boys with an ease that spoke of someone used to being in charge. When two boys started a heated conversation, he got between them and quickly de-escalated the situation.

She'd never seen him with teens but wasn't surprised at how well he did. She would have guessed he would have the patience and personality to step in and take control without being overbearing or diluting the fun.

She turned away and resumed her walk home. As

she reached Kathy's house, she realized she'd let herself get carried away before. Lawson was someone special. Yes, she wasn't ready for love, but it was too soon to worry about that. They were having a good time as they got to know each other. That was what dating was for. It was perfectly fine to have moments of panic, but she wasn't going to let the emotion define her decisions.

As for staying or going, she needed to make that decision on her own, without thoughts of Lawson influencing her. Because they weren't a sure thing. So maybe the question was, if she and Lawson broke up, would she still want to stay in Wishing Tree? And if she didn't, then maybe that told her everything she needed to know.

CHAPTER EIGHT

JUST ENOUGH CLOUDS lingered through the evening to produce a perfect sunset. Shaye walked next to Lawson, her hand in his as they strolled through the neighborhood where he'd grown up.

He pointed to a modest ranch-style home. "My friends and I TPed that house when I was nine. My dad wasn't happy when he found out and made me go back and help with the cleanup the next day. Toilet paper is not easy to get out of bushes."

She smiled at him. "Did you learn your lesson?"

"Absolutely. I never did it again."

"But you found other ways to be bad."

He chuckled. "It depends on how you define the term. I was a regular kid, so it's not like I stole a car and went hot-rodding."

"Car theft would be crossing the line."

They'd had a quiet dinner together at Blitzen's Pub, enjoying fish and chips and imported lager. Conversation had flowed as easily as ever, as they'd talked about their respective days working on people's gardens.

She was still confused about what she wanted for her future, but she had to admit the more time she spent with Lawson, the more she knew he was one of the good guys. Just as important, being around him made her happy. She enjoyed his company, liked hearing his opinions. They made each other laugh, and when he touched her, the tingles were impressive.

She still knew she was going to have to make her decision about staying or going, independent of how she felt about him, only she was afraid that untangling him from her life wasn't going to be easy.

They turned the corner, and he pointed to the large park surrounding a very small lake.

"The town's outdoor ice-skating rink," he said. "At least, in the winter."

"It's pretty here."

There were lots of trees, picnic areas and a playground for the kids.

"On weekends and the week before Christmas, they set up booths selling things like hot chocolate," he told her, pulling her toward a cluster of trees. "The music changes every night." He grinned. "Ice-skating to hip-hop is kind of a challenge."

"Not if you're a really good skater."

"True, but for the rest of us, it's not pretty to watch."

They stepped into the darkness of the trees. Lawson didn't go far before leaning against a sturdy trunk and drawing her close. She wrapped her arms around him as he cupped her face. And then he kissed her.

It wasn't the first time, but she sensed more passion in his touch. They were in relative privacy, or maybe it was they were more comfortable with each other. Unlike the other times, he didn't hold back. Instead he claimed her lips with a level of desire that stole her breath.

Caught up in the feel of his mouth, his tongue and the heat they generated, she instinctively moved closer, pressing her body against his. She felt the hard lines of his chest, the thickness of his erection, and she wanted more than this. She wanted him.

But she didn't say that, nor did she suggest they take things inside. As much as she would like to make love with Lawson, she knew they weren't ready. She needed to get her head together first and make a few decisions. But it was nice to want him, to feel the desperate ache of need.

After a few minutes, they drew back. His eyes were bright with need.

"You take my breath away," he murmured.

She smiled. "I was thinking the same thing."

"I want you." He shook his head. "That's information, not a request. I want you, Shaye. In my arms, my bed, my…" He stopped talking, as if internally editing his words, then returned his attention to her. "I'm enjoying getting to know you."

My what? What had he been about to say? His life? His heart? Happiness and concern fought for dominance and had to settle on an uncomfortable truce.

"I'm enjoying getting to know you, too," she said, hoping her unease didn't show. She wasn't sure how to tell him he was moving too fast without sounding mean.

He touched her cheek. "All right. Let's get you home before I start begging. You'd be forced to let me down gently, but I'd be crushed, and I suspect my tears would upset you."

"I don't think you cry very often, but I appreciate the visual."

He put his arm around her as they walked out of the park. "I tend toward those high-pitched little sobs that make your voice catch."

She laughed. "You are so lying."

"Maybe a little."

LAWSON FOUND HIS sister folding laundry in the family room. There were piles on every chair and on the sofa.

Adien shook her head when she saw him. "No judging. I can't seem to catch up this week, and Jack has been working as much overtime as he can get."

"I don't judge," Lawson said, walking over to the sofa and grabbing a towel. "You want everything in place for when the baby comes."

She rubbed her back. "Three kids. What was I thinking?"

"That you want a big family."

"I know, but right now, it feels overwhelming."

"Call Mom."

"And have her descend? No, thanks. I'm playing that card after this one makes an appearance."

"Let me know what I can do to help."

She pointed to the stack of towels he'd started on the coffee table. "Keep doing that and I'll be happy." She looked at the clock. "You're home early from your date."

Lawson had wanted to stay out later with Shaye, but she was getting to be a little too tempting. He knew he had to go slow, but every time he was with her, he wanted her more and not just for sex.

"I'm falling for her."

Adien looked at him. "I can't remember you ever saying that about anyone else you dated."

"I haven't."

"So it's the real thing?"

"It is for me."

His sister smiled. "For what it's worth, I like her a

lot. She does a good job at the pie shop. She's honest and hardworking. The customers adore her. More than one has stopped by the store to talk about how sweet she is."

His sister's assessment only confirmed what he already knew.

"I'm not sure she's staying," he told her. "Her plan was to settle in Seattle." He told her what Shaye had said the first day they'd met. "Wishing Tree is a pit stop, not a destination."

"Maybe she's changed her mind. Or maybe she will. Toby offered her my job."

Hope flared. "Did she take it?"

"Not yet."

Hope died. "So she hasn't made up her mind yet, and I don't know what that means. Is she being careful, or is she just using me to pass the time?"

"I doubt it's that."

"I don't know. Sometimes I think she's as into me as I'm into her, and other times I have no idea what she's thinking." He finished with the towels and moved on to the kids' clothes. "There was a guy back home. He treated her badly. I know she's still working through that."

"Don't worry about another guy," Adien told him. "You're going to measure up to anyone."

"I just don't know what she wants. I don't think she knows, either." He looked at his sister. "What if she leaves? What if the plan is more important than what we've started?"

"Maybe you should wait for the bad thing to happen before you start worrying about it. Lawson, this isn't like you. You don't usually anticipate trouble."

"Shaye matters. I don't want to lose her."

His sister put down the T-shirt she'd been folding. "You're in love with her."

Words he didn't want to hear but wouldn't run from. "Yes."

She smiled. "Good for you."

"Not if she leaves."

His sister picked up the shirt. "I want to tell you to convince her to stay, but we both know that won't work. She has to want to make a home here or not."

"I won't try to influence her decision. Not after Cori."

Because when his ex-girlfriend had started to express doubts about them and their future, he'd done everything he could to convince her she would be happy in Wishing Tree. He'd pushed and she'd pushed back. They'd ended up fighting way too much. By the time they'd broken up, the fighting had ended. There hadn't been anything left to say.

With time and maturity, he'd seen that. Now he knew that Shaye had to make her own decision based on what she believed to be best for herself. If she wanted to stay, then he would woo her until she fell in love with him or told him it wasn't going to work. But if she left, he would let her go without saying a word. There would be no attempts to change her mind.

"I wish I knew which way she was leaning," he admitted.

"Bring her to dinner Sunday," his sister offered.

"With the family? No way."

"Why not? It's big and loud, and she'll have fun. And you'll see her in a different setting. If she can't handle the craziness, then she's never going to marry you anyway, so you might as well find out now."

"I'm not ready to share my time with her." If she was leaving, there weren't that many days left. Selfishly he wanted to spend them all with her.

Adien's gaze was steady. "You know I'm right. Invite her to dinner and see what happens. The evening will answer a lot of questions."

His sister *was* right—a fact he didn't much like. "I'll see if she wants to join us."

"Try to be at least a little enthusiastic when you ask her," she teased.

"With any luck, she'll say no."

Shaye absolutely should have said no, she thought as she walked beside Lawson. It was too soon to be meeting the parents, not to mention the other members of his family. But when he'd asked, she'd been swept by an incredible longing to be a part of what he'd described as *general chaos over a rib roast*. She'd been on her own long enough that the thought of real family time was irresistible.

She'd taken over Kathy's kitchen for the morning and had made sugar cookies that she'd carefully iced and decorated. Given that it was Christmas in July, she'd created Santa hats, Christmas trees and ornaments, then had wondered if they would see the humor in her gift or just think she was weird.

Thankfully the delivery of the newly painted red car had been a nice distraction. She'd spent the afternoon starting the reassembly process before having to stop to get ready for her date.

Lawson's parents lived close to what had been the old downtown, before the retail area had moved to The Wreath. The house was a big, sprawling, three-story beauty on an oversize lot in a neighborhood filled with families. The front yard was dotted with tricycles and balls. A stuffed bear sat by the front door.

As they climbed the porch steps, Lawson looked at her. "I need to tell you something."

Her already nervous stomach clenched. "Yes?"

"We're not having a roast. My folks are barbecuing burgers. There will be some salads and stuff, but there's no roast. I hope that's okay."

She stared at his serious expression. "I don't know. That changes everything. Maybe I should come back another time."

"Understandable. I lured you here with false pretenses. I'm sorry."

Before she could think of something funny to say in return, the front door opened, and a dark-haired woman in her fifties waved them inside.

"Lawson, what are you doing? You don't leave your guest on the porch like that. What will she think about how I raised you?" The woman smiled. "You're Shaye, yes? I'm Norma. Come on, come on. The party's in back."

Shaye found herself hustled through the house to the kitchen. She passed through large, comfortable rooms and high ceilings, then she was in what was obviously the heart of the home.

Adien stood at the biggest stove Shaye had ever seen, stirring a huge pot. Another woman, about her age, had a baby on her hip. Through the big bay window, Shaye could see more children running through the backyard.

"Everyone," Norma said in a loud voice, "this is Shaye."

Adien turned and smiled. "You made it. Welcome. I

hope you brought earplugs. We're loud." She laughed. "That's my sister Sabrina. Mom, let's avoid giving her the kids' names. There are too many."

"Nice to meet you," Sabrina, as pretty as Adien, said with a weary smile. "They're a little wild today. I apologize in advance."

"Nice to meet you, as well." Shaye turned back to Lawson's mother. "I made some cookies. I decorated them in honor of Christmas in July."

"Oh, you bake!" Norma looked at her daughter. "She bakes. That's good." Norma set the container on a table overflowing with food. "Let's go outside and meet the rest of the family." She looked at Lawson. "You'll have to watch your father with the burgers. He doesn't like to cook them enough for the kids."

"Dad knows, Mom."

"He knows, but does he listen?" Norma linked arms with Shaye. "A five-year-old doesn't want a raw burger, am I right? It's not good for them. Yes, we get the meat from a local rancher, but still. Cook the food. They're babies. Be kind to their tummies. Not that he's the one who they come to when they have to poop for three hours in the middle of the night. No, then it's the mother. Always the mother."

Shaye honestly didn't know what to say as she went outside with Norma. She met Lawson's father and both his brothers-in-law but she wasn't sure which man went with which sister. Something that would sort itself out over the course of the afternoon.

Henry Easley was tall and handsome, with a charming smile. The man obviously adored his wife which, after so many years of marriage, was lovely to see.

She was invited to join a game of croquet with the

older kids—all of whom were still under the age of ten. Lawson stayed with her, helping her keep names straight and settling a couple of disputes about the rules.

The sun was warm, the sky clear, and the sound of laughter and happy conversation added to the party atmosphere.

"Is it like this every weekend?" she asked him when the game ended and they all lined up for lemonade.

"We do the big dinners about once a month," he said. "My parents always host, but my sisters take turns cooking. In the summer, we usually barbecue like we are today, but when it's colder, the meals are a little more formal."

"And with the roast you lied about?" she asked, her voice teasing.

"Yes, with that."

She looked around at the kids running everywhere and his dad talking to his sons-in-law. "You must have missed this while you were overseas."

"More than I can say."

She believed him. While this wasn't anything like her small family had been, she still felt the same kind of love and support. This was what she'd been missing in her life. A family. Belonging.

His mother appeared at the back door. "Shaye, I need your help in the kitchen." She shooed Lawson away. "You can talk to your pretty girl later. Now it's my turn."

Lawson grimaced. "You don't have to answer anything you don't want to. Remember that. I'll check in on you every ten minutes."

She laughed. "I like your mom. Don't worry. I'll be fine."

Once in the kitchen, she was put to work peeling carrots for the veggie plate. Norma positioned herself close.

"So, Shaye, tell us about yourself. You've been married before?"

She nearly dropped the carrot she'd been holding. "What? No."

"Any children?" Norma held up a hand. "I'm not judging. I'm asking. You can have children. It's fine."

"Mom!" Adien shot Shaye a sympathetic look. "Could you at least try to be subtle?"

"What's the point in that? I want to know if she has children. I like children. It would be nice."

Shaye cleared her throat. "No, um, children."

"But you want them?"

"Mom!" Sabrina joined in with Adien. "Stop."

Shaye grinned, kind of liking the free-for-all grilling. If she could handle this, she was tougher than she'd realized.

"I like children very much and would like to have a few of my own one day."

Norma smiled at her daughters. "See, a good answer. What about prison? Have you been?"

Shaye couldn't help laughing. "I have never been arrested, so no prison time for me."

Lawson walked in just then. "Mom, what are you asking? Prison?"

"Your father and I saw a show about young people in prison. It's not a good place to be. You should avoid it."

"Thanks for the tip," he said, taking the peeler from Shaye. "We're going back outside."

"She wants babies," his mother said. "That's a good thing. I said it was good, and I know you agree."

He eased Shaye out of the kitchen and onto the back porch. "I am so sorry."

She laughed. "Don't be. I like that she's direct. You always know where you stand with her."

"Yes, but don't say that like it's a good thing. Next up she'll be grilling you about our sex life and telling you to make sure I always wear a condom."

"But we don't have a sex life," she said, intending the remark to be funny, only to realize it wasn't at all. Longing filled her, and she swayed toward him.

He stared into her eyes. "I'm very clear on that. You know why, don't you?"

"Yes."

"Tell me."

She smiled, confident in her answer. "Because you care about me and us and you want both of us to be sure. Sex too early tends to change things and not always in a good way."

"Yeah," he said softly. "That."

CHAPTER NINE

SHAYE ENJOYED WATCHING Lawson interact with his family. The love they shared was obvious, even from a distance. There was plenty of teasing and jokes, but also concern and support. Lawson might be the third in age, but somehow he was the head of the group of siblings. His sisters obviously looked up to him and wanted to know what he thought, and his brothers-in-law considered him a friend.

She liked that. She liked how his mother said what she thought and how his father still chased his mom to steal a few kisses. It was the perfect way to spend a few hours, and while she should have been delighted to be part of things, as the evening progressed she found herself sinking into a bone-crushing sadness that she couldn't seem to shake.

Yes, being with Lawson was great, and she liked his family, but it wasn't hers. No matter how many hugs she observed, her parents would never hug her again. She had no siblings, no extended family. At the end of the day, she was completely alone. And while that was awful to think about, risking caring again seemed so much worse. She simply didn't have it in her to give her heart again and have something bad happen. She couldn't deal with one more loss.

Having her previous boyfriend behave so badly had

hurt her pride and made her feel awful, but her heart hadn't been touched. He hadn't had the ability to steal his way inside enough to truly matter. But Lawson was different—she could love him. And then what? What if he didn't love her back? What if he did, and things progressed, and then he changed his mind? What if he died? What if they couldn't have children?

There was too much potential for her to be emotionally devastated, and she wasn't going to go there. Not again. It wasn't worth it. Better to stay separate and not risk the pain.

With the acceptance of that as her life's destiny came the need to run. She couldn't stay here, couldn't pretend. Only she wasn't going to tell Lawson the truth—not now. Not like this. So she excused herself from the kitchen and went out back to find him.

He was talking with his father but stepped away as soon as he saw her.

"What's wrong?"

Because he could read her that well.

"I think I'm getting sick," she lied, pressing a hand to her stomach. "Maybe something I ate. I don't know, but I'd like to go home."

"Of course. Give me one second."

He returned to his father's side and spoke to him. Henry glanced at her, his expression concerned, then he handed over a set of keys to his son. Lawson came back to Shaye.

"I'll drive you," he said. "It'll be quicker." He put his arm around her and guided her through the side yard. "You left your handbag in the living room. We'll go in through the front to get it." He gave her a worried smile.

"Less questions that way. When I get back, I'll explain to my mom what happened."

She came to a stop and looked at him. "I should tell her myself."

"You don't want to do that. She'll grill you about what's wrong, give a lot of unsolicited advice, and it will take an extra twenty minutes to get out of here."

"Thank you."

The smile turned genuine. "Of course."

He escorted her to the car and quickly delivered her to Kathy's front door.

"I'm going to check in on you in a few hours," he said. "I hope that's okay."

Because he cared. Because he wanted her to be all right. He really thought she was sick, rather than a coward who was too scared to accept what he offered.

She nodded and quickly escaped, before she confessed her flaws and saw the affection in his eyes change to contempt.

Kathy was gone, and the house was quiet. Shaye hurried up to her bedroom and changed into yoga pants and a T-shirt. She stretched out on the bed, suddenly feeling sick to her stomach—perhaps her body punishing her for the lies.

"I didn't have a choice," she whispered into the silence. "Everyone would have been upset."

She would have ruined the evening. This was better. She would lie low for a while, then end things with Lawson. She only had a few days left at her job. Once that was done, she would leave for Seattle and start over there.

This time she would be smarter. This time she wouldn't get involved with anyone. She would keep to herself and stay emotionally safe. If she didn't care, she couldn't love. Without love, there would be no loss. It was a sensible plan. A lonely one, but that was very little to pay for an intact heart.

TWO HOURS LATER, Shaye received a text from Lawson asking how she was feeling. She couldn't stand to tell him they were finished just yet, so she said her stomach was much better and asked him to tell his parents how sorry she was to miss out on the dinner.

An hour after that, Kathy knocked on her closed door.

"I heard you weren't feeling well," her landlord called from the hallway. "I have chicken soup and Sprite downstairs, if either of those would help."

Shaye thought about telling her to go away, but knew she couldn't repay Kathy's kindness that way. She rose and crossed to the door.

After pulling it open, she said, "I'm feeling a little better. Thank you."

Kathy looked at her and sighed. "Oh, dear. This isn't good, is it? Why don't you come downstairs and tell me what happened?"

Shaye followed dutifully. Once they were in the kitchen, Kathy put water in the kettle and set it on the stove, then started assembling a plate with cheese, crackers and some sliced nectarines. When the tea was ready, she put a mug in front of Shaye, then took a seat at the island.

Shaye nibbled on a piece of cheese to buy time, but eventually she knew she had to speak.

"I miss my mom and dad."

Kathy nodded slowly. "Of course you do."

She fought against tears. "We found out about my dad when we got a call from his supervisor, telling us he'd been rushed to the hospital. Thankfully, I was home for spring break. By the time we got to the emergency room, he was gone. It was just so fast, and there was a surreal quality to the whole day. My mom was so quiet, so still until we got home, and then she lost it. She cried for days."

Shaye wrapped her hands around the hot mug. "That's what I remember most. Her pain. It was a living creature in the house. She couldn't function. I arranged the funeral, made the calls. She'd always had health issues, and after my dad passed, she didn't get out of bed for three days. Finally she got up and tried to help, but then she would start crying."

Kathy rubbed her back. "That was a lot for you to deal with on your own."

Shaye nodded. "Her friends helped. Mine didn't know what to do. No one else had lost a parent, and they mostly hovered. Plus, I'd been living somewhere else since I'd started going to college. I felt disconnected from what was happening, but I knew I couldn't leave my mom on her own. I left school and my apartment there and moved back home."

"You were her rock."

"I tried to be." She thought about that time. "It was strange to be back, especially with him gone. We just kind of clung to each other, waiting to hurt less. I got a job and reconnected with my high school friends."

"But you lost the ones you'd made at college. The ones who were more in tune with your future plans."

Shaye stared at her in surprise. "Yes. How did you know?"

Kathy smiled. "The benefits of age, my dear. I've seen a lot. Then your mom left you."

"It was bad. She hadn't been feeling well or sleeping. One morning, she wasn't up, and I was so relieved she'd finally gotten some sleep. Only, when I checked her, she was gone. She'd died in the night."

She didn't remember much about that morning. She supposed that was her brain's way of protecting her from yet another loss.

"I called the paramedics, and they called the coroner. Given her health issues and my dad's passing, no one was surprised, except for me." Tears burned. "I didn't think she'd leave me."

"You know she didn't have a choice, right? It's not like she willed herself to die. You were her only child, and she loved you. She would have stayed if she could."

"I tell myself that, and most days I believe it." She looked at Kathy. "I can't do it again. I can't survive another broken heart. I don't have it in me. Lawson is... He's incredible and wonderful, and I'll never meet anyone like him again. I know that. I know I'm going to regret losing him, but I can't deal with any other option. I'm not that strong. I just want to go be by myself. If I don't care too much, I can't get hurt. That's better."

"Safe," Kathy said, squeezing her hand. "So much safer. Lonely, but that's the price you pay."

Shaye pressed her lips together. "I can't tell if you're agreeing with me or humoring me."

Kathy's expression was kind. "I understand what you're feeling, and I know why you're making the choices you are. I'm not humoring you. I'm sad you're giving up the chance to have something wonderful in your life based on the assumption that you're a weak person."

Shaye pulled back her arm, hurt by the words. "Why would you say that?"

"Because it's the problem. You just said you're too weak to handle the pain of loss. At least you know your limitations."

Shaye didn't like the sound of that. She wasn't weak. She'd held it together through the death of both her parents. She'd dealt with their estates, had sold the family home and, when her boyfriend had turned out to be a jerk, had driven across the country, by herself, to start over.

"I'm not weak. I'm not."

"So, afraid?"

Wrestling with fear sounded better than being weak. "Yes, I'm afraid."

"Of not being strong enough to handle something bad happening?"

"I guess." Although *not being strong enough* sounded an awful lot like *being weak*. She shifted, uncomfortable with the conversation.

Kathy smiled. "I know you expect me to tell you that you can't run away from loss, so I'll just point out that it has a way of finding you, regardless of how well you hide. It's a part of life."

Kathy's gaze locked with hers. "Love is worth it. That I know for sure. Was I devastated when Douglas died? Of course. That pain will be with me always, but it can't take away the thousands of days we spent together. I'll always have the laughter, the love, my children and grandchildren. I know you've suffered a lot. Having said that, I must tell you you've learned the wrong lesson. We can't hide from life. What's that old saying? Something about reaching for the stars because even when we fail, we've aimed so much higher than we did before." She smiled. "I have that all wrong, but you know what I'm saying."

Shaye did, and she didn't like it one bit. "I'm still leaving," she said stiffly. "I have to."

"Then, I won't try to convince you otherwise, but I do have a request."

"What?"

"Stay long enough to ride in the classic car parade with me. I'm so grateful for the work you've done. I want you to share in the glory. Just stay through the parade. Please."

Shaye nodded slowly. She would stay for her job and for the parade, and then she would leave. Maybe she was making a mistake. Maybe she would regret it. But right now she had to protect herself, and there was no way to do that if she stayed.

LAWSON STARED AT his phone. He'd read the text so many times he had it memorized, but he still looked at it over and over again, as if by sheer will the words would change. Only, they didn't.

I can't see you anymore. It's not for the reasons you think, although I'm not sure that matters. I'm leaving after the car show and moving to Seattle. I'm sorry. I never meant to hurt you. Please believe me when I tell you I'm the problem. I'm not who you think.

And that was all. There was no real explanation beyond the cryptic message, no offer to talk or to see him again. Nothing. Just her ending things.

He spent the rest of the day with a knot in his gut. He went through the motions of doing his job, all the while aware that the very thing he'd hoped would happen—he and Shaye falling in love and spending their lives together—was lost forever.

About once every five minutes he took out his phone to call her. About once an hour, he started for his truck to go talk to her. Each time, he stopped himself. She'd made up her mind, and he would respect that. He wasn't going to try to convince her. That wasn't his place. He'd learned that very hard lesson with Cori.

The irony was that if she asked him to go with her to Seattle, he would consider the move. He would think about giving up his dream of buying the auto shop, of living close to his family, because being with Shaye was more important than both. But she didn't ask, and he knew better than to offer.

There was nothing to do but endure the rest of the day, then head home and wait for the worst of the pain to pass. It should only take a couple of years. But even then, he knew he would spend the rest of his life sure that Shaye had been his true soul mate. He didn't think a guy ever got over something like that.

THE MORNING OF the twenty-fifth dawned with a perfect blue sky. By ten, the temperatures were already close to eighty degrees. Shaye sat in the window seat and stared out at the beautiful mountain view. Just one more thing she was going to miss when she left Wishing Tree.

She'd accomplished a lot in not very many days—mostly because she wasn't sleeping and could work late into the night and start again early. The Mustang was back together and looking glorious with its candy-apple-red paint job.

She'd started the engine two days ago. It had caught immediately and had rumbled just the way it should. There was nothing so satisfying as the growl of a V-8 in a beautiful car.

The moment should have thrilled her—it was the culmination of so much hard work. Only, she'd been alone in the garage. Kathy had been out with friends, and there had been no one else to share her triumph. No one to cheer with, no one to join her on that first drive.

She hadn't heard from Lawson—not since she'd sent her breakup text, and he'd responded with a gentle *I'm sorry, too, but I'll respect your wishes. You won't hear from me again.* Which was just so like Lawson. He wouldn't push, he wouldn't yell. He would simply let her go.

She missed him. Not just with working on the car but in every other way possible. She missed seeing him and thinking about seeing him. She missed laughing with him and having him kiss her. She missed *them*. And while she was thinking about missing things, she was also missing Paisley and Dena. She'd been a total coward and had joined them for dinner without mentioning that she was planning on leaving. A truth that made her feel small, but she hadn't been able to face the questions and the hurt she knew she would see in their eyes.

Instead she'd lied to them, then had gone home and cried herself to sleep.

Leaving hurt. She was already packed and had loaded most of her things in her truck. But every trip downstairs had been like a blow to her heart. She would miss Kathy and the house and her room. She would miss her job and the silly town.

She stood and gave the room one last check to make sure she hadn't forgotten anything. Once she got to Seattle, she would feel better. Once she started her new life, she could forget about this one. She would get used to being lonely. The alternative was to…to…

She stood in the middle of the bedroom, trying to figure out what the alternative was. To care? To risk losing again? Did she really want that? Was it worth it?

"Shaye, it's time."

Kathy's voice drifted through the open door. Shaye grabbed her purse and stepped out on the landing, then carefully closed the door behind her. She was done. There was no going back. Only forward.

THE CLASSIC CAR parade was bigger—or possibly longer—than Shaye had expected. There were at least three dozen entries. Everything from a sputtering Model T to an elegant 1934 Buick Eight to an iconic 1955 T-Bird, made famous in the old movie *American Graffiti*.

The lineup was arranged by the owners drawing a number from a hat. Kathy's Mustang was number fifteen, right in the middle of the parade. Kathy had arranged for the car to be driven by a very excited high-school senior whose hands practically trembled as he ran his fingers along her glossy hood.

"She's a sweet ride, Mrs. Vieira."

"Thanks, Elliot. I think so, too. Shaye here finished the restoration my husband had started."

Elliot's face showed his shock, but he managed to nod and say "You did a great job."

"Thank you."

"We'll be riding in back," Kathy said, pointing to the car. "And aren't the booster seats clever? See how they get locked in with the seat belts? And there's a place for us to hang on. We'll be up a bit and able to wave at the little people."

Despite her heavy heart, Shaye laughed. "The little people?"

Kathy grinned. "You know. The ones who can only watch us sail by."

Shaye and Kathy climbed into the back seat and strapped themselves in. The booster seat was secure, but Shaye felt like she was riding a camel. Still, she was determined to enjoy her last day in Wishing Tree. When the parade was over, she was leaving town.

Elliot started the engine, then flashed her a grin. "I love this car."

"Me, too," Shaye admitted.

They waited a few minutes, then the car in front began to move.

The parade route started and finished in The Wreath. They went north on West Mistletoe Way, by the park that had the ice-skating rink in winter, along Red Cedar Highway and around to String of Lights Park, then back to The Wreath.

Crowds lined the entire route, and right away Shaye saw people she knew. That nice couple from Nevada, the ones who'd been buying lunch from her for the past three days and tipped so well, waved and called out to her. A block later she saw Paisley, who hooted as Shaye drove by. She saw Dena with an older couple. Her parents, Shaye guessed. They looked happy together.

She saw families she recognized by sight if not name and dozens of tourists. Everyone was smiling and waving, having a wonderful time on the beautiful summer day. Everyone but her.

The more they drove, the worse she felt. Her body was heavy with sadness, and she was finding it harder and harder to breathe. She didn't want to give this up. Not any of it. She wanted to stay and be a part of the town. She wanted Christmas in July and then Thanksgiving and the entire month of December. She wanted to see the giant Advent calendar and be there when the first snow fell. She wanted friends and something more than being alone for the rest of her life.

By String of Lights Park she heard a familiar voice and saw the entire Easley clan, including Henry and Norma, waving frantically and calling out to her.

"You'll have to come back for dinner," Norma yelled. "We miss you." Norma frowned. "Are you crying? Shaye, what's wrong?"

Shaye touched her cheek and found it was wet with tears. She *was* crying, and she had no idea why. The only thing she knew for sure was she had to find Lawson before it was too late.

"He's waiting at The Wreath," Kathy said softly. "I asked him to be there when we got back."

Shaye stared at her. "Why would you do that?"

"Because I don't believe in giving up hope."

Shaye leaned over and hugged her friend. "What was I thinking?"

"You were alone and afraid. You thought you didn't have anyone, but you were wrong. You have us, Shaye. We're going to be your family for the rest of your life. You'll see. It's going to be wonderful."

"Thank you."

"You're welcome. Now, wave to the nice people."

Shaye gave a strangled laugh and turned back to the crowd. She waved and waited, aware of how painfully slow the parade was going. Finally she couldn't stand it any longer.

"Let me out," she told Elliot. "Stop the car. I'll run the rest of the way."

Elliot did as she requested. Shaye fumbled with the seat belt, then scrambled out and started running. She cut across Noble Street and down Gingerbread Lane, entering The Wreath from the north.

The crowd had grown, but she was undeterred. She hurried to the finish line and scanned the faces until she found the one that filled her heart with so much love, she knew she would never feel empty or alone again.

"Lawson!"

She ran toward him. He turned and saw her. Their eyes locked, and for a second she saw how much he'd been hurting and what she'd done to him. Then his expression brightened, and he was running toward her.

"I'm sorry," she said, pressing her hands to his chest. "I'm sorry. I was so wrong. I was scared, and I let that fear define me. It wasn't you, it was me. I didn't think I could handle one more loss. Only, I got it wrong. Love gives you strength. Love is what makes life worth living. You offered me so much more than I could have ever imagined, but I didn't see it that way."

She paused. "I'm not making any sense, am I? I just want you to know I was wrong to think leaving was the answer. It's not. I want to stay. I want to make my life here in Wishing Tree, and I'm hoping you'll still want to go out with me. I think we have something special between us, and I want to see where it goes."

He smiled at her, a handsome, sexy smile full of

promise and hope and something that looked at lot like love—not that she was going to assume anything.

"I'm in love with you," he said simply.

Her heart fluttered, and her knees went weak. "I love you, too."

"Then, you want to get dinner later?"

She laughed and threw herself at him. He caught her and held her like he was never going to let her go.

EPILOGUE

THE OCTOBER DAY was cool and crisp. The blue sky provided the perfect backdrop to the reds, yellows and oranges of the changing leaves. Shaye breathed in the scents of fall as she walked the trail with Lawson. They were on what she feared was their last hike of the season. She would miss their weekly treks but knew they would start up again in the spring.

They were on one of their favorite trails. The steep path ended at a flat outcropping that offered a stunning view of the town and the mountains beyond. They came up here often and thought of it as *their* special place.

After realizing she would be a fool to leave Wishing Tree and reconciling with Lawson, Shaye had settled into life in the town. She'd accepted the job at Judy's Hand Pies and had signed a lease with Kathy. She would be applying to college in the spring, with the idea of starting the following fall, once she'd established her residency.

Paisley and Dena had forgiven her for almost-leaving, and now the three of them were good friends who spent many a girls' night together. Shaye was hoping one or both of them would find a great guy so they could double date.

Lawson's family had welcomed her as one of their own. She and Norma were close and getting closer, something Lawson teased her about, but she didn't care. She loved being part of a big, loud family.

The last few yards of the climb were steep, forcing her to pay attention to her feet and her breathing rather than her thoughts. She rallied for the last bit and emerged on the big, flat area, out of breath and laughing.

"I always worry I won't make it," she admitted, leaning against Lawson. "Why doesn't it get easier?"

"Because without the effort, the view wouldn't be as good."

She kissed him, then led the way to their favorite boulder. They climbed up on top and took their familiar seats to look out at the valley below.

From here they could see the town. The Wreath was a real circle, with the businesses around it. The colors of the trees blended with roofs, and beyond the buildings were the mountains.

"It's going to look so different in the spring," she said, helping Lawson shrug off his backpack. They usually brought a picnic lunch with them. It was a little chilly for dining alfresco, so today they were just going to have a snack and then head back down.

"I'm looking forward to sharing the view with you then," Lawson said, pulling out plastic champagne glasses.

"Those are very fancy," she said, then laughed when he drew out a bottle of champagne. "So not water?"

He looked at her. "No. It's our last hike for a while. I thought we should celebrate."

"I'm all for that."

He expertly popped the cork, then poured. "I had an

interesting talk with Kathy this week," he said, smiling at her. "About her house."

"What about it?" Shaye felt her stomach drop. "Oh, no. She's going to buy one of those retirement condos, isn't she? I want her to be happy, of course, but I'll hate leaving that house. I love it."

"I know you do. I was thinking we could buy it. For the two of us now and for our family later."

Before she could figure out what he was saying, he drew a ring box out of his backpack.

"I love you, Shaye. You're the one I've been waiting for. I want to spend the rest of my life showing you just how much you mean to me and making you happy. Will you marry me?"

The diamond solitaire sparkled in the afternoon light. Her heart thudded in her chest, and there was a muffled ringing in her ears. Love, happiness and most of all hope filled her until she knew it was very possible she would float away.

"Yes," she said, hugging Lawson. "Yes, I'll marry you. I love you so much. For always. You're where I find home."

"We'll find home with each other, Shaye. For the rest of our lives. That's my promise to you. For always."

"For always," she echoed, knowing she was right where she belonged. In a quirky little town called Wishing Tree.

* * * * *

Can't get enough of Wishing Tree?

Please turn the page for an excerpt from
Home Sweet Christmas, *the witty and heartfelt*
second book in #1 New York Times *bestselling*
author Susan Mallery's Wishing Tree series
about two friends who unexpectedly find the
person—and the place--in which they belong
this Christmas.

CHAPTER ONE

"YOUR TEETH ARE LOVELY, Camryn. Did you wear braces as a child?"

Camryn Neff reminded herself that not only was the woman sitting across from her a very wealthy potential client, but also that her mother had raised her to be polite to her elders. Still, it took serious effort to keep from falling out of her chair at the weirdness of the question.

"No. This is how they grew."

Hmm, that didn't sound right, although to be honest, she didn't have a lot of experience when a conversation turned dental.

She refocused her mind to the meeting at hand. Not that she knew for sure why Helen Crane, leader of Wishing Tree society, such as it was, and sole owner of the very impressive Crane hotel empire, wanted to meet with her. The summons had come in the form of a hand-written note, inviting her to the large, sprawling estate on Grey Wolf Lake. Today at two.

So here Camryn was, wearing a business suit that had been hanging in her closet for over a year. The dress code for Wishing Tree retail and the dress code for the job in finance she'd left back in Chicago were very different. While it had been fun to dust off her gorgeous boots and a silk blouse, and discover her skirts still fit, she was ready to get to the point of the invitation.

"How can I help you, Mrs. Crane?" she asked.

"Helen, please."

Camryn smiled. "Helen. I'm happy to host a wrapping party, either here or at the store. Or if you'd prefer, I can simply collect all your holiday gifts and wrap them for you."

She casually glanced around at the high ceilings of the sitting room. There was a massive fireplace, intricate molding and a view of the lake that, even with two feet of snow on the ground, was spectacular. And while there were lovely fall floral displays on several surfaces, there wasn't a hint of Christmas to be found. Not in Wishing Tree, the week before Thanksgiving. Those decorations didn't appear until the Friday after.

"I have some samples for custom wrapping paper," she said, pulling out several sheets of paper from her leather briefcase. "The designs can be adjusted and the colors coordinated with what you have planned for this holiday season. Wrapped presents under a tree are such an elegant touch."

"You're very thorough," Helen murmured. "Impressive." She made a note on a pad. "Are you married, dear?"

"What?" Camryn clutched the wrapping paper samples. "No."

Helen nodded. "Your mother passed away last year, didn't she?"

A fist wrapped around Camryn's heart. "Yes. In late October."

"I remember her. She was a lovely woman. You and your sisters must have been devastated."

That was one word for it, Camryn thought grimly, remembering how her life had been shattered by the loss. In the space of a few weeks, she'd gone from being a relatively carefree, engaged, happy junior executive in Chicago to the sole guardian for her twin sisters, all the while dealing with trying to keep Wrap Around the Clock, the family business, afloat. The first few months after her mother's death were still a blur. She barely remembered anything about the holidays last year, save an unrelenting sadness.

"This year the season will be so much happier," Helen said firmly. "Victoria and Lily are thriving at school. Of course they still miss their mother, but they're happy, healthy young adults." The older woman smiled. "I know the teen years can be trying but I confess I quite enjoyed them with Jake."

Camryn frowned slightly. "How do you know about the twins?" she asked.

Helen's smile never faded. "It's Wishing Tree, my dear. Everyone knows more than everyone else thinks. Now, you're probably wondering why I invited you over today."

"To discuss wrapping paper?" Although even as Camryn voiced the question, she knew instinctively that was not the real reason.

Helen Crane was close to sixty, with perfect posture and short, dark hair. Her gaze was direct, her clothes stylish. She looked as if she'd never wanted for anything and was very used to getting her way.

"Of course you'll take care of all my wrapping needs," Helen said easily. "And I do like your idea of custom paper for faux presents under the tree. I'll have my holiday decorator get in touch with you so you two can coordinate the design. But the real reason I asked you here is to talk about Jake."

Camryn was having a little trouble keeping up. The order for wrapping and the custom paper was great news, but why would Helen want to discuss her son?

She knew who Jake was—everyone in town did. He was the handsome, successful heir to the Crane hotel fortune. He'd been the football captain in high school, had gone to Stanford. After learning the hotel business at the smaller Crane hotels, he was back in Wishing Tree, promoted to general manager of the largest, most luxurious of the properties.

They'd never run in the same circles back when they'd been kids, in part because she was a few years younger. She'd been a lowly freshman while he'd been a popular senior. Her only real connection with Jake was the fact that he'd once been engaged to her friend Reggie.

Helen sighed. "I've come to the conclusion that left to his own devices, Jake is never going to give me grandchildren. I lost my husband eighteen months ago, which has been very hard for me. It's time for my son to get on with finding someone, getting married and having the grandchildren I deserve."

Well, that put the whole "did you wear braces" conversational gambit in perspective, Camryn thought, not sure if she should laugh or just plain feel sorry for Jake. His mother was a powerful woman. Camryn sure wouldn't want to cross her.

"I'm not sure what that has to do with me," she admitted.

Helen tapped her pad of paper. "I've come up with a plan. I'm calling it Project: Jake's Bride. I'm going to find my son a wife and you're a potential candidate."

Camryn heard all the words. Taken individually, she

knew what Helen was saying. But when put together, in that exact way, the meaning completely escaped her.

"I'm sorry, what?"

"You're pretty, you're smart. You've done well at Wrap Around the Clock. You're nurturing—look how you've cared for your baby sisters." Helen smiled again, "I confess I do like the idea of instant grandchildren, so that's a plus for you. There are other candidates, of course, but you're definitely near the top of the list. All I need is confirmation from your gynecologist that you're likely to be fertile and then we can get on with the business of you and Jake falling in love."

"You want to know if I'm fertile?"

Camryn shoved the samples back in her briefcase and stood. "Mrs. Crane, I don't know what century you think we're living in, but this isn't a conversation I'm going to have with you. My fertility is none of your business. Nor is my love life. If your plan is genuine, you need to rethink it. And while you're doing that, you might want to make an appointment with your own doctor, because there's absolutely something wrong with you."

Helen looked surprisingly unconcerned. "You're right, Camryn. I apologize. Mentioning fertility was going a bit too far. You're the first candidate I've spoken to, so I'm still finding my way through all this." She wrote on her pad. "I won't bring that up again. But as to the rest of it, seriously, what are your thoughts?"

Camryn sank back on her chair. "Don't do it. Meddling is one thing, but you're talking about an actual campaign to find your son a bride. No. Just no. It's likely to annoy him, and any woman who would participate in something like this isn't anyone you want in your family."

Helen nodded slowly. "An interesting point. It's just they make it look so easy on those reality shows."

"Nothing is real on those shows. The relationships don't last. Jake's going to find someone. Give him time."

"I've given him two years. I'm not getting younger, you know." Her expression turned wistful. "And I do want grandchildren."

"Ask me on the right day and you can have the twins."

Helen laughed. "I wish that were true." Her humor faded. "Do you know my son?"

"Not really."

"We could start with a coffee date."

Camryn sighed. "Helen, seriously. This isn't going to work. Let him get his own girl."

"He's not. That's the problem. All right, I can see I'm not going to convince you to be a willing participant. I appreciate your time." She rose. "I meant what I said about the wrapping. I'll arrange to have all my gifts taken to your store. And my holiday decorator will be in touch about the custom paper."

"Is the holiday decorator different from the regular decorator?" Camryn asked before she could stop herself.

Helen chuckled. "Yes, she is. My regular decorator is temperamental and shudders at the thought of all that cheer and tradition. He came over close to Christmas a few years ago and nearly fainted when he saw the tree in the family room."

She leaned close and her voice dropped to a conspiratorial whisper. "It's devoted to all the ornaments

Jake made for me when he was little. There are plaster handprints and little stars made out of Popsicle sticks. My favorite is a tuna can with a tiny baby Jesus in the manger tucked inside. There's bits of straw and a star." She pressed both hands to her heart. "I tear up thinking about it."

Baby Jesus in a tuna can? Helen was one strange woman.

Camryn collected her briefcase and followed Helen to the front door. Helen opened it, then looked at her.

"You're sure about not being a part of Project: Jake's Bride?"

"Yes. Very." Camryn kept her tone firm, so there would be no misunderstanding.

"A pity, but I respect your honesty."

Camryn walked to her SUV and put her briefcase in the backseat. Once she was behind the wheel, she glanced at the three-story house rising tall and proud against the snow and gray sky.

The rich really were different, she told herself as she circled the driveway and headed for the main road. Different in a cray-cray kind of way.

She turned left on North Ribbon Road. When she reached Cypress Highway, she started to turn right— the shortest way back to town. At the last minute, she went straight. Even as she drove north, she told herself it wasn't her business. Maybe Jake knew about his mother's plans. Maybe he supported them.

Okay, not that, she thought, passing the outlet mall, then turning on Red Cedar Highway and heading up the mountain. She might not know Jake very well, but Reggie had dated him for months. Reggie was a sweetie who would never go out with a jerk. So Jake had to be a regular kind of guy, and regular guys didn't approve of their mothers finding them wives.

Besides, she doubted Jake needed any help in that department. He was tall, good-looking and really fit. She'd caught sight of him jogging past her store more than once and was willing to admit she'd stopped what she was doing to admire the view. He was also wealthy. Men like that didn't need help getting dates.

The sign for the resort came into view. She slowed for a second, then groaned as she drove up to the valet. Maybe she was making a mistake, but there was no way she couldn't tell Jake what had just happened. It felt too much like not mentioning toilet paper stuck to someone's shoe.

If he already knew, then it would be a short conversation. If he didn't care, then she would quietly think less of him and leave. If he was as horrified as she thought he might be, then she'd done her good deed for the week and yay her. Whatever the outcome, she would have done the right thing, which meant she would be able to sleep that night. Some days that was as good as it was going to get.

JAKE CRANE STOOD at his office window, gazing out at the mountain. The air was still, the sky gray. About six inches of fresh powder had fallen overnight. His two o'clock meeting had been moved to next week and sunset wasn't for two and a half hours. There was no reason he couldn't grab his gear and get in an hour or so of snowboarding, then return to work later and finish up. One of the advantages of his position was the ability to adjust his hours, if he wanted. Except, he didn't want to go snowboarding.

Oh, he loved the sport, the rush of speed, the trick of staying balanced, testing himself on the mountain. He enjoyed the cold, the sounds, the sense of achievement as he mastered a difficult run. He was a typical guy who enjoyed being outdoors. Just not by himself.

He had friends he could call. Dylan had the kind of job where he, too, could take off if he wanted and make up the time later, and Dylan was always up for snowboarding. Only that wasn't the kind of company he was looking for. He missed having a woman in his life.

He'd been avoiding that truth for a while now. Given his incredibly disastrous track record, he'd sworn off getting involved. As he saw it, the only way to keep from screwing up in the romance department was to not get romantically entangled. An easy, sensible solution. What he hadn't counted on was being…lonely.

Sex was easy. He could head to Seattle or Portland, meet someone, have a great weekend with her, then head home. No commitment, no risks of breaking her heart, no getting it wrong. Except he'd discovered he didn't enjoy those kinds of relationships. He wanted more. He wanted to get to know someone and have her get to know him. He wanted shared experiences, laughter and, worst of all, commitment. He wanted what other people made look easy.

But if he got involved, he would completely mess up. Or he could turn into his father, and he refused to do that. So he did nothing. A solution that was no longer working for him, which left him where he'd started. Staring at the mountain with no idea what to do with his personal life.

The phone on his desk buzzed.

"Jake, there's a Camryn Neff here to see you. She

doesn't have an appointment, but says it's about something personal."

Camryn Neff? The business community in Wishing Tree was small enough that he knew who she was. She owned Wrap Around the Clock—a store that sold wrapping paper, and wrapped and shipped gifts for people. The hotel referred guests to her when they wanted items they'd bought sent to friends and family or simply shipped home.

He knew her well enough to say hello at a business council meeting, but little else. He thought she might have younger sisters.

He pushed a button on his phone. "I'll be right there."

He crossed the length of his large office and stepped out into the foyer of the executive offices. Camryn, an attractive redhead with a cloud of curls and big, brown eyes, stood by Margie's desk.

Wishing Tree was a casual kind of place, so he was surprised to see her wearing an expensive-looking suit and leather boots with three-inch heels. Her posture was stiff, her expression bordered on defensive. Camryn hadn't stopped by to sell him wrapping paper, he thought, wondering what was wrong and how he'd gotten involved.

"Hello, Camryn," he said easily.

"Jake." She seemed to force herself to smile. "Thanks for seeing me on such short notice. I wasn't sure I should come, but then I couldn't not talk to you and…" She pressed her lips together. "Can we go into your office?"

"Of course." He motioned to show her the way, then followed her inside. He pointed to the corner seating area, where the couch and chairs offered a more informal setting.

"Can I get you something to drink?" he asked. "Coffee? Water? Bourbon?"

At the last one, she managed a sincere smile. "I wish, but it's a little early in the day for me. Plus, I'm not a bourbon kind of woman. Brown liquor isn't my thing."

"We have a nice selection of vodkas in the main bar."

Camryn chuckled and relaxed a little in her chair. "Tempting, but no."

Jake had taken a seat on the sofa. He leaned toward her and asked, "How can I help you today?"

Her body instantly tensed and the smile faded. She crossed and uncrossed her legs. "Yes, well, I wanted to tell you something. It's not my business, really." She paused and met his gaze. "It would have been if I'd said yes, but I didn't. I want to be clear about that."

"Please don't take this the wrong way, but so far you haven't been clear about anything." He smiled. "Except not liking brown liquor."

"I know. I'm sorry. I'm trying to find the words. I should just say it. Blurt it out."

He considered himself a relatively easygoing guy who could handle any crisis, but she was starting to make him uncomfortable. What could she possibly want to tell him? Not that she was pregnant—they'd never been on a date, let alone slept together. He doubted she needed money. The store was successful and if she did need a loan, why would she come to him? While they knew a lot of the same people, they didn't hang out together, so an issue with a mutual friend seemed unlikely.

"I saw your mother today."

Jake held in a groan. Those five words always meant trouble and mostly for him.

Camryn met his gaze, her brown eyes filled with sympathy and concern. "She invited me to the house. I didn't know why but hoped it was to buy custom wrapping paper. We can design nearly anything and have it printed. In fact, I have some ideas for custom paper for the resort. I've been playing with the logo and there are—"

"Camryn?"

She blinked. "Yes?"

"My mother."

"Oh, right. That." She swallowed and looked at him. "She wants to find you a wife. She had a plan. It's called Project: Jake's Bride. She's interviewing women as potential candidates. Apparently, she's done waiting for you to find someone on your own."

He stood, then wasn't sure what to do. Pace? Run? Shout? His mother had always been a meddler, but this was bad, even for her. Project: Jake's Bride? Seriously? *Seriously?*

"She wants grandchildren," Camryn added helpfully.

He sank back on the sofa and resisted the urge to rest his head in his hands. "She's losing her mind."

"I don't think so. She's very lucid and completely in control. I wasn't sure if you knew."

He stared at her. "I didn't know."

"Yeah, I can tell by the look on your face."

"Horror and murderous rage?"

She smiled. "You're not mad. Resigned, maybe. You love your mom, so you can't hate her. But I get this isn't ideal."

Jake collapsed back against the sofa. "The woman is trying to find me a wife, Camryn. I think *not ideal* undersells the moment."

He swore silently as he realized he had no idea what he was going to do about the problem. Telling his mother to back off was the equivalent of looking at the sky and discussing the weather. The exchange was frequently unsatisfying and ultimately futile.

"I'm shipping her off to Bali. She enjoys tropical weather. I'll buy her a nice condo, supply a staff. She can take up painting. Like that painter." He paused. "What's his name? Oh, Paul Gauguin. But that was Tahiti, not Bali. Which is fine. They're both beautiful this time of year."

"What makes you think she'd agree to go?" Camryn asked. "Your mother seems highly invested in your personal life."

"I'll trick her. I could do that." He would tell her he was eloping and wanted her there for the wedding. Then he would lock her in the newly bought condo and—

He looked at Camryn. "Why did she tell you all this?"

She ducked her head, but not before he saw color flare on her cheeks. "She, ah, thought I would be a good candidate."

Jake hadn't realized the situation could get worse, which he should have. When it came to Helen Crane, that was always a possibility.

"My mother invited you to her house to discuss the possibility of us marrying?"

Camryn nodded slowly. "Although she did say she thought we should start dating first. Get to know each other."

"You're defending her?"

"No, it's just she was impressive, and talking about it like this makes her sound…"

"Outrageous? Impossible?"

"A little. I understand why you're upset. She actually wanted me to provide proof of fertility, which is what set me off."

Proof of— He stood again, only to realize there still wasn't anywhere to go.

"I'm sorry about all of this," he said stiffly. "That she butted into your life and dragged you into one of her crazy schemes. I'll make this go away."

Somehow. There had to be a way to get her to stop what she was doing.

Camryn rose. "There are other candidates. I don't know who they are, but she mentioned them. Some might have kids. She said my younger sisters were a plus. She called them instant grandchildren."

He held in a groan. Other candidates? Unsuspecting women who were going to be approached by his mother?

She looked at him. "She's lonely, Jake. She lost her husband less than two years ago and she's by herself in that huge house. I know she has friends and a life, but it's not like having a husband around. Wanting grandchildren is pretty common at her stage of life." She held up a hand. "Still not defending her. It's just, I get what she's doing and when you think about it, she's really very sweet."

"Then we'll let her find you a husband. See how sweet she seems then."

Camryn laughed. "Point taken. Anyway, I wanted you to know."

"I appreciate you coming here and warning me. I owe you."

Her eyes brightened. "Really? Because I could bring

some custom wrapping paper samples by for you. They'd look lovely under the dozens of trees I know you'll be putting up."

"Sure. Make an appointment with Margie and bring them by. We support local whenever we can."

"Then I'll see you again, soon. Samples in hand."

"I look forward to it."

He escorted her out of his office. Once she'd left, he turned off his computer, grabbed his coat and then headed for the door. He paused by his assistant's desk.

"I'm going to be gone a couple of hours. Text me if there's an emergency. Otherwise, I'll be back around four."

Margie, a forty-something brunette with three teen-aged sons and a husband who adored her, frowned. "You okay, boss? You look, I don't know, stressed maybe."

"I'm fine," he lied. "I'm going to stop by and see my mother, then I'll be back."

Margie sighed. "I hope when my boys are grown, they're as good to me as you are to her."

Jake only nodded, because he couldn't say what he was thinking. That the whole Bali/Tahiti plan made the most sense, but if she wouldn't agree, he was going to hire some kind of keeper. And take all her electronics away. And possibly her car. He understood she was missing his father and he wanted to be there for her, but there was no way in hell he was letting her move forward with Project: Jake's Bride. Not now. Not ever. No. Just no.

Don't miss Susan Mallery's Home Sweet Christmas*!*

Also by Synithia Williams

The Jackson Falls series

Forbidden Promises
The Promise of a Kiss
Scandalous Secrets
Careless Whispers
Foolish Hearts

For additional books by Synithia Williams,
visit her website, synithiawilliams.com.

Look for Synithia Williams's next novel
The Secret to a Southern Wedding
available now from Canary Street Press.

THIS TIME FOR KEEPS

Synithia Williams

Dear Reader,

I listen to a few podcasts on personal growth, finance and development. A few of them have talked about the pitfalls of hustle culture. According to *Forbes*: "Hustle culture puts work at the center of life. Long working hours are praised and glorified. Time off is seen as laziness. If you are not hustling, you are failing." Basically, burnout is life!

Michaela Spears, the heroine in *This Time for Keeps*, has built a financial empire but at the expense of her relationships and mental health. It took her father's sickness for her to go for a second chance with the one guy she let go. As she learns to let go of hustle culture, she gets a chance to define what happiness really looks like for her.

I hope you do the same as Michaela and make taking time for yourself and your care a priority. Great start by picking up this book!

Happy reading,

Synithia W.

CHAPTER ONE

MICHAELA SPEARS TOOK a deep, fortifying breath as she stared at the front door of her parents' house. She'd only been home a week, and hiding her concern behind a facade of cheer was harder than she'd anticipated. She didn't know what was wrong with her. She'd been able to push forward, smile and keep her chin up for most of her life. It was how she'd built a successful financial management empire that allowed her to come home and make sure her parents didn't have to worry about a thing while her dad recovered from a kidney transplant.

Yet, lately, keeping her head up, grinning and bearing it, not showing any sign that she couldn't handle things was becoming harder and harder. Maybe because she'd always viewed her parents as strong and capable. They were the ones who'd encouraged her to never call in sick to work unless it was completely necessary and drilled into her head that there was no excuse for laziness. But seeing her dad recovering after living his life following those same principles made her question a lot of things.

All those vacations he'd said he couldn't take. All the times he'd gone to work knowing he didn't feel well. Every excuse he'd made about why he wouldn't complain about work because he was lucky just to have a job. They all ran through her mind now and she wondered, what was it all for? What about all the vacations he'd never take if that kidney transplant hadn't come through?

Watching her dad's recovery had her reflecting on her own life. The things she'd lost in her *work hard, play hard* lifestyle. Not things—a person.

Michaela shook her head and squared her shoulders. She'd focus on that situation soon enough. Right now, she just needed to make sure her dad hadn't tried to get out of bed in the fifteen minutes it had taken her to run by the pharmacy and pick up his prescription.

She opened the door and went down the hall to the main bedroom. As soon as she saw him out of the new adjustable bed she'd purchased and hobbling toward the window, she was reminded that she and her dad were not going to make it. The man was too stubborn for his own good.

"Daddy, what in the world!" Michaela dropped her designer handbag and the prescription at the door and rushed across the room. "Why are you out of bed?"

Willie Spears grunted and swatted at Michaela before grimacing. Sweat beaded across his brow and added a sheen to his dark brown skin. His curly gray hair was matted from lying in bed for a long time. Although he was obviously in pain, defiance was most dominant in his dark gaze.

"I want the curtains open," he said in a shaky voice.

Michaela took her dad's arm. Despite the recent surgery, his still felt strong and steady under her hands. Probably part of the reason why he refused to sit still. Her dad rarely sat still, so being bedridden was driving him wild.

She gently eased him back into the bed. "Why are you worrying about the curtains?"

"I needed light," he said, as if she should know why he was defying the doctor's orders.

"And you couldn't wait a few minutes for me to get here. Where is Mom?"

Willie let out a sigh and rubbed his side. "Her boss called about a file she couldn't find, and your mom went into work. You know that office can't run without her."

Of course her mom would go in if her supervisor called her. Her mom was just like her dad. They never took a day off and had enough leave time accrued that they could both take months off without worrying about a paycheck. But who was she to talk? Her last vacation in Bali had been fun…when she wasn't spending time writing, making conference calls and checking in with her staff.

"This is exactly why you need a nurse," Michaela said. "You can't be trusted to recuperate on your own." Michaela crossed her arms and tried to give her dad the same "do what I told you" glower that she'd received as a kid, but judging by how unbothered he seemed, she guessed it wasn't working.

She got why he wanted to move around. Her dad was usually a very active sixty-five-year-old man. He still worked full-time as the head of building maintenance for the Peachtree Cove School District, and couldn't resist taking on the repair jobs himself, despite having a team of technicians reporting to him who could handle almost anything. When he'd had to start dialysis, he'd tried to power through and find ways to continue working despite the fatigue the procedure cost his body. But no matter how much he wanted to push himself, he wouldn't be able to just hop up and resume normal activities after a kidney transplant. Even if in his mind he believed the six to eight weeks of recovery time was just a suggestion.

"I'll be fine. You didn't have to come home for this."

Michaela wanted to reach out and rub his head but shoved her hands into the pockets of her red off-the-shoulder jumpsuit instead. Rubbing her dad's head as if he were a kid would only make this harder.

"Did you really think I was going to stay in Atlanta and wait for you to give me updates about your kidney transplant?" She cocked her head to the side and raised a brow.

Her dad frowned. "Well, you didn't have to spend money on an in-home nurse."

Michaela waved a hand and crossed the room to pick up her purse and prescription. "I know mom would have taken off work, but she'd be just as bad as you are at sitting around the house and following instructions. One quick call with her supervisor would turn into an hour and you obviously can't be left alone for more than ten minutes. I didn't want to hear about you falling out of the bed because you tried to play Superman with your recovery."

Willie grunted and crossed his arms, then grimaced after the sudden movement. "You're just as hardheaded as your momma."

Michaela only grinned at her dad. "And you're both secretly glad I'm here. So stop grumbling and let me take care of you for once. That's part of the reason I made all this money."

She examined the Swarovski-crystal-studded handbag before placing it carefully on the coffee table.

Thankfully, none of the crystals had fallen off when she'd frantically dropped it to the floor. Most of the time she was more careful with her things, especially her sparkly things. But seeing her dad struggling to cross the room had put the bag at the bottom of her "things I care about" list.

Willie wagged a finger at her. "I hope you made all that money to take care of yourself. We never wanted you to spend your money on us."

"Maybe so, but that doesn't mean I can't spend my money however I want. And, right now, I want to spend it making sure you're taken care of while you recover."

She grinned and scrunched her nose up like she'd done since she was six. As usual, the silly face worked and the line between her dad's brows disappeared and the stubbornness in his gaze was replaced with a loving "what am I going to do with you" look. The vise that clamped around her heart when she'd entered the room eased. She wasn't a doctor, but she was pretty sure frowning and being upset wasn't going to help her dad get better faster.

"I can't believe you're going to stay here while I recover," he said. "Don't they need you at your company?"

Michaela shrugged despite the same question racing through her head twenty times a day since she'd returned home to Peachtree Cove. "I hire competent people, so I don't always have to be there. I can work from anywhere. Besides, I'm kind of tired of Atlanta. I'm ready for something different."

That was one of the things Michaela loved about her business. She could work from anywhere. And she'd worked hard enough over the years to save enough money so that she'd feel comfortable taking time off.

Even though every time she'd tried to go on vacation, she ended up working, she promised herself this time she wouldn't check in so much. It was true she had hired smart people that she trusted. She shouldn't feel guilty for making sure her dad was being cared for while he recovered.

Her dad chuckled and shook his head. "You never could sit still. Must be nice to be a millionaire."

"First of all, I get that from you and Momma. Second, I'm just a fledgling millionaire. That's not a big deal," she said with a shrug.

He narrowed his eyes. "Quit saying that. Be proud of what you built. You don't have to downplay your success for me or anyone else."

"I know, I know." Michaela sat on the edge of the bed.

He always told her that. Back when she'd tried to diminish getting straight A's if a friend of family member hadn't, her dad was the first one to tell her not to be ashamed of succeeding. *If you did the hard work and earned something, then never pretend like it doesn't matter. If you do that, others will do the same.*

"It's still hard to believe sometimes," she admitted. "I never thought the word *millionaire* and my name would go in the same sentence."

Although her bank account proved it, Michaela sometimes still had to wrap her mind around the fact that she'd melded her love of investing and teaching into a profitable business. A multimillion-dollar business. Twelve years ago, when she'd been paying off student-loan debt while working a going-nowhere public relations job for a nonprofit, she'd been blessed to attend a conference where the keynote speaker talked about how he'd earned financial freedom through investing wisely. The talk was enough to inspire her to sign up for his class, and even though all of his methods didn't work for her, Michaela had taken what she'd learned and done her own research on budgeting, finance and investing.

She was a quick learner, and soon found ways to get her financial life in order, which then allowed her to begin investing. She'd started making money and re-investing her earnings to grow them even more. Her work in public relations meant she was good at breaking down complicated things into simple, easy-to-understand nuggets, so she'd helped others learn how to get their financial lives in order, too. That turned into a budgeting and finance business that later expanded into classes for women who were interested in making their money work for them. Word of mouth, combined with her active social media presence, the creation of a series of online workshops and classes, and her continued smart investing, eventually grew so quickly that she was now considered a budget and financial guru with a podcast, a book deal and more money than she'd ever expected to earn in her lifetime.

"I'm not surprised," her dad said. "You were always a hard worker. You worked just as hard to get what you've got now. I always knew you'd turn out okay."

"Even when I had to text you begging for a hundred dollars to cover my car insurance that time after graduation?" She pursed her lips and tried to look doubtful, but she believed every word he said. He'd never told her anything different.

Her dad chuckled softly. "Even then."

She reached over and patted his leg beneath the blanket. "Would you believe me if I said I kinda want to put down roots back here in Peachtree Cove?"

Michaela was proud of the time and energy she'd put into growing her business. She'd watched her parents work hard every day and couldn't imagine a life where she wouldn't need to hustle hard every day either. But she was exhausted. There weren't enough long-weekend vacations, facial masks or binge-watching days in the year to shake the feeling of being burned-out. She felt like she needed to readjust some things but didn't know how to start. Quitting wasn't an option, but living like she had before wasn't sustainable.

"I wouldn't believe it one bit," her dad said without batting an eye or hesitating.

Michaela let out a surprised laugh. "I'm serious, Daddy! I think I'm ready to settle down."

If only she'd realized that sooner. It shouldn't have taken watching the man she cared about propose to another woman or her dad needing a kidney transplant for her to come to that conclusion. Whoever had said hindsight was twenty-twenty deserved their own million dollars.

Willie shook his head. "Girl, stop with all that settle-down mess. You're rising to the top. Don't look back now."

"Look back how?"

"You got out of Peachtree Cove and became even more successful that we could have imagined. Why in the world would you want to move back to a small town?"

He tossed her words back at her like a fastball. She'd thrown that question out there plenty of times when family or old friends asked if she'd ever move back home. She'd been so eager to escape her small town. Maybe it was her dad's illness, or her hope for a second chance to be with the man she wanted, but the idea of coming home indefinitely didn't made her immediately want to roll her eyes.

"You and Momma are here," she said softly.

"We've always been here," her dad said dryly. He raised one brow. "Which is why I don't believe you really want to move. You're upset because I got sick. Don't worry." He patted her hand. "I'll be better in no time, and you'll be back to taking over the world again."

The doorbell rang before she could respond. The conversation could wait for now. Her dad could be right. A lot had happened in the past two years to shake up her thinking. She needed to be sure before she did something rash without thinking about how moving to Peachtree Cove would affect her business.

"That's your nurse," she said, getting up from the bed.

"I don't need a nurse," her dad grumbled.

"You really want me to take you to the bathroom or give you a sponge bath?" she asked with a raised brow.

Her dad scowled and waved her away. "Go answer the door."

"That's what I thought." Michaela laughed softly and headed to the front.

Her dad didn't want her in charge of his personal needs, but she knew the argument against a nurse wasn't over. He'd tried to convince his doctor that working from home was not only necessary but completely doable as he recovered from his kidney transplant. *Slowing down* simply wasn't in his vocabulary.

Hell, it wasn't in hers either, but she was tired of always working. Sure, hustle culture had gotten her where she was today, but she'd pushed herself for twelve years and what did she have to show for it? Okay, yes, there were the millions of dollars in her bank account. She wouldn't underrate that, but what was the end game? When was enough going to be enough? Her vacations were for social media content, her friendships were with other entrepreneurs who lived off caffeine and the challenge of overcoming the next obstacle, and her longest "relationship" with a man hadn't really been a relationship at all. More like a series of casual hookups when her schedule collided with his—the guy she'd known that one day she'd want to spend her life with despite never making the time to actually date him. One of the biggest sacrifices she'd made for her success.

You've still got a chance in that arena. The hopeful thought whispered through her head.

Even though it was a long shot, as someone who never gave up, the idea of a second chance brought a smile to her face. Khalil lived in Peachtree Cove. Their parents were mutual friends and the two had grown up always seeing each other, but she'd known she'd liked him when they'd both returned home for the holidays freshman year of college. They'd been dating other people, but the spark she'd felt when she'd seen him then outshined anything she'd felt for the boyfriend whose name she couldn't even remember now.

They hadn't kissed until after they'd graduated college. Both were single by then, but she was leaving to spend the summer interning at a marketing company in New York. He'd visited her six months later, and that was the first time they'd slept together. They'd decided to keep things casual. Well, she had. Her life, her career, was more important than the boy from home. And that was how their relationship had proceeded from then on. They both dated other people, but she always came back to Khalil. Until Khalil made it clear he was no longer waiting for her to settle down.

I'm getting married, Michaela. I hope you'll be happy for me.

The memory still played in her mind when she opened the door to welcome the nurse she'd hired to help her dad.

"Hell-oooh!" Michaela's jaw dropped when she locked eyes with the man on the other side.

Maybe some angel in heaven had heard her and decided to help her along. That had to be the reason why the man standing in blue scrubs that fit so perfectly they seemed stitched onto his broad shoulders and sculpted arms stood in the doorway, facing her. She'd come back to Peachtree Cove with hopes of reconciling with him. She'd hoped to convince him she was ready for more than casual hookups. She hoped he believed her this time.

"Khalil, you're my dad's nurse?" she asked in a breathy, excited voice.

Khalil gave her the smile that had made her heart skip a beat since she was nineteen-years old. Earlier than that, if she was honest with herself. "Yep, I'm your dad's nurse. What's up, Michaela?"

Michaela grinned. Thank heaven for whatever angel was on her side today.

CHAPTER TWO

KHALIL DAVENPORT DRANK in the sight of Michaela Spears standing in her parents' doorway. When he'd accepted this job, he'd known he was playing with fire and was going to get burned…again. Yet, there he was. Standing here looking at the woman who always left him with scorch marks on his heart.

His best friend, Brandon, thought he was foolish for taking the job as Mr. Spears's home nurse, knowing he would be around Michaela again. Knowing he'd never been able to resist her before. But this time was different—he was prepared. He'd always expected too much of her and he wouldn't make that same mistake again. He knew exactly what they'd meant to each other because it was just what she'd first promised him: a good time with no strings attached.

Khalil tried to remind himself of that, as his heart flipped in his chest at the sight of the bright smile on her face. He was not going to fall for Michaela again. His feelings for her had already ruined one relationship. If he didn't get her out of his system, she'd continue to dismantle his life.

And I'd enjoy every minute.

"I didn't know you were doing home nursing," Michaela said, breaking into his thoughts.

She looked as good as ever in a red off-the-shoulder

jumpsuit that accentuated her full breasts and hips. A head wrap in a matching color covered her dark hair. She wore a red lipstick that seemed to stand out against her golden-brown skin like a beacon. Luring him to lean in closer and see if she still tasted as sweet as he remembered.

"I do it part-time when I'm not working in the emergency room," he said when his brain remembered to respond to her comment. He pointed to the doorway. "Can I come in? It's kind of hot out here."

She immediately stepped back. "Oh, sure, come in."

He crossed the threshold and her arms spread wide for a hug. He didn't even think of not hugging her. Hugging Michaela was like coming home. They'd known each other most of their lives. He leaned in and wrapped his arms around her. She was an inch or two shorter than him, but her curves seemed to fit against his body perfectly. Her perfume was the same, a Burberry scent that was as bright and light as her personality. She squeezed him tight. A part of him, the old him, wanted to believe she'd missed him just as much as he'd missed her.

He pulled back before the thought could take hold and drag him under. This was the same woman who, two years before, had toasted his engagement and thrown him an engagement party. The engagement may not have lasted, but the memory of knowing Michaela hadn't batted an eyelash when he was about to marry someone else remained.

Michaela looked up at him with sparkling brown eyes and a beautiful smile. "I was worried when I hired an in-home nurse, but I feel a little better knowing it's you."

"When I saw the request, I immediately volunteered to look out for your dad. I was happy to hear that Mr. Spears finally landed on the kidney transplant list, but I knew that recovery would be hard for him. I thought he'd feel more comfortable if I was a part of that recovery."

"Maybe he'll sit still, too."

Khalil laughed, knowing Mr. Spears would not be happy about being bedridden for weeks. "That, too. Plus, my parents wanted me to check in and make sure he was okay."

She placed a hand on his arm and squeezed lightly. "Thank you and your parents. How are they?"

Her touch sent electric currents through his body. He wanted to shift so her hand would fall away, but worried she'd notice. He was keeping his distance but didn't want to make it obvious. If he did, she'd ask why, and he was too proud to let her know how much letting her go had hurt. He hadn't expected for his heart to break a little when she hadn't cared about him getting engaged. Proposing to someone else had him convinced he was finally over her. Silly of him.

"They're good," he said easily. "Both retired now and spending their time traveling and visiting my brother and his kids in Charlotte."

"I'll have to go by and see them." She took his hand in hers. "Come on and see Dad. I don't want to leave him alone for too long. He was trying to get out of bed earlier."

She tugged him toward the back of the house. He pulled on his hand in an effort to let go of hers, but she didn't let go. That was how it was with them. They touched, held hands and hugged all the time. Even when they hadn't been hooking up. He thought he was ready to handle this, but his confidence wavered.

They were down the hall a few seconds later and entering the main bedroom. Michaela's dad sat propped up in the bed. He spotted Khalil and his face lit up.

"Khalil, what are you doing here?"

Khalil was glad for the reason to quickly drop Michaela's hand and crossed the room. "I'm going to be one of your home nurses."

Mr. Spears's eyes crinkled from his broad grin. "I heard you were doing that on the side, but I didn't expect you to be helping me out."

Khalil placed a hand on Willie's shoulder. "Well, when I heard that you were getting a nurse, I couldn't help but come over and lend a hand. I got to make sure you're good."

He grunted and pushed Khalil's hand off his shoulder. "I don't really need a nurse. I'll be all right."

Khalil didn't take the words or the gesture to heart. Mr. Spears had always been an independent person who was constantly moving. He empathized with the man's frustration. "I'm sure you'll be all right, but it never hurts to have someone help out. Just consider me as your backup."

"Mm-hmm, that's just what you're saying to try and make me feel better."

Khalil grinned and lightly bumped his should. "Did it work?"

Mr. Spears raised a brow. "Not a bit, but if I have to have someone nursing me then I'm glad to know it's you," He finished with a light chuckle.

He looked from Khalil toward Michaela. "Did you know he was coming?"

Michaela shook her head and sat on the edge of the bed. "I didn't. I was just as surprised to see him as you were."

"I would have thought you'd set this up," her dad said.

Michaela's brows rose. "Why would I set this up?"

"Because you always liked having Khalil around. That's why, and don't even pretend any different."

"I wouldn't pretend. I do like having Khalil around." Michaela winked at him.

Khalil's stomach clenched. She was a big flirt. It was one of the things he liked about her. Her openness and free-spirited attitude. Michaela had always been ambitious and gone after everything she wanted. He'd always known she was going to be bigger than Peachtree Cove, bigger than him, and his dreams of staying and giving back to the community that raised him. Nothing could contain her, and he'd been a fool for ever thinking he could tie her to him.

"Good, because you'll be seeing a lot of me," Khalil said. "I'll make sure you're eating right, that you're taking your medication and changing your dressing, and I'll be watching the healing."

"And you can't complain, Daddy." Michaela patted her dad's feet. "You have to follow Khalil's directions."

Mr. Spears grunted. "Who said I was going to complain?"

"You were complaining before he got here," Michaela countered.

Willie looked at Khalil. "Only because I didn't know who they were sending over. I feel better having you here. I know I'm in good hands."

"I'm glad you feel that way, Mr. Spears. You know

you're just like family." Mr. and Mrs. Spears were his older brother's godparents and like an aunt and uncle to Khalil. His parents and Michaela's parents had known each other for years and often got together for summer cookouts, birthdays or game nights. He cared about them nearly as much as he cared for his own parents.

"So are you." He sighed and shook his head. "I'd hoped you might be my family one day. I thought you might be able to convince Michaela to stick around longer."

A lot of people had thought that about him and Michaela. Hell, there were several times over the years when they'd hooked up when he'd thought the same, but he and Michaela always wanted different things. Now, even though he was beginning to think that he might need to branch out from Peachtree Cove, he knew nothing would ever change between them.

"I don't think anyone can make Michaela stick in any one place for too long," Khalil said. "She's like the wind. Gotta keep moving."

Michaela scoffed. "You two can stop talking about me like I'm not here. I'm not the wind. I just had to see what's out there in the world. Now that I've seen it, I'm ready to stay in Peachtree Cove a little longer."

Khalil met her eyes. His heartbeat sped up even as his brain said not to get caught up in her words. He'd heard that before. The *I'm tired of the rat race and ready to settle down* speech she'd given lip service to once or twice before. He'd believed it once. Had even asked her to stay and start a life with him. She'd been gone two weeks later.

That was when he'd let go of the dream of Michaela wanting what he wanted. He didn't resent her for chasing her dreams and pursuing greatness. How could he? Peachtree Cove was a small town, and many had fled its borders for bigger things. He was even entertaining the idea of leaving as well. Even if he took the thought of leaving and made it a reality, no matter where he ended up, he couldn't expect her to follow.

"I'll believe it when I see it," Mr. Spears said without any malice.

"Same for me," Khalil said.

Michaela's shoulders straightened. "I'm for real this time. I'm going to stay in Peachtree Cove."

Khalil ignored the conviction in her voice and the longing in his heart. No more pining after Michaela. He looked at Mr. Spears. "Let me check your incision and go over what our routine will look like for the day."

Mr. Spears huffed but nodded. "Okay." He looked at Michaela. "Can you give us some privacy?"

Michaela hesitated for a second. Her eyes met his before she sighed and stood. "Sure."

She gave him one long look, before she went out and closed the door.

"You know, I always hoped you two would end up together," Willie said not two seconds after Michaela left the room.

Khalil wasn't surprised by the comment. His parents felt the same way. He was used to them asking about him and Michaela. The questions had stopped when he'd gotten engaged two years ago, but now that the engagement was off, he should have expected them to start up again. Especially with him working with her dad.

"Michaela and I are better as friends," Khalil said hoping that Mr. Willie wouldn't get his hopes up.

"Is she the reason you and your fiancée broke things off?"

Khalil narrowed his eyes at the older man. "Going straight for the tough stuff, huh?"

Just like his parents, Willie didn't hold back his curiosity. It was the million-dollar question. Why had Khalil and Jackie broken up? She'd known what he wouldn't admit. That he loved her but wasn't in love with her enough to make a marriage work.

Willie shrugged. "Just asking."

Khalil shook his head. "We broke up for other reasons."

His parents had asked if his friendship with Michaela had played a part in the breakup, but Khalil wouldn't confirm or deny. Once again, pride wouldn't let him admit how much of a hold she'd had on him. Instead, he told everyone an abbreviated version of the truth: that it was Jackie's decision, and he respected her choice.

"Which means you and Michaela can try again," Willie said, as if that were the natural next step.

Khalil looked at the closed door and shook his head. He wasn't going to let that thought get a chance to take root in his brain. How would he move forward if he kept looking back? He focused on Willie. "That ship has sailed, Mr. Spears. Now, let's look at your incision and focus on why I'm here."

CHAPTER THREE

MICHAELA TRIED TO wait patiently to get a chance to
talk to Khalil. He was a good nurse and spent most of
his time looking after her dad. Which was cool. That
was what she'd hired him for, but still… He was there.
Under the same roof as her. The man she'd come back
to try to get a second chance with.

Or was this a third chance?

Honestly, maybe this was their fourth chance.

The number of chances didn't matter. They'd gone
back and forth for years, with occasional hookups in
between seeing other people without ever truly being
together. Now the time seemed right. He was single. She
was single. He was settled and she was tired of being
constantly in motion. The fact that he was the nurse
assigned to her dad had to be fate stepping in to show
them they belonged together. He and her dad may not
believe that she was serious about sticking around in
Peachtree Cove, but she'd prove them wrong.

Once, three years ago, Khalil had asked her to take
their relationship from casual flings to a serious commitment. She'd wanted to say yes, but she'd also just
kicked off her Build Wealth Academy, a program that
brought together experts to help people take control
of their finances and lay the foundation to financial
freedom. She hadn't thought she'd have the time to be

in a long-distance relationship. The pain on Khalil's face when she'd said no had haunted her for the following year. She'd missed him every day that her Academy grew. When they saw each other a year later, she planned to ask him to give them another chance. Instead, her heart was broken.

I'm getting married, Michaela. I hope you'll be happy for me.

She wasn't conceited enough to believe that she could waltz back into his life a year after his engagement ended and win him over. She hadn't approached him shortly after his breakup because she'd worried he'd be heartbroken, or worse, she'd be a rebound. When she'd returned home, she'd worried he would no longer feel anything toward her. That fear drifted away when he'd smiled at her and the spark of attraction that was always there when he looked at her lit up his eyes when she'd answered the door.

So, instead of stalking outside her dad's bedroom and preventing Khalil from doing his job, she did what she normally did when she needed to occupy herself: she worked. She took a video call with her business partner, Noreen. She recorded a few clips with some of her thoughts on the latest finance headlines and saved them for posting later on social media. Then she worked on a few articles she'd promised to magazines and coordinated with her company's social media manager on the right information to go with the posts they'd planned for the week.

What was supposed to be a day relaxing and focusing on her dad had turned into another full day of work. The sound of a throat clearing from the door of the dining room made her look up from her laptop to where Khalil stood.

"Hey, I'm about to head out in a little bit," Khalil said. "I want to touch base with you before I go."

Michaela sucked in a breath. He was leaving so soon? She glanced at the time on her laptop and realized that it was nearly seven o'clock in the evening.

"Already?" she said, noticing how disappointed she sounded.

He grinned and stepped farther into the room. He leaned against the wall next to the door and crossed his arms. The muscles of his biceps flexed and strained against the blue scrubs he wore. She'd known from his social media content that he looked good in scrubs but seeing it in person made her mouth water. "The night nurse will be here soon. Once I go over what I did for the day with Mr. Willie then I'll be out."

She'd requested twenty-four-hour assistance for her dad. She wasn't staying at her parents' place. Her mom had turned Michaela's old bedroom into a sewing room, so she had booked a room at the local bed-and- breakfast, The Fresh Place Inn, owned by one of her former high school friends, Tracey Thompson. The room was just a place for her to sleep, but she wanted to be sure someone was always with her dad.

"Will you be back tomorrow?"

He nodded. "Tomorrow and the next day. Then I go back to my shift at the emergency room this weekend."

She frowned in confusion. "When do you get time off?"

His broad shoulders lifted in an easy shrug. "Not often. I'm trying to be like you when I grow up."

She frowned. "What do you mean?"

"I'm trying to get my professional life in order. Now that I've graduated with my doctorate in nursing, I've got to come up with a way to pay off those student loans. I covered what I could, but they still leave a dent. That, and I didn't go back to school just to keep doing what I always did. I'm looking for opportunities to help get my money together."

"You just finished school, but you're still working two jobs. When do you sleep?"

Khalil chuckled and shrugged. "I get a few hours here and there. I'll be done soon. Besides, you understand how it is. You've got to hustle hard to get to the top. You talk about that all the time."

Michaela cocked her head to the side. "And I've got the burnout to show for it. Besides, I follow that thirst trap you call an Instagram account. You're always posting pictures of you making time to chill."

Khalil's brows rose and a teasing grin spread across his handsome face. "My page is not a thirst trap."

"Yes, it is! Nothing but pictures of you either in the gym, chilling with your boys or wearing your scrubs and looking all sexy. You've got nearly fifty thousand followers and most of them aren't there for those healthy-living tidbits you throw in here and there. That, sir, is the definition of a thirst trap."

Khalil shrugged but chuckled. The deep rumbling sound echoed through her midsection. "Hey, I've gotta do what I've gotta do. I have a few endorsement deals from my Instagram account. Money I put right back into paying for school. Now that I'm *Doctor* Davenport, I may not have the time to post as often."

Michaela nodded slowly. "Hmm… Doctor Davenport. I like the sound of that."

His body stilled. And a fire Michaela had witnessed hundreds of times before heated his gaze. "I like the sound of that, too. Especially coming from your lips."

Michaela's heart bounced from her chest to her feet and back again. She forced herself to take a deep breath and tried not to overreact. This didn't mean he'd immediately believe she was ready to give them a shot. Still, she had to bite her lip to stop the huge grin trying to spread out over her face.

"Just my lips or from your adoring fans?"

"Just yours, Michaela." He said her name slowly, letting every syllable roll across his tongue.

Energy hummed between them. That wasn't new. She and Khalil always had awesome chemistry. It was one of the reasons she'd never been able to fully get him out of her system, no matter how many times they separated. Her body came alive and seemed to hum whenever he was within a few feet of her. She'd once believed the feelings would fade, or that over time she'd eventually get over him. But that never happened. No matter how much time passed, or how much she tried to convince herself she didn't have time for a relationship, Khalil made her think differently.

"I'm leaving here soon," she said. She swallowed hard and gathered the confidence to say her next words. "I can come by your place and...catch up."

There, she'd done it. She put the invitation out there. She wouldn't have done it so soon, but the way they vibed, the way he looked at her, it all felt so familiar. Like years, rejection and a broken engagement hadn't happened. Like they'd done so many times before when they'd come back to each other.

He watched her for several tense seconds before saying, "I don't think we should do that."

Michaela blinked, surprised and a little embarrassed. No matter what happened, or how much time passed, she and Khalil had always found their way to each other. She thought she'd lost her chance when he'd gotten engaged. As much as she'd fantasized about being evil and confessing her feelings before he walked down the aisle, she also never wanted him to be alone or unhappy. She'd swallowed her hurt feelings and pride and tried to be happy for him. She'd even thrown him a damn engagement party, but when she'd heard the engagement was off, she hadn't felt a moment of guilt for celebrating.

"Why not?"

"Because, Michaela, we can't keep doing this."

It wasn't the words but the seriousness of his tone that made her stomach drop. The smile that had originally played across his lips was gone. The spark in his eyes extinguished.

Her heart raced and her fingers tightened around the pen in her hand. She tried to appear calm as her biggest fear seemed to play out. That Khalil was really and truly done with her.

"Doing what?" Her voice was light and shaky despite her efforts at composure.

"Getting together and pulling apart. It's time for both of us to move on."

"I thought you did that two years ago." She knew the words were harsh, but she didn't care. He blinked and looked away. The spark of guilt she hadn't felt when she'd celebrated the end of his engagement poked at her now. She pushed it away.

To his credit he didn't look away for long. His gaze

didn't waver as he watched her. "Two years ago was the start."

Michaela frowned and stood. "Quit talking in riddles and just say what you mean."

"I mean that we can't keep going back and forth, Michaela. We both want different things."

She crossed the room to him. "That was before. I meant what I said earlier."

He uncrossed his arms and shifted his stance. "You meant what you said all the other times, too. You're just thinking that because your dad is sick."

"I was thinking this before my dad got sick." She stood close enough to him for them to almost touch. The minuscule distance did nothing to lessen the current vibrating between them. "I've been thinking about this, about us, for a long time."

He sucked his teeth and gave her a doubtful look. "Since when? Since I said I was getting married? Because if that's the case then I know it's not real. You're just reacting to the fact that I was off-limits for a while."

She put a hand on her hip and pointed a finger with her other hand. "Oh, so you're telling me you forgot what I said before you told me you were engaged?"

His brows drew together, and he glanced away. That was what she thought. He hadn't forgotten. Neither had she. She'd gone to him and said she wanted them to really be together. To stop the back-and-forth, hooking up here and there. She'd wanted him. It wasn't until after her confession that he spoke the words that replayed in her mind constantly.

I'm getting married, Michaela. I hope you'll be happy for me.

The pain from back then dug into her heart again

today. Then she'd wanted to cry, scream, tell him no, he couldn't get married because he belonged to her. She'd done none of that. After all, she'd refused him just a year before. Pride wouldn't let her beg. So she'd asked him who she was. Then listened as he'd told her about this perfect woman he'd found. Her world had shattered, but instead of ruining his happiness she'd celebrated his good news. Tried to support him and his decision.

That was then. Today she wasn't going to pretend. Doubt had kept her from accepting what he'd offered once. Pride had kept her from fighting for the love she'd held in her heart later. Neither of those mattered to her now. She didn't doubt her feelings, and pride wouldn't replace the joy she felt when she was in his arms.

He shook his head. "That was different." The bass had left his voice now that she'd drawn up the memory.

She placed a hand on his chest. His heart beat nearly as fast as hers and he sucked in a quick breath. "That was different?" she asked in a quiet voice. "How? Because the way I feel hasn't changed."

He shifted from foot to foot again but didn't move away from her. He looked away and took a deep breath before meeting her eyes again. "We keep doing this and one of us always ends up getting hurt."

He didn't pull away. Emboldened, Michaela placed her other hand on his chest. "Then let's not hurt each other anymore." She ran her hands from his chest to his shoulders.

"Stop playing with me, Michaela." There was steel in his voice even as the fire in his eyes heightened.

Didn't he realize that she'd never played with him? That she'd never lied to him or hid her feelings? She'd put her drive, her ambition, her need to have more at the top of her priority list for so long. Even neglecting herself to be more successful. She'd lost him once because of that. Lost herself. She wasn't going to lose either of them again.

"Who says I'm playing?" she asked in a soft voice. "If you don't want me—" she leaned in closer until her breasts brushed against his chest "—you can always push me away."

His hands moved to her waist. For a second, she feared he was going to put distance between them, but then his grip on her tightened.

"You're no good for me." The words came out in a low, grumbling voice.

She didn't get a chance to counter the statement because he pulled her flush against him and lowered his mouth to hers. Michaela didn't resist. She trusted herself in Khalil's arms. She was safe in his embrace. The familiar taste and feel of his mouth against hers made her heart swell and her body tingle. She loved kissing him. Loved the confident way his lips moved over hers, and the sensual glide of his tongue as he tasted her. Making her knees go weak.

She tightened her arms around his neck and pulled him even closer. She didn't have to guess about his next move. She knew what he'd do, and he didn't disappoint. His strong arms wrapped around her waist; one hand palmed her behind as the other pressed into the small of her back. Making sure all parts of her front were cemented to his. The hard press of his desire against her stomach was all the proof she needed that he was just as lost as she was. That despite what he said, the feelings between them were far from over.

You're no good for me.

What he'd said cleared the fog of happiness in her mind. She pulled back. Khalil's eyes remained closed for two heartbeats before they opened and met hers. Her breathing was choppy and uneven as she stared into his hooded eyes.

Everything was there. The desire. The familiarity. The excitement. But something else was there, too. Distrust. He wanted her, but he didn't believe her. Her throat constricted and her fingers released the grip they had on his shirt.

"Why did you say that?" she whispered. Did he really believe that? Had all the years they'd known each other mean nothing? Did he regret the time they'd shared?

Pain flashed in his eyes. His lids lowered and he took a shaky breath. They were so engrossed in each other that Michaela didn't notice the sounds coming from the back door of the house until the house alarm beeped. Her mom was home. That was the only person who would possibly be entering from the back the house.

They pulled apart. Kahlil pressed a hand over his mouth. His nostrils flared and his intense gaze bore into hers. Michaela tried to control her breathing, to not look as if she'd just gotten off an emotional roller coaster, but every part of her body was on hyperalert. It was always like that when he kissed her. All she wanted was to jump back into his arms and feel his body against hers again.

Not if he doesn't trust you.

Her mom came around the corner. "Oh, Michaela, you're here, and Khalil! Willie told me you were his nurse. I'm glad it's you."

Khalil dropped the hand from his mouth and smiled at her mom. Michaela's eyes widened and she brought a hand to her lips. His mouth was red. The lipstick she'd put on that morning, and which lasted all day, had transferred to him. Which meant her face had to be just as bad as his. Flames of embarrassment heated her cheeks. She was supposed to be taking care of her dad, not making out with Khalil.

"I was just about to leave," Khalil said, oblivious to the red lipstick on his face.

Michaela's mom raised a brow. "Looks like you had a good day, huh." She looked from Khalil to Michaela. A teasing glint brightened her mom's eye. Michaela suppressed a groan. Did she want Khalil back? Yes. Did she want her parents to get their hopes up before she was sure things would work out? Hell no.

"He did great, but he really has to go." She tugged on Khalil's arm and tried to turn him away from her mom. "Umm… Khalil, will we see you tomorrow?"

He looked down, caught a sight of his palm then brought his hand back to his mouth. He rubbed his lips and more of her lipstick spread across his face and onto his palm. Eyes wide, he looked at Michaela. She tried to give him a reassuring smile, but to be honest, with her lipstick on his face he looked like the Joker and she was probably just as bad.

"Yeah, I need to go," he said. "Mrs. Spears, I'll see you tomorrow." He hurried out of the dining room.

"Good to see you, Khalil. Tell your mom and dad I said hey," her mom called out.

"Will do," he said before dashing toward the front.

After the door closed, her mom looked back at her. "I guess your dad wasn't the only person he was seeing after."

Michaela walked over to the dining table. She grabbed one of the paper towels she'd used earlier.

She turned her back on her mom and tried to wipe her mouth. "I don't know what to say."

Her mom laughed. A second later her hands patted Michaela's back. "Don't say anything. I always wanted you two together. Maybe now I'll get my wish."

Michaela stopped wiping her mouth. Her shoulders relaxed and she turned her head to look at her mom, whose brown eyes were filled with compassion and love. Michaela had never said anything about how much she hated that Khalil had gotten engaged, but she'd always wondered if her mom knew. They'd never told their parents they were hooking up. Mostly because if they'd admitted to being together then their parents would put matchmakers around the world to shame with their efforts to get their kids down the aisle.

But when Michaela had called home to give her mom Khalil's good news two years before, her first words had been *I'd always thought one day he'd marry you*. In a moment of weakness Michaela had replied *Me too*.

Her mom hadn't brought it up when Michaela had thrown Khalil an engagement party. She'd just been the first person to call her and let her know when Khalil's engagement ended. Her dad and Khalil may doubt that she meant what she said, but her mom didn't.

"That's my wish, too," Michaela admitted.

Her mom squeezed her shoulder. "Next time remember to take that lipstick off before you kiss him." Her mom pointed. "No need telling the whole world what your intentions are. Now wash up while I go check on your dad."

Tears pricked her eyes and Michaela nodded. She didn't think she could love her mom any more than she already did before that moment. "Yes, ma'am." She turned toward the bathroom.

"And, Michaela," her mom called.

She looked back. "Yes?"

"Protect yourself, too. Don't make it too easy. He did get engaged to someone else. I know you want him back, but be sure it's right before you jump, okay?"

She wanted to argue. To say that this time was the right time. But the words didn't come. He'd said she was no good for him. If he believed that, was there any hope for them? What if he was no good for her? Something she'd never considered before until she glimpsed the concern in her mom's eyes.

She nodded. "Yes, ma'am." Her mom gave her another nod before turning to go check on her dad. Michaela went to wash her face. Her mom was right. She'd hurt Khalil, but she'd only been honest with him for her reasons for turning him down. Before she jumped, she needed to make sure that their connection was strong enough to hold them together.

CHAPTER FOUR

MICHAELA SAT AT one of the tables in the middle of A Couple of Beers, a cool brewery in downtown Peachtree Cove. She raised her glass of sour ale and grinned at her longtime friend Kaden sitting across from her. She and Kaden had met in fourth grade and been fast friends all through high school. College and adulthood had made keeping up less frequent, but when the two reconnected, it was as if no time had passed.

"To friendships that last," Michaela said.

Kaden clicked his glass against Michaela's. "I can't believe I put up with you for this long." He rolled his eyes but there was no malice in his voice, and his gaze sparkled with the same mischief they had when the two had hung out as teens.

"You put up with me? I'm the one who kept you on the straight and narrow," Michaela teased before taking a sip.

"Straight and narrow my behind," Kaden replied. "Let's just tell the truth. Both of us were too much."

Michaela grinned at the memories. The two of them had spent a lot of time in high school sneaking into parties and looking for ways to have fun. "That's what made us best friends."

"Even after I transitioned?"

Michaela pursed her lips. "Now it just means I get a guy's opinion on things."

When Kaden transitioned five years ago, Michaela had been surprised, but she'd accepted her friend and been proud of Kaden for living his truth.

Kaden laughed and shook his head. "You always were the person to point out the benefits in any situation."

Michaela shrugged. "That's part of the reason I'm successful. I can find the silver lining in just about anything."

"I love your optimism."

"It's gotten me where I am today. How's the baby?"

Kaden's eyes lit up. "She's beautiful and doing just fine. She's almost a year old already. Where did the time go?"

"You tell me. It seems like you just had her," Michaela said, thinking about when Kaden had first sent pictures from the hospital of him holding his new baby.

"That's how I feel." Kaden sounded just as amazed at how quickly time passed as Michaela.

"Do you want any more kids?"

Kaden lifted a shoulder. "I don't know. I'm still getting used to being responsible for one tiny human. Not sure if I'm ready to add another one to the mix."

"I remember when you wanted five kids."

Kaden pursed his lips and shook his head. "That was a long time ago. I think two will be my limit if I have any more. What about you? You wanted two or three kids."

Michaela sighed and sipped her beer. "That was before I got so busy building my business. I can't imagine having a kid and keeping all of this going."

"People do it. I think you'll be able to make it work."

"But do I want to make it work? Finding someone I'm willing to have kids with is hard enough. Do I really want to add in being responsible for the life of another person while I'm hustling every day?"

"First of all, you already know who you want to have kids with if you ever chose to," Kaden said, raising his brows then taking a sip of his beer. "Besides, if you two ever did come to your senses, decide to get together and somehow manage to take the time to have kids, I'm sure you would find a way to figure it out. You're too stubborn not to."

Michaela didn't bother pretending she didn't know who Kaden was referring to. Her friend knew all about Michaela's longstanding on-again, off-again, never-quite-able-to-connect relationship with Khalil. Kaden had probably guessed Michaela would try to get back together with Khalil while she was back in town.

"I may know that, but that doesn't mean anything. I thought I could prove to Khalil that I was serious about making things work out between us, but he's kept his distance."

Despite the kiss they'd shared in her parents' home, all she could remember was him saying she wasn't good for him. She'd assumed convincing him to give her a chance might be harder after his broken engagement, but she hadn't thought he would believe she was bad for him. The realization hurt more than his engagement. Had she been the only one emotionally invested all these years? Had the time he'd asked her to be with him just been a whim?

Kaden's eyes widened and he leaned forward. "How can he avoid you when he's taking care of your dad?"

"Oh, he can find a way. I appreciate how focused he is on my dad's recovery, but he's making sure to keep away from me. I thought it was fate that brought him to me, but since that first night he's kept his hands to himself and avoids being alone with me."

"But he kissed you," Kaden said, sounding just as affronted as Michaela. She'd told her friend about the kiss earlier.

"We kissed, but that's been it. I know he still wants me. I can feel it. I can see it. But he doesn't want to want me."

"You know," Kaden said slowly, a slight frown on his face, "I can understand where he's coming from."

Michaela leaned forward. "Hold up. You're supposed to be on my side."

"I am always on your side, but that doesn't mean I can't see *all* sides. From where Khalil is standing, I can understand why he may not think this time is any different from before."

"This time is completely different from the other times," Michaela said emphatically. "I'm looking for ways to step back at work. His engagement ended. There's no reason why we can't try this for real now."

"Yeah, *you* know that. You're the one who had the epiphany, but that doesn't mean he had the same breakthrough. Or maybe his breakthrough was different."

Michaela settled back in her chair, absorbing Kaden's words. "Do you think he doesn't want me anymore?"

"I don't know about all that. I mean, he did kiss you. But wanting you may not mean he wants to invest in anything serious with you."

"Damn Kaden," Michaela said, pouting.

Kaden shrugged. "You wanted my opinion. You both

spent most of your twenties hooking up whenever you came around each other and dating other people when you were separated. He always wanted to put down roots here in Peachtree Cove. You wanted to fly away and do your own thing. There's nothing wrong with what either of you wanted. Now you've both grown up. It's time to get to know the people you are now. Not the young bucks just hooking up whenever you came into each other's orbit."

"What if it's deeper than that? What if he's really done?" The thought made her chest ache. She rubbed her hand over the spot. She tried to imagine her life without Khalil and it made her eyes burn.

"I can't answer that question. The only way to find that out is to talk to him."

"How can I talk to him if he's avoiding me?"

Kaden looked then pointed behind Michaela. "No time like the present."

Michaela peered over her shoulder to where Khalil walked through the door. He hadn't come to her parents' house today. It was his day off before he worked in the emergency room over the weekend. He looked good in scrubs, but she also loved the way he looked in his casual clothes. The short-sleeved light blue T-shirt and dark shorts made him appear more relaxed but no less sexy.

She and Kaden sat at a table in the middle of the bar, so he saw them soon after he walked inside. Michaela lifted a hand and waved. He waved back before going to the end of the bar.

"So, are you going over there?" Kaden asked.

Michaela tore her gaze away from Khalil. "We're

hanging out. I can't ditch you for him." She glanced back at the bar.

Kaden laughed and finished his beer. "Don't use me as an excuse. I need to get back home anyway. You go ahead and handle that."

"What if he really doesn't want to try with me again?" She hated how scared she sounded, but she was afraid. Afraid that the window of opportunity they'd once had was closed.

Kaden stood and squeezed Michaela's shoulder. "Then you accept it. It'll hurt, but you'll be okay. You always find a way to bounce back."

KHALIL WASN'T SURPRISED when Michaela joined him at the end of the bar. They could still be cool with each other even if they weren't together. Her not coming over to sit next to him would have been weird. He didn't want their relationship to be weird. He still wanted her in his life; he just wasn't sure if he could handle anything more than friendship without getting too wrapped up in thinking they could be more.

Joshua, the bartender and part owner of A Couple of Beers, came over just as Michaela sat. "Can I get you another beer?"

Michaela waved a hand. "Nah, I'm good for now, but I'll take some water."

Joshua nodded. "Got it. What about you, Khalil?"

"What's good on tap?" he asked.

"We've got a new pale ale from a Georgia brewery that's pretty good," Joshua replied.

"I'll give that a try."

"Got it," Joshua said before walking away to make their drinks.

Khalil turned toward Michaela next to him. "You ditching Kaden?"

She shook her head. "Nah, he had to get back home to the baby."

"I thought you'd get back to your parents?"

"I came out because they forced me out," she said with a laugh. "Apparently all I do is work and hover. They want me to get out and have some fun."

"There may be some truth to that statement," he agreed. When she frowned, he explained. "You are either always on a call, video chat or drafting up something."

"It takes a lot to keep the business growing." She didn't sound defensive but there was a tightness to her voice.

"Your business has grown a lot. You are now the guru of financial advice. How much larger do you want it to be?" He kept his tone light. He didn't fault her for wanting to be successful. But sometimes her drive for success seemed to come at the expense of Michaela's personal needs. He worried about her but didn't want his concern to come across like he was trying to hold her back.

"If you really want to know, I think I've hit the 'how large do I want to be' portion of my life." She paused to smile and thank Joshua, who had returned with their drinks. After he walked away, she continued, "I've pretty much done everything I wanted to do and more. I got myself out of debt. I've taken what I learned and used it to help other people get out of debt, save and invest wisely. I've created a network to help others, and I even wrote a book. I've made enough money to support me for the rest of my life."

"Are you saying you're ready for retirement?" he asked doubtfully. He couldn't imagine Michaela sitting still for the next fifty years.

She shook her head and frowned. "I'm too young to retire. That's part of the problem. I don't want to keep working at the pace I've been going, but I don't know how to slow down either. It seems like working hard to get somewhere means you have to keep working hard to get the next thing, you know?"

He nodded, understanding what she was saying. "Why do you think I got my doctorate in nursing? Sometimes it seemed like having one degree wasn't enough to get ahead. So I went as far as I could go."

"I thought you were always good with what you had. I didn't realize you felt like you had to go for more."

He laughed softly before taking a sip of his beer. "I had ambitions, too, Michaela. They may not be as big as yours, but they were there."

"I didn't mean it like that."

He reached over and brushed her hand resting on the bar. Her skin was soft, and the brief touch made his hand want to linger. He pulled back before succumbing to the urge.

"I know you didn't. I'm just explaining my side. There are opportunities happening in Peachtree Cove. The hospital system is thinking of expanding the emergency room to a full hospital. They have plans to build a timeshare next to the ER."

She frowned. "Time-share? Like vacation property?"

He shook his head. "No, it's just a term they used. They've added on a space next to the emergency room, and different doctors and specialists can use the offices on a rotating basis. It's allowed us to get better health care in Peachtree Cove without having to travel to Augusta or Atlanta. I'd like to work for one of the specialists using the time-share. That way I can still be close and give back."

"That's pretty cool. When will it be complete?"

"End of the year, though I've heard some rumors about budget cuts and potential delays. Which means, now I've got to face the possibility of looking outside of Peachtree Cove to achieve my dreams."

"You're thinking of leaving?"

He took a long breath. "Thinking about it."

He'd been thinking about leaving Peachtree Cove a lot lately. Since the breakup of his engagement, he'd felt stymied. Stuck in the same place, doing the same thing, building a dream he'd had since he was a teen that was going nowhere. He finally understood why Michaela had left all those years ago. It was the other reason why he wasn't ready to jump into anything too quickly. If she was honest about staying, how would she react knowing he was ready to go?

"But you love it here. You can't leave Peachtree Cove." She spoke as if him leaving Peachtree Cove was unthinkable. Maybe to her it was.

"I do, but I have to accept that there are limited opportunities. Do I just wait around and see if the hospital really expands, or do I go after opportunities elsewhere? You know how that is."

"I do. I'll be a little selfish and hope the plans for the hospital expansion happen quickly so you can stick around."

"We'll see," he said, not committing either way. His decision would be his. Not because of Michaela. "It would be a good thing for the town."

"And for you. You'll be contributing to the town. While I know you're currently giving back through your thirst-trap tendencies on social media, you can do so much more for the world." Her lips lifted with the teasing words, and she took a sip of her water.

Khalil chuckled and shook his head. "I told you that I'm not a thirst trap. I just post pictures of me doing everyday stuff. That's all."

"Uh-huh, sure. I don't think your followers are there for the everyday stuff. You don't mind having all those people following you for more than your nursing tidbits?"

"It doesn't bother me that much."

"That much? So it does a little bit?"

He shrugged. "I started that account in undergrad and just posted random pictures. Then later I focused more on my nursing studies. I did not expect it to blow up like that. I just went with it. The exposure and the occasional gig work as an influencer helped with tuition. I didn't think much of it until my account became one of the reasons me and Jackie didn't make it."

Michaela's brows drew together. She turned on her seat to face him fully. "Were you replying to the people sliding into your DMs?"

Khalil narrowed his eyes at her. "Come on, Michaela. You know me better than that. I'm not going to follow up with any other woman when I'm in a relationship." He'd made a point to ignore his direct messages.

"Then what was it?"

"Just me being out there, I guess. She said if I loved her then I wouldn't post pictures online."

"Okay, I know I teased you about being a thirst trap, but your pictures aren't suggestive. I mean, you have the occasional post-workout selfies that I would argue are thirst-trap adjacent, but overall, the rest of your pictures are you in your scrubs or hanging out with friends."

"It was after the *Gossipfeed* article came out listing me as one of ten 'hot male nurses' to follow. She thought I submitted my account, but I don't care about *Gossipfeed*. I didn't even know they were putting together an article like that." Irritation entered his voice at the memory of her accusation.

"She didn't seem like the jealous type. She was always nice to me and good with us being friends."

Khalil shook his head. "No, she wasn't. She hated every minute of that party you threw for us."

Michaela's eyes went wide. "And you still let me do it?"

He threw up a hand. "I didn't know she hated it until after. When you offered, I told her I'd already said no. I wasn't going to let you throw us an engagement party."

"I remember. You were adamant. Kind of hurt my feelings." She pouted with the words even though humor reflected in her eyes. Damn, she was cute.

"I couldn't let the woman I…" He cut off. She raised her brows and Khalil reconsidered his words. "I couldn't let someone I used to hook up with throw me an engagement party."

"Except, we were never officially together, but we were always friends. Us hooking up always kind of just…happened. No rules, no expectations."

"I know." And he'd always hated that about their relationship. The long-term friends with benefits. Having Michaela but never really having her. "Anyway, I told her I said no, and then she got upset. Said it would look like she was jealous or couldn't handle being around you. So, I agreed to the party. Later, when we broke up, she used that as another reason why. She said I was with her but that my heart wasn't really with her. She felt like a fill-in."

"Was she right?"

Khalil looked into Michaela's eyes. The truth was in the tightening in his gut just from making eye contact with her. No one did to him the things Michaela did. No one had a hold on him the way she did. He'd wished it were different a thousand times, but something about this woman was in his blood.

All things he wasn't ready to admit now, if ever. Michaela didn't want to be tied down. Never wanted to get married. Didn't want the sleepy small-town life. She'd literally built her own financial empire to avoid returning to it. He would always be a convenient layover in her jet-setting life, but never a permanent stop. He was the one stuck in the same spot.

"She wasn't a fill-in." He took a sip of his beer and looked away.

"Are you okay?" Concern entered her voice. "I mean, are you still upset after the breakup?"

"I was right after. I kind of felt like a failure. I couldn't even make the one thing I always wanted out of life work. But she was right, if I couldn't delete a simple social media account because she asked me to then I wasn't really in love. I cared about her, but it was better finding out we couldn't make each other happy before we got married versus after."

"How are you now? Seeing anyone?"

"Nope. I've finished school and I'm making plans for my next step. Time to focus on the reason I've worked so hard this far in the first place. Which means continuing to ignore any offers in my DMs."

She gave him a small smile and leaned closer. "What about the people sliding up next to you at the bar? Are you ignoring them, too?"

His heart rate picked up. He clenched the bottle in his hand to avoid reaching out and touching her. "We'll always be cool with each other, Michaela."

He kept his voice even. Tried to ignore the memory of their kiss popping up in his head. Tried and failed. He'd been thinking of that kiss every day. The sweet taste and feel of her in his arms. It would be so easy to fall back into what they'd been before. To sleep with her again knowing she would walk away afterward. His body craved hers, but his heart… His heart needed the distance.

"You said I was bad for you. Have you always felt that way?" The teasing was gone, and her tone was serious.

He heard the hurt and confusion in her voice. The sound made him want to take back the words, but he couldn't. All he could do was try to clarify what he'd meant. "Going back to you, expecting things that I know won't work, that's what's bad for me. I can't, I won't, keep doing that."

She was quiet for a few seconds before asking, "So, being cool with each other is all we can be? Nothing more than that?"

The sounds of the bar faded. All he saw was her sitting in front of him. Looking at him with eyes that wanted everything he was willing to give. He wanted to believe in that look. So even though he should tell her no, his emotions spoke for him instead. "I don't know, Michaela. A lot of that depends on you."

CHAPTER FIVE

MICHAELA SPENT THE next few days thinking about what Khalil said. What they became was up to her. She knew what he'd meant by that. He was still interested. But, after his broken engagement, she understood why he'd be hesitant to believe that she was for real. Of course he'd be hesitant to jump into a new relationship.

Except, they weren't new. They were familiar with each other. They'd just never really dated. Their past hookups had been about sex and vibes. Mostly at her insistence. He wanted more than that. Maybe he'd always wanted more. She understood what he meant. They couldn't keep playing this back-and-forth game. Otherwise, they'd continue hurting each other. Proving they could be more than just sex and vibes was on her?

If Michaela loved anything, it was a challenge. She'd started Operation Date Khalil the next day. She would prove they could be more. She was going to woo him.

She spent the next few weeks doing just that. Starting with sending him texts during the day. Not just "what you doing?" but texts asking his thoughts on something she'd seen on television or links to interesting podcasts she listened to. He responded and the conversation would typically carry on throughout the day. She'd followed that up by dropping off lunch for him at the ER when he'd texted that he survived off vending-machine sandwiches and protein bars during the day. She didn't stay long so she wouldn't take up his time, but she saw the appreciation in his eyes. The texts and lunches turned into phone conversations and that was when she asked him to hang out with her when he had time. They'd meet at the bookstore, have coffee one morning or she'd join him watching television while her dad took a nap.

She intentionally did not try to turn the dates into something sexual. They didn't have any trouble in that department. Operation Date Khalil was about taking Kaden's advice. She was going to get to know who Khalil was today without hormones fueling their interactions.

The plan was working. After a month, he was more relaxed around her, and she'd discovered that Khalil was even more fun to hang out with than before. She decided to step things up a bit and ask him out on an official date. Which was how she found herself meeting him at the art gallery downtown. The gallery owner taught wine and art classes on the weekends, so she'd signed them up. She'd opted for a daytime class versus a night class. She wanted things to move along between them, but she didn't want to push too far. A day class felt like it was more about having fun versus being romantic.

She spotted Khalil crossing Main Street and smiled and waved. He returned the action, and her heart skipped a beat. Khalil's smile made her want to run to him, throw her arms around his neck and kiss him deeply. The one drawback of Operation Date Khalil was that she couldn't do that. With each date she wanted Khalil more, but she couldn't tell if he viewed them hanging out as proof they could work out as a couple or proof that she belonged in the friend zone.

"Were you waiting long?" he asked when he reached her. He didn't try to hug her. Before he would have hugged her. Now he kept physical contact to a minimum, which only made her crave his touch even more.

She shook her head. "No, just got here. Are you excited?"

He glanced at the door of the art gallery. "I'm interested. I've never painted before."

"Really?"

He nodded. "Not since art class in elementary school. I heard that the classes here are cool, but never had a reason to try it out. If I suck don't laugh."

Michaela pressed a hand over her heart. "I promise not to laugh if you don't laugh."

"I thought you had done this before." He walked to the door and held it open for her.

"I've done a few guided art classes before. That doesn't mean I'm good at creating art. Luckily, I picked a class with an easy painting."

They went inside the gallery. The art studio had opened just a year before in Peachtree Cove and was part of the revitalization of downtown. The owner, Jackson Bowman, had relocated to the area when he'd decided he wanted to pursue his love of painting in a place that supported the arts but wouldn't stretch his budget. The gallery was part of a growing creative community in Peachtree Cove that included the local theater, an art studio, a pottery studio along with several new bars and restaurants that hosted local musicians or poets for readings.

Jackson waved and greeted them when they entered.

He was a white man in his midforties, with kind gray eyes and a dusting of grey at the temples of his dark hair.

"Just pick a seat anywhere," Jackson said. "We'll get started in just a few minutes."

"Thanks," Michaela said and glanced at the ten chairs set up in two rows facing the back of the room. Small easels holding blank canvases sat on the tables in front of each. Another chair with a standing easel faced the rows of stations.

Five people were already sitting. When Michaela spotted one of the women there, she grinned.

"Halle, hey!"

Halle turned and grinned at Michaela. They'd gone to high school together, and even though they hadn't been best friends, they had hung out a few times and had both been in the school's teacher prep program for students who were interested in going into education. Michaela had turned her love of education into teaching adults how to budget, save and invest. Halle followed the path laid out for them in the program, becoming a teacher and now the middle school principal.

"Michaela, hey girl! And Khalil, ready to be artsy?" Halle asked, pointing at the chairs next to her.

"I'm ready to try," Khalil said, giving the canvases an unsure glance.

"It's easy," Halle said with a shrug. "Shania and I have come here at least three times, haven't we?" Halle looked at the young girl sitting to her left.

Shania held up three fingers. "I think this is our third time."

Michaela's eyes widened. "Is that your daughter?"

"It is. Shania, this is Ms. Michaela. We went to high school together and she's in town for a little bit."

Shania waved a hand. "Nice to meet you."

"Nice to meet you, too. How old are you now?"

"Just turned thirteen. I'll be in eighth grade next year."

Michaela's jaw dropped. "Wow! Everyone's kids are making me old."

Halle laughed and shook her head. "How do you think I feel? How long are you in town for?"

Khalil pulled out the seat next to Halle for Michaela to sit in. After she was settled, he moved to the one next to her. Michaela's answer was for both him and Halle. "I'm not here for a little bit. I just put in an offer on a house."

"You did?" Halle said excitedly.

Khalil stopped mid squat into his seat. "You did?"

Michaela nodded. "I did."

"But aren't you, like, a millionaire?" Shania asked, sounding astonished.

Halle swatted at her. "Don't be counting other people's money."

Michaela chuckled and waved off the comment. "She's right, and it doesn't bother me to talk about it. I've worked hard for a long time to grow my business. Now I'm ready to take a few steps back and enjoy what I've built. Having my dad get sick really brought that home to me."

"Well, I for one would love to have you back," Halle said. "We need to keep the new ideas flowing around here. And new donors for the school's booster club," Halle said with a wink.

Michaela laughed. "Still ready to raise money for a cause."

"Always."

"Then let's talk. If I'm going to be here, then I want to invest and give back to the town."

"Sounds like a plan."

Shania said something to Halle, who focused back on her daughter. Michaela turned to Khalil.

"Did you really buy a house?" he asked.

She hadn't wanted to tell him until she found the place she wanted. She was going to make sure he understood this time was about actions and not just words. "It's not final, but yeah. I made an offer."

"What about your place in Atlanta?"

"I don't plan to sell it. My business is based in Atlanta, so I'll have to go back occasionally. When that happens, it'll be nice to stay in my own place versus a hotel."

"You've got two houses?"

She held up three fingers. "Three. I bought a condo on the Gulf coast last year. I mostly use that as rental property, but I'd like to spend some time there in the summers. I love the beach."

He blinked. "Three houses?"

She nodded. "Yep."

He stared then shook his head and grinned. "You say that like it's normal."

"Believe me, it still feels surreal."

"You really have worked hard over these last few years. You don't really need anything."

Michaela shook her head. "That's not true. I'm proud of what I've got, but all of that hard work came from a place of thinking I had to hustle 24/7 to feel safe and secure. It would be nice to have a safe place that doesn't require me to run all the time."

She held back the rest of what she wanted to say. That she wanted him to be her safe place. Her calm when the work became too much. But was he ready to be that for her?

The corner of Khalil's lips lifted in a half smile. "You may find that place sooner than you think."

JACKSON STOOD IN front of the budding artists and smiled. "How did your paintings turn out?"

Khalil squinted at his and tilted his head. He'd tried to relax and let an artistic side he'd never indulged take over, but still worried his painting would be the worst in the class. When he glanced over at Michaela's, Halle's and Shania's paintings of a full moon over snow-covered hills, his was like theirs. He hadn't done as bad as he thought.

Michaela smiled at him. "You did pretty good!"

"It's all right," he said, trying not to show how much her praise made him want to puff out his chest. "Not as good as yours, but pretty good."

"We've got to hang them up somewhere," she said.

He thought about the inside of his place and wondered where he could hang it, then shook his head. "Nah, I did all right, but it's not display worthy."

Michaela reached over and placed a hand on his arm. "Yes, it is. Let's go to your place after this and I'll find the perfect spot."

"You want to go to my place?"

He knew she'd thrown out the words with no underlying meaning. In the weeks since he'd said what they became was up to her, she'd spent time hanging

out with him and having fun, but she hadn't tried to resume their sexual relationship. He'd assumed she'd decided to keep them as just friends. He should be happy
about that...except spending time with her without sex
on the table only made him realize how much he liked
being around her. That his feelings for Michaela were
more than sexual.

"Yeah, I'll come to your place," she said with a
shrug. "Let's go when we're done."

He searched her face for flirting or inuendo, but only
saw excitement about the possibility of putting up his
painting. This was good. This was what he'd wanted.
For them to be cool. For him to keep his heart from
engaging with a woman who obviously didn't want to
settle down.

Except, she didn't seem as against settling down anymore. She was doing more than paying lip service to
the idea of sticking around Peachtree Cove. She'd donated to the hospital and agreed to join their citizen advisory board. He'd heard she'd confirmed to speak at
the Business Guild meeting in three months. Now she
was buying a house. Her third house, but still, a house
in Peachtree Cove.

His original plans were wavering. He was beginning
to wonder if maybe, just maybe, this time with Michaela
could be something more than just a fling.

The class wrapped up and everyone cleaned their stations before gathering their belongings to leave.

"Don't forget that I have these classes on the third
Saturday of each month. Be sure to come again," Jackson said.

Michaela grinned before shaking his hand. "I will."

Halle waved her phone toward Michaela. "Give me your number. When you come back, we will, too."

He waited for Michaela to find an excuse to avoid giving her number. She'd never liked sharing it with people she wasn't going to see often and kept her contacts limited to business associates and close friends.

"Sure!" Michaela said, grinning before rattling off her digits for Halle. "I'll be in town now, so call me. We can go for drinks or hang out sometime."

Halle nodded while she saved Michaela's number. "Sounds like a plan."

When Halle turned away to leave, Michaela looked at him. "What?" she said, reaching for her cheek. "Is there something on my face?"

He shook his head. "Nah, just...you don't give out your number often."

Michaela shrugged. "Halle is cool, and I'll need people to hang out with now that I'll be living here. I can't expect you to always entertain me."

"I don't mind entertaining you." The words were out before he could think about what he was saying.

Michaela's smile softened and she reached over to squeeze his forearm. "Remember you said that when you're sick of me." She dropped her hand. "Come on. I'll follow you to your place."

Khalil's heart jumped in his chest. From the touch or her saying she'd follow him to her place, he didn't know or care. He managed to rein in his thoughts before they could get out of hand and he started imagining things happening at his place that she wasn't thinking about. Things like kissing her, holding her and making love to her again.

"Yeah, sure," he said in a thick voice. "It'll only take a few minutes."

By the time they got to his place, he'd gotten his wayward fantasies under control. He'd set the tone for their relationship, and she'd followed his lead. The last thing he wanted was to come across like he was playing games.

"You've got a nice place," Michaela said once they were inside.

He lived in a modest two-bedroom home in a newer subdivision a few minutes away from downtown. "Thanks." He led her from the foyer into the family room connected to the kitchen. "When I bought the place, I thought of it as a nice starter home. But now I think I'm pretty settled in."

"You originally planned to move?"

"I figured I'd need something bigger after the wedding. We both talked about kids. Two bedrooms may not be enough."

"Ahh…that makes sense."

An awkward pause filled the space at the mention of his failed engagement. She had the same question in her eyes that she'd had back when he'd first told her the reason why he and Jackie had broken up. Had their relationship played a role? It hadn't, but he thought about what he'd do if Michaela asked him to get rid of his "thirst trap account," as she called it.

You would've deleted it fast as hell.

He held up his painting before that thought could shake him more than it already had. "Where do you think I should hang this?"

She walked over and took it from him. "Hmm…let

me see." She went to a blank space on the wall next to one of the windows and held it up. "Maybe here."

He came up behind her. "That could work."

She stepped back and bumped into him. Khalil steadied her with a hand on her waist. Her body stilled. The soft curves of her ass pressed into his crotch. The air around them thickened. He didn't let her go and waited for her to pull away. She didn't.

"Were you thinking of another spot?" he asked quietly.

"I kind of like this spot," she said in a soft voice. She leaned slightly into him. The intoxicating scent of her perfume and the underlying sweetness that was just Michaela drifted around him like a silk string and squeezed. His fingers tightened on her waist.

"Why do you like this spot?"

"It's comfortable."

He frowned. "Comfortable?"

Michaela looked over her shoulder at him. "I like being comfortable. Being safe. I haven't felt that way in a long time."

"This spot makes you feel safe?"

She nodded, and her eyes dropped to his lips before meeting his again. "Maybe it isn't the spot. Maybe it's just your touch."

Heat rushed through him like an out-of-control forest fire. "My touch, huh? I thought we were talking about the painting."

"I was. But then… I can't think of anything else when you touch me."

His fingers dug into her hips. He didn't push her away. He held on to her as the last bit of his reasons why he shouldn't start up with Michaela again flew out the window. He didn't understand what it was about this woman, but he couldn't resist her. "Michaela—"

She turned away and sighed, her head falling to the side. "I know, I know. You don't want to hook up with me again. I get it. We never worked out before. We kept missing each other in the past, but I can't help but feel like we don't have to keep missing each other."

Pride told him to hold out. To stick by what he said. But when she tried to pull away, another emotion pushed pride aside. He lowered his head and kissed the side of her neck.

CHAPTER SIX

MICHAELA WANTED TO flip with joy when Khalil's lips pressed into the sensitive spot where her neck and shoulder met. She'd held back and tried to be patient. To let him come back to her and avoid coming on too strong. She wasn't interested in only a casual hookup. She'd thought she'd have to wait longer, but the soft kiss on her neck was the sweetest ending to her longing.

A soft sigh escaped her as his strong hands gripped her hips. He held her body tight against his. He didn't have to worry about her slipping away. She was all in for this. For him.

Khalil ran the tip of his nose across her skin and breathed in deep. "You smell so good."

"You always say that." Her voice shook, her body trembling with anticipation that had built from the moment she'd seen him standing on her parents' porch.

"Because it's true. Do you know what you do to me?"

"What I do to you? You're the one who does things to me."

"What do I do to you?" he asked in a desire-thickened voice. His lips closed around the pulse at the base of her throat. The slightest bit of pressure as he gently sucked.

"Drive me wild," she said in a half moan. "Make

me forget everything but the feel of your hands on my body."

"Like this?" His right hand shifted, and the warm heat of his palm cupped her breast. Michaela shivered and nodded. His fingers traced over her hardened nipple and pinched softly. "What about that?"

She sucked in a breath. "Yes."

He pushed his hips forward. The solid weight of his desire dug into her back. "You do the same thing to me. No matter what happens, I can't forget you, Michaela." His voice shook almost as much as hers. The emotion threaded into his words clenched her heart.

Michaela reached back and clutched his thigh. "Then don't."

He groaned, his body trembling as he hastily tugged her dress up. His hands roamed over her body confidently. As if the last time he'd touched her was only three days ago versus three years. He knew just how to drive her to the brink. His fingertips played across her stomach, making her gasp then chuckle from the ticklish movement. The humor was quickly swallowed by need as he went back to lightly sucking against her neck while one hand palmed her breast and the other pushed down her underwear.

Michaela turned into mush in his arms. She let herself be carried away by the current of ecstasy he created with each caress and kiss. This was what happened whenever they came together. She didn't have to be strong, powerful or in control. She could trust herself in his arms. She could relax and let him take the lead, because she knew Khalil only wanted to give her pleasure. There was no hustle or struggle here. Just happiness and joy.

That was all he'd ever wanted. She'd once believed letting go and succumbing to the feelings he incited in her would somehow mean she was being weak. That she had to want the career more than she wanted the man. Not anymore. As his fingers slid between her thighs and caressed her while his voice murmured in her ear, she knew she wanted and could have both. *Would* have both.

"Tell me how you want me," he whispered in her ear.

"From behind," she said without hesitation. She never hesitated to tell Khalil what she wanted. Even though he knew what she liked and how to touch her body, he never assumed or pushed her. The other reason why she could trust herself in his arms.

His body shook with his light laughter. She didn't care. She was eager to have him and wasn't afraid to let him know it. From the way his body trembled as he touched her, she knew he felt the same.

Khalil spun her around and kissed her deeply. Michaela wrapped her arms around his neck and kissed him back. What felt like too quickly, he broke the kiss. Her protests stopped when he took her by the hand and led her to his bedroom. Michaela bit her lip and smiled to stop herself from giggling.

They quickly undressed once they crossed the threshold. Clothes removed with an urgency that spoke to their desire. Khalil took a condom out of the nightstand and he moved to open the package, but Michaela took it from him.

He raised a brow. "Are you still okay with this?"

"Let me do this." She opened the package and stepped forward. His lids lowered and his breathing stuttered as she slid the condom over his thick length.

His large hand palmed her ass while the other cupped the back of her head. "You want to take over?"

She shook her head. "I just want to touch you. Now make love to me like only you can."

He kissed her hard and Michaela clung to him. Her heart, her body, every part of her willing to give him anything just to keep this moment forever.

Khalil turned her around and bent her over the bed. She bit her lip, this time not to stop giggling but in eagerness. She'd waited so long for this. He didn't tease her or make her wait. Khalil grabbed her hips and pushed into her. Her head fell back, her eyes closed as the pleasure seeped into every corner of her body. He started slow, letting her body get used to the feel of him stretching her. When she pushed back, he followed her lead and increased the pace.

Michaela's mind went blank from everything but the feel of Khalil's hands on her hips and the slide of him oh so deep inside. She let go, turned herself over to the pleasure and let him drive her to the brink. She could do this all day, but her body had other ideas. As if sensing she was close, he bent forward and kissed the back of her shoulder.

"You feel so damn good. I could make love to you forever."

Her heart flipped as emotion and pleasure became a thousand tiny bubbles in her veins. She squeezed around him and as her body exploded with her orgasm, one thought came out as a cry on her lips. "You can have me forever."

CHAPTER SEVEN

KHALIL STARED AT the email on his cell phone's screen. His fingers tightened around the phone and his heart rate picked up. He'd never been so excited and conflicted at the same time.

"Nurse Davenport. Khalil!"

Khalil blinked and looked up from the screen. Brandon Greene, one of the ER nurses and his good friend, looked at him with a mixture of humor and confusion on his face.

"Huh?" Khalil said.

"I had to call you about three times. Everything good?"

Khalil nodded. "Kinda, but what's going on? Do you need me?"

Brandon shook his head. "No, I'm about to go downtown on a coffee run. Did you want anything?"

Khalil shook his head. "I'm getting off in a few and don't want to be up all night."

Brandon grinned. "Must be nice. Now that you've got that PhD, you're getting the better shifts."

"Hey, I can't complain. Working the day shift on weekends is worth it after working my butt off to finish school."

"When do you come back?"

"Later next week. I'll be helping out home nursing with Michaela's dad."

Brandon frowned. "I thought you were going to give up the second job."

"I was, even though the funds help pay off the student loans. But…" He glanced down at his phone before turning it face out toward Brandon. "I may have to quit anyway."

Brandon squinted at the phone. His lips moved as he quietly read the words on screen. Then his eyes widened, and he grinned. "Yo, for real! You've got the job!"

"Shh," Khalil, said motioning for Brandon to lower his voice. He glanced around but thankfully no one was close to them. "I mean, they want to bring me back in to discuss options."

"Discuss options, man, that means you're hired. This is great! You said you were ready to move on to a larger hospital."

Khalil sighed before sliding the phone into his pocket. "I know. It's great."

Brandon's eyes narrowed. He eyed Khalil with suspicion. "Hold up. You don't seem as excited as I thought you would be. I thought you were ready to get out of Peachtree Cove."

"I am. I was." He shrugged. "I don't know."

"What's going on. You've been itching to start over. You said your life was stunted after breaking off the engagement. Now you're hesitating." Brandon crossed his arms and squinted. "Wait a second. Is this about Michaela?"

Two nurses came around the corner. Khalil grabbed Brandon's arm and pulled him down the hall in the opposite direction.

"Aye, man, hold up," Brandon exclaimed as Khalil dragged him away.

"Come on. I can't have you spilling all my business in front of everyone." Khalil checked to make sure no one else was following them.

"You don't have to drag me."

Khalil let him go once they were out of earshot. "My bad."

"Yeah, your bad." Brandon straightened his scrubs before leaning in and grinning. "But I'm right. This is about Michaela."

"I don't know. I mean, I was ready to get out of Peachtree Cove. I felt like I was just sitting here. Doing nothing."

"And now you're doing her, so that's different?" Brandon said with a laugh.

Khalil pushed his shoulder. "No! It's not because I'm *doing* her. It's because she's…she sees potential in the town."

"You've always seen potential in the town. You're the one who changed your mind after your engagement was broken off. Suddenly, Peachtree Cove was too small, and you weren't living up to some new standard." Brandon rolled his eyes with the words, not bothering to hide his disdain.

Khalil couldn't fault his friend for his feelings. He had said all those things and meant them after the breakup. He'd wondered if he was sitting still waiting for something that would never happen versus living his life. "I did feel like that."

"Why, though? I never understood that."

Khalil shrugged. "I don't know."

"You do know, you just don't want to admit it."

Khalil cocked his head to the side. "Oh really. Since you know me so well, then why do you think that?"

"Look, man, I've known you since we both started nursing school. You were hung up on Michaela then and you're hung up on her now. You've wanted her and maybe a small part of you thought that maybe moving up to a bigger job would help you get her."

Khalil shook his head. "It wasn't about Michaela."

"Then what was it about? Jackie never once said you weren't amounting to much. She was supportive of your job. You were the only one who thought you needed more."

"Because I saw everyone else doing more. And not just Michaela. All those other people who finished up their nurse doctorate. They moved on to bigger jobs and had these big plans. All I wanted was to stay in my small town and continue working at this ER. I felt like I wasn't aspiring enough. That I was settling." Or worse, that he was afraid to try for something else.

"Look, everyone doesn't have to hustle hard to get to the top of some mountain. It's cool to be happy where you're at."

Khalil knew that. He hadn't bought into the hustle culture before. But now, with this opportunity in front of him, he had the first feelings of doubt. Had not buying into the "hustle culture" also meant he'd limited himself?

He pulled out his phone and looked at the email again before looking to his friend. "Do you think I should take it?"

Brandon shrugged and shook his head. "I can't tell you what to do. Now, ask me if I think you can do it?

The answer is yes. I know you can do it." He slapped a hand on Khalil's shoulder. "It's on you to figure out if you should take it."

"Boy, YOU BETTER take that job!"

Khalil stopped in the middle of helping Mr. Spears put on his basketball shorts before walking around the house for exercise. The man spoke with such force that Khalil almost dropped the shorts.

"Hold still, Mr. Spears, before you fall," Khalil said.

He put his hand on Khalil's shoulder to stabilize himself. "I'm not gonna fall. You got me."

Khalil laughed as he helped Mr. Spears get his legs in the shorts and pulled them up. "There you go."

"Now, about that job," Wille said immediately. "Why aren't you going to take it?"

Khalil let out a laugh. Mr. Spears was definitely where Michaela got her determination from. Once he was set on something, he didn't get easily distracted. "I didn't say I wasn't going to take it. I said I was thinking about if I should or if I should stay here in Peachtree Cove."

"Look, I love Peachtree Cove as much as the next person, but you were looking forward to this job, weren't you? It sounds like what you've wanted for a long time. I think you should go for it."

"I also like working here. Things are growing and so is the hospital. There could be opportunities for me in Peachtree Cove."

Talk about the hospital expansion had come up again today. As if making the decision wasn't hard enough for him as it was. Fate had a funny way of playing with his emotions lately.

"Yeah, but I'm a big believer in not counting your chickens before they hatch. You've got an offer already at a bigger hospital with more responsibilities. Do you have anything similar here?"

Khalil shook his head. "I don't." There was talk of expansion, but that was all it was. Talk.

Willie stopped the slow pacing they were doing around the room and looked Khalil in the eye. "Then why are you holding out for something that may or may not happen?"

Khalil couldn't look away from Mr. Spears's direct stare. Just like when his dad gave him the look, he felt compelled to admit what he was really feeling. "What if I go there and I can't do the job? I've worked in a small hospital system all my career. It's not even really a full hospital. More of a stand-alone emergency room. I might not be able to handle things."

Willie put a reassuring hand on Khalil's shoulders. His eyes softened with understanding. "You can do anything you put your mind to. It might be hard but that doesn't mean you can't do it."

The confidence in Willie's voice was exactly what Khalil needed. Sure, his friends and family would tell him that he could do the job. They were going to support him no matter what. But Mr. Spears was a straight shooter. If he thought something was a bad idea, then he would say so. He'd talked Khalil out of one or two dumb decisions when he'd been younger. That was the reason why he felt comfortable talking to him about his thoughts.

"You're right. Thank you, Mr. Spears."

Willie smiled and squeezed his shoulder. "Anytime."

Khalil helped Mr. Spears walk toward the door. He opened it, and they went into the hall.

"Now that we've got that out of the way, want to tell me the real reason you don't want to go?"

Khalil frowned. "What you mean? That's the only reason."

"Mm-hmm," Willie said skeptically. "Are you sure this doesn't have anything to do with my daughter."

"What would anything have to do with me?" Michaela stepped into the hall.

Khalil sucked in a breath. He'd thought she was working at the coffee shop that morning. Otherwise, he wouldn't have brought up his concerns. He didn't want her to know he was struggling with this decision.

"Nothing," he said.

Willie pointed at Khalil. "He's not sure about taking a job in Atlanta."

Her eyes widened. "You got a job in Atlanta?" she asked, excitement filling her voice.

"I was called in to discuss options," he said.

"That means you got the job. That's great!" She clapped her hands.

He blinked. "You think so?"

She nodded. "Yeah, I mean, you mentioned wanting to work for a larger hospital. You're finally getting the chance to do that. When are you going to meet them?"

"Next week," he said hesitantly.

She did a hip shimmy. "Let's celebrate. I went over to Books and Vibes this morning and brought back some croissants."

"You're speaking my language," Mr. Spears said, perking up even more. He shuffled forward toward Michaela.

Khalil followed behind them to the kitchen, as his conflicting emotions rattled around inside him. As much as he'd denied it to everyone else, Michaela was a small part of the reason he was considering turning down the job. He'd applied before she'd come back to town. He hadn't even considered them being together again. He'd gone after the position because he'd wanted a change. To challenge himself. But with her here, a part of him was happy to settle in again. He'd thought she would want him to stick around with her, but instead, she supported him leaving. Had he been wrong to think their making love meant something more? Were things just like before? Was she ready to let him go so soon after they'd come back together?

CHAPTER EIGHT

MICHAELA SPUN IN a circle before running her fingers down the valley between her breasts. She undulated her hips and moved her body back and forth in a sensual glide. Soft music played in the background, and she wore a barely there lacy camisole as she gave Khalil one of the sexiest dances of her life. She was ready for him to jump up from the bed, wrap her in his embrace and drag her back to bed in his arms.

That didn't happen. Khalil watched her, but he wasn't seeing her. A line formed between his brows and his eyes weren't focused. She sucked in a breath after giving what she thought was a riveting performance and he wasn't even paying attention.

Michaela placed her hands on her hips. "What's wrong?"

He blinked and his gaze focused on her. "Huh?"

"You're not into the dancing?"

"Um…yeah. It's sexy." He tried to smile but it didn't quite reach his eyes.

She cocked her head to the side. "You are not acting like it's sexy." She crossed the room and stood at the end of the bed. "I mean, I was doing this to celebrate your big news and you don't seem interested."

"I am interested."

"But?" Because she could hear a *but* in his voice.

His shoulders lifted as he sighed. He sat forward and crossed his legs. "I just didn't expect you to be so happy about me leaving."

Michaela blinked several times. "What? Why wouldn't I be happy? Isn't this what you wanted?"

"Yeah, but... I thought we were starting over again. I found out about the job and you're ready to push me out of town right when you're back in town."

Michaela shook her head. Was he being serious? He couldn't be serious. She crossed her arms beneath her breasts. She couldn't be flattered when his eyes dropped to her chest. "Are you really telling me that you're ignoring this fantastic sexy show I'm putting on because I'm *too* happy about you getting the job?"

He had the decency to look slightly ashamed. His eyes darted away for a second before his shoulders squared and he nodded. "I'm just saying, you didn't seem to care about me leaving."

Michaela narrowed her eyes. "Khalil, do you really think that I'd be the type of person to hold you back just because we're dating?"

"I mean, I thought you'd at least show some sadness or something at the thought of me moving away when you're deciding to move here."

"Why? I'm not going to be some possessive girlfriend who expects you to give up your dreams because of me. I won't stop you from accepting an opportunity just because it'll take you physically away from me. Atlanta isn't that far away. I'll be there a lot for my business anyway. I don't really see how this is going to hurt us."

He stared at her for several seconds before speaking in a rush. "I don't know if I really want the job."

She pressed her fingers to her chest. "Because of me?"

"No. Why is everyone thinking this is just you?" He spoke in a way that said he'd been asked that question more than once.

"Then what is it? Because you just ignored me being hella sexy and you wanted me to be sad about you taking this job." She sat on the edge of the bed, her earlier frustration draining away at the sight of the uncertainty in his expression.

Khalil reached over and took her hand in his. "It's not that I want you to be sad. It's just… I applied for this job on a whim. I thought that I needed to try harder. Do more. But honestly, I like where I'm at and what I'm doing."

She knew that he loved what he did. That had been obvious for as long as she'd known him. "Are you saying you want to stay at the emergency room in Peachtree Cove?"

"I didn't think I had a shot at this job, but it felt like what I should be going for after finishing my degree. I wasn't sure I had a chance, but they're offering it to me. At first I worried I wouldn't be able to do the job."

She could understand that. Feeling nervous about a new opportunity was common. She squeezed his hand holding hers. "Why wouldn't you be able to do it? You completed an entire doctorate degree in nursing and you're one of the smartest, most compassionate people I know. Of course you can do the job."

"But other doubts are hitting me. Am I really applying myself here in Peachtree Cove? Am I trying hard enough. I like where I'm at, but a part of me feels like since I have this chance that it would be wrong of me not to take it."

She scooted closer to him. "Look, I can't tell you what to do. You've got to figure that out for yourself. I understand how hustle culture will make you think you have to work harder and push harder. In the end that can drive you into the ground. But sometimes you have to push a little harder to get to a different place. You've just got to know when enough is enough."

"I like my life right now. I like helping people. I like being a part of getting things done. This job will be more management, less patients."

"If you take the job it doesn't mean you have to stay there until you retire. Give it a try and see how you like it. Then you can always come back here if it doesn't work out."

"There's no guarantee they'll take me back."

"I went to the citizen advisory board meeting the other day. They want people who are part of the community to work at the hospital. They'll take you back. Who knows, maybe you'll go there and come back and have so much experience that you'll bring good things to Peachtree Cove."

He considered her words for a second before taking a deep breath. "I'm sorry I messed up your dance."

She smiled before leaning forward and kissing the corner of his mouth. "You didn't mess it up. You just ignored me and dented my pride a bit," she said. When he frowned, she laughed. "I'm joking. It's normal. You get a new opportunity and wonder if it's the right thing. Even though I was the person who always chased every opportunity, I was nervous about each new thing. Challenging myself to try something I hadn't done before helped me build what I have now."

"You think I should do this?"

"I think you should challenge yourself. You've only known Peachtree Cove and this system. There's nothing wrong with that, but you've got an amazing opportunity. Don't dismiss this chance because you don't think you can do it. They don't just offer people jobs for fun. They offer it to people they think can do it."

He placed his hand on the back of her head and pulled her forward for a kiss. "Thanks for the pep talk," he murmured against her lips. "I needed to hear that, but I've been too worried to say what was really bothering me."

"That's what girlfriends are for. Now—" she gave him a sexy grin "—do you want me to get back to the dance?"

Heat filled his dark gaze and melted her like chocolate. "Forget the dance. Just get over here."

Michaela laughed and wrapped her arms around his neck as he pulled her down on the bed. "I won't argue with that."

CHAPTER NINE

MICHAELA LISTENED AS the president of the hospital's citizen advisory board wrapped up the meeting and reminded everyone about the next one. This was Michaela's second time attending and she enjoyed participating. Khalil had been right—the hospital had a lot of plans to expand and offer more services in Peachtree Cove. Dr. Imani Kemp, whom Michaela had known in high school, was back in town and today talked about a women's health fair she'd helped organize. Michaela had signed up to sponsor the health fair. After her dad's kidney transplant, she wanted to make sure that others in town had the opportunity to access life-saving screening.

She checked the time on her cell phone as she got into the car after the meeting to go to her parents' house. Khalil would be home from work in an hour or so and then she'd head to his place. He'd traveled to Atlanta the day before to meet with the hospital about taking the job and asked for twenty-four hours to consider the offer before answering. Michaela had meant everything she said to him. Even though a part of her hated to see him leave Peachtree Cove just as she'd decided to move there, a larger part of her couldn't hold him back when he was ready to try something different.

Her cell phone range as she drove home. A picture of

her friend and business partner, Noreen, grinning while flipping the bird popped up on her car's dashboard. Smiling, Michaela tapped the button to answer the call.

"Noreen! What's up, lady!"

"Hey, Michaela! How are you handling things in small-town Georgia?" Noreen asked, sounding like she couldn't imagine enjoying Peachtree Cove. Michaela could picture Noreen rolling her bright, expressive eyes and scrunching up her nose as she shook her head. Noreen had grown up in Chicago, was not nostalgic for small-town life at all and couldn't fathom why Michaela had chosen to stay.

"Things are going well. I'm just leaving the citizen advisory board meeting before going back to my parents' place."

"You are really determined to become a part of the town, huh."

Michaela laughed at the disbelief in her friend's voice. "I told you I was. Did you think I was joking?"

"Girl, you know stores closing at seven and town fairs aren't my ministry. But that's not why I called. I've got fantastic news." Noreen sang the last part, her voice rivaling any professional singer out there.

"What news?" Excitement creeped into Michaela's voice. When Noreen sang while talking, then she knew she was either in for a good time or learning something that would be life changing.

"The Build Wealth Academy not only has a waiting list for the next cohort, but National Bank wants to sponsor, which means we can offer a second cohort! On top of that, I've got us a meeting with a representative from the College Accreditation Association. I ran into a member of the review committee at that conference last week and mentioned our interest in having our financial management program becoming accredited so we can teach it at local colleges and students can earn credit. They're interested! Michaela, we can expand it even further!"

"Oh my God, Noreen, you did that?" Michaela's cheeks hurt, her smile was so big. Of course Noreen had made the connection and followed through. Her partner had more drive than Michaela at times. Their love of seeing how far they could go and passion to succeed had made them great friends and they'd managed to play off each other's strengths.

"Yes, I did," Noreen said, pride in her voice. "So, that's why I need you to get back over here so that we can prepare for the meeting and get to work taking the academy even further."

Michaela was excited about the possible expansion, but she wasn't ecstatic. This was something she'd usually be squealing about and immediately begin mentally rearranging her schedule to see how she could get back and start making plans. Instead, all the things she'd have to cancel in order to make this happen gave her pause. She was presenting to the Business Guild in two weeks. That Saturday she was doing a painting class with Halle. Her dad's next checkup was in a few days. She wanted to do that more than she wanted to get back and work on this amazing opportunity.

"Look, I just got back to my parents' place," she said, trying to keep her enthusiasm at a Noreen-approved level. "Let me check on my dad and then I'll call you back later to talk about it more, okay."

"Aww, really? You want to get off the phone now? I thought you'd be ready to hash this out."

"I would, but I literally just got here. Dad is still recuperating, and I don't like spending time around him talking work. I'll call you later. I promise."

"Fine, that's cool. Just be sure to call me as soon as you can. I can't wait to get started on this. I know you are, too, right?" Noreen asked expectantly.

Michaela let out a strained laugh. "Me, too. We've really got to figure this out."

The call ended and Michaela let out a heavy sigh. The need to rush back and help Noreen battled with her wish to stay in Peachtree Cove. She got out of the car and went inside. Her parents were sitting together on the couch. An old black-and-white movie played, but they weren't focused on the television. They spoke to each other in low voices, giggling and smiling at each other like newlyweds.

Michaela sighed and grinned. She hadn't seen her parents spend so much time together in a long time. She was happy to see them still together and in love after forty-plus years of marriage.

"What are y'all watching?" she asked, coming into the room.

Her mom looked over at Michaela. "*Sergeant York.* It's on the classic movie channel and you know your dad loves this movie."

"I do," she said. "I just came to check on you both after the citizen advisory board meeting. I don't want to interrupt date night."

"You're not interrupting," her mom said.

Her dad raised a brow. "Says who? She's dating Khalil and understands."

Michaela laughed and raised a brow. "Oh, you kicking me out?"

Willie wrapped an arm around his wife. "Things were just heating up."

Michaela shook her head and held up a hand. "All right, that was too much information." She laughed. "I'll get ready to go."

"Make some popcorn before you go," her dad said.

"Get work out of me first. I see how you do it." She walked over and kissed the top of his head. To see him recovering, smiling and ready to spend the night cuddling with her mom on the couch after his surgery was a blessing. She'd happily make all the popcorn he wanted.

Her dad patted her hand then gruffly pushed her away after his limit of being fawned over. Michaela exchanged a grin with her mom before she went into the kitchen and pulled out a bag of microwave popcorn. Her mom came into the kitchen holding two empty glasses just as Michaela set the timer.

"How was the advisory board meeting?" Mary asked. She went to the fridge and pulled out lemonade.

"It was good. Imani Kemp is putting together a women's health fair. I agreed to sponsor it. I think we can do a lot to help them be more involved in the community. It's exciting."

"I'm glad to see you get involved. I wasn't sure if you really were planning to stay in town like you said." There was no judgement in her mom's voice, just curiosity.

"I meant what I said. It's just harder than I thought."

"Hard how?"

"Noreen called." She updated her mom on the good news and potential expansions. "Now I don't know what to do."

"What do you mean?"

"I'm walking away right when things are growing even more. I feel like I'm giving up and letting Noreen down."

"You're not giving up," her mom said, matter-of-fact. As if it were easy to walk away from a business she'd worked on for over a decade with Noreen. "You're just pivoting focus."

"I know." But it felt a lot like bailing.

Mary raised a brow. "You sure? Because it doesn't sound like you're sure."

"I mean… I know I'm ready to slow down, but it feels a lot like I'm letting a lot of people down by staying here. That I shouldn't walk away from this opportunity."

"Why are you thinking like that?"

"I'm not a quitter. No one I know is. Khalil is stepping up. You're still working."

Her mom held up a hand. "Don't pull me into this. Your dad and I worked hard all our lives because we had to. We had a kid to raise and a roof to keep over our heads. Your dad had to learn the hard way to slow down. Seeing him go through this…" Her mom sighed and shook her head. "Well, now I'm ready to put in my retirement papers and spend more time with him."

"But you worked for years. I've only worked this hard for a few. I could do more."

"You can, but who says you have to do more of what you've been doing? You put in a lot of time and energy to get what you have. There's nothing wrong with slowing down so you can enjoy it. Your business can still go forward without you directing everything."

"Huh?" Michaela asked, confused. How was her business going to keep growing after she stepped away? She'd planned to work more remotely and travel back when needed. Maybe delegate more. But she still needed to be involved in the running of things. Or else everything she'd worked to build would be gone.

"Huh? her mom repeated with a grin. "I mean what I said. You don't have to oversee this. You can still take a step back and let your business grow. Or you can sell it because it's worth something and live off the money. You've got options. Consider them."

"Mary," her dad called from the kitchen. "Bring your fine tail back in here. We're getting to the good part."

Michaela shook her head and took the popcorn out of the microwave. "You better go before he comes and gets you."

"That man can be demanding. But he sure knows how to love a woman." Affection filled her mom's voice as she placed the glasses of lemonade on a tray.

"Okay, Mom, too much information." She held out the popcorn bag. "Enjoy date night."

"Oh, we will," she said with a sparkle in her eye. "And remember what I said. If you mean what you say about stepping back, then figure out a way to make it happen. You came here to help with your dad, but you're still working just as hard, and stretching yourself with the obligations here. Eventually, you're going to be right back where you started. Burned-out. Baby, you don't have to live like that."

CHAPTER TEN

KHALIL SMILED WHEN he saw Michaela's car parked in his driveway later that evening. She'd texted to say her parents were having date night and asked if he minded if she waited for him at his place. He'd quickly sent her the codes to get into the house through the garage and to turn off his alarm.

Knowing she was there waiting for him when he got home after getting off work made the last part of his shift fly by. The idea of curling up on the couch with Michaela and talking about their day held an appeal. Once, he never would have dreamed they would have shared that type of relationship, but now that they had it, he couldn't imagine not being with her like this.

He found her inside pouring ramen noodles from a pot into a bowl on the counter. "You're just in time," she said. "Dinner is served."

Khalil came up behind her and wrapped his arms around her waist. "You're making dinner now?" He kissed the side of her neck.

"Don't get used to this. I don't plan on making cooking a habit."

He squeezed her tighter. "I don't need you making dinner. I just like having you around."

She turned in his embrace and wound her arms around his neck. "How was your day?"

"It was good. I had an interesting call today."

"What was it?"

"The hospital executives called me up. They found out about my interview in Atlanta. They said they don't want to lose me and offered me a promotion."

Her eyes widened. "Are you for real?"

"I am," he said with a laugh. He'd been just as shocked as she looked. "They want me to back up the doctor and see patients in the new internal medicine practice office they're adding to the hospital. According to them, I was already being considered for the job. They just didn't plan to offer until the facility was complete, but they didn't want to lose me after finding out I was getting other offers."

Michaela raised her brows. "Do you want it?"

He'd thought about it a lot. Thought about the offer they'd made in Atlanta. The new responsibilities he'd have at a larger hospital would be a perfect step in his career. But when he'd talked to the administrators today, he'd known his answer.

"I do. I've decided to take their position instead of going to Atlanta."

He watched her face and waited. He worried she might think him staying in Peachtree Cove would mean he was giving up or settling for less.

Michaela grinned. "Good."

"Good? I thought you were okay with me leaving."

"Yeah, I'm okay with you leaving, but it doesn't mean I'm not happy about you being here. What made you decide to stay?"

"After talking it over with a few people, I realized that I'm not trying to impress anyone. It's not that I was afraid to try, but that I really am happy where I am. You were right, getting offered the job means I can handle it. That was even more clear during the interview. They said I was perfect and knew exactly how they wanted me to fit, but I interviewed them, too. The added stress, increase in hours isn't what I want to deal with every day. Plus, when I asked them about the work environment they brushed it off and said changed the subject. That was a red flag. I'd gotten wrapped up in the idea after graduation that Peachtree Cove didn't have what I wanted, but that was wrong. I like working in this community. I want to continue to give back here. Staying isn't about giving up—it's about giving back to the place I love."

Michaela lifted up on her toes and kissed him. "I'm happy for you. Really, I am."

"Thank you."

She took a deep breath before sliding her hands from around his neck to his chest. "I got a call today from my business partner. The financial academy we started is doing great, and we got an offer to expand. It's something I've worked so hard for. It's everything I ever wanted."

Khalil hugged her tighter. "That's great!"

She nodded but her face didn't show the level of excitement he'd expected. "I know. Noreen wants me to come back immediately and start working on things."

Khalil's smile faded. Dread became a heavy weight in his chest. "You're leaving?"

"I considered it. I thought that not handling things meant I was being lazy or letting people down, but then I realized, I'm happy. Being close to my parents, volunteering on the advisory board, spending time with you.

I worked hard so that I can enjoy life. If I don't ever try to enjoy it, then I'll spend my life working."

"What about your business?" He knew she still cared about it no matter if she wanted to take a step back. She wouldn't be able to walk away completely.

"I called Noreen back. I'm going to make her CEO of the Academy," she said confidently. "She can oversee the upcoming cohorts and the expansion, and I'll just stay on as an adviser and consultant."

"Is she okay with that?"

"She was a little disappointed, but she was also excited about the opportunity. I don't have to be there for every part. I can let others grow. Then I can focus more on my writing and speaking engagements that are related to financial planning. I can still do what I love and teach people, but I'll have more time to enjoy this thing called life."

"Are you okay with that?" he asked.

Michaela didn't hesitate. The grin on her face was bright and happy. "I am. It's kind of like what you said. I thought about the opportunity and then I thought about what I'm doing here. I always did what felt right for me. Peachtree Cove, my parents, you. You all feel right. I want this time with you."

"You sure?" he asked. Even though he believed her, he just wanted to hear it again.

"I'm sure. I love you, Khalil. Of course I want to start a new chapter with you."

For the first time in his life, Khalil felt like his knees would give out. He pulled her tighter against him, happiness and contentment swelling inside him. "I love you, too, Michaela."

She squealed and leaned up to kiss him. "So, we're doing this?"

"You're damn right we're doing this."

*****

Wish you could spend a little more time in Peachtree Cove?

Please turn the page for an excerpt from Synithia Williams's
The Secret to a Southern Wedding,
filled with southern charm, good friends and bad decisions. This first book in the Peachtree Cove series is the story of a woman determined to stop her mother's impulsive wedding to a man she barely knows, only to find herself irresistibly drawn to the groom's son.

CHAPTER ONE

IMANI LICKED HER lips and reached out, flexing her fingers open and closed in a "gimme" fashion toward her lunch time savior. Loretta worked behind the counter in the hospital's busy lunch line. Her black hair was covered by a hair net and laugh lines creased the dark brown skin around her nose and mouth.

Loretta shook her head and smiled. Imani didn't care. She was starving and Loretta had exactly what she needed.

"I made sure to put one to the side for you today," Loretta said handing over the red and white checkered food boat with a golden-brown, fried corn dog in the middle.

"I owe you big time, Loretta," Imani grinned as she snagged the corn dog and placed it on her tray. "I just knew I missed it."

"You're the only person I know who gets so excited when we have corn dogs in the cafeteria," Loretta said. "Most of the doctors prefer the fancy stuff."

Imani shook her head. "Give me a corn dog and mustard any day over fancy. How's your daughter and the baby?"

Loretta's smile broadened, revealing one gold tooth. "They're doing great. I'm so glad I told her to come see you instead of that other doctor. Thanks again for fitting her into your schedule. I don't know if she would have made it without you."

Imani's cheeks warmed and so did her heart. "Of course, I'm going to fit her in. You always save the best corn dogs for me." They both laughed before Imani sobered. "Seriously, I'm glad they're okay. Tell her to call the office if she needs anything."

"Will do, Dr. Kemp," Loretta said with a bright, grateful smile.

The man next to Imani in line cleared his throat. Loretta threw him an annoyed look. Imani shrugged and waved a hand. "I'll see you tomorrow."

She moved on down the line and grabbed a handful of mustard packets and a bag of baked potato chips before scanning the crowded seating area for her lunch partner. She spotted Towanda Brown, a doctor from the hospital's orthopedic practice sitting in a corner near one of the windows.

Maneuvering through the filled tables, Imani kept her eyes down to avoid eye contact as she made her way through the maze of bodies, seats and chairs toward her friend. Still, she received several points and stares with whispered "yeah, that's her. the hospital's chosen one" along with a few waves from some of the less cynical doctors and nurses for her to sit with them at their table. Those who caught her eye she gave a polite node before pointing toward Towanda.

She sat with her friend and sighed. "Sorry I'm late."

Towanda shrugged. Despite having not run track in over ten years, Towanda still had the tall, muscular figure that once had her on the fast track for the Olympics before an injury ended her career. Her sienna skin was as line-free as it had been when Imani first met her, and she wore her hair in braids that were pulled back in a ponytail at the base of her neck. She looked closer to thirty-three than her actual forty-three.

"It's crazy busy today, but I knew you'd make it for corndog day." Her friend grinned and pointed to Imani's tray.

"Loretta never lets this day go by without saving me one," Imani said.

"That was before you helped her daughter. I'd be surprised if she doesn't make extra just to pack up and deliver to your office."

Imani chuckled while opening a package of mustard to put on the corndog. "I would've helped her daughter despite her support of my corndog addiction. She was seeing a doctor who ignored all her fears. I was just happy to let her know that her concerns were valid and that I wasn't going to gas her up with fancy talk."

"And that's why you're the hospital's doctor of the year," Towanda said pointing behind Imani.

Imani didn't look over her shoulder. She knew what was there. Her face was plastered all over the hospital right now on signs, cardboard cutouts, and the television screens throughout the hospital that ran with news and updates. Was she proud of being named the hospital's doctor of the year, kind of. She'd spent so much of her life trying to become an obstetrician patients could rely on and trust, did that translate to being comfortable as the "face" of the hospital system for a year, not one bit.

"Can we not talk about that right now?" Imani squirted mustard down the length of her corn dog.

"Why not? It's something to be proud of."

"And I am proud, I just don't want that to become all I am. Especially when we know the hospital administration's guilt about the last few doctors of the year may have had something to do with it." She raised a brow.

The last four years hadn't included a female doctor of the year at all and only two women were nominated. Ever since Guardian Heath merged with Mid-State Health to become one of Florida's largest health systems, the strives made to diversify prior to the merger were lost as profits and popularity became a thing. Imani hadn't believed she'd had a chance of winning when she learned of her nomination against a heart surgeon and oncologist.

"You won because you're the best and that's all we're going by," Towanda said.

Imani shrugged. "Fine, I'm the best. Now can we talk about something else."

Talking about being the hospital's doctor of the year meant thinking about how the obstetrics unit now pushed her in front of every camera they could find to draw more clients to the practice. Imani, who'd previously been a liked and well-respected member of the practice, but never thrust forward as the only Black doctor for diversity points, was suddenly a double commodity. She didn't like that.

Imani took a bite of her lunch. The savory mixture of the mustard with the hotdog wrapped in corn meal batter made her groan with pleasure. "This is soooo good."

Towanda's brows rose and she eyed Imani curiously. "Can we talk about how after watching you go in on that corn dog and moan like a porn star, I don't know why you haven't caught a man, yet."

Imani tried to glare at her friend but could only cover her full mouth and suppress a laugh. She chewed and swallowed hard. "Corndogs, unlike a lot of men, don't disappoint."

"Chile please. Everything disappoints eventually."

"Corn dogs never disappoint," Imani took another bite.

"Even microwaved ones?" Towanda asked.

Imani scrunched her nose and shivered. "Touche. Thanks for reminding me nothing in life is perfect."

She'd once believed in perfection. That she'd had the best life ever. That reality had been shattered harshly and abruptly one fall afternoon.

Her cell phone vibrated in the pocket of her white lab coat. She pulled it out and smiled when she saw the text icon from her mom.

"Who is it?" Towanda asked.

"My mom. She only texts with town news or a funny video she found online."

Towanda grinned. "You still care about town news?"

Imani nodded and clicked on the text. "I mean, I don't live in Peachtree Cove anymore, but that doesn't mean I don't like hearing what's going on with all the judgmental people in town."

"The people couldn't be that bad."

Imani grunted and didn't answer. The same people who'd loved her parents had been quick to talk about them when her dad and his girlfriend decided to put a deadly plan in place to separate Imani's parents for good. So, maybe it was petty, but Imani indulged in her mom's texts about the trials and tribulations of the people ready to cast judgment on her family all those years ago.

Imani opened the text, preparing for the funny video

or latest update, but frowned at what looked like an invitation instead.

"Everything alright?"

Imani zoomed in on the invitation and nearly dropped her phone. She had to read the words out loud to be sure her eyes weren't deceiving her. "You're invited to the wedding of Linda Kemp and Preston Dash. What the hell is this?"

Towanda leaned forward and tried to see Imani's cell. "Your mom's getting married?"

"No. She couldn't be. My mom isn't even dating."

At least, her mom never talked about dating. Her mom hadn't dated since the disaster of her last marriage. She hadn't been able to trust anyone since. Not that Imani blamed her. Getting almost killed by your husbands and his mistress tended to do that to a person.

"Who in the world in Preston Dash?" Imani muttered and why was her mom be marrying him? In a month! This didn't make sense. It had to be a prank. She called her mom immediately. The phone went straight to voice mail.

Imani stared at her cell phone. "Seriously?"

"She didn't answer?"

"This has to be a joke," Imani said. The watch on her arm vibrated. "Damn." She pressed the button to stop the alarm reminding her that she needed to be back upstairs in the practice in time for her next patient appointment.

"You're probably right," Towanda said. "Your mom wouldn't get married without telling you?" The question in Towanda's voice was the same question in Imani's heart.

"My mom wouldn't get married, period," Imani said.

She shoved the rest of the corn dog into her mouth and jumped up. She pointed toward the exit.

Towanda nodded. "I know. Go ahead. We'll talk later. Let me know what your mom says."

With her mouth full, Imani nodded and hurried out of the cafeteria. She shoved the bag of chips into the pocket of her lab coat and chewed the rest of the food in her mouth after dumping her trash into the can. On the way to the elevator, she texted her mom back.

This is a joke, right?

She watched her phone and waited for her mother's response. There was nothing as she waited on the elevator. Nothing as she boarded with a group of people. Still nothing as she tried to avoid eye contact with the others as they slowly realized the face smiling back at them from the picture plastered on the elevator doors was her. In the background the throwback song, How Bizarre by OMC, played from the speakers. Imani hummed along and watched her phone. The doors opened, thankfully, before the dots were all connected between her and the life-size photo, and Imani quickly got off. Her phone finally buzzed as she approached the door to the practice.

No joke. Come home. We'll talk.

What kind of response was that? Her mom wouldn't answer her call, but she'd text back telling her to come home. She'd just talked to her mom a few days ago. She hadn't mentioned anything about getting married or even gave a hint of there being a special person in her life. A few months ago her mom mentioned Imani's cousin Halle said something about getting on a dating app for seniors, but Imani had immediately shot that down. No way was her mom about to be played by some random guy online after all she'd been through. Now she was talking about marriage? After she'd vowed to never trust another man again. Something wasn't right.

She was preparing to dial her mom's number again when she walked through the door of her office.

"Oh thank goodness, Imani, you're here!" Karen, the receptionist behind the desk exclaimed.

Imani looked up from her phone to Karen. The receptionist had a bright smile on her face as she pointed to a man holding a camera next to the desk. The white guy wore a blue polo shirt with the logo from a local news station on the breast pocket and khakis. His dark hair was stylishly cut, and he grinned a hundred-watt smile at her.

"Dr. Imani Kemp, it's great to meet you. I'm here for your interview at one," the man said.

Imani looked from him to Karen behind the desk. "I have a patient at one."

The door behind the reception desk opened and Dr. Andrea Jaillet came out. Tall, red hair with bright blue eyes and a super sweet personality that wasn't manufactured, Andrea was someone that was nearly impossible to dislike.

Andrea beamed. "Imani you're here, great. We've moved your patients around to other doctors so you can do this interview. Isn't is great. The news wants to feature our doctor of the year."

Imani's phone buzzed again. She glanced down.

Dinner Saturday at 2. You'll meet your step-father then.

She looked from the text to Andrea's smiling face, to the reporter and his camera. The chorus of "How Bizarre" played on loop in her head. All she'd wanted was a corndog. What in the world had happened to her perfectly normal day?

CHAPTER TWO

CYRIL DASH STARED at the digital wedding invitation on his phone and scratched his chin. The rough hairs of his beard were longer than usual. He'd need to get it trimmed soon, but the brief thought of future trims immediately faded as he read the words again.

"Are you for real?" He looked up from the invitation to his father sitting on a stool across from him at the bar.

It was just before ten in the morning and Cyril's bar, *A Couple of Beers*, wouldn't open until noon. His dad usually came over on his days off from the hardware store where he worked part time. Typically, Cyril enjoyed listening to his dad give an update on the latest happenings at the hardware store or his plans to go fishing with some of the other retirees in the area over the weekend. His dad hadn't had much opportunity to enjoy life in the past decade and any sign of him relaxing and being happy made Cyril happy. He wanted his dad to be happy. He was not prepared for his dad to jump headfirst into happiness by getting married in a month.

Preston Dash grinned from ear to ear. His brown eyes sparkled with a joy Cyril hadn't seen in years. The lines in his golden-brown skin deepened and he rubbed his hands together as if anticipating the upcoming conversation. Dressed in a blue, linen short set with the gold chain he always wore glinting around his neck, his dad looked like the confident, laid-back version of himself Cyril worried he'd never see again.

"I'm for real," Preston said in his deep, scratchy voice. "Linda Kemp and I are getting married in November."

Cyril tapped the thick paper invitation on the bar. "You two just started dating. How are you already getting married?"

"When you know you know," Preston said with a shrug.

"Okay, I get that, but isn't this kind of sudden?" His dad and Ms. Kemp had only been dating for a few weeks.

His dad waved a hand. The lights over the bar glinted off the gold, signet ring with the letter P engraved on the surface he wore on his right ring finger. He'd stopped wearing a wedding ring after Cyril's mom died. "You and I know more than anyone else that life is short. I'm not taking anything for granted, including believing I've got a lot of time on my hands."

Preston grabbed the clean towel draped over his shoulder and went back to wiping down the bar. "But still..." Cyril tried to balance the shock of his dad's announcement with the worry easing into his chest. Marriage? Seriously?

"But still what? When we moved here, we agreed we weren't looking back and would start over." His dad slapped his chest. "This is me starting over. You did the same thing when you opened this bar."

Cyril stopped wiping the bar and cocked a brow. "Come on now, we both know starting a bar isn't the same thing as getting married."

"Why not? They're both a big commitment. You had

to put a lot of time and money into this place and look at what you've accomplished. You've turned it into a success."

"I just had my first year out of the red, and that was barely out of the red and you know it."

Yes, he'd worked hard to open a bar. A dream he'd had but never pursued before they'd left Baltimore three years ago to move to Peachtree Cove, Georgia. Back in Baltimore the idea of running his own business, much less opening a bar, had seemed as likely as hopping a taxi to Mars. Something that would be cool, but never going to happen. The struggles of getting his dad's name cleared and finding out the truth about what happened to his mother made dreams seem wasteful.

Yet, here they were. His dad was free. They'd started over in a small but vibrant town. Cyril had not only opened a bar, but he'd survived his first two years. Still.

"Have you told her about mom?" He tried to keep his words light despite the heavy burden they held.

The smile on his dad's face dimmed and his gaze slid away from Preston's. "I told her enough."

Cyril's brows drew together. He glanced around the bar even though he knew they were alone. He could count his staff on two hands and have plenty of fingers left over. *Couple of Beers* employed a few locals as bartenders and served several craft and traditional beers on tap along with whatever seasonal beer Cyril brewed up in the back. He didn't have to worry about a bunch of people overhearing, but his business partner and friend, Joshua, would arrive any minute. Joshua knew their story, but Cyril still wasn't comfortable talking about their past with an audience.

He leaned closer to his dad. "What does 'told her enough' mean?"

"It means that I told her your mom died and we moved to Peachtree Cove a few years afterward for a fresh start."

Cyril waited for more. When he got nothing, he scratched his head, tipping back the camel-colored fedora he wore over his short, faded hair. "Dad, there's a lot more to that story."

Preston grunted and waved off Cyril's words. "I know that, but the rest of that story only causes problems. I don't want her to look at me with the same suspicion that our family and friends gave me. That part of the story is over. We've finally got closure and I don't want to bring it up anymore."

"You can't just brush aside everything else."

Preston shook his head and scowled. "Why can't you just be happy for me. I never thought I'd find a woman who would make me feel the way I felt with your mom. I've finally got that and I'm finally ready to look forward to the future. Why can't you be happy for me?"

Guilt fought the worry in his heart. "I am happy for you."

"Then act like it," Preston said in a stern voice.

Cyril held up his hands defensively. Guilt won every time. "I'm acting like it."

"No, you're not you're questioning me."

"I just want to make sure you're good. You know I'm here for you. I've always had your back. I'm being cautious."

"Don't worry. I'm good. Besides, Linda's got demons in her past of her own that she doesn't want to talk about. I understand that more than anyone. We both agreed that we're starting over and not looking back. Trust me, son. I know what I'm doing. I just want you to be happy for me."

Cyril looked into his dad's eyes and sighed. He hadn't seen his dad this excited about anything in years. If he were being honest, he'd opened the bar hoping it would make his dad remember the good ole days. Back when Preston and Cyril's uncles would sit in the back yard of their home and talk late into the night about any and everything. Cyril and his cousins would hover in their periphery, soaking up the advice of the coolest men they knew. He'd learned a lot about life, relationships, and family watching his dad and uncles' relationship.

Relationships that were violently broken with the unexpected death of Cyril's mother. Sides were chosen, ties severed, and damaged almost beyond repair. *A Couple of Beers* was a nod back to that happy time. But even that hadn't made his dad smile the way he had since meeting Ms. Linda Kemp.

"I'm happy for you dad," Cyril said honestly.

"For real?"

Cyril nodded. "For real. Whatever you need just let me know."

"Will you be my best man?" His dad asked with a hopeful smile on his face.

Cyril placed a hand over his heart. He never thought he'd hear those words from his dad. Never thought his dad would ever get married or love again. To see the joy and excitement on his face after years of pain and heartbreak brought a swell of emotion through Cyril's chest. "Of course, I will."

He reached out a hand and his dad slapped it. They clasped hands and his dad rose so Cyril could hug him over the bar. When they pulled back his dad looked away and quickly wiped his eyes. Cyril smiled and grabbed one of the glasses from behind the bar.

"How about a drink to celebrate."

Preston waved a hand. "You know it's too early for me."

"That's why I'm only giving you a taste."

Preston narrowed his eyes and pointed at Cyril. He tried to glare but ended up laughing. "What you put together now?"

"It's the last of my winter blend. I'm going to put it on sale so I can make room for the spring blend I'm working on." He went to the tap and poured a small amount of the cinnamon infused lager he'd brewed for the winter.

"Look at us. You've got the bar. I'm getting married. Who would have seen this seven years ago?"

Cyril shook his head. "I always believed things would work out."

"You never doubted me once?"

Cyril handed his dad the glass. He held on when his dad would have taken it and met his eye. "Never once."

When his mother was murdered and the cops immediately tried to pin it on Preston, Cyril refused to believe it. His dad had loved his mom and Cyril had witnessed that love every day. Was their marriage perfect? No. Something that had come to light during the investigation, but despite being witness to his parent's flaws Cyril never believed his dad would hurt his mother. It had taken way too long to prove that, but they had. Now they were here and happy. He'd do anything in his power to protect his dad's happiness. He deserved it after losing so much.

The sheen returned to his dad's eyes, and he blinked several times. "You gonna give me this beer."

Cyril chuckled and let go. "Take it."

There was noise from the back of the bar. Cyril looked that way as Joshua came into the main area. Joshua was about five years younger than Cyril's thirty-eight years, with his hair cut short on the sides with dreads at the top that he wore in a ponytail. His circle wire rimmed glasses enhanced his expressive eyes, and he wore a black *Couple of Beers* t-shirt with a pair of distressed jeans.

Shortly after opening Couple of Beers Cyril realized that while he loved beer, he did not love managing the books. He'd immediately looked to hire a business manager and Joshua, who'd grown up in Peachtree Cove, left for college in Atlanta before returning home, was the first person he'd interviewed. They'd immediately clicked, he liked Joshua's laid-back vibe and his thoughts on ways to market as well as manage the business. Three years later and they were not just partners but friends.

"What's up, Mr. Dash," Joshua said coming over to shake Preston's hand. "What are you doing here so early?"

Preston raised his glass. "I'm just here to give my son the good news."

Joshua's brows rose and he glanced at Cyril. "Good news?"

Cyril nodded his head in his dad's direction. "That's his news to tell."

Joshua turned back to Preston. "Don't leave me out. What's going on?"

Preston grinned from ear to ear. A sight Cyril would pay to see over and over again. "I'm getting married."

Joshua's eyes nearly bugged out of his head. "For real? To Ms. Kemp?"

Preston nodded. "The one and only. You know since we moved here I think I figured out the secret to why so many people move south."

Joshua raised a brow. "What? Lower taxes?"

Preston laughed but waved a hand. "Nah, all the sweet southern women. Find one and marry her quick." He pointed to both of them.

Joshua shook his head. "I'll leave that to you."

Cyril waved a hand. "I've got to get you through this wedding first before I even think about getting married."

Preston grinned. "You've got to not only get me through the wedding, but since you've agreed to be my best man I need you to convince Linda's daughter to go along with the wedding."

Cyril's smile dropped and he frowned at his dad. "Say what now?"

Don't miss Synithia Williams's
The Secret to a Southern Wedding,
available now!

BEST MAN NEXT DOOR

Stefanie London

Dear Reader,

I hope you enjoy Sage and Jamie's story. My inspiration came from a documentary about the haute couture fashion world. But rather than the glamour of a runway show, I was fascinated by the endless repetition and quest for perfection *inside* the atelier. I wondered who might be drawn to such a meticulous, challenging career, and thus Sage was born.

Of course I needed the perfect hero to be the one to help her heal the wounds from her high school days, when she was bullied. Jamie's big heart and kind spirit are exactly what Sage needed. I wrote a large chunk of this book late at night while my husband was very ill in the hospital, and it was his fighting spirit and ability to make friends even in his most dire moments that made me want to write a hero who was goodness through and through.

So I hope this second chance happily-ever-after lifts your spirits as it did mine.

Stefanie

To Justin, for fighting.

CHAPTER ONE

BEFORE TODAY, JAMIE HACKETT had thought he'd already faced death.

Like the time he dove off a cliff on a dare, plunging into the ocean with the speed of a bullet. Or the time he'd come face-to-face with a territorial goose who'd gone apeshit at him for getting too close to her goslings. Or when his car skidded across a patch of black ice in the middle of winter and he'd narrowly missed crashing into a big oak tree.

He'd been cool as a cucumber, every single time.

But it turned out he hadn't *really* faced death. Now that he'd confronted it for real, he understood what it felt like.

Jamie glanced around the sterile white hospital hallway, feeling weirdly disconnected from it all. If someone had told him he was floating in the air, watching everything happen from above, he would have believed it. Giving himself a shake, he reached one hand to his opposite arm and pinched himself. Hard. He winced from the pain.

Still alive.

But the quicker he was out of here the better.

His mom stood at the administration desk, her shoulders hunched. Exhaustion seeped into her posture and made her look even smaller than usual. When she turned to face him, he noticed her blouse was buttoned wrong and her curly ginger hair was sticking out in all directions like it always did when she didn't have time to style it.

"Ready to go, hon?" She tried to smile, but her eyes were watery and the dark shadows circling underneath made her look hollowed out.

You did that to her.

He nodded.

"Your dad has gone to get the car so he can meet us out front." She slipped her arm into his and held him close, her fingernails biting into his skin, as if she was worried he'd float away like a discarded balloon if she didn't hold on tight enough. "No need to rush—we'll walk slow."

"You didn't have to wait around. I could have gotten a cab," he said quietly. He kept his gaze averted from the goings-on around him, not wanting to see the people being wheeled about and the elderly folk shuffling along, walking their fluid bags like strange, lifeless pets.

It freaked him out.

He was thirty-two for crying out loud. Thirty-two with his whole life ahead of him. With *decades* ahead of him.

"Jamie Hackett, if you think I would let my child come home from hospital in a cab then I don't even know..." Her voice broke as she shook her head, still clutching him tightly. He could hear the tears she was holding back, companions of the ones she'd been shedding ever since she'd arrived at the hospital yesterday. "Of *course* we were going to take you home."

There was no point arguing. Patty Hackett was an overprotective mama bear at the best of times, let alone when one of her own was hurt. Although really, aside from a few stitches in the back of his head and some chest pain that felt like a couple of boulders had been propped there, Jamie was walking away from this situation a lot better than he could have.

A lot better than what *would* have been if his best friend hadn't saved him.

When they made it outside, Jamie sucked in as much air as his lungs would allow, and even though doing so burned, he had to clear the hospital smells from his nostrils. It was warm and sunny out, with a clear blue sky and not a cloud to be seen. The perfect early summer day.

Perfect like it had been the previous evening when he'd decided to get a good sweaty workout in. Perfect like when he'd jogged across the gym floor, warm sunshine streaming in through the windows and the high-quality shock-absorbent flooring cushioning his feet. Perfect like when his fists had sailed at the heavy punching bag, the repetitive pounding motion better than any form of therapy he'd found to date.

Perfect…until he'd almost died.

Jamie shook the dark thoughts from his head as his father pulled the family SUV up in front of the hospital's pick-up area. His mom rushed forward to open the passenger side door for him.

"I can open the door myself, okay?" he said. He hated seeing her worry like this. Hated knowing that he caused it. "You don't need to wait on me."

"Just get in the car, James," she sighed and shot him a look that told him there was no point arguing. It was easier to do what he was told. And if she was calling him by his full name, it meant she was a hair away from clipping his ear.

So he climbed into the car without another word.

"Son." His father looked over to him with a crinkled brow. "Let your mother fuss. She needs it."

Jamie nodded. "You're right."

His father turned to face the road as the back door opened and Patty climbed in, scrambling to hoist her small frame up into the giant SUV like she always did. The ride home was filled with rapid-fire questions from the back seat.

Why didn't you tell us you were stressed out?

Should you be talking to a professional about your problems?

Is it happening again?

The last one made a weird acidic taste burn in the back of his throat. No matter how many years he put between himself and The Great Breakdown of his early twenties, he was frequently reminded that nobody would ever forget it happened.

Because when you were a world-class athlete, your failures didn't only become gossip—they became lore.

"The doctor said you need to keep your stress levels down and take a break from work," his mother relayed. "This could happen again. She said that panic attacks can be triggered by working too much and not getting enough rest, and—"

"I know, Mom. I was there."

"We care about you, Jamie." His father's voice was gruff. "This isn't about blame or trying to make you feel bad. You know that, right?"

Despite everything that had happened in the past, his parents had never once made him feel like he was to blame for what had happened...even if he himself had felt like a giant failure.

"Yeah," he said. "I know."

"And the doctor said we need to keep an eye on you for the next twenty-four hours to make sure there are no complications," Patty continued. The car rolled smoothly along the highway, other vehicles passing them at a rapid pace thanks to his dad's careful—read: slow—driving. "I got your sister to set up the spare bedroom at our place. And don't bother protesting about going home by yourself because I won't have it."

Jamie glanced at his father, who simply shrugged as if to say, *she's the boss.* Too right. Nobody was under any illusions about who was head of their household, that was for damn sure.

"Wouldn't dream of it, Mom. But what about—"

"Flash is staying at Clay's house," she said without letting him finish. "He said we could leave him there until you were ready to go home."

Whenever Jamie wasn't feeling himself, the first thing he wanted to do was to hang out with his dog. They really *were* man's best friend. No doubt Jamie's business partner, Clay Harris, would spoil him rotten with treats and belly scratches, so it wasn't like he'd be sad having a sleepover.

Jamie watched the scenery roll along outside the window. Soon they were approaching Reflection Bay, the town where he'd spent most of his life—a town that wasn't even big enough for its own hospital.

He'd driven along this road so many times he'd lost count, watching the silvery blue of the ocean flicker between patches of green and rugged cliff faces, the tourist-favorite red-and-white lighthouse rising up in the distance. It was the same as it had always been and yet…it felt different now.

Everything felt different.

FORTY-EIGHT HOURS after returning home from the hospital, Jamie was "discharged" from the Hackett Family Hospital. But not without needing to pass a rigorous interrogation from his mother. If someone had overheard the conversation, they might mistake Patty Hackett for an actual doctor rather than the elementary school art teacher she was.

But now that Jamie could taste the sweet air of freedom, he was happier than ever to be alive. Especially since he had been reunited with his canine best friend.

"Isn't it glorious? The sun is shining. The birds are singing." Jamie glanced down at his dog, Flash, who ambled with the kind of gait that could only be described as "walking under duress." "Oh, come on, bud. It's not *that* bad."

The chunky fawn-and-white bulldog looked up at him with imploring eyes as if to say, *please make it stop*. Flash, named in the most ironic fashion, hated working out as much as Jamie loved it. In fact, it was somewhat of a local joke that the two fittest guys in town had adopted the laziest dog ever as the mascot for their gym.

But Jamie loved Flash with everything he had. The dog might not be able to move faster than a drunk snail, but he had a heart of gold. Flash was always happy to see Jamie, never judged him for working too long or for stressing out too much about his business, and loved nothing more than just hanging out. No expectations, no bullshit.

That was love.

The pair ambled along the street. His business, Reflection Fitness, sat right at the end of the main strip, on a corner. It never failed to make pride surge through Jamie's veins to see what he and Clay had built together. Their goal had been to create a gym that catered to *all* the people in their small town, leaving no one to feel like they didn't belong. Reflection Fitness had clients who were training for big goals like marathons and fitness competitions, as well as clients like Jamie's grandpa—who was combating osteoarthritis with regular, low-intensity workouts—and Jamie's favorite personal training client—a bubbly woman in her forties who'd decided to try weight lifting after years of thinking cardio was the only option for women. They had a trainer on staff who specialized in pre- and postnatal fitness and another who ran classes for seniors aimed at improving joint mobility. They had built the gym to be accessible for clients with mobility needs. It was important to both Jamie and Clay that everyone who came to the gym felt welcomed and catered to.

"Let's get you inside where there's some air-conditioning, huh?" Jamie looked down at Flash, who was taking each plodding step with great effort. To be fair to the dog, it was unseasonably hot for so early in the summer. "We're almost there."

Jamie turned the corner to access the gym from the back door, which led directly into the office he and Clay shared. He tried not to take Flash through the front if he could help it, in case anyone working out had asthma or allergies. But when Jamie got to the door and tried to turn the handle, he found it locked.

"Weird," he muttered.

The back was usually open if Clay was working,

which he should be, given the hour. But perhaps he'd stepped out.

Jamie tried unlocking it. Only…the key wouldn't fit.

"What the heck?" He tried again. No dice.

He stared at the key, wondering if the knock he'd taken to the back of his head had done more damage than he'd realized. But no, it was definitely the right key.

Befuddled, Jamie walked Flash around to the front of the gym, where a sleek set of glass doors opened to a small reception area. The space was light and welcoming, with a big potted plant and a white couch in one corner. An old black-and-white photo hung on the wall, showing Clay and Jamie in their high school days, arms around each other—a tennis racket in Jamie's hand and a basketball in Clay's.

"Jamie!" The receptionist, Sara, brightened when she saw him. She wore a blue Reflection Fitness uniform polo shirt and her long, dark brown hair hung over her shoulder in twin braids. "How are you feeling?"

"Never better," he replied breezily. "And thank you for sending those flowers to Mom's place. That wasn't necessary."

"Everyone was thinking about you." Her brow wrinkled. "We were all so worried when Clay told us what happened!"

Ugh, Clay. The guy had a big mouth.

"I told him to keep it quiet," Jamie muttered. "In any case, I appreciate the gesture. Mom commandeered the flowers right away for her living room."

Sara laughed. "That's why I picked tulips. I had a feeling she would end up with them."

Mama Hackett was a favorite among the staff since she often made oatmeal cookies, energy balls and other healthy treats for everyone who worked at Reflection Fitness.

"Is Clay in?" Jamie asked. "I tried the back door, but I think something's wrong with my key."

"Uh…" Sara's expression turned strange, and she reached for the phone on the desk. "Let me call him through."

"It's okay, I'll head in." Jamie had his swipe pass on hand, like always, and he tapped it against the electronic reader which activated the gate into the gym.

The screen flashed red and made an angry *beep* sound.

First his key didn't fit the lock and now his pass wasn't working. What the—

"Jamie."

He looked up and saw Clay striding through the gym toward the foyer, a no-nonsense look on his face. At six foot five with shoulders that could bridge two cities, Clay had the perfect build for the sport he'd loved as a child—basketball. He had dark brown skin, warm eyes and close-cropped curly black hair. Usually, Clay would be flashing his signature charming smile—a smile that had won over just about every cheerleader the guy had ever encountered in his high school and college days. A smile that, now, was conspicuously absent.

"You locked me out." Jamie shook his head in disbelief. "You *changed* the locks on the office without telling me?"

"Outside, now." Clay pointed to the front doors as he strode through the gate. "We're not doing this in front of the clients."

Sara dropped her head and pretended to bury herself in work, ignoring Jamie's gaze pleading for support.

He let out an irritated huff. "Fine."

The two men walked back outside and Jamie felt a pang of guilt as Flash made a noise of protest about returning to the hot summer day. The trio rounded the corner away from the front of the gym so they could have it out.

"This is for your own good, Jamie." Clay held up his hands, signaling he didn't want a fight. Despite being strong enough to beat most men in anything physical, Clay was a gentle giant with a big heart.

He was also, however, stubborn as an ox.

"We're *partners*, Clay. You can't lock me out of my own damn business." Jamie gestured with his free hand toward the building next to them. "That's…that's got to be illegal."

Clay folded his arms across his chest. "I had a feeling you wouldn't take this seriously. The doctor said you need to rest and your mom told me to keep an eye on you, because she's worried, too."

Typical Patty. Jamie made a sound of disbelief. "I rested."

"For *two* days." Clay shook his head. "That's not enough."

"Man, it was nothing. You're overreacting."

"I am *not* overreacting. Do you have any idea what it's like to walk up on your best friend lying unconscious on the floor? I thought you'd had a heart attack or something. I thought you were dead."

He felt terrible for putting Clay through that, but he was already feeling vulnerable about this whole thing. He couldn't let his friend see how much it had shaken him.

"So dramatic." Jamie rolled his eyes.

"See, this—" Clay circled a finger at his face just like his mom used to when they were naughty kids "—is why I know you're not listening to what the doctor said. You came right here to go back to doin' exactly what you were doin' before."

"Building our business?" he replied, biting back his frustration.

"Running yourself into the ground. Wake up, Jamie." Clay shook his head. "You might not be so lucky next time."

"It's my call to determine whether I'm ready to come back, not yours."

"It sure is, because I won't give you a new key until I'm sure you're actually taking this thing seriously."

Jamie's mouth popped open. "You can't do that!"

"Sure I can. It's my name on the lease, remember?"

Oh yeah. *That.* He'd been meaning to get that bit of paperwork updated for almost three years now, but it was one of those things that kept falling off his to-do list in favor of more impactful items. Besides, he'd always thought Clay would never do him dirty, so it didn't seem like a big deal.

"It's *our* business, no matter what the lease says."

"Jamie, I'm doing this because you're my best friend. I want you to take care of yourself." Clay looked genuinely concerned. "Coach always used to say a heart that pumps too fast is no better than one that doesn't pump at all. Rest is as important as work."

Jamie let out a groan. "Sitting at a desk isn't exactly strenuous. I just need to answer some emails—"

"And then you'll just need to look at some spreadsheets and make some calls and then some new client will come to you with a sob story and you'll squeeze them in even though you said you weren't going to take on any more PT clients yourself." Clay shook his head. "I know your tricks, man. Don't try to play me."

"But what about the clients I have—"

"I split them up between the other trainers. It's already done."

"You called everyone already?" Jamie scrubbed a hand over his face. "I told you I didn't want anyone to know."

"I said you were helping me plan stuff for the wedding. Best man shit." Clay grinned and Jamie found his anger withering away. It really *was* hard to hate the guy when he smiled. "You're loyal like that."

He let out a strangled noise of frustration. "I'll call the locksmith myself."

"Then he's gonna have to get through me."

Jamie considered his options. Anyone who didn't know Clay might be too intimidated to try changing the locks against his wishes and anyone who *did* know him would be too charmed to want to try. Fact was, his best friend had him over a barrel.

"What am I supposed to do with myself, huh?" Jamie hated the panic in his voice. Who on earth felt panicked at the prospect of time off?

"I don't know. Play ping-pong with your dad, go up to the Cape, sleep in. You're a big boy—you'll figure it out."

Clay's hand came down hard on Jamie's shoulder, earning him a soft grunt. There was no reasoning with the guy, that much was clear.

Maybe Clay and his mom were right and this was serious. Jamie *could* have died. When he'd woken up in the ambulance, everything had flashed before his eyes—his whole life. His family. Work. His failed professional tennis career. His business. Long hours at his computer after longer days on the gym floor. Chasing the next thing, expanding the business, more clients, more money. Never satisfied. Always restless.

Was *that* all his life was about?

He'd always been hyper competitive, driven, and ambitious. But what if he *had* died the other day? What would he have left behind?

Jamie realized then that Clay was looking at him, as if waiting for him to speak. "No sweat. You want me to chill for a bit, fine. I can do that. You'll see this isn't a big deal."

But even as he brushed off the severity of the incident, he knew the earth had shifted beneath his feet. What he'd thought was solid ground was now loose earth and uneven terrain. He needed to find his footing again. He needed to get himself straight. Most of all, he needed to prove to everyone that this *was* just a one-off. That he *could* handle pressure—unlike when he was younger.

Because he couldn't ever go back to being Jamie Can't-Hackett ever again.

CHAPTER TWO

THE VIDEO BLURRED for a second as the person holding the camera phone shifted, but the visuals soon came back into focus. A large opulent church was filled with people. To one side, light streamed in through an intricate stained-glass window, glowing shades of blue, red, yellow and green like the inside of a kaleidoscope. A priest stood in front of an altar and before him, a bride and groom. Her dress was a masterpiece—Leavers lace and Swarovski crystals and Italian silk and a fourteen-foot train and more than one hundred delicate handmade lace roses.

Sage Nilsen knew every single detail of the dress because she'd made it with her own bare hands.

The bride stared lovingly at the groom, who wore an impeccably fitted black tuxedo. It was a magical wedding moment. Two people, so in love.

"If anyone present knows of any reason that this couple should not be joined in holy matrimony," the priest said, his voice tinny through the phone's tiny speakers, "speak now or forever hold your peace."

A hush fell over the church, save for the nervous titter of someone in the front pews. These words, so often spoken, felt like nothing more than ritual. Because nobody would *dare* protest at a wedding, right? What kind of person would ruin someone's special day like that?

"I have a reason."

Gasps rippled through the church and the camera swung, searching out the devil who dared to speak up. You couldn't see the bride anymore, but Sage remembered her panic as though it was yesterday rather than two weeks ago. The blood had drained from her face, turning her bronzed skin as white as the custom-made wedding dress that cost her—or rather, her future husband—several hundred thousand dollars. Then two splotches of red appeared on her cheeks, mortification mutating into molten rage.

"She's cheating on you with the best man!" The camera shook as it settled on Sage's face, the groove between her brows so deep you could lodge a coin there. "Don't marry her."

The video cut off at that moment.

Sage buried her face in her hands as her younger sister, Emma, sat silently beside her. For a moment, neither of them said a word. In reality, it wasn't the first time Sage's lack of social awareness had caused her problems. She never knew how to deal with situations properly, never knew when it was appropriate to speak out or shut up.

After she found out the bride's secret she'd shared it with her boss, who'd told her to keep it quiet. It wasn't their business, she'd said. Not their place to interfere.

Only the bride had insisted they come to the wedding. That's how she'd ended up at the church, the secret suffocating her from the inside, like she was a champagne bottle vigorously shaken so that the truth exploded out of her at the worst possible moment.

Why are you like this? Why couldn't you have done

the normal thing and written him an anonymous email or something?

"You did the right thing," Emma said, her hand landing on Sage's back and rubbing in comforting circular motions.

The video had been shared all over YouTube, Twitter and TikTok, and had even made it onto some mainstream media sites. People had used it to share their own wedding horror stories and Sage's rarely updated Instagram account had been flooded with internet trolls.

Thankfully, her online footprint was barely a smudge and people hadn't been able to find her outside Instagram. She didn't have any other social accounts or publicly listed emails, nor did she have any friends who might turn her over to the wolves. For once, her hermit ways had paid off.

Sage, however, had been promptly fired from her position as senior seamstress and was told never to set foot into the atelier again.

"The right thing?" She let out a barking laugh. "The right thing would have been to keep my trap shut and let the wedding go ahead so I wouldn't lose my career, my professional reputation and my entire life in one fell swoop."

The wedding dress maker who ruined a wedding… talk about a situation made for the headlines. This was exacerbated by the bride and groom, who lived in the spotlight. She was a fashion influencer with two million followers, and he was a blue blood with a pedigree surname, Ivy League education and a hefty trust fund. A trust fund now protected from cheating hands, since he'd walked out of the church, leaving the bride sobbing at the altar after she confessed her sins.

Thanks to Sage, he'd dodged a bullet. Sage herself, however, had everything to lose and nothing to gain... and that was exactly how it played out.

"Who's going to hire me now?" Sage tossed her hands in the air. "The couture industry is small. Everybody knows everybody and I'm on the do-not-hire list. Permanently."

"I'm sure that's not true." Emma squeezed her arm and offered an encouraging smile. "But maybe this is the opportunity you need to strike out on your own! You're an amazing designer and you don't need to spend your whole life working on other peoples' visions. You could work for yourself."

Sage snorted. "Yeah, and who is going to buy a dress from the woman who's all over the internet for ruining a wedding, huh? Doesn't exactly fit the happily-ever-after image."

"You did the right thing," Emma repeated with conviction. "Letting him marry someone who clearly doesn't love him would be wrong."

"Of course you would say that, Miss Bride-to-Be."

Emma shook her head adamantly, several strands of her fine white-blond hair escaping her ponytail. "I would still say it even if I wasn't getting married myself. Morals are morals, Sage. You're not a good person if you're only good when it's convenient."

While her sister had a point, there were *so* many other ways Sage could have handled the situation. When the bride was in the atelier for a fitting, she'd taken a call. The boss had stepped out to grab lunch and the bride mustn't have known that Sage was still there, quietly sewing silk flowers and being invisible, like always.

The bride had boasted to the caller about screwing her husband's best man.

There hadn't been a single ounce of remorse in her voice. Sage could have spoken up then. Or she could have told the groom when he came to make the final payment on the dress. Or she could have done literally a half dozen *other* things than shouting it out in the middle of a wedding ceremony.

"I'm shocked you haven't seen the video until now. It's everywhere." Sage picked at a loose thread on the duvet of her childhood bed.

Her father had kept the room exactly as it had been when Sage was a high school student—all the girlie pink-and-white decorative accents and, most importantly, her beloved Mr. Stinky, the teddy bear with one eye who looked like he was permanently giving you the stink face. Sage reached for him and hugged the bear to her chest.

"I didn't go searching anything out," Emma replied. "People have been talking about it, sure. That's small-town life. But there are *plenty* of people who thought you did the right thing."

Sage wasn't sure she agreed. But for now, wallowing wouldn't achieve anything, and she didn't want to ruin her sister's prewedding glow by being a sad sack.

"Want to see your dress?" she asked, changing the topic and forcing a smile for her sister's sake.

Emma's eyes lit up. "Yes!"

Sage climbed off the bed and went to the vintage armoire that had once belonged to Sage's grandmother, Inger. A white garment bag bearing her former employer's company logo hung from one of the doors. Sage cringed. If it wasn't for the hundreds of hours she'd spent on her sister's dress, then she might have thrown the damn thing in a plastic bag just so she didn't have to be reminded of her poor life choices.

She drew the zipper down slowly, revealing the dress inch by inch. So far, her sister had only been to New York once in the early stages of the design process to look at fabrics and sketches and for them to go shopping in the garment district for materials.

"It's beautiful," Emma breathed as Sage carefully shrugged the garment bag off the hanger to fully reveal the dress. "You've shown me every step of the way on Skype but…"

"It's something else in person, isn't it?"

"It really is."

That was probably the most heartbreaking thing of all. Sage might be lacking in a lot of areas—social skills chief among them—but she was *good* at her job. No, not good. Excellent. Dedicated to mastering the craft, sucking up tips and techniques and wisdom from all the older women she'd worked with like a sponge seeking moisture. She lived, breathed and dreamed sewing.

It was everything to her.

"Let's get you into it," she said as she began opening the tiny buttons that ran down the back.

Emma stripped down to her underwear facing away from Sage, and then she carefully stepped into the dress and pulled it up. Sage closed the buttons that trailed along Emma's spine. Seeing her sister wearing one of her own creations brought Sage so much joy that her troubles were momentarily forgotten.

"I still can't believe you wanted me to make this knowing you wouldn't be able to try it on until it was too late to really fix it if it didn't fit." She reached for-

ward to check on one of the delicate lace flowers that
gave the dress's outer layer a subtle 3D effect.

"Well, it fits like a glove." Emma turned to her,
splaying her hands across her stomach.

The dress did, indeed, fit like a glove. It had a floor-
length A-line skirt and a nipped-in waist, all of which
was covered in a gauzy overlay with floral detailing that
extended up into the bodice. Sheer, scalloped lace straps
left a daring vee of skin in both the front and the back.
Since Emma wasn't busty, it showed some skin without
risking anything peeking out where it shouldn't. Sage
had hand-beaded tiny shimmering Swarovski crystals
into the center of the flowers on the outer layer, just
enough to give a subtle sparkle without looking over
the top.

But maybe it *could* be a little more sparkly.

Her brows narrowed as her critical mind kicked in.
To Sage, anything short of perfection was unacceptable.

"Okay, I'm ready to see it." Emma let out a shaky,
excited breath.

Sage reached for the armoire's door and pulled it
open, revealing a long, narrow mirror inside. The sincere gasp and the flutter of Emma's hands at her mouth
filled Sage with joy. *This* was why she would always
love doing bridal wear. There was something so magical about this moment—the grand reveal.

And in those moments, Sage wasn't the high school
weirdo who couldn't speak without stumbling over her
words. She wasn't the girl who skipped prom because
she couldn't get a date. She wasn't the loner in New
York City with no friends and nothing but her job to
keep her occupied. She wasn't the odd woman who sat

in the park and spoke to squirrels because they were the only ones who didn't judge her.

She was talented. Special.

"Sage…" Emma shook her head, tears glittering in her eyes. "It's beautiful. I'm speechless."

"Now I *know* I did a good job," she teased. Her sister had been known as Queen Chatterbox for a reason when they were growing up. "You look amazing. Clay is going to fall off his feet."

"Thank you." Emma threw her arms around Sage's neck and squeezed. "It's even more special knowing you made it."

"I hid a little surprise in there, too." She stepped back and crouched down, lifting the underside of the dress's hem, where she'd embroidered Emma and Clay's initials and the date of their wedding in white thread so it could only be seen upon close inspection.

"Oh my gosh," Emma squeaked. "It's everything I hoped it would be. I take back how angry I was when you left me here to move away."

Sage laughed and gently disentangled herself from her sister's arms, so as not to damage the dress. "I forgive you."

Emma *had* been devastated when Sage announced she was moving to Paris after school to chase her dreams of being a wedding dress designer. Sad as it had been to leave her family behind, Sage loved every minute of honing her skills and learning the "detective work" and problem solving of couture sewing. Eventually the homesickness had gotten too much, and she'd returned to America, finding a job working for one of the most sought-after couture bridal designers in New York City.

Everything had been going according to plan…

She shoved the sad thought to one side. While she was here, her job was to make her sister's wedding as special as possible. But no matter how hard she tried to focus on all the good things that were happening around her, the dire consequences of her outburst lurked in the back of her mind. She could only bury her head in the sand so long.

Eventually, it would be time to head back to New York and pick up the pieces.

CHAPTER THREE

SAGE HAD BEEN dreading dinner from the moment she woke up. Normally, a beer and some battered fish at Mayberry's, an English-style pub, would be cause for her salivating all day long. But not today.

"Do we *really* have to do this?" Sage asked as Emma slotted her car between two trucks parked on the main strip. "Can't I have dinner with you and Clay only? He's the one who's joining our family and I am *here* to celebrate it. I think he's great. But I don't need to hang out with the best man, too."

Emma glanced over with an amused expression as she killed the engine. "How many times did you change your outfit?"

Heat crawled up Sage's cheeks. "None. I threw on whatever was least wrinkled from the suitcase."

Liar, liar, pants on fire.

Sage had changed her outfit a total of five times. A cute blouse and ankle booties? Too small-town. Chic black dress with leather side panels that she'd made herself? Too New York. Pretty vintage wrap dress with a floral print? Too obvious she was trying to look cute. Jeans and sneakers? Not cute enough.

Ugh!

Option five stuck, because by then she was running late and Emma was hollering at her to get going.

"Why did Clay even have to pick Jamie freaking Hackett as his best man anyway?" she grumbled.

Emma chuckled as they got out of the car. "Oh, maybe because they've been best friends since they were five years old and Jamie is like a brother to him. You know, the usual reason you pick someone to be a best man."

The pub glowed with warmth—golden light spilled onto the sidewalk, music floated from the open-air beer garden, and baskets of flowers hung on either side of the door, above which sat a Medieval-style sign. Sage caught sight of her reflection in the big windows. She'd curled her white-blond hair and decided it looked too overdone, so she'd brushed the curls out until her hair looked like she'd spent the day at the beach. The final outfit was a T-shirt dress in a classic navy-and-white stripe, white sneakers and a vintage designer denim jacket that she'd picked up in a cramped charity shop a few years back for an absolute steal.

Comfy, chic but still casual.

Would Jamie see right through her carefully constructed attempt to appear as though she wasn't nervous about seeing him?

"I don't even know what you're worried about," Emma continued as she grabbed Sage's hand and dragged her toward the pub's entrance. "He's a great guy."

A great guy you've loved since you were in diapers and who rejected you when you asked him to prom because he was popular and you were the high school loser.

"Don't even *think* about bringing up the prom thing," Emma added.

That was the downside to being super close with her sister—she could never get away with lying about anything.

"It's awkward." Sage tugged her hand out of Emma's grasp.

It wasn't that she hated Jamie Hackett. Frankly, it might be easier if she did because as an emotion, hate was crystal clear, with boundaries easily drawn and an unwavering fire to keep her on course. But that wasn't how she felt. Because when Jamie had rejected her, it'd been done with kindness. And maybe a little pity.

So what she really felt was shame, which was sticky and uncomfortable.

"Maybe I should go home," Sage said. "You know, I've had a headache ever since the flight. I should probably—"

"Do *not* bail on this." Emma narrowed her eyes.

"It could be serious."

Her sister folded her arms across her chest. Unlike Sage, who'd toiled for a good hour and a half over what to wear, practical Emma had thrown on the same thing she always wore—a pair of light blue jeans that showed off her legs, a plain pastel-colored T-shirt and matching Converse high tops. Today's color was lilac.

"Sage Audhilda Nilsen." Emma shook her head. "If you really thought it was serious, then you would have said something earlier."

Chastened, Sage hung her head.

"Now, you're going to come into this pub, have a drink and play nice because you're my sister and you love me. Got it?" Her tone left no room for argument.

Letting out a big sigh, she nodded in defeat. "Fine."

"This wedding really means a lot to me and you're

my best friend in the whole wide world." Emma's expression softened. "Since Mom isn't with us and Dad is kind of baffled by anything beyond the idea of walking me down the aisle, you're all I've got."

"Half the damn town is coming to this wedding." Sage looped her arm through her sister's. "You're hardly alone."

"You, Dad and Clay are the most important ones to me. Everyone else has to get in line."

They walked into the pub together. It was already a little rowdy inside, since it was after eight, and there had undoubtedly been people drinking since the early afternoon. The pub was run by an American woman and English man and was a strange blend of the two cultures—with fish and chips *and* jalapeño poppers both occupying a spot on the menu.

Sage spotted a group of women from her high school days sitting together. They looked like the result of a cloning experiment, each with the same softly curled and ombre highlighted hair, matching cowboy-inspired boots that had undoubtedly never encountered anything of a bovine nature, and manicured fingertips in every boring shade of nude and shell pink possible.

Sage avoided their eyes as she and Emma walked past, but she was sure she heard someone whisper "wedding wrecker" at her. Or maybe that was just her social anxiety talking.

She spotted Clay and Jamie even before they'd gotten close to the table. It had been years since she'd seen either one of them, because the last time she'd come home for a visit, Emma and Clay were still keeping their relationship under wraps. Now it was barely a year later and they were already getting married. It had all happened so fast.

But Emma was like that; life came easy to her. Relationships came easy. She was the outgoing, confident sister and people loved her. No wonder she'd snagged one of the most well-loved guys in town.

"Hey." Clay hopped down off his stool and swept Emma into his arms, pressing a hungry kiss to her lips.

Emma was tall for a woman, but next to Clay, she didn't look it. She was, however, totally and utterly smitten. Despite always feeling a little envious of how her sister breezed through life, Sage was truly happy she'd found love. There was no one more deserving than Emma.

When they broke apart, Clay reached out for Sage and gave her a warm hug. "It's good to see you."

"You too, Clay. It's been a long time."

Her eyes darted across the table to where Jamie sat and her mouth suddenly grew dry. He looked even better than she remembered, his lanky teenage athleticism morphing into broad shoulders, thick muscular arms and his face developing sharp, masculine angles. His hair gleamed with a red fire and his smile was warm and genuine, like always. It was the smile that had gotten to her as a young woman, letting her think he felt something for her. Letting her believe that her desires were reciprocated. Letting her believe that their friendship was progressing to the next level.

But it turned out that the most popular jock in school would *never* fall for the social outcast like all those teen movies said. It was just a fantasy. Nothing more.

IT TOOK EVERYTHING in Jamie's power not to let his jaw drop to the ground.

It had been a *long* time since he'd seen Sage Nilsen and, boy, had time been kind. Her hair was a gleaming shade of ultra-pale blond and it fell in messy waves past her shoulders. Her skin was porcelain fair and her eyes a silvery blue, giving her the look of a Nordic princess or a character out of a long-ago written fairy tale.

Back in high school, she'd been mercilessly teased for how pale she was. Cruel names like Ghost Girl, Casper and even Bloody Mary. He'd been at a party one time when someone had suggested they do a seance to see if they could conjure her out of thin air to prove she wasn't really human. It was only Jamie's protest that the idea was boring and juvenile that stopped it from happening.

Why did some people slide down to the bottom of the social hierarchy without doing anything wrong? While others, like himself and Clay, climbed to the top for no more reason than hand-eye coordination. Athletes were revered in their small town, while shy creative types were not.

"It's good to see you, Sage." He nodded at her, and her icy eyes flicked over him, an obligatory smile quirking the corners of her mouth for a flash before they returned down. Expressionless.

Okay, so she wasn't pleased to see him.

He'd been hoping that the past would be the past when it came to his and Sage's last conversation almost fifteen years ago. He still remembered it like it was yesterday—she'd come to his house, dressed in a pretty yellow dress that he knew she'd sewn herself, with little white flowers embroidered on it. Her hair had been long and shiny, her lips slicked with a cherry-tinted gloss.

How anyone could look at her and think her any less than beautiful was beyond him.

But when she'd shyly asked him to prom, her eyes shining with sincerity, it had almost cleaved him in two to say no. He was taking someone else—a cheerleader. They were both athletes, highly competitive, nominated for prom king and queen. They were a good match.

And, as much as he liked Sage, he knew that showing any kind of romantic feelings toward her would only thrust her even more into the unwanted spotlight. If he took Sage to prom, it would be no better than drawing a target on her back so that all the girls who swanned around him would swoop in to put her back in her place.

Even Clay had thought it was a bad idea when he brought it up. "They'll eat her alive, Jamie. You know that," he'd said.

But he knew the rejection would sting and when she'd looked at him, confusion swimming in her watery eyes, he'd felt like the biggest asshole on the face of the planet. During prom, he'd tried to seek her out to apologize only to find out she hadn't come. Couldn't get a date, people said. Who wanted to take someone who couldn't even read a whole sentence aloud in English class without nervously tripping over her words? Someone who shunned parties and sporting events to sit inside with her needle and thread?

After graduation, she disappeared. Last he heard, she was living in New York…until it seemed that she'd landed herself in the unwanted spotlight after all.

Oh yeah, he'd heard *all* about the wedding thing.

Personally, he thought it took an unshakable moral

center to speak up like that, but not everybody agreed. Some speculated that she was in love with the groom— a jealous other woman rather than someone trying to do the right thing. Others claimed it was wrong to speak up during the wedding and that she should have said something sooner.

Everyone was an expert when it wasn't their ass on the line, that much he knew from his days as a pro-athlete. It was easy for some armchair specialist to judge from the sidelines, but few knew what it was actually like to be out in the open, taking a risk, while the world looked on.

"I need Emma for a minute. Wedding stuff," Clay said, taking his fiancée's hand. They were having their wedding reception in the pub since it was where they had their first date. "Order whatever you want and we'll be back in a bit."

Jamie clocked a flash of panic in Sage's face as she looked to her sister, who simply shrugged. But as best man and maid of honor, they wouldn't exactly be able to avoid one another for the next few weeks. Especially since Emma had decided that she wanted Jamie and Sage, and the rest of the bridal party, to perform a dance on the special night.

"So…" Her eyes darted around, almost as if she was wondering whether she could dive through the window to escape being alone with him.

"I hear you're living in New York now," he said, trying to break the ice.

"Mmm-hmm." She didn't offer anything else. The silence settled awkwardly and Sage drummed her fingers against the pub's high wood table. "And you're back here."

"Yup." His early retirement from tennis and subsequent return to his hometown wasn't exactly a topic he was eager to dive into.

"Cool, cool." She bobbed her head and the conversation petered out entirely.

They sat there for a moment, avoiding eye contact, and the silence made Jamie shift on his stool. One thing was clear: if he and Sage were going to be able to work together effectively on their wedding tasks, the air *had* to be cleared.

"Look," he said, leaning forward. "I'm probably the last person you want to see, but we're here for Emma and Clay's sake. I want the wedding to go well and that means you and I need to put our differences aside."

"We don't have any differences," she said, but her body posture indicated otherwise. She was so far back on her stool that he was surprised she hadn't fallen off it.

He sighed. It would be easy to point at Sage and call her defensive, but Jamie knew her history. He knew she was deeply scarred from years of schoolyard bullying that caused her to withdraw deeper and deeper into herself as she got older. In her mind, he was probably just another person who'd rejected her. Winning her trust wouldn't happen with a simple "hi, how are you?" after fifteen years of not talking.

Why do you even care? She's not part of your life.

But that wasn't how Jamie operated, not anymore. His own experiences of being bullied by the media while his sporting career fell apart had given him insight into how she must have felt being a point of ridicule for all those years.

It hurt. It left marks. And it wasn't easily forgotten.

"Then why do you look like you're wondering how

strong those windowpanes are?" he asked, smiling so she knew he was trying to make light of the situation. "Thinking about making a grand escape?"

"Guilty," she admitted with a small smile. There was a flicker of warmth in her eyes, but it was gone as quickly as it appeared.

Around them, the pub was full of life. People having dinner, catching up, making friends. He was pretty sure the two people next to them were on a date. When was the last time he came out for a drink? He couldn't even remember.

"I probably wouldn't want to see me, either, if I was you," he said with a shrug. "I get it."

Her brow furrowed and he sensed a slackening in her defenses. "I expected you to act like nothing ever happened and to think I was weird for being standoffish."

Well, there was some honesty at least.

"Why's that?" He cocked his head.

"It *was* a long time ago. I guess most people wouldn't hold on to something for so long." She looked down at her lap. "And it wasn't like you owed me anything."

There she went again, assuming she was going to be judged.

"Words hurt. Trust me, I understand that now."

Her eyes searched his face, a spark of curiosity like a distant flash of lightning. When they were kids, living next door to one another, Sage hadn't been like this—so hidden away, so protective of her thoughts and emotions. That came later, after her mother died. He remembered her vividly from before that, when they were six years old and she was always sewing dresses for her Barbie dolls and making up stories and playing make-believe. It was a crying shame that had been ridiculed out of her.

"You're right," Sage said with a serious nod, like she was really thinking about what he'd said. "The most important thing is making sure that Clay and Emma have a wonderful wedding. How hard can it be?"

He bit back an amused smirk. She must not know about the dancing lessons that Emma had planned. But Jamie was smart enough to hold his tongue. Leave it to Emma to deal with the fallout. Because it was one thing to sit across the table and share a drink in mixed company, but getting up close and personal on the dance floor was something else entirely.

The thought of being close to her, holding her hands, her waist, sent a thrill through him. Tonight, she looked sweeter than a summer cherry pie in her little T-shirt dress and her hair all mussed, and Jamie found himself suddenly happy for a distraction from his current woes.

And that was a new feeling, indeed.

CHAPTER FOUR

"YOU WANT ME to do *what*?" Sage shook her head in disbelief.

Her sister must be joking. Surely.

"It's just a few dance lessons, no big deal." Emma leaned forward, poking her tongue out the side of her mouth as she wrote someone's name in perfect calligraphy on a place setting card.

"No big deal?" Sage pressed her fingers to her temples. "Am I dancing with Jamie?"

Emma didn't look up as the nib of her pen glided smoothly across the luxuriously thick card stock. "Well, yeah. He's the best man."

"Oh god, it's going to be like the prom that never was."

That got Emma's attention. Her head snapped up and her mouth popped open as the calligraphy pen hovered motionless. "Oh my god, I didn't even think…"

Sage scrubbed a hand over her face. What Jamie had said last night was true, however. This was all about Emma and Clay's most special day. All Sage was doing by freaking out was making her sister feel bad for something that wasn't her problem.

"Hey, if you want my two left feet ruining your wedding reception, that's on you." Sage shrugged and tried her best to sound like she was simply teasing her sister instead of freaking out. "Don't say I didn't warn you."

At that moment, Emma's bridesmaid, Hailey, came into the room, carrying a box. The three of them were having an afternoon of wedding preparations.

"That's the last of the jars," Hailey said, making a slight *oof* sound as she set the box on the floor. "We'll have these place settings done in no time."

"You guys are the best." Emma looked up and gave a grateful smile. "It's so much work to do this stuff yourself. But Clay and I are trying to be sensible about how much we spend."

"Smart." Hailey nodded. "I went to a wedding last year where the bride spent almost ten thousand dollars on her dress alone. I can't even imagine."

Sage concentrated on her work as she pierced a piece of silk with her needle and carefully pulled the thread through before depositing a small, glimmering bead onto it and securing it back down—she needed every spare moment to make sure her own dress was done for the wedding, since Emma's gown had been her main focus these past few months.

"Sage, tell Hailey about some of the dresses you've made," Emma said, trying to bring her into the conversation. For most of the day, she'd worked quietly while the other two women chatted.

Until the subject of the dance lessons was brought up, that was.

"You're a fashion designer, right? Emma said you were living in Paris for a while and now you're in New York." Hailey smiled. "That sounds very glamorous."

Hailey wasn't a local. In fact, she lived three towns over. She and Emma had become friends at work, as they were both EMTs, and Sage hadn't met her before. She seemed nice and knew nothing of Sage's reputation in town, nor anything about the "wedding incident."

She tried not to cringe at Hailey's genuine curiosity. A few weeks ago, she would have been only too happy to talk about getting her dream job working in *haute couture*.

"I'm not a designer." She forced a smile. "I'm what's called a *les petites mains* which translates to 'the little hands,' and we help the designers to execute their vision. I do a lot of hand beading and fine embroidery work, although I do know a lot about garment construction, of course."

"Enough to make a wedding gown."

"And this."

Sage held up the dress she was working on. Emma wanted the women to pick dresses that suited their own style and figured Sage would want to wear something of her own creation anyway. Her only request was that the dresses were a neutral shade—something like silver or gold or a soft shade of bronze. Sage had picked a champagne shade.

The dress was slim-fitting with a knee-length hem and a sexy vee at the back and sleeves that fell over her shoulders like tiny silk waterfalls. It was made from a fine silk, which Sage had interlined for stability, and the entire thing was covered in a design made from dazzling sequins and clear crystal beads that glimmered like diamonds.

The materials should have cost a small fortune, but one of the best things about her old job had been the industry contacts. The silk had been a designer deadstock fabric and the beads had been purchased in bulk through one of the suppliers they used at the atelier where Sage had worked. A dress like this could sell for thousands in a high-end boutique, but there was a clause in her contract that prevented her from selling her work independently.

A clause that no longer applies since you got fired.

"It's *beautiful*," Hailey breathed. "I love glitzy things."

"Me too." Sage touched the dress, running her thumb gently over some of the beadwork. "It's a labor of love."

"How do you have the patience for it?" Hailey shook her head in wonder. "That must take forever."

"Working with my hands is actually the thing that gets my brain to be quiet." Sage had always been a high-strung person, especially after her mom died when she was still a kid. She had loads of nervous energy and her mind always seemed to race, replaying every awkward thing she did over and over. But the rhythmic motion of working with needle and thread soothed her. "It's almost…meditative."

"She has a real gift," Emma said, gently waving a place card back and forth so the ink would dry faster. "I keep telling her it's time to make her own designs. She's too talented to be hidden away in a back room."

"One step at a time," Sage muttered, turning back to her work. "Let's get through this wedding first and then I'll think about what's next."

For now, she had too much on her mind to even *consider* the idea of starting her own business. Like how that afternoon, she was going to be taking part in a dancing lesson with Jamie. Like how she would have to touch him and be close to him and sway in time with the music like she'd wished to all those years ago. Like

how being back home was no better than pouring salt
into a long-festering wound.

*Two weeks, that's all you have to do for your sis-
ter. Then you can go back to New York and lick your
wounds while you figure out what's next.*

But for the first time in Sage's life, the "what's next"
was a big black hole of nothingness. Years of being
safe and invisible in the back room of the atelier disappeared and nothing she could do would get it back.
Everything she'd worked for was gone and she had no
one to blame but herself.

"Oof." Jamie grunted when Sage once again stepped
on his foot.

She cringed. "Sorry. Sorry."

"It's okay." His hand twitched at her waist, holding
her but with light pressure like he wasn't exactly sure
what to do. "Let's try it again."

They were standing in the middle of a dance studio—normally used for tiny tots ballet classes, if the im-
ages on the walls were anything to go on. Sage looked
at a picture of a chubby-cheeked toddler wearing a tutu
and leotard, staring unsmilingly, her eyes so piercing it
looked as though her photo were actually staring back.

"Let's take it from the top," the dance instructor said.
Her name was Courtney and she'd been in Sage's gradu-
ating class, a former cheerleader who now ran the dance
studio. She'd made a huge fuss of Jamie when they all
walked in, and Sage had noticed her eyeing him when
she thought no one was looking. "And…step left, step
right. Move to your partner and clasp hands, then we
begin one, two, three. Left, two, three."

Sage accidentally went right, grunting when she realized her mistake as Jamie tugged her in the other direction. The comment she'd made to Emma about having two left feet wasn't an exaggeration. In fact, it felt like she had pumpkins instead of feet. Or maybe cinder blocks.

"Then turn slow, two, three, four. Not too fast, Sage!" The dance instructor clapped to get her attention and Sage's cheeks burned as she was called out for making an error. "Everybody back to the front. Keep in time with the music."

Sage stumbled slightly on the heels she was wearing. Emma had told them all to wear the footwear they were planning to be in for the wedding, to make sure they knew what the dance moves would feel like, and Sage was mightily regretting the pencil-thin stilettos she'd picked up on sale at Saks a few months ago. Yes, they made her legs seem a mile long, but they were shoes best suited to standing still for photos. Or maybe luring someone into bed.

Not this *left, two, three, four* crap.

The music cut out and Sage's shoulders slumped. She was *never* going to get this! And last night her biggest worry had been how it would feel to have Jamie standing so close to her. She didn't even have space in her brain to stress about Jamie what with her lack of coordination tripping her up. Tripping them *both* up.

"It seemed better," Jamie said encouragingly. To his credit, he was a very supportive partner and hadn't once complained in the last two hours about her stepping on his feet, or going left when they were supposed to go right, or missing the beat of the music and getting him off time. "I think we're starting to get it."

"Oh, you're getting it just fine," she said, trying to

mask her embarrassment. "Must be all that natural
rhythm you have from tennis."

He chuckled. "A good forehand isn't much help on
the dance floor."

"Just natural talent then."

"I'm full of it." He shot her a cocky grin, which
made her snort.

"You sure are," she replied with a smirk.

"Hey!"

She laughed and it didn't feel forced. Jamie was *exactly* as she remembered—funny, gracious, warm, without a hint of ego or self-entitlement that many others
would have in his position. Even when he was the top
dog in school, he'd never hesitated to stick up for the
nerds and the weirdos. He'd never shunned anyone who
tried to talk to him or purposefully made someone feel
left out.

That was the thing she'd always loved about him—
the decency that ran bone deep.

*Loved? Get a grip. You were young. No teenager
knows what love is.*

"Let's call it there for today's lesson," Courtney said,
clapping her hands together. "We've got the first part
of the routine looking pretty good and when you come
back in a few days' time, we'll work on the second part.
In the meantime, I suggest you all practice…a lot."

Courtney's eyes drifted to Sage and a wrinkle formed
between her brows. Flushing, Sage hoped that nobody
else noticed the pointed message. If Emma wasn't her
little sister *and* her best friend, she would have walked
right out of the dance studio and never gone back. This
wedding was going to be the death of her! As if coming home wasn't hard enough.

"Practicing is a good idea," Jamie said, nodding studiously. He'd also been that jock who did well in school. It was unfair for one person to be good at so many things. "Why don't you come around to my place tonight?"

Sage blinked. "Uhh…"

"I'll get Courtney to send me the music and I can clear some space in my living room. Clay will rib me forever if I mess up." Jamie gave a sheepish laugh as if it were totally him who needed the practice and not her.

Before Sage could respond, Courtney walked over. She was wearing a pair of tight lilac leggings which showed off her toned dancer's legs and a flowy black tank top that hung low on the sides to expose a bright pink sports bra beneath it. She barely reached Sage's chin, but she still carried herself as if she were the tallest person in the room.

It was an enviable skill.

"It's *so* good to see you, Jamie." She reached out to touch his arm. "Gosh, I was so worried after I found out what happened."

Jamie winced and Sage raised an eyebrow. She was *really* out of the loop on town gossip and Emma hadn't said a word about anything to do with Jamie, other than him being the best man.

"To think what might have happened if Clay hadn't found you…" Courtney pressed a hand to her chest, leaving her other one still resting on Jamie's arm. "I can't even begin to think how terrifying that must have been."

"It's more terrifying having to keep talking about it," Jamie said with a joking tone, although Sage noticed that his smile didn't quite crinkle the edges of his eyes like it usually did.

"Well, I for one am *so* grateful that you're okay. Would be a huge loss to this town if something happened to you." She was practically batting her eyelashes at Jamie and Sage had to fight the urge to roll her eyes. Courtney was, as Sage's dad would say, subtle as a brick through a window.

"I appreciate the concern, Court." Jamie nodded and gently removed her hand from his arm.

"You know, I was thinking," she said, flashing him a brilliant white smile. "I would be *more* than happy to help you practice this routine for the wedding."

"Wouldn't it make more sense for me to practice with my partner?" Jamie replied, raising an eyebrow.

Courtney looked over to Sage, her mouth tightening. "Well, technically the man leads in this kind of dancing, so it makes sense for you to really have the steps well-memorized. That would be more effective with a skilled partner."

Sage didn't take the comment as an insult. Fact was, she *wasn't* a skilled dancer. If anything, she found Courtney's blatant interest—which was clearly unreciprocated—to be kind of amusing. In high school, she'd never been short of a date and it must be truly confusing for her not to have a guy responding with enthusiasm.

Why wouldn't Jamie be interested? Courtney was attractive—she had long dark brown hair, full lips, a great body and loads of sex appeal. But Sage could read Jamie's disinterest like it was a truckload of frozen Coke being poured over whatever fire Courtney was trying to stoke between them.

"As much as I appreciate the offer, Sage and I already have a date lined up for us to practice." He nodded, then he looked to Sage. "Eight o'clock at mine. I'll text you the address."

And with that, he turned and walked out of the studio, catching up with Clay and the other groomsman, leaving Courtney looking completely baffled.

I'm just as confused as you are.

For some reason, it felt like Jamie was up to something. But what, she had no earthly idea.

CHAPTER FIVE

JAMIE HAD TIME before Sage was due to arrive at eight.
At least, he *hoped* she would come, since he hadn't exactly given her the option to RSVP. But one, they really did need to practice. He wasn't a great dancer and
Sage was…well, the girl had loads of creative talents,
but rhythm wasn't one of them. And two, if he didn't
find something to occupy his time, he was going to
drive himself up the wall.

It turned out that without work, Jamie's life was kind
of boring.

Already that day he'd taken Flash for a walk, then
he'd gone for a run and done some resistance training
in his basement home gym. Then he'd gone to see his
mom until it was time for the dance lesson. After that
he'd come home, meal-prepped his lunches for the entire week, vacuumed and swept the whole house, done a
load of laundry and now he was so bored he was thinking about taking Flash for another walk.

But as soon as the dog heard the jingle of the leash,
he'd moved at a very un-Flash-like speed to go hide
under the bed. Not even a piece of jerky had been able
to coax him out.

Sighing, Jamie looked at the clock for what felt like
the hundredth time that day. How was he going to do
all this again tomorrow? And the day after? And the

day after that? If Clay wanted to push him to the brink of his mental control, then this was certainly a good way to go about it.

Resting was the worst.

What he needed was a project. His mind immediately sprung to the storage room in the basement. It was full of old junk—rarely used sporting equipment, boxes of old textbooks and school yearbooks, probably old Halloween costumes and decorations and other crap he didn't need. That sounded like a good place to start.

He abandoned his attempt to lure Flash out for another walk and headed downstairs, grabbing a box cutter from the kitchen and munching on the piece of jerky as he went. Clay could push his buttons all he wanted; Jamie was a resourceful guy. If work was taken away from him, then he would *find* something to do.

Jogging down the stairs to his basement, Jamie made a beeline for the storage room. It was a weird size— larger than a normal cupboard, but much too small to house anything more than a single desk, chair and a filing cabinet. But Jamie had a great office upstairs, so this room had become a bit of a dumping ground.

There were piles of cardboard boxes that had come from his parents' place when he'd moved into this house, since they were sick of storing his stuff. Hasty marker in his mother's handwriting indicated what was inside. He probably should have gone through it all a long time ago, but life kept him busy...usually.

He took the box cutter and opened the first box marked *childhood 1*. He was expecting to find stuffed toys and old video game consoles. But instead, it was a box of trophies. He pulled one out. A gold man was poised mid-serve atop a wooden base with a plaque declaring *James Hackett, The Boys 14-and-Under Champion* from some tournament he could barely remember.

Not because it wasn't important. Every win had been important back then. But there had been so many. Weekend after weekend, they'd driven all over the place. Hours and hours in the car, grinding out matches, scooping win after win.

The box was full of little gold men with rackets, gleaming tennis balls, cups and stars and all other symbols that signified glory. His mom had kept every single one. She'd probably envisaged him having some custom cabinetry installed so he could display them all, as if they were something to be proud of. Instead, they were a reminder of everything he'd sacrificed over the years—missing out on birthday parties and dances and lazy weekends gliding around a lake on the back of someone's boat. They were glittering regrets. A representation of swinging big and missing hard.

He returned the trophy to the box and closed the lid. Maybe this was a bad idea.

Upstairs, the doorbell sounded and Jamie almost jumped out of his skin. How long had he been down there, staring into this box and letting all his unwanted memories come to the surface?

"Coming!" he called out as he headed toward the stairs. Sage's arrival had come at exactly the right moment. He needed a distraction now more than ever.

When he pulled open the door, Sage stood on his doorstep wearing a different outfit than earlier. She'd pulled the top half of her white-blond hair away from her face but left a few strands falling down. In the early evening light, her hair had an almost pink tint to it, as if it had absorbed the setting sun. On her feet were a pair of flat sandals but she had her high heels poking out of a tote bag. And she wore a wrap dress in a buttery shade of yellow. Something about it struck a chord of memory in him. She'd come to his doorstep wearing yellow once before—the night she asked him to prom. He wondered if she remembered.

"Wow." The word popped out. "I mean, that dress is really nice."

That dress is really...nice? Gee, you're a Pulitzer winner waiting to happen, huh?

"Thanks." Her lip twitched with amusement. "I made it myself."

"Of course you did."

She flushed. "Ready to practice?"

"As ready as I'll ever be."

JAMIE HELD THE door open, motioning for Sage to head inside. Her stomach fluttered with nerves. She could already tell from the outside of his home that it would be *worlds* away from her cramped Manhattan apartment, where every surface was cluttered with the sewing items that wouldn't fit in her tiny cupboard and a wardrobe literally bursting at the seams with all her handmade clothing.

And don't even mention the cockroaches.

Jamie's house looked like it had been ripped from the pages of an interior design magazine. It was built to fully capture the swath of green wooded area behind the house, large windows making it feel like you could touch the leaves without leaving the room. The house was open-concept with a large kitchen to one side, a dining area and two large comfy sofas in a deep forest-green flanking a coffee table with raw edges that looked as though it was handmade. A huge canvas hung on the wall behind the dining table, showcasing an abstract painting of a tree with a person siting beneath it. The furniture was comfortable, lived-in and unpretentious, with tones that captured the landscape. Deep green and warm woods to represent trees, creamy whites to reflect the clouds and the occasional pop of grayish blue to reflect the storms that often rolled through their town, even in summer.

"Your home is…" She shook her head. "It's beautiful."

Jamie looked like he was holding back an amused chuckle. "You sound surprised."

"A lot of single guys have that real bachelor pad feel to their homes. You know, all white and chrome and Xbox controllers everywhere." She shrugged. "You've got style."

"Thanks." He grinned, clearly pleased with her reaction. "I spent *a lot* of time in hotel rooms and airports when I was playing tennis and I promised myself that when I had a home of my own, I'd make it a haven that focused on things that made me feel at ease."

"Greenery always calmed you," she said, looking out the back windows toward the pines and oaks. A memory bubbled to the surface, of her finding Jamie in the woods after he'd lost an important tennis match. She'd gone looking for him, finding him sitting at the base of a tree, much like the figure in the painting, and they'd sat quietly while he mourned the loss.

"You remember that?" Something sparked between them, a little frisson of electricity. A stirring of chemistry.

But Sage didn't want that connection with him. Not

now. Not when she was going to get the hell out of here as soon as the wedding was over. Not when he'd already broken her heart once before. Not when her life was already *far* more complicated than she wanted it to be.

"Apparently I fill my brain with all kinds of random information instead of the stuff I need to remember, like the password to my online banking." She forced a laugh. "So, uh, dancing. We should practice."

If he noticed her awkwardness, he didn't say anything. Instead, Jamie did what he always did—smiled and smoothed things over. "Let's do it."

He'd already pushed the dining table out of position to make space for them and connected his phone to a Bluetooth speaker. He tapped the screen and the music from their dance lesson filtered through the room. Emma had picked some indie song that Sage didn't recognize, but the vibe was nice. Slow, a little sensual, romantic. Sage swallowed and ran her palms down the front of her dress, hoping she didn't have sweaty hands.

The dance class had been nerve-racking because everyone could see her. But being here, alone with him, stirred other kinds of nervous feelings.

She changed into her high heels and placed her flats in the tote bag she'd brought with her.

"I've set it to play on loop, so I figure we keep going until we've got it," he said, walking toward her.

"Uh-huh. Sure."

I'm doing this for Emma. I'm doing this for Emma. I'm doing this for Emma.

Jamie stopped right in front of her and reached for her hand. The late evening light pouring in through the windows made his hair look like glowing embers and his eyes look like uncut pieces of emerald. He held her gaze in a way that should have made her want to glance away like she usually did when someone looked at her closely.

But she didn't. Instead, she held the eye contact and allowed herself to be pulled closer to him. His other hand settled at her waist, the contact warm and welcome, and he led her into the dance, confident to be in the driver's seat.

Without the pressure of Courtney's critical eyes or Emma's hopeful looks or the feeling that everyone was judging her, Sage found herself following Jamie's movements with ease. He talked through the steps and she listened, letting her body move without restraint. Every so often, she stepped the wrong way—one time tugging left when she should have gone right, and another stepping forward instead of back. Her body had brushed against his, setting her insides aflutter. She'd recovered quickly—hopefully quick enough that he didn't notice the effect he had on her. That he *still* had, despite all the years behind them that should have doused the flames.

Eventually it felt like they were moving closer, hips brushing, hands lingering. The music played on and on while the sun dropped low in the sky outside and Sage found her world shrinking to only this moment. It was like everything else melted away—the music, the past, her insecurities, her career woes. Everything.

"See, you're a great dancer," he said, his voice husky. "I knew it was in there."

"Hardly." She dragged her gaze away for a second.

"You undersell yourself, Sage. With everything." He shook his head.

"I think I adequately sell myself," she replied. "Not everybody can be amazing."

It was a sad truth that most people didn't want to believe. Not everybody could be the star, the standout, the number one. In fact, the world was mostly full of ordinary people like her. Sure, she was exceptionally talented with a needle and thread. But beyond that? She was average. Unremarkable. Forgettable.

"Bullshit," he said.

Her breath hitched, their electric energy shimmering like tiny fragments of crystal. The way he looked at her—so intimate, so full of longing, tinged blue with regret—was like drinking a glass of champagne too quickly. It made her feel light-headed, dizzy, free.

"I think you're amazing," he said. "I always have."

His words, though quietly spoken, were like snapping a thread with two hands. Jamie leaned forward, sliding his palm along her jaw and around to cup the back of her head. She didn't resist. Their noses brushed and her lips parted, her desire free-flowing.

They hovered for a moment, ready to drown in anticipation, and Sage let her eyes flutter shut, blotting out the light. Jamie's warm breath brushed over her skin, followed by the soft yet firm pressure of his lips. Her hands caught his shirt, curling so she could tug him closer as his tongue darted across the seam of her mouth, encouraging her to open to it. And she did.

Her whole body pulsed with sensation. A sigh rose up from deep inside her, and she leaned farther forward while Jamie's hands began to explore her body. He skimmed over her shoulders and down her arms, tracing the dip at her waist and the flare over her hips. It was so good to be touched. To be learned and understood.

This was what she'd dreamed of all those years ago.

And where did that end up, huh? Happily-ever-after? Yeah right.

Her inner voice jolted her back to reality. What did she think she was doing? Kissing Jamie would lead nowhere good. At a minimum, it would cause awkwardness at Emma's wedding, which was not a very sisterly thing to do. At worst, if she fell for Jamie again…

That's not going to happen.

Sage had faced enough drama and ridicule lately. She certainly didn't need to pile on by opening her heart up to anyone from this town, especially him.

"I, uh…well, yes…" She stepped backwards, her words coming out jerky and tight. "Thanks for your help, James."

He raised an eyebrow. "James?"

"Good dancing." She patted him on the chest and wanted to curse herself for being such an awkward turtle. "See you at the dance studio."

Without giving him a chance to respond, she rushed toward the front door, teetering in her high heels as her ankles wobbled precariously. She was halfway down his driveway before she realized she'd left her sandals behind, but there was no way she was going back for them now. Not with that kiss lingering in the air and in her mind.

It would be best for them both if she pretended like it never happened.

CHAPTER SIX

THE FOLLOWING DAY, Jamie walked to Sage's father's house, a tote bag containing her sandals dangling from his hand and Flash's leash in the other. The stocky dog lumbered forward slowly and Jamie was more than happy to kill time. What else did he have to do? Since he hadn't dared go back into his storage room after discovering all those old trophies, he found himself bored and aimless again.

Hence the personal shoe delivery.

The Nilsens' house hadn't changed a bit over the years—a tidy front yard with a sunflower-yellow mailbox that demanded attention, and a cluster of garden gnomes having a meeting between two bushes. By comparison the house next door, his childhood home, looked nothing like it used to. The current owners had taken out his mother's shaggy ferns and replaced them all with stuffy white roses and neatly-trimmed box hedges.

At the Nilsens' front door, he bounced on the balls of his feet a few times before raising his hand to knock. But before he had the chance to bring his knuckles down, the door opened and Emma stood there, yelping in surprise.

"Oh my gosh, you scared me." She pressed a hand to her chest and laughed.

"Sorry about that." Jamie rocked on his heels. Flash

looked up at Emma and wagged his tail. Well, maybe *wagging* wasn't quite the right word. His tail was a coil that was wrapped up tight like a cinnamon roll and it kind of rocked back and forth.

"Oh, look at this handsome fellow." Emma reached forward to give Flash a rub on the back and she cooed at him lovingly. "What are you doing here, anyway?"

"Is, uh… Sage around? She left her shoes at my place yesterday after our practice session."

Emma's eyes flashed with curiosity, and she looked like she was about to grill him. But then she quickly glanced at her watch.

"I can take them," she offered.

"I was hoping to chat to her for a minute. Wedding stuff," he lied, cringing at how unconvincing he sounded.

Her eyes narrowed but then she nodded, the need to be punctual winning out over her desire for information. "She's in the living room. Go on in."

"Thanks."

Emma lifted her hand in a wave as she headed to her car and Jamie returned the gesture before walking into the house. Emma was still living at home since she and Clay had decided not to move in together until after the wedding, which seemed a bit traditional to Jamie. But to each their own.

As soon as Flash made it inside, he melted down onto the cool tile floor.

"I'll be right back," Jamie promised. "Don't you go anywhere."

Fat chance. If Flash could lie in one spot for the whole day, he totally would.

Padding softly toward the house's main living room,

he spotted Sage sitting on the couch, sewing something by hand. The fabric shimmered in the glow of the late afternoon sun thanks to hundreds of small beads collecting the fiery golden light and reflecting it back in a blaze of red and gold. He could only imagine what it would look like on, with her lithe body giving meaning and shape to the dress and the pale champagne-gold color highlighting her fair skin and hair, making her look more angel than human.

For a moment, he watched as Sage dutifully worked. There was something magical about the actions she took—the needle piercing the silk, pulling the thread through and plunging the needle back in again. It was the same action over and over and over, and she worked with the fluidity of a ballet dancer.

Her attention to detail never failed to enrapture him, and she took such care with each single stitch that it was like she was painting a beach one grain of sand at a time.

"Emma, is that—?" She looked up from her work, eyes widening. "Oh, hi."

"Hi." He held up the bag before placing it on the ground. "You left your shoes yesterday."

Since Sage looked mildly panicked, Jamie thought better of jumping straight in to talking about the kiss. Never mind that he wanted to blurt out how much he enjoyed it and how he wanted to do it again. How he'd been thinking about it all night after she fled his house like a startled rabbit.

But brute force was not the approach to use with someone like Sage. She needed a softer touch.

He walked into the room and dropped down into the sofa chair to her left. The couch and coffee table were scattered with items, including a red container full of pins, some spools of thread, a tiny pair of gold scissors that didn't even look properly sized for human hands and other assorted sewing items. "Is this what you're wearing for the wedding?"

"Yep." She gave a little tug on her thread and Jamie noticed she was wearing a silver thimble on one finger. "But only if I can get this hem finished."

Now that he was closer, he could see the detail of what she was doing better. It appeared that she made four or five stitches and then tugged on the thread, pressing the little fold of fabric with her fingers as it seemed to almost zip up, before moving on to the next lot of stitches.

"It's called a rolled hem," she said, as if sensing his curiosity. "We use it a lot for fine or sheer fabrics to keep the edge neat while maintaining the floaty nature of the fabric."

"Wouldn't it be quicker to use a machine?" Back in the good old days, when his grandmother was still alive, she would whip up all manner of things on the noisy machine she kept in her spare room. The thing had clattered like it was punching a needle through steel.

"Quicker, yes. But hand stitching gives a much more delicate finish. In fact, the bulk of the work I do is by hand." Something flickered across her face, but it was gone before Jamie could really understand what she was thinking. "Lots of beading and embroidery, mostly."

"And you make your own clothes outside work?"

"Sometimes." She secured her current thread with a few stitches in place and then snipped the end off with the small pair of scissors. "It's very time-consuming and can be expensive. But I felt like my sister's wedding was a special event worthy of a new dress."

"I'm sure it will look incredible on you." The words rushed out of his mouth.

Sage looked up at him, the sunlight flickering in her eyes and catching on the fine angles of her face. She was unusually beautiful. Wide-eyed with high cheekbones that gave her an almost strange, ethereal look. A strand of her pale hair tumbled free of her ponytail, and she tucked it behind her ear.

"Uh...well, thanks."

"About yesterday—"

"We don't need to talk about it." The smile plastered on her face was as brittle as old plastic. "We got caught up in the moment. The music was romantic and weddings do have a certain magic about them. It's totally understandable."

Jamie wasn't sure he agreed. "I wasn't caught up in the music."

She blinked. "Then it must have been something else. You know certain types of light can really have an effect on people's mood."

He sighed. Sage was like a clam shell: one little prod in a direction she didn't like and she snapped shut so tight he had no hope of prying her open. "Anyway, I just wanted to make sure everything was cool between us given we're going to be spending some time together before the wedding."

"Everything is perfectly fine, absolutely. One hundred percent normal and fine and we never need to mention the kiss again. It didn't happen." She looked down to her work and worried a bead back and forth with her thumb. "Thanks for bringing my shoes."

"My pleasure."

Jamie was already twitching with the idea of having to go home with nothing to do. That morning, he'd tried to convince Clay to let him come back to the gym's office just for an hour or two, but the guy stonewalled him. Again.

"Do you feel like getting some fresh air?" He blurted the question out. "I have to walk my dog and I thought... maybe you'd like to come."

"You have a dog." Sage's eyes lit up. If there was one way to that woman's heart, it was with a four-legged creature. "Is he here?"

"Yeah, he's chilling by the front door." Jamie smiled, a seed of warmth rooting in his chest. "Come on, he'd love to meet you."

FIFTEEN MINUTES LATER, Sage had a dog leash in her hand, an adorable roly-poly bulldog plodding in front of her and a handsome man at her side as they headed down the street toward the center of town. Was it her imagination or did the sun feel brighter and the sky look bluer?

Maybe this is what life feels like for people who have their shit together.

She glanced at Jamie covertly, using her sunglasses to hide her eyes. He was wearing a pair of light blue jeans which looked perfectly old and worn-in with a white T-shirt and a pair of white trainers. It was a simple outfit—certainly nothing fashionable, especially by New York standards—but damn if he didn't look as tasty as her favorite gingerbread croissant from the Dominique Ansel Bakery.

Flash paused to sniff something and she slowed to

let him do his thing. Jamie's dog was so lovable and sweet, and it made her chest immediately pang for the fact that she lived in an apartment where she wasn't allowed to have pets.

"Are you on vacation at the moment?" Sage asked.

Jamie laughed and raked a hand through his reddish hair. "That's a complicated question."

"If your vacation is complicated, then you're doing it wrong," she replied, raising an eyebrow. Flash abandoned his sniffing—which sounded a lot more like snorting—and they continued on their walk.

"Well, it's a forced vacation…in effect." He let out a long breath. "I, uh…had a health incident."

"Really?" She looked at him directly this time, brows furrowed. Jamie looked healthy as a horse. The guy was a professional athlete at one time, and he looked just as fit now. "What happened?"

As Jamie recounted the story of his hospital visit as a result of hitting his head on some gym equipment when he fainted after a panic attack, Sage's eyes grew wider and wider. She was no stranger to panic attacks and had experienced a handful in her life. The one she'd had after her boss called to fire her had left her on all fours, the room spinning around her. It was an awful feeling.

"I'm *so* sorry. That sounds really scary," she said, shaking her head. "Gosh, even the most successful and confident of us can have a moment like that once in their lives. You'd never know."

Jamie looked at her a little strangely and Sage had the feeling that she'd somehow put her foot in her mouth without realizing it. Wouldn't be the first time. Nor the last, she suspected.

"You really don't know what happened with my tennis career, do you?" he asked.

Sage chewed on her bottom lip. "After I got out of this town, I was pretty desperate to pretend it never existed. I buried myself in work overseas and never looked anyone up."

Not even him.

He bobbed his head slowly. Sure, she'd wondered why Jamie was back home running a gym instead of playing in Grand Slam tournaments across the world. It had been widely known when he was a child that he had professional-grade talent and had big things in front of him, but Sage also knew a lot of athletes suffered injuries and other things out of their control that ended their careers.

"I, uh… I lost it."

She cocked her head. "What do you mean?"

"I cracked under the pressure and totally lost myself. I botched a huge game where I was ahead and should have won because the crowd got under my skin. I smashed my racket and people started booing me. Then I refused to do the press interviews afterwards and the tournament officials issued a big fine and threatened to ban me from competing there in the future." He raked a hand through his hair, his eyes fixed far in the distance like he was reliving the moment. "It all went downhill. The internet started calling me Jamie Can't-Hackett and I… I became a meme. To 'pull a Jamie' meant to flip out and quit. Everywhere I went, people criticized me."

Sage's mouth hung open. She could scarcely imagine it, because the Jamie from her memories had always had a legion of fans. He'd been hot property—young, good-looking, athletic, talented and with a kind personality like the cherry on top.

"I became a villain and a joke."

She could hear the tremor in his voice, the regret. The sadness. He'd lost something very dear to him.

"One day I'd had enough and…" He shook his head. "I walked out of a match and never went back."

She blinked. "Like, never again?"

"I haven't touched a tennis racket since." He glanced at her, his green eyes deathly serious. "So, uh, this was not my first time dealing with high-pressure stress and letting it get to me."

She wanted desperately to reach out and hug him. Sage understood, more than anyone, what it was like to have everyone point and laugh at you. To make you into a caricature. A joke. It was a great cruelty.

"You really picked yourself up and made the best of it, huh? Emma's told me all about the gym and how well it's doing." Her sister hadn't mentioned Jamie, specifically, but she'd talked a lot about what he and Clay were trying to achieve. "Sounds like you're doing really well."

"Until the freak-out." He let out a self-conscious chuckle. "That's why Clay is forcing me to take some vacation time. He doesn't want me to spiral again."

"He's a good friend."

"He's a pushy friend," Jamie grumbled.

As they walked, Sage felt her reserve continuing to melt. Jamie had been through a lot, and he was so open about his troubles. Maybe it was because the whole world had seen it happen in real time, so he thought there was no point hiding it. Or maybe it was because he knew she would understand.

And she did.

It was part of the reason being home was hard, because it was like opening up all those old wounds. She still felt like an outsider when she came home—with no friends to visit or favorite places to go, and bad memories on every corner.

But being with Jamie now reminded her of all the times they'd hung out as kids, with him climbing the fence to play with her or her splashing around in his pool. Those were the times she never felt like an outcast...and for the first time since she'd returned, this place really did feel like home.

CHAPTER SEVEN

A FEW DAYS later was the next dance rehearsal and Sage found herself unexpectedly having a great time. It seemed the extra practice session with Jamie had really paid off. When Courtney did a recap of the last lesson, they found their rhythm quickly and earned an impressed thumbs-up from Emma, as well as a curious eyebrow raise from Clay.

For the entire class, Jamie and Sage encouraged one another and worked as a team, counting the beats and helping each other memorize the steps. Gosh, it had been so long since Sage had been part of any kind of partnership—romantic, platonic *or* in the workplace. She missed the camaraderie and connective feeling of sharing a goal. Her career was solitary. Yes, she worked with her boss and other seamstresses to execute bridal designs, but Sage was heavily into the detail and on a day-to-day basis, she spent a lot of time alone in her corner of the atelier, quietly sewing and beading, lost in her own thoughts. Silent. Lonely.

But this…this was surprisingly fun.

"One, two, three and sidestep. Turn, back, turn, back." Jamie muttered the steps to himself as they moved in time to the music, a look of utter concentration on his face. It was quite adorable, seeing a guy as muscular and masculine as Jamie getting right into the semi-cheesy dance moves.

Muscular, huh? You noticed that?

Oh boy. How could she not?

Not that Sage was hung up on peoples' looks—she cared more about all the stuff underneath—but she'd be lying through her front teeth if she said she hadn't felt a flutter in her tummy looking at Jamie in his jeans and fitted gray Henley T-shirt, sculpted arms on display and his reddish hair tousled from running his fingers through it.

"You're taking this so seriously," Sage said, stifling a smile.

"As my mom always says, if it's worth doing then it's worth doing properly," he replied with a grin.

Cue heart melting in three, two, one...

What was more attractive than a confident guy who quoted the life lessons from his mom? Maybe that was the sexiest thing of all about Jamie—that he was a genuinely good person whose insides *absolutely* matched his outsides.

"Okay, everyone," Courtney called from the front of the studio. "Let's take it from the top."

Sage shifted from one foot to the other, cringing as her shoes rubbed against the backs of her heels. A blister was forming. But that sharp little snap of pain went right out of her head the moment Jamie stepped forward and reached for her, one hand settling at her waist and the other clasping her hand. Her palm was pressed against his, their bodies lined up. It was hard not to think of their kiss when they were close like this, to imagine the feeling of his lips brushing hers and the sweet relief as she gave into the pull between them—

Stop it before you start emitting pheromones!

She held her body tall, forcing her mind back to the task at hand. But as they danced, his body occasionally—innocently—touched hers and his gaze held her captive. For a moment, she let herself stare back, imagining they were back at his place, alone. Her mouth ran dry, attraction surging through her with rapid speed as they moved together, steps in time and rhythm matched. She let one hand settle on his chest, fingertips grazing the soft cotton of his shirt.

How easy it was to let the rest of the world fall away when he looked at her like that—eyes like emerald fire.

It was only the clearing of Courtney's throat that yanked Sage back into the present, where she realized that the rest of the class was staring at them...and the music had stopped. Eyes widening, Sage dropped Jamie's hand and stepped away from him as if she'd accidentally touched a burning pot. In her peripherals, she caught that he had a slight bit of pink to his cheeks. Emma was looking at her with one brow arched so high it was at risk of shooting off the top of her head.

It was quite a sensual song, so who could blame Sage for getting a little googly-eyed while dancing, especially when she had the most handsome man in the whole town as her dance partner?

Sage cleared her throat and avoided eye contact with Jamie.

"Well, that's it for our second lesson. We'll have one more next week a few days before the wedding," Courtney confirmed. She was wearing a pair of high-waisted hot pink leggings today and a white cropped T-shirt that showed off her tanned stomach. Her dark hair was loose and hung around her shoulders in soft curls. "The last part of the routine brings together what we learned in parts one and two, so no new steps to be learned. Rest assured, I will make sure you all look great to help Emma and Clay celebrate their special day. Thanks, everyone."

The class began to dissipate and Emma made a bee-line for Sage, hooking a hand around her arm and tugging her away from the group. "What the hell was that all about?"

"What?" Sage tried to appear nonchalant, but her sister wasn't about to let this go.

"You know exactly what! Dancing with Jamie Hackett like you two were…" She mimed fanning herself. "That was *hawt*."

"Stop it," Sage hissed. "We were just trying to get the steps right."

"Bullshit."

"We were!"

Emma grabbed her sister by the shoulders. "Are you two—"

"No." Sage shook her head vehemently.

Don't mention the kiss. Don't mention the kiss. Don't mention the kiss.

"I didn't even finish my sentence." Emma's mouth curved into a triumphant smile. "But your defensiveness is very telling."

"I went to his house to rehearse. That's it." Sage brushed Emma's hands from her. "Nothing happened."

"Well, if you *want* something to happen, you might want to speak up." Emma's eyes drifted past Sage, causing her to turn to see what her sister was looking at.

Courtney stood next to Jamie, her hand resting on his arm and her body craned toward his. Clay walked past

Jamie and gave him a subtle nudge in the ribs that made Sage's stomach churn. She whipped her head away.

"I *don't* want anything to happen. I'm not looking for a relationship, especially not in *this* town." The words rushed out before she could stop them and she cringed when a little bit of hurt splashed across her sister's face.

But Emma brushed it off, like she always did. Even though she had loads of friends and loved this town, she understood why Sage didn't. "Who said anything about a relationship? I'm talking about a little...you know, sexual healing. It's good for stress."

Sage snorted. "You my doctor now?"

"I *do* work in the medical field, so that's basically the same thing," she joked. "But seriously, he's so clearly into you. You two dancing today was...*whoa*."

"It's just dancing." Sage blushed.

"Stop being shy and go for it. Lord knows you've had an awful time of things lately. Don't you deserve a little fun?" Emma knocked Sage's elbow.

"You just want me to fall in love with someone here so I stay." She folded her arms across her chest and Emma made a guilty face.

"Is it so bad that I want you around more? You're my big sister. I love you."

Sage's annoyance softened. It really was hard not to adore her baby sister. "I love you, too. My living else-where doesn't change that."

"I know. But I'm also looking out for *you*. You need some joy in your life! It's been nothing but work, work, work for years and I know it will be like that again when you find another job," Emma said. "So why not have a good time while you're here?"

"I'm a little out of practice when it comes to having a good time."

Sage glanced back at Jamie and found that he was looking at her. Their gaze connected and she caught sight of the confused expression on Courtney's face. It made a little seed of anticipation unfurl in Sage's chest, as Jamie abandoned his conversation with Courtney and strode right over to her, eyes hungry and a smile on his lips.

"Want to practice again?" he said. "It seemed to work a treat last time."

She remembered the feeling of his hands all over her as his mouth came down to hers. "It sure did," she croaked in response.

Emma squeezed her arm. "I think that's a *wonderful* idea. I'm so thrilled you're all taking to this dancing thing like ducks to water. I was worried everyone might hate it."

"It's your big day," Jamie replied affably. "We're just here to make you two look good."

"Well, you know what they say…practice makes perfect," Emma said with a cheeky smile as she walked away, leaving Sage standing with Jamie. "With *all* things."

If Sage had been holding something in her hands, she likely would have thrown it at her sister.

"What's that all about?" Jamie asked.

"Just Emma being Emma." Sage shook her head. "Come on, let's go practice. Maybe we can take Flash for a walk later."

Jamie's face lit up. "That sounds great."

Dog walking was about the most "fun" she was willing to have right now. But even as she drew a line in the sand mentally, something in her gut told her she might not be so able to resist Jamie if things heated up again.

JAMIE DROVE THEM back from the dance studio to his place, which was on the other side of town. It was a bright, sunny day and they rolled the windows down. He caught Sage snuggling back into the passenger-side seat, looking more relaxed than he'd seen her since she returned to Reflection Bay.

"What was Courtney talking to you about?" she asked out of nowhere as they drove.

"Oh, she…" He frowned.

Courtney had been making her interest known for some time. Jamie was an "eligible bachelor" around town—as much as he hated the label—and she used any excuse to flirt with him. He'd been her trainer at the gym until she'd gotten a little too suggestive, and he'd ended up passing her off to one of his employees under the guise of needing to cut back his client list to focus on growing the business.

Fact was, she wasn't his type. She was attractive, sure, but she could be a little…mean. He didn't like that.

While they were in the studio earlier, she'd come over to him and made a petty comment about Sage, calling her by one of the nasty nicknames she'd had in high school. When Jamie had shut it down and defended Sage, Courtney had quickly moved the conversation to them having dinner and he'd extracted himself, saying he was busy with work.

Now let's hope she doesn't find out from Clay that I'm on involuntary vacation.

"She's always flapping her gums about something." He hoped Sage didn't pick up on any of the tension in his voice. He had no intention of telling her that the high school mean girl had grown up to be a mean adult. "She's a client at the gym."

"Right." Sage nodded, but her brows were slightly furrowed, like she'd picked up there was something he wasn't telling her.

"It's been a long time since you were home, right? I don't recall seeing you around here for ages."

"It's not a happy place for me," she replied. "There are a lot of bad memories here."

Good call on keeping your trap shut about the Courtney thing.

"I'm sure you miss your dad and your sister, though." He glanced over to her as they paused at a stoplight. She was looking out of the window.

"Yeah, I do." The words sounded heavy. Sad. And he longed to reach out and grasp her hand, to comfort her in some way. "I miss them so much."

"You shouldn't let a few bad eggs keep you away then."

"I promised myself when I left this town that I was never coming back." She let out a laugh. "I was just so happy to be leaving and putting everything behind me. I never thought about how much I was sacrificing."

"Promises can be changed."

"You mean broken?"

"No, I mean changed." He navigated the quiet residential streets, thinking about how he could name almost every family in every home. But at one point, he had been like her—desperate to spread his wings and go someplace new. "I promised myself one day that I would be world number one and that obviously didn't happen. But I don't think of it as a broken promise, but rather what I wanted out of life changed and so I let my promises change with it."

A smile ghosted over her lips. "You're very smart, Jamie Hackett."

"Not just a pretty face, eh?" He laughed.

"Not at all," she said, her tone serious. "Of all the jocks who were just in it for the social kudos, I knew you were different. You had drive, ambition."

"So did you. You still do, I'm sure."

"Not much point having drive and ambition without a job though, is there?" She pulled a face. "I screwed up. Big-time."

"You spoke up when you thought something was wrong."

"Ah, so you *do* know what happened. Everyone's talking about it, I bet." She seemed to burrow deeper into her seat, like a turtle yanking back into its shell.

"People can say what they like, but it takes a brave person to stand up and say something uncomfortable for no benefit of their own."

"Or a person with a penchant for bad decisions," she quipped.

"What are you going to do now?" he asked. "Maybe this is your chance for something more."

"You sound like Emma."

"It's a good life being your own boss." He shrugged. "It's hard work, for sure. But I suspect you're working hard already."

She nodded. "I am."

"Nobody can fire you if you work for yourself," he pointed out. "And the freedom is good. You get to make all the decisions instead of being told what to do."

Like being forced to take part in media interviews

where journalists would pick him apart with their questions and bait him with insults just to get a click-worthy headline.

"Trust me, I know how rewarding it is to turn the ashes of one failed thing into the success of another," he added.

"And you let the past go?" she asked. "Just like that?"

He thought of the boxes of trophies in his storage room, all the memories locked away like demons he'd tried and failed to exorcise. It was hypocritical to get all ra-ra with Sage about moving on with her life when he still had his own doubts to deal with.

"I wouldn't say that. But bad memories don't have to hold you in place forever."

He slowed his car as the turn to his street came up and he eased around the corner. A large dogwood tree stood proud in his front yard, shading the sidewalk and road with its large branches and yellow-green leaves. He pulled up to his house and killed the engine.

"I came for dance practice, not a psychoanalysis," she said. But she hadn't moved from his car. Dappled sunlight poured in through the windscreen and it occurred to Jamie that he hadn't actively thought about work since they got in the car, even though they'd driven right past the gym.

That was the effect Sage had on him—she engrossed him. Intrigued him. Captivated him. She was like a puzzle he wanted to figure out.

And right now, much to his surprise, there was nowhere else he'd rather be.

CHAPTER EIGHT

Jamie got out of the car and Sage followed, almost like she was drifting after him, unable to stop herself. Listening to him speak so passionately about turning his life around…it inspired her. He was brave enough to try again after a massive public failure (although she didn't really think of it as such) and he'd found his place in the world again.

Maybe she could do the same.

"I appreciate the pep talk," she said as he unlocked the door and let them inside. He threw his keys onto a small table in the entryway and Flash ambled over to say hello. "Sincerely."

She bent down to give the goofy dog a little loving. His stumpy, knotted tail rocked back and forth, and she laughed. A prickle of intuition crawled down her spine and she looked up, catching Jamie staring at her. Clearing her throat, she stood and brushed her palms nervously down over her stomach.

"You're capable of way more than you think you are," he said.

He looked like flame and smoke. Like every fantasy she'd ever tempted to life in the wee hours of the morning when she couldn't sleep and her bed felt impossibly cold and empty because she was so afraid of rejection that she never allowed anyone to get close.

Except him.

Back when they were young, before she had fully closed herself away, she had let him in.

"Do you regret what you did?" he asked.

"Speaking up at the wedding?"

"Yeah."

"I regret that it made me lose my job, but…" She looked down. "I'd do it again. It felt like the right thing."

It was hard to admit it, knowing how much it had cost her. But she would never be able to stay silent while someone else was taken advantage of. That wasn't her nature.

"But maybe I'd go about it a different way," she added.

"Wouldn't life be easier if we could be content with having no morals?" He quirked a smile and it almost broke her. "I couldn't live like that, though."

He was a good man. Full-hearted and emotionally intelligent and… So. Damn. Hot.

She should leave—go back to her dad's house and practice on her own. Because Jamie was tempting her with things she couldn't have, things she'd promised herself she'd stay away from. He was a small-town guy from the place that broke her.

Before "the wedding incident," her world had been perfectly uncomplicated—she had a job she loved, a tiny but clean apartment, respect from her industry peers. Yes, her social calendar was emptier than Old Mother Hubbard's cupboard, but that left more time for sewing. Then it all came crashing down and she had to come to the one place that *always* made her feel like a loser.

Maybe that was why she connected with Jamie so

well…he knew what it was like to lose everything you'd been working toward.

"The world would be a better place if more people were like you, Sage," he said, stepping closer. The air sparked between them.

"My capacity for bad decisions should *not* be romanticized," she said, trying to make light. But his green eyes were smoky and dark, full of something she desperately wanted to give in to.

"You don't make bad decisions," he said.

"How would you know?" The question was supposed to put some distance between them, but instead it drew him closer. It engaged him. "You don't know me as I am now."

"I know you're talented. I know you go after things even if you don't know whether you'll succeed. Like moving to Paris to get a job in fashion. That's brave, Sage. Most people would look that kind of fear in the eye and turn tail."

The words warmed her deep inside—because she'd never *ever* looked at her insecurities like that before. She'd always seen herself as being a step behind everyone else. Struggling to catch up. Never the smartest or the prettiest. Hard work was her crutch, her only chance to make something of herself.

Driven purely by the feeling of being painted anew, she rose onto her tiptoes, curled her hands into his shirt and pulled him down to her, kissing him softly. Her lips brushed over his in a way that felt like tugging on the ribbon of a perfectly wrapped birthday gift. It was silky and sensual and it spoke of treasures inside.

He turned them so Sage was backed up against the wall, wedged between hard granite and harder man.

His hands pinned her in, strong arms keeping her delightfully captive as she clung to him, his lips meeting hers. Harder this time. More insistent. She sucked in the scent of him and reveled in the press of his lips, creating sparks in her bloodstream.

Her mind blanked as Jamie's hand slid up over her ribcage to cup her breast. He had the slightly roughened hands of someone who used them often. Working hands. Competent hands. And the extra friction ratcheted up her senses until her body sang like a siren.

"I wasn't expecting this," he said.

"Me, either."

"But you want it, right?" His lips were at her neck. "I'm not reading things wrong?"

"I want it." Her voice was so raspy she almost didn't recognize it. "I want you."

His hand went to her thigh and skated under the hem of her dress. She pressed into his touch, her body wound so tight she thought she might crack from the pressure. She'd almost forgotten the thrilling rise of her pulse when she let someone get close. When she let someone in.

"Like this?" He brushed his fingers over her thigh so lightly it was almost like a breeze. When her eyes flashed up to his, she found his lips pulled into an indulgent smile, eyes blazing. He was torturing them both. Making them both ache with want.

"Are you teasing me, Jamie?"

"Maybe I'm teasing myself." Jamie's throaty laugh sent bold, unrestrained heat barreling through her. "It's hard to tell."

"Then stop teasing."

The transformation in his face—the widening of his

pupils, the intensity in his brows and the parting of his lips—made her weak at the knees. He inched his hand higher, and Sage wished that she wasn't wearing any underwear right now. Because even thin cotton felt like too much of a barrier. Like too much between them. She let herself sag back against the wall, with one arm hooked around Jamie's neck in case her legs gave out. It had been so long since she'd felt like this—liquid and wanton and free.

"I want to take you to bed."

"Yes," she whispered into his ear.

He led her through the house, down the hallway and to a door right at the end. Inside was a huge bed covered in soft white-and-blue linens, a modern canvas hanging above it with abstract splashes of slate gray, silver and navy, and a dog bed in the corner of the room with a plush toy sitting on the nest of blankets inside.

"Let's get you out of that dress," he said, gently turning her to face him. His hands drifted to the ribbon tied into a floppy bow at her waist. "Stunning as it is."

"Thanks," she said, unable to stop a smile. "I made it myself."

"You're so talented, Sage. Beautiful and talented."

He untied the bow, pulling on the ends of the long ties so they slithered out of place and slackened the fabric wrapped around her body. There was something so sensual about it, this slow undressing. It was like being laid bare. Stripped of everything that held her back. Like he was helping to discard her insecurities, one by one.

When he got to the part where the tie went through a small hole at her waist, his brow furrowed and she laughed, brushing his hand aside and taking over.

"Women's clothing is so much more complicated than men's," he said, letting out a self-conscious laugh.

"Don't tell me you struggle with bra hooks, too."

"Guilty." He put up both hands.

"I can do it."

Sage was *not* a seductress at all. She was quiet and methodical and detail-oriented, and she let others take center stage. But right now, it was as if she had a whole Broadway theatre to herself and there was only one person in the audience: him.

She pulled the tie loose, watching as Jamie's eyes tracked the widening vee of skin. By the time she slipped the tie completely loose and the dress opened up like a robe, Jamie had jammed his hands into his pockets as if trying to physically restrain himself from touching her. It was fun to put on a show. She'd never felt like that before. With a shrug of her shoulders, she let the open dress slip to the floor and land in a pool around her bare feet.

For a moment, neither of them moved and the only sound in the air was their labored breathing. His eyes roamed her body, lingering on the delicate lace cupping her breasts and the matching fabric riding low on her hips. She reached behind herself and felt for the clasp of her bra—unclipping it and slowly peeling it from her skin. Her underwear followed.

He reached forward and gently grabbed her wrists, bringing her hands to his lips so he could kiss her knuckles. Then he released her to let his hands roam— over her shoulders, her arms, her hips, her waist, her ass.

"Your turn," she whispered.

He tugged at his Henley T-shirt and pulled the hem out of the waistband of his jeans before lifting it over his head. Muscles flexed—abs starkly defined and his body lean and strong. Sage felt a small surge of insecurity at her own skinny, soft limbs, but she whisked the thought away. He was the kind of guy who could have whoever he wanted, and he wanted to be here with her.

That meant something.

Jamie discarded his jeans and underwear. He was glorious naked—all sharp angles and smooth freckled skin. Reddish hair dusted his legs and arms. He was a far cry from the lanky boy she remembered from high school who always had a tennis racket in his hand and a band of sunburn across his nose.

"I'm glad you're here, Sage," he said, coming closer and sweeping her loose hair back over her shoulders. "It's…it's been good to see you again."

"Same," she admitted.

Jamie wrapped her up in his arms and drew her back to the bed, his lips coming down to hers. Sage let her mind go blank as she gave into sensation. Into feeling. Into being. The last few weeks had been utterly miserable and it was so freeing to do something for the sake of pleasure and nothing more.

And instead of feeling an imbalance—him the superstar athlete and her the weird, shy girl—they felt equal. Matched. Compatible. He understood her doubts and her problems, and she understood his. The desire was mutual and even, and for a brief moment, she understood the way her clients looked at the men and women they loved on their big days.

It felt real, all of a sudden. More than sequins and tulle and horsehair hems. More than technique. It felt… passionate.

"I'll grab a condom." He pressed a quick kiss to her

lips and left her to scoot beneath the covers, burrowing down into the soft, cozy bed.

Jamie fished out a box from the side of his bed and opened a silver foil packet, taking a moment to sheath himself. Then he pulled her close under the covers, dragging her body on top of his.

"Ready?" His eyes were hungry and her heart fluttered in her chest.

"I was ready a long time ago."

He trailed kisses down her neck. Then he pushed into her, slowly. So very slowly. It was wonderful and torturous at the same time and Sage bit down on her lip to stifle a cry. She clamped her eyes shut. Goodness, she'd forgotten how good this could feel. How intense and perfect.

She pressed one hand to the center of his chest, letting her head loll backwards so that her hair tickled the curve of her butt. Undulating, she dug her knees into the soft mattress on either side of him and rocked her hips this way and that, getting accommodated to the feeling of him. She leaned back, lost in sensation, and his hand drifted between their bodies. When his thumb found the apex of her sex, her eyes fluttered shut and fireworks danced behind her lids, shimmering and otherworldly.

With each sensual rock of her hips, she met him. Joined with him. It was impossible to do anything but ride the waves since her mind had blanked everything that wasn't him.

"Yes." She groaned as he circled the pad of his thumb over her sex, applying more pressure. Teasing her. Coaxing her. "That's so good."

She felt her muscles tighten as her mind narrowed to a pinpoint of euphoria. Release broke like a champagne cork popping—it was sharp and sudden and wonderful. She gasped, arching against him as she rode the ripples of pleasure, her cries uncensored and her nails scraping against his skin.

Then his hands were in her hair, his mouth hot on hers, body solid beneath her. He moaned against her neck, the vibrations skittering through her body and fracturing at the last second in a billion glittering shards as he followed her over the edge, clutching her tight like she was his only tether to earth.

CHAPTER NINE

IN THE LEAD UP to the wedding, Sage found herself in Jamie's arms more often than not. After the first time, she'd slid out of his bed with every intention of leaving—only Jamie had caught her hand and asked her to stay. He'd tempted her back to bed where they'd cuddled, kissed and eventually made love again. That night, she'd sat on the couch, giving belly rubs to Flash while Jamie made them a simple yet delicious dinner of salmon pasta.

She'd left before midnight and lied to Emma and her father about where she'd been. But the lie hadn't lasted long because Jamie had called on her the next day with both her dad and Emma home to witness it. And the one after that. And she'd slept over, telling herself to be careful and keep her heart safe, all the while her inner teenage self was aglow with belonging and the feeling of being desired. Aglow with finding a deep connection with a man she admired and respected.

But all good things come to an end.

"I have to go," Sage said, reluctance hanging heavy in her voice. "Emma and I are going to have a girls' night of pre-wedding activities. She said something about mud masks and pedicures and cheesy Netflix rom-coms."

Jamie was lying in his bed, the duvet covering him

up to almost his belly button. The top half of him was bare, red hair gleaming like embers in the early evening sunlight that filtered through the window. His arms had a distinct line at the bicep, white above and pink below from where he'd gotten a little burned while they had a picnic in the nearby national park. They'd eaten fruit and cheese and laughed as Flash snored like an eighty-year-old man beside them.

It was by far the most romantic—yes, even with the doggy snoring—afternoon she'd ever had. Of course it was playing on her mind that their time was short… In truth, it was playing on her *a lot*.

"Can we clone you so I can send one version home to your sister and keep the other one here with me?" His hand reached out and encircled her wrist, pulling her back to the bed. It was oh so tempting.

"Other than destroying the natural balance of life, cloning me would be a terrible idea because the world can only handle one of me screwing up." She laughed.

"I was talking more about screwing than screwing up." He grinned and there was a wolfish glint to his expression.

Sometimes screwing and screwing up are one and the same.

Try as she might, it was hard to think of their time together as a mistake, however. Although she knew it was going to hurt when it came time for her to leave because this past week had been…

Everything.

No other relationship she'd ever had with a man had come close. Emma said that was because she dated losers, but Sage knew it went deeper than having bad taste.

She *knew* most men were losers when she picked them, but part of her had figured that was the best she could do.

Jamie had shattered that ideal. If only he didn't live in the one place she loathed with all her being.

"I really can't stay, sorry. I would *much* prefer to be here with you than slathering mud on my face."

Jamie got out of the bed and cupped the back of her head, coaxing her lips open with his for a brief, but delving kiss. "Don't say that. I know you love spending time with your sister."

"Spending time with Emma, yes. Partaking in beauty routines with dubious effectiveness? Not so much," she sighed. "I don't know where this week has gone."

Jamie released her and they both pulled on their clothes slowly, as though they were literally dragging their heels toward what they knew was coming. Sage opened the bedroom door to find Flash lying like a lump outside, fast asleep. Clearly whatever burst of energy had him pawing at the door had passed as quickly as it came. For some reason, it made tears spring to her eyes.

What she wouldn't give to stay here forever…

Forever? *That's a big word when you've only been sleeping together a week.*

Ah, but that was a lie on some level. Because they were not merely having sex, and her relationship with Jamie could be counted in decades, rather than days. They may not have crossed the boundary from platonic to romantic until recently, but the admiration, respect and friendship had been there since they were children.

"How soon after the wedding are you flying out?" he asked.

Sage swallowed, aware his green eyes would miss nothing. "The day after."

"Couldn't wait to get out of this place, huh?" His voice made it sound like the words were a joke, but his eyes showed no signs of humor.

Sage wasn't sure how to respond. If someone had posed that question a week ago, she would have said "heck yeah" without thinking twice. But being home with her family lately had been so soul-soothing and being with Jamie…well, she'd never felt so good.

"You know why I feel that way," she said softly, her eyes downcast.

He cradled her to his chest. There was an intimacy to the way he held her, a realness. This wasn't simply a case of two people who were physically attracted to one another—it went deeper than that.

"Don't you believe in second chances?" he asked, his voice muffled into her hair.

"This town used up every chance I'm capable of giving."

"What are you going to do in New York?"

"Try again," she said. "I want to get a foot back into the industry and start rebuilding my reputation."

Despite Emma's insistence that she should start her own business, Sage wasn't confident that was the best next step. What if she tried and failed? What if she really *had* been cast out of the bridal industry just like she'd been cast out by the bullies at her high school? Putting herself out in the world—putting *her* designs out in the world—was a scary thing. She wasn't ready for that kind of rejection.

"Whatever you set your mind to, I know you can do it," he said.

Silence settled between them. It felt like so much was going unsaid.

I really like you.

She couldn't bring herself to utter the words because they would only cause more pain. She and Jamie had come together too late in life, when her scars were already scabbed over and healed. She couldn't risk picking at them again because what if she wasn't capable of healing this time? What if she never recovered?

As sad as it was to say goodbye to someone who'd always had a piece of her heart, it was better to risk a single piece than put the whole damn organ on the line.

CLAY AND EMMA'S wedding was every bit of fun Jamie had hoped it would be. He'd grinned like a fool through the entire ceremony, thrilled for his best friend to be taking such an important leap. He'd also found himself sneaking a million glances at Sage, who was so beautiful she outshone everyone in the room.

Even the bride, in his humble opinion.

She'd flushed as the wedding MC had announced them into the pub as maid of honor and best man, and she'd nailed every single move in the first dance, their practice paying off if the cheers were anything to go on. The pub was decorated with dozens and dozens of twinkling lights strung from the roof, making it feel like they were outside standing under the stars. Everyone was eating and drinking and being merry, but it seemed that Sage was doing her best to avoid him.

His gaze drifted across the room to where she was standing, drinking champagne and talking with her father and an older woman. Everyone was dressed in their finest. But Sage…well, she looked as though she'd stepped right out of his wildest dreams.

She wore the dress he'd seen her sewing the day

he dropped off her shoes. It was cut close to her body, showing off her willowy shape in champagne fabric covered in what looked like thousands of tiny beads or sequins. From the front it looked modest, with feminine fluttering sleeves that reminded him of angel wings. But the second she turned around, the magic happened. A deep vee exposed most of her back, with a strand of glimmering beads draped across her bare skin keeping the dress in place.

How he'd stopped his jaw from hitting the ground when she'd walked down the aisle was a legitimate miracle.

Only now, the reality of her imminent departure was settling in.

"Hey, best man!" Emma walked over, a glass of champagne in her hand, cheeks pink with joy. Her white dress looked romantic and pretty—although that was based on Jamie having zero knowledge about wedding dresses. All he knew is that Sage had made it and everyone had gasped when Emma appeared as the bridal music started. "Are you having a good time? *I'm* having a good time! Did you know I got married today?"

Jamie snorted and eased the champagne flute out of Emma's hand. The woman weighed a hundred and thirty pounds soaking wet and he had no idea how she got people onto stretchers in her day job. Clearly she was also a lightweight when it came to adult beverages.

"That's enough of that or you won't get to the most important part of the wedding night," he said.

She giggled. "That's rude!"

"I was talking about the cake cutting." He grinned.

"Sure." She swayed a little and poked him in the chest. Jamie, meanwhile, caught Clay's attention and

motioned him over. Emma might need a little black coffee and some fresh air to help counteract the effects of the champagne before they got to the speeches.

Everyone in this town loved Emma, however, so even if she was a bit tipsy people would still be happy to hear from her. He'd always wondered how that universal love had never extended to Sage—probably because Sage had always been shy and introverted, whereas Emma had been that little kid who wanted to pat every dog and talk to every stranger and make every friend wherever she went.

"You have to tell Sage that she should stay here," Emma said, nodding seriously like she was imparting him with a top secret mission. "And not go back to New York."

"Don't you think that's her decision?" he asked gently.

"But I know she wants to be near family and she wants to fall in love," Emma said, the words a little blurry around the edges. But her pale green eyes were filled with sincerity. Those two women loved one another fiercely, there was no doubt about that. "And she wants to design her own dresses and be creative. But she's scared."

"She shouldn't be scared," he said.

"Exactly." Emma threw her hands in the air. "But she's too stubborn. Won't listen to me even though I'm her sister and I know everything about her."

"So why do you think she's going to listen to me?" he said with a laugh.

"Because you are the one person who never teased her in school. You were always nice to her and she told me she loved you when she was ten. I remember it, clear as day." Emma nodded and Jamie noticed that she had a sparkly clip in her hair that was dangling a little precariously. "She said, *I love Jamie Hackett and we're going to get married one day.* Word for word."

Jamie laughed. "Ten-year-olds say a lot of things."

"She needs someone to believe in her. Someone that's not me or Dad, because she thinks whenever we encourage her that we just say it because we're family."

Clay arrived and slipped an arm around his bride's waist, smiling indulgently down to her. "Okay, Mrs. We're going to get you some sober juice."

"*Tell* her, Jamie," Emma implored him. "Tell her now or that will be it. She'll be gone for good."

Clay looked at him quizzically, but Jamie waved him away. He had bigger fish to fry than Jamie's love life. Although Clay had texted him the previous day to ask if he was dead because he hadn't seen or heard from him since the last dance lesson—something that was practically unheard of. Being best friends and business partners, they were in constant contact. But Jamie had told Clay that he was finally doing what everyone wanted: relaxing. Enjoying himself. Doing something other than work.

And it had been glorious.

Tell her, Jamie. Tell her now or that will be it. She'll be gone for good.

He turned his gaze back to Sage and for a moment he saw her as a young woman—wide-eyed, cautious but authentic, on his doorstep asking him to prom. What might have happened if he'd said yes that day? If he'd done what he wanted instead of being worried about how it might look? What people might say?

Don't you believe in second chances?

He did. Jamie knew more than anyone the power of starting over, of reinvention and dusting oneself off. If he could do it with his career, then he could do it with anything. *She* could do it with anything.

All he had to do was be brave enough to voice his feelings aloud.

CHAPTER TEN

SAGE WASN'T SO sure how long it had been since she'd felt *this* happy. Watching her baby sister walk down the aisle, pure joy shining out of her face like beams of sunshine, in a dress that Sage had made, was probably in the top three moments in all of Sage's life. Emma had squeezed Sage's hand when she'd passed her the bouquet to hold while the vows were read and mouthed "I love you, sis," instantly making Sage tear up.

Gosh, how she'd missed her family.

Through the entire ceremony, she glanced around the church at so many people she hadn't seen for years. More distant relatives, like her cousin who was a good decade older than her, and her elderly aunt and uncle. She'd watched her dad cheer when Emma and Clay kissed. She'd watched her new brother-in-law only have eyes for his beautiful bride, their love real and tangible and intoxicating.

And she'd seen Jamie sneaking glances at her...just like how he'd looked at her yesterday afternoon when he'd left her with a lingering kiss at his front door.

It felt like another world. Another dimension. A place where she was someone else, with the life she'd always wanted—her dream career, her dream man, her loved ones close by. Her chest was already aching at the thought of going home tomorrow, knowing the shit-storm that awaited her in New York. Not to mention the loneliness.

Feeling suddenly—and uncharacteristically—overcome with emotion, Sage excused herself from chatting with her father and her aunt to head to the restroom. She hurried as best she could on her stilt-like heels and almost stumbled into the sink area. Her pale eyes were glistening with tears but there was a hopefulness in her expression that hadn't been there before.

Maybe she wouldn't leave it so long between visits next time.

You could always change your flight? Move it out by a week or two. Have some more time with your family. With Jamie.

Temptation swirled in Sage's stomach. But before she could think too much about what those inner thoughts meant, there was a loud giggle right outside the washroom. Sage ducked into one of the pub's toilet stalls. A second later, the sound of two sets of high heels came into the restroom.

"My god, Courtney, you're such a flirt tonight. How much champagne have you had?" a lilting voice teased.

"Enough to tackle Jamie Hackett to the ground and rip his clothes off in front of everyone," Courtney replied, her voice more musical than normal. She was tipsy, but not drunk. The night, however, was still young.

"Did you see him making eyes at Emma's sister during the ceremony?"

"At Sage? Puh-lease. She's *so* not at his level. Don't you remember how weird she was in high school, always stuttering and going red in the face if anyone looked in her direction? I always thought she was a bit…you know."

Since Sage couldn't see the gesture or expression Courtney was making, she wasn't exactly sure what the message was…although her tone said it was nothing positive. Sage's cheeks heated up. So much for Jamie trying to convince her people in this town had changed as they got older. The bullies were still mean. People still judged.

And Sage was still someone to be mocked.

"I always felt sorry for her," the other woman said. "Emma was so popular and fun. Must have been hard not living up to your younger sibling."

Sage wasn't sure what was worse—Courtney's un-filtered disdain, or the other woman's pity.

Courtney made a snorting sound. "Look, the fact is that humans have a social hierarchy and someone like Jamie Hackett will never choose the school freak. It's a fact."

Tears flooded Sage's eyes, but she remained quiet and still in her stall, her feet drawn up and out of view, hoping that neither of the women would notice anyone was there. But she wasn't upset because she believed Courtney—the fact was, Jamie *had* chosen her. He'd kissed her and touched her and made her feel special. He wasn't the issue.

It was everyone else.

Because even if Jamie declared that he loved her and wanted them to be together…it would have to be here, in this town. With these people.

And she would never be accepted.

JAMIE FOUND HIMSELF hanging around outside the wash-rooms after he'd seen Sage go in. He really wanted to corner her so they could talk. He *needed* to tell her how he felt, and she'd been slipperier than an eel all night.

But it sounded like there was a conversation going on inside the washroom. Two women were close to the door and he got snatches of what they were saying.

"…humans have a social hierarchy… Jamie Hackett will never…the school freak. It's a fact."

"Don't be so mean…" There was a second voice. "She never…unfair. How would you…"

He frowned and stepped closer to the door, trying to hear more fully, aware that he probably looked like some creeper trying to spy into the women's bathroom.

"Ever since you had kids, you've become such a bleeding heart, Jo." Courtney's voice was like nails on a chalkboard.

"I would hate for my daughters to be treated like how Sage was," Jo replied, sounding sad. "I regret how we were back then."

The door suddenly swung open and two women almost walked smack into him. He stumbled back, righting himself with a hand to the wall.

"Jamie!" Courtney's face lit up and she made a show of flicking her long dark hair over one shoulder. Frankly, he thought it made her look like a horse. "I've been hoping to catch you for a dance. You really showed off your moves tonight."

He looked at her, fury billowing inside him. He knew for a fact that Sage hadn't come out of the toilets after she'd gone in, which meant she was probably hiding in the stalls listening to every word Courtney and Jo said.

"Let me be clear," he said, stuffing his hands into his pockets so he didn't ball his fists. "I'm not interested. I will *never* be interested. Because what matters to me is whether or not someone has a good heart and I'm afraid you don't."

Her mouth popped open into a glossy O of surprise. Beside her, Jo's eyes widened until she looked almost like a cartoon character.

Without waiting for a response, he pushed into the women's bathroom, pulled the door shut behind him and leaned against it so she couldn't follow him inside. All the stall doors were shut and he couldn't see any feet dangling down. If he hadn't been watching the door like a hawk, he might have thought she'd already gone.

"I know you're in here, Sage," he said.

Nothing.

He counted to fifteen before he tried again. "I'm happy to make everyone in this place pee their pants waiting if that's what it takes to talk to you."

There was a resigned sigh from one of the stalls and two stilettos slid into view in the gap beneath one door. The sound of a bolt sliding open was followed by the squeak of hinges as Sage pushed the door open. Her eyes were a little red and her makeup had some smudges.

But she was still the most beautiful woman in this pub. In this town. In this whole hemisphere, he'd wager. At the very least, when it came to the space in his heart, she was the only woman who fit.

"Courtney is—"

Sage held up a hand. "I don't want to stoop to her level by slinging insults. I'm not here to talk badly about anyone."

"Fair." He nodded. That was Sage in a nutshell— she held herself with grace and morals, no matter what. "They're wrong about you."

"Are they?" She looked at him as she washed her hands, the water dotting her pale skin and her dress glittering under the overhead lighting.

"Of course they are." He blinked. "Surely you don't really believe that someone like her—who has *never* taken the time to get to know you—would have a single clue about who or what you are."

A smile tugged at the corner of her lips. "You're passionate."

"About you, I am." The words came out in a rush, like a spirit leaving his body, exorcised by need and want. "I knew I had feelings for you when we were young, but these past two weeks…"

The past two weeks should have been some of the worst in his life—locked out of his job, humiliated that the pressure had gotten to him once again. Instead, he had two weeks of lazy days in bed with Sage, dancing lessons and spending time with Flash. It was like life had shoved him toward a mirror and for the first time in forever, he'd seen what his life had become…and all it was missing. All he wanted it to contain.

"Sage, am…am I alone in feeling this? Was this just a fling for old times' sake?"

Her pale eyes were glossy, and she shook her head, scattering her curled white-blond hair around her shoulders and making her glittering earrings shudder. "No, it's not that at all."

The lingering resistance in the air stopped him from latching on to her statement.

"But I'm going back to New York to try to salvage my career." She sucked in a breath and drew her shoulders back, clearly drawing on something inside her.

"And your life is here. You have a thriving business, a family who loves you—"

"*You* have a family who loves you here." He hated the desperation in his voice. But he had the very real fear that Sage would disappear just like she did after high school, vanishing like a tendril of steam, never to be seen again.

Something told him that if she left for New York, she wouldn't ever come back.

"What do you want me to do, Jamie? Try and build a life and a business here, in a place where no one will ever take me seriously?" She looked at him incredulously. "How do you think that will go?"

The door rattled behind Jamie, but his weight kept it firmly in place. "Occupied for, uh…maintenance."

There was a disgruntled sound on the other side of the door but the person went away.

"This is going to sound ridiculous after what you just heard Courtney saying, but you underestimate this place," he said. "I know it was rough for you when we were in school—"

"Rough?" She laughed, and the sound was slightly delirious. "Did you know that Ginnie—your prom date—cut off my ponytail once? Remember when I turned up to school with that pixie cut all of a sudden?"

He remembered. She'd looked like a '60s fashion model.

"I didn't *want* a haircut. Ginnie and Courtney held me down on the floor of the locker room after gym class and cut my ponytail off." Tears gathered in her eyes, and he could see the panic and fear she must have felt in that moment. "Another time they opened up a tin of dog food into my school bag. Do you have any idea what it's like to be treated as though you're not even human?"

There was a ferocity in her voice, like a lion's roar. Her pain was sharp and fresh even though these events had taken place more than a decade ago.

"I would *never* try to diminish your experience, Sage. You know that." He shook his head. "Kids can be assholes, no doubt about it. But Courtney is a one-off. Most people grow up and they become adults and... it's different."

But...was it?

Maybe now bullies used words instead of scissors and dog food. But the intention was still the same—to humiliate her. To undermine her.

"This place was good to me after I left the tennis world. I came home and people welcomed me with open arms even though I felt like I failed everyone."

"It's different for you," she said, folding her arms across her chest. "For people like you."

"For people like you, too," he said, his green eyes imploring her to hear him out. "What about Mrs. Carver?"

The woman who'd lived across the street when they were young had no family of her own and was always kind, baking cookies and letting the neighborhood kids play with her dog, Henri. He knew she'd often babysat Sage and Emma after their mother died.

"And Mr. Marchesi, who ran the convenience store?"

He'd seen the older Italian man slip her packs of gum or small candy bars when they went to buy milk, because the Nilsen family didn't have much to spare for such luxuries.

There *were* good people in this town.

People like his client Lisa, who donated one of her

personal training sessions each month to her neighbor, who couldn't afford to pay for a membership themselves. People like the folks who'd opened their homes to strangers who were stranded in a freak blizzard the previous Christmas.

"What are you trying to say, Jamie?"

"*I* like you, Sage. A hell of a lot."

Her heart thumped unevenly in her chest.

"I like you too, Jamie. I always have."

The words should have filled him up. They should have smoothed over his heart like warm toffee, filling in the cracks and dents. But it sounded a hell of a lot like goodbye.

"Then let's give this a try," he said, trying to keep her with him. Trying to convince her. "Maybe we could try long-distance? You could be in New York and…"

"Yeah, because *that* works for so many people. Not. And besides, what happens when I never want to come home and see your family for Thanksgiving or Christmas, huh? Are you okay losing all those holidays to come and see me? And if I always expected you to come to New York and I never return the favor…well, that isn't fair."

She was right. It was easy to see how it might work for a year or two, but over time, it would pull at the threads of their relationship, disintegrating them one holiday and special event at a time.

"I regret more than anything not telling you how I felt when you asked me to go to prom with you," he said. "I wanted to say yes so badly."

"It's in the past." Her voice was soft, her shell already closing around her.

"But the past seems to be the present for you." He

reached for her arm and squeezed, wanting more than anything for her to see how much he cared. "You're acting like coming home is reliving all those bad times, which means you haven't put it behind you. You haven't realized that you're not the same person anymore. People like Courtney are the ones who are stagnant and stuck in the past. You… You're a successful, competent, talented woman in charge of her destiny."

"I am," she said, tears in her eyes. "And that's how I know my destiny isn't here."

"It could be."

"Do you have any idea what I would give to be able to stay here—to be five minutes down the road from Dad and Emma, to open Christmas gifts with them, to pop in whenever I felt like it? I miss them so much."

"What if you gave it a shot?" he asked. They both knew what he was really asking—what if she gave *them* a shot?

"Sometimes the only answer is to move on when something isn't working. You of all people know that's true," she said. Hurt flashed through him, but he held himself strong. "The only thing that will bring me back here is my dad or my sister needing me. That's it. Otherwise, I'd be happy never to set foot in this place ever again."

"Sage, please…"

"Let me go, Jamie." Her lip quivered. "Let me leave this place so I can pick up the pieces and put myself back together again."

It hurt like hell to step aside and hold the restroom door open for her, but there was no convincing her. She needed to be the one to make the decision to stay.

"I'll miss you even more than I did last time," she said softly, leaning in to kiss his cheek before she exited. Then she was gone.

CHAPTER ELEVEN

Two days later...

JAMIE STOOD IN the middle of his house, discombobulated. Everywhere he looked now he saw Sage. Saw them dancing in the middle of his living room, saw her walking next to him on the street, saw her bending down to pet Flash, saw her in his bed. In his shower. On the wicker chair on his back porch. It made him feel like an ice cube rattling around in a cocktail shaker while some unseen hand jostled him up and down, left and right.

Flash plodded over to him and looked up with his perpetually sad eyes.

"I know, bud. I miss her, too."

In truth, Flash was probably just angling for treats. But it helped Jamie feel like he wasn't the only one mourning Sage's departure. He knew Emma was. Clay said she'd been quite hungover the morning after the wedding, and she'd cried over her sister leaving. If only Jamie had been able to convince her to give this place another shot. Why did she have to let the past dictate the future?

Flash made a whining sound at Jamie's feet and then plodded away from him, heading downstairs into the basement. Weird. He followed the dog, curious as to what his canine best friend was up to. The dog walked right over to the door of the storage room and, to Jamie's utter surprise, raised a paw to scrape at the wood like he wanted inside. He'd never done that before.

Why did she have to let the past dictate the future?

Strong words from a man who'd literally boxed up his past and left it to rot. It was totally hypocritical of him to judge Sage for not being able to put the past behind her when he hadn't been able to do it, either.

Flash looked at him imploringly.

"It's finally time." With a renewed sense of hope budding in his chest, he walked over to the door and pushed it open.

The boxes sat, untouched since the last time he'd been inside, his failures preserved.

"Want to hang out while I clean this place up?" he asked, and Flash ambled over to the far side of the room where it was coolest. Settling into a lump-shape in the corner, he promptly fell asleep. "I'll take that as a yes."

If he wanted to be the kind of person who inspired and helped others, then it was time he faced his own demons. Working one box at a time, he unpacked all the old memorabilia—trophies, medals, a tennis ball signed by Lleyton Hewitt, his first ever kiddie tennis racket, framed photos of him at his first Wimbledon, clippings from newspapers carefully stored in protective sleeves. It felt like a lifetime ago.

And for the first time since he'd last set foot on to a tennis court, Jamie smiled when he looked at these things. They no longer felt like markers of failure, but memories of something he'd cared passionately about for a time. They were goals held by his childhood self, dreams he'd nurtured as a teenager. They were something to be proud of, rather than hidden away.

He held a racket in his hand—one he'd had freshly strung right before he quit—and wrapped his fingers loosely around the grip, giving it a little spin. The weight was familiar, the noise of his fingertips over the strings like an old song he'd not quite forgotten. Maybe he'd see if Clay wanted to hit the courts with him once he got back from his honeymoon.

Sage might not ever know this but talking to her about her past had helped him with his. It had helped him to see he was doing the same things that she was, being ashamed of something that was simply the past.

"I hope she comes back one day," he said to no one in particular. And if she did, he would tell her that their short time together had meant everything to him.

Sage sat on her couch, her laptop balanced on her knees as she hung her head in her hands. *Another* rejection.

We have received a large number of applications from qualified individuals and thus, we regret to inform you...

Blah, blah, blah.

Not only had Sage been frozen out of the couture world, but now she was being rejected from bridal sales assistant jobs as well! Granted it had been many years since she worked in a sales capacity but still... she knew everything about wedding gowns there was to know. She'd bet her last ten bucks that the second they searched her name, "the wedding incident" would put a big black mark on her application.

Maybe it was time to change her name. Surely the process wasn't that hard—she could pick something new and start over. Samantha Nilsen had a nice ring to it. Or maybe Sara. Or Sienna. Or she could pick an entirely new initial all together.

The possibilities were endless.

At that moment, another email appeared in her inbox. The subject line read *your beautiful dresses*. The email was from a guest at Emma and Clay's wedding wanting to know how to book an appointment to talk about Sage designing her a dress. It was the fifth one in the two weeks since she'd been back in New York. All of them were from guests of the wedding, other twenty- and thirtysomething women who were getting married in the next year or two wanting to know if she was open for business.

"I'm not open for *that* business." She clicked the red X on her browser.

It was getting ridiculous—two of the women who'd contacted her wouldn't even *look* at Sage in high school. Not mean girls exactly, but other non-popular types who'd turned a blind eye when Sage was being bullied for fear of becoming targets themselves. Could she blame them? Not really. Perhaps if she were in their position, she would have stayed quiet, too.

But you spoke up at the wedding when it came with no benefit to you.

Good point.

Sage hadn't responded to a single request, although she'd been working on a new design sketch based on one of the emails that came with some inspiration photos that had gotten her creative juices flowing. She looked across the tiny living area of her apartment to her sewing desk, which was currently buried under two bolts of silk, another of point d'esprit, two large cones of thread, an unopened order of sequins and costume pearls, and every type of fabric shears, thread snips, duckbill scissors and other cutting implements known to man. Oh, and at least five different pin cushions and containers. The itch to sew was there—the need to create and craft and perfect swelling like a storm inside her.

But not one job application had yielded any positive response and asking her former employer for a reference was *not* going to happen.

Before Sage could wallow too much more, the sound of her Skype ringtone cut through the quiet air. It was her dad. Emma had helped him to download and use Skype a few years back and it was the main way he and Sage kept in touch. Putting on a smile, she answered the call.

"Hi, Dad."

"What's wrong?" he asked in his gruff voice. His gray hair was a mess, like it always was at the end of the day when he took off his cap after work. It stuck straight up on one section, which Sage had always jokingly called his "cockatiel" look.

"Who said anything was wrong?" she asked.

"Your face said it," he replied, frowning. The action made his fuzzy caterpillar-like eyebrows knit close together. "What's going on?"

Filip Nilsen might be a man of few words, but he could read his daughters like they were books on his shelf. There was no point trying to hide anything from him.

"I'm frustrated," she said with a sigh.

"Tell your old pappa everything."

"I feel like no matter what I do in my life, I end up a

laughingstock." To her mortification, her voice shook. "Everywhere I go, I mess up and people hate me."

"Skatten min," he said, and she smiled at the way his Norwegian accent became thick with emotion. He'd called her "his treasure" ever since she was a little girl. "People always fear what they perceive is different, but nobody ever made an impact on the world by being the same as everybody else. You are thoughtful and introspective and sensitive and creative...just like your mother was. They are wonderful qualities."

She had to look away from the screen for a moment, lest her tears spill onto her cheeks. "I wish she was here."

"Me too." Silence stretched on for a few heartbeats and Sage had to look back at the screen to make sure the connection hadn't dropped. "I know losing her so young was hard on you girls, especially you."

Sage had been two weeks shy of her ninth birthday when her mother was knocked off her bicycle by a passing car. To lose her mother so suddenly had devastated Sage, and she'd gone from being a vibrant, happy young girl to...something else. Only Jamie had ever been able to get her to smile after that, when he poked his head over the fence and pulled silly faces.

"She would have been so proud of the woman you've become, Sage."

But...would she? Sage looked around her apartment that, apart from the sewing station, bore no personal touches. No photos, no art, no cute succulents or quirky travel finds. Any spare cash she had went into sewing materials and her idea of picking up a souvenir on vacation was buying some antique lace in Paris or vintage sewing shears in London or deadstock fabrics from job-bers in the LA Fashion District.

Everything in her life went to sewing…and now she couldn't even do that.

You could, though. You have five emails of willing clients sitting in your inbox waiting for a response.

Back home.

"And I'm proud of you, too," he finished. "That dress you made for Emma…she has never looked more beautiful. It was a work of art."

"Thanks, Dad. Emma would have looked good in a potato sack, though."

"Yes, but your mother would have come back from the afterlife to haunt me if I allowed that," he replied.

Sage burst out laughing. Her father never failed to cheer her up with his dry sense of humor. "I think you might be right."

"Can I give you some unsolicited advice? I know you're all grown up now and you're more worldly than I will ever be, but hear an old man out?"

"I'll always listen to what you have to say, Dad," she said, settling back against the couch. She had to resist the urge to close her eyes and imagine they were sitting at his dining table together.

"Stop worrying about what everyone else is doing and saying and do what *you* want." He leaned close to the camera as if to emphasize his point. "If you said screw all those nasty people in the world, what would you be doing?"

She let her eyes flutter shut and the image was sharp and bright—a familiar set of woods, with strong trees and a carpet of green beneath her feet. Laughter, her father's rough hand in hers, Emma by her side. A house with plenty of space, her sewing machine by a window. Another hand in hers, smoother...but still with a few calluses. Red hair. Green eyes.

She could practically smell him, that perfect mix of faded aftershave—just a whiff—and fresh air and a hint of soap. And feel him, the way his hand curved around her waist as they'd danced and how his lips had encouraged hers to open. Jamie. The boy she'd always loved.

Everything about the fantasy screamed one thing—*home*.

"I would come home," she said.

You have a family who loves you here. People like you, too... I *like you, Sage. A hell of a lot.*

Jamie's words rung in her ears. For her, it was more than like. It always had been. What if it could be more for him, too? He'd asked her to stay, even offered a compromise. That meant something...didn't it?

"Your mother said something before she died," her father said, his eyes misty. "It was almost like she knew something was going to happen. She told me that I had to live like I wasn't going to have a chance to do things over, that I had one life and it needed to mean something. My life has always meant raising you girls the best I could and guiding you to find your purpose in life. For Emma, it's about helping people in their darkest moments. But for you—you help people to shine in their brightest ones. You're two sides of one coin."

Sage sniffled. "That's such a nice way of looking at it."

"You deserve those bright moments, too. And you have to take them. You can't wait for someone to hand them to you."

He was right. For a lot of her life Sage had been passive, allowing the opinions of others to guide her like they were the ocean and she was merely a buoy bobbing around, waiting to be pushed this direction or that. Her career was the only exception—the one area she allowed her passion to guide her. But everything else in life—friendships, relationships, hobbies—had all fallen by the wayside.

"You give good advice," she said, reaching out to touch the screen, wishing she could hold her dad's hand. She knew more than anyone how fleeting life could be. How easily ripped from one's grasp. What if one day he wasn't there anymore? Would she regret avoiding her home? Wasting time she could have spent close to him?

"It comes with being old," he said, shooting her a wry smile.

"It comes with being *you*." She nodded. "I love you, Dad."

"I love you too, *skatten min*."

As she ended the call and closed her laptop, she sank back against the couch. Her apartment walls felt smaller than ever—but were they small like a prison or small like a protective barrier? She wasn't sure anymore.

All she knew was that something needed to change.

CHAPTER TWELVE

Two weeks later...

SAGE FELT A strange mixture of anxiousness and relief as she pulled her rental car into the driveway of the home she'd grown up in, the back seat and trunk piled high with everything she owned. Granted, most of it was her extensive wardrobe, dressmaking supplies, her industrial-strength sewing machine, serger, several bolts of Italian silk she couldn't bear to part with and one single box for her meagre kitchen supplies. Coming home was…big.

Prior to Emma's wedding, Sage would have told anyone that she'd rather ram a stiletto into her ear than *ever* move back to Reflection Bay. But now she looked at the place with fresh eyes. Why had she allowed her high school reputation to follow her around for so many years? Her own mentality had been the quicksand sticking her in place and sucking her down into doubts and fears. Jamie's impassioned speech at the wedding had opened her eyes—*she* was the one holding herself back. She was the ceiling above her head.

Could she really find the kind of success she wanted making wedding gowns in a little town the size of a postage stamp? That was unknown. But what she *did* know what that she was ready to try. One time, she'd traveled all the way across the country to visit a woman who handmade silk flowers with such realism they could be mistaken for the real thing. If people traveled to that woman for her talents, why couldn't they travel to Sage?

Besides, she was sick of feeling like she was losing the chance to spend time with her father. He was getting older and the hands of time stopped for nobody. She missed him and Emma fiercely.

And Jamie?

She'd missed him too, these past weeks. As inconvenient as the feeling had been, she couldn't deny its existence. But it had taken a new perspective to help her see that she was at risk of losing something wonderful.

And like a sign from the universe, the day she'd Skyped with her father, she'd received an email that felt like it was the final shove in that direction.

Sage,

I got your email from your old boss. I know you've had a lot of scrutiny for speaking out at my wedding, but I wanted to say thank you for speaking up when you did. I had no idea that Julia was cheating on me, and it turns out this was not the first time. Or the second or third. You've saved me a world of pain from marrying someone who would never uphold our vows and I cannot adequately express my gratitude.

Most people probably wouldn't have had the guts to do what you did. I have no idea how I can ever repay you. All I can do is hope that you have a life of good things waiting in front of you. I hope we both do.

Thomas

Her life in New York didn't feel like a life with good things ahead of it. But coming home did. Coming home to her family, to Jamie, to the possibility of starting her own business and designing her own dresses and being her own boss where nobody could ever fire her again.

That felt like a life with good things.

She pushed open the car door in time to see her dad come out of the house, ruddy-cheeked and grinning from ear to ear. "You're finally home."

Her dad held his arms open and she rushed forward, allowing herself to be pulled into a bear hug. She was never going to let her doubts keep her away from her family ever again.

As for Jamie…well, all she could do was hope that she hadn't missed her chance with him. Maybe now that they'd both said "no" when they really wanted to say "yes," they'd be back on equal footing. And maybe now that she could finally separate the past from the present, she could be the kind of girl who took the bull by the horns to have it all.

JAMIE AND FLASH finished their walk through the wooded area behind his house, taking the trail all the way down to one of the lakes. It was mercifully cool today and the dog seemed happy to be outside again, though the walk had clearly tuckered him out. Before his health scare, Jamie would *never* have taken time to get some fresh air and do something as leisurely as a Flash-speed walk for the fun of it. In the old days, he would have preferred a few rounds with the punching bag and some free weights and then running a few miles on the tread-mill to get the "real exercise" in before he walked Flash.

But lately he'd started to see that a slower pace was… regenerative.

After the walk, he ventured back into his former storage room—now memorabilia room—to admire the new display cases with all the most important parts of his history. He was no longer going to pretend like that part of his life didn't exist. Jamie was proud of what he'd achieved in his tennis career, even if that part of his life was over. Just because he hadn't achieved all of his goals didn't mean that none of it counted. Thanks to Sage, he could see that.

Jamie grabbed a quick shower before heading to the pub to meet Clay. He'd returned from his honeymoon with Emma the evening before and Jamie had promised he wouldn't set foot into the gym while Clay was away. And he hadn't. He'd left the business in the capable hands of his wonderful staff members. For the first time in as long as Jamie could remember, work had been the last thing on his mind.

The warm glow of the pub's interior lighting beckoned him inside and he was already looking forward to downing a few beers with his best friend. The place was packed, with every table cluttered with glasses and plates, raucous laughter ringing in the air and a good vibe of general merriment making Jamie smile as he tried to locate his drinking buddy. He spotted Courtney sitting with some friends, wearing a dress that was made for catching attention, and she looked in his direction, her smile dimming. They hadn't spoken since Clay and Emma's wedding.

The only woman on Jamie's mind these past few weeks had been Sage. He'd picked up the phone to call her *so* many times before chickening out. He found

himself wanting to share every little thing with her—
the cool bird he'd spotted on his walk, the funny things
Flash did in his sleep, a great new song he'd heard on
the radio.

She hates this place. She's never coming back.

And Jamie could never leave. His business with Clay
was super important to him and Jamie couldn't bear
the thought of being away from his family, either. His
life was here.

He just wished that life included her, too.

But he also understood why this was a place of bad
memories for her. Just like it had taken him a long time
to be able to unbox his trophies and be proud of his
past, she had to change her perspective on this place
or else it would always be a demon to her. And nobody
could force her through that process. It had to come
from within.

He spotted Clay perched on one of the high tables,
wearing a brightly colored and very patterned shirt that
would look ridiculous on anyone but him.

"Hey, man," Jamie said, clapping his hand against
Clay's in greeting. Clay patted him strongly on the back.
"Cool shirt."

"You like the drip?"

"I do. It's wild, but it suits you." Jamie slid onto one
of the stools.

As he got settled, Clay pulled something out of his
pocket and slid it across the table. It was a key.

"What's that for?" Jamie asked.

"It's for the new locks at the office."

"Ah, so I've been granted access again?"

"I heard from the crew that you kept away while I
was gone. In fact, Sara told me she saw you and Flash

by the small lake having a picnic." Clay raised an eyebrow. "And you were just...sitting there."

Jamie chuckled. "I was getting my zen on."

"Now I *know* you've changed."

"You were right, you know." Jamie let out a sigh. "Not to lock me out against my will, but... I'm glad you did. I needed the time. Work was starting to overtake everything and I wanted so bad to see our little gym soar that I was putting a stupid amount of pressure on myself."

"It *will* soar," Clay said with a confident nod. "And we don't need to kill ourselves to make it happen. Good work stands out."

"True." Jamie scooped up the key. "But I'm glad to be back."

"Me too, bro."

He was about to grab the menu when he noticed a figure hovering close by. He blinked. Then shook his head. A woman wearing a pretty floral dress, white-blond hair falling softly around her shoulders, and a tentative smile dancing on her lips.

"Sage?" He blinked. Had he gone *too* zen and started seeing things?

"Hi, Jamie." She fiddled with the strap on the bag hanging over one shoulder. "Can we talk?"

"I, uh...have to do a thing." Clay bailed before Jamie even had the chance to process what was going on.

Jamie slid off his stool. "Yeah, sure. Outside?"

"We can talk here."

A few tables away, he spotted some people watching them. Folks he knew from high school—former cheerleaders, football players, party animals. They all watched on with undisguised curiosity. But Sage didn't seem to notice them. In fact, her gaze was so intense it felt like the only thing she could see was him.

"What are you doing here?" he asked. "I thought you said that…"

The only thing that will bring me back here is my dad or my sister needing me. That's it. Otherwise, I'd be happy never to set foot in this place ever again.

"Is your dad—"

"He's fine." She held up a hand to halt his concern. "I'm back…for me."

He frowned. "Why?"

"When I got to New York, I realized that living there was more about *not* being here. By going back there I was…running away. Just like I did when I finished school." She shook her head. "I never wanted to leave my family, but I felt like I had to go somewhere else if I wanted to be a different person. If I wanted any chance of being successful then it couldn't happen here where people would always see me as an outcast."

"You shouldn't regret pursuing your dreams," he said.

"I don't. And I don't regret going to Paris or New York." She bit down on her bottom lip. "But I *do* regret keeping away from Reflection Bay when I didn't want to, just because I was scared of what people would say if they saw me here. I let my insecurities separate me from my family. I let bullies chase me out of town for good."

It made Jamie want to throw something. The way she'd been treated was abhorrent. To think, all the years she'd lived away from the people she loved because she was frightened of being ridiculed…

"What changed?"

"Spending time with you recently was the first time I realized that nobody is perfect."

He raised an eyebrow and let out a self-conscious laugh. "Why do I feel like I should be insulted?"

She waved her hands as if trying to scrub the words away. "What I mean is… I've always thought you were perfect. A golden boy. That you could do no wrong. I thought your success was carved into stone a long time ago and that was it. Who we were as kids were who we would become as adults, which meant I was *always* destined to be the outcast."

He shook his head. "That's not how life works."

"I know—you *showed* me that. You lost something very dear to you and yet you picked yourself up and made a new path with the gym. You pivoted and you were resilient. You *changed* your course when the old path didn't suit you anymore."

"Yeah." He bobbed his head. "I did."

"And you came back here even when you were worried that people might point and laugh." Her eyes glittered. "That was so brave. I have always wanted to be brave like that."

"But you *are*," he said huskily. "You moved to another continent all on your own. You forged a career that took you all over the world. You made something of yourself."

"But I've been holding myself back." She shook her head. "Hiding in the back of an atelier, working only behind the scenes, never pushing for promotion or recognition. Never betting on myself. But you've shown me what can happen when you bet on yourself, Jamie. You've shown me that it's possible to pick yourself up and try again."

"So you're back? For good?" He almost couldn't believe it. "For *you*?"

She nodded. "I'm going to start my own business, make my own bridal gown designs. I'm going to bet on myself like you did with the gym."

"I'm so happy for you."

Tears sparkled in her eyes. "Thank you for helping me see that I could come home."

He wanted to pull her in close and wrap his arms around her. But then he remembered where they were—in the middle of the town watering hole with packed tables around them. What if she'd come to tell him her plans as a friend? What if she was trying to establish boundaries?

"I, uh…" Suddenly he felt like the one who was tripping over his words. "Clay let me back in the gym today."

Sage laughed. "That's good news."

"I guess I proved I wasn't going to have another meltdown." He raked a hand through his hair. "But I'm glad he did what he did. I need to make some changes. No… I am *going* to make some changes. I'm cutting my client list down and taking more days off."

"I'm so glad to hear that."

"I may have helped you, but…you helped me, too. Doing the dancing lessons with you and spending time together was the first time I'd looked forward to something other than work in a long time. It made me see what I might miss out on if I kept going down the same path."

"I'm proud of you." She smiled and it was like pure afternoon sunshine—warm, rejuvenating. Healing.

He couldn't let this conversation finish without

knowing where she stood—where *they* stood. Because the part of his life he'd neglected—relationships, love—it felt so important now. So critical.

But it meant nothing without her.

"I know you're making a lot of changes and it's a huge upheaval coming back here. And I know you might still be tempted to hide in the shadows for a while…" He let out a breath. "But I meant what I said. You have *always* been special to me, even though I was too chickenshit to tell you in high school. What we have…it's not just a teenage crush."

"It sure as heck was a crush for me," she said, gazing up into his eyes. "I was just hoping that one day you would notice me sitting alone in the cafeteria. Maybe I'd wear the right dress and bam! Suddenly I'd be the girl of your dreams."

"This isn't one of those movies where the girl takes her glasses off and suddenly the guy sees that she's beautiful. I've known you were beautiful the whole time."

"Jamie, I've cared about you since we were kids. Now that I'm home…" She looked up at him and his heart felt like it was about to burst. "Can we try again? I'd hate to think I blew it because I was too scared of what people might think. I… I want to be with you."

"I want to be with you too, Sage."

She pushed up onto her tiptoes and wrapped her arms around his neck right there in front of everyone. Without hesitation. Without her eyes darting around, worried about who was watching. In that moment she was taking the wheel of destiny, and it seemed like she didn't care one bit who saw.

There was no stopping her now.

He bundled Sage up in his arms and held her tight, crushing his lips to hers, kissing her in front of the whole town. There was cheering in the background and he was pretty sure he heard Clay yelling "Get some!" But none of that mattered. What mattered was that their kiss was heaven. It was fire and sunshine and all necessary things. And all the regrets he'd held—about rejecting her and his sporting career being cut short and being Jamie Can't-Hackett—all vanished into dust.

She'd shown him there was more to life than chasing success. Than work. Than goals and deadlines and contracts and profit. He wanted to indulge in life's pleasures now. With her. And he wanted to see her soar.

"I'm so glad you're back," he whispered, planting kisses along the edge of her jaw and sliding his hands into her hair. "I've missed you for so long."

"I've missed you, too." She tipped back her head, staring up at him with eyes open and full of love. "Thank you for giving me my home back."

"You got it back yourself. That was all you." He leaned in to kiss her again. "And I can't wait to see what you can build here."

As his lips brushed hers, the din of the pub—the music, the laughter, the clinking of glasses—all faded away. Second chances were life's blessing. A do-over. A fresh start. A way to learn and grow and find joy after loss. He knew, without a shadow of a doubt, that he and Sage would never take that for granted.

The past was finally where it belonged, and they had their eyes fully on the future.

* * * * *

Please turn the page for an excerpt from
The Dachshund Wears Prada, USA TODAY
*bestselling author Stefanie London's hilarious
and heartwarming story of a social media
consultant who goes from working with movie
stars to baby-sitting a foul-tempered
Dachshund—and falling for her owner.*

CHAPTER ONE

Theo Garrison had never felt so uncomfortable in a suit in all his life, which was saying something, given an ex-girlfriend had once asked him if he exited the womb wearing a three-piece. But today it felt like his signature outfit was suffocating him, despite being tailored to his exact measurements. He reached up to his shirt collar and hooked his finger over the edge, tugging in a desperate attempt to find relief. But none came.

Maybe it wasn't the suit at all.

Maybe it was being surrounded by two hundred people. *Too* many people, for such an event. Theo avoided large gatherings where possible. But not today. Today, he was here to honor his grandmother, and she never did anything without a crowd.

Not even dying.

He tugged at his collar again. The sun beat down relentlessly and agitation prickled along his skin as the priest talked about his grandmother's life. The weight of curious eyes made him antsy. He hated being watched. Hated that people looked at him as they might a reptile in an enclosure, tapping on the glass to see how he'd react. Thankfully, Etna Francois-Garrison had been commanding most of the attention today, which Theo was sure had been her goal.

Otherwise why choose to be buried in a Valentino ball gown?

The casket—now closed after a viewing period earlier that morning—was pure white, lined with pale pink silk and studded with glinting stones that Theo was pretty sure were real diamonds. Frankly, as executor of his grandmother's estate, he'd barely even looked at the list of requests when it had come time to sign off. Whatever his grandmother wanted, she would have. No request too outrageous. It was the last time he'd ever get to say yes to her. The last time he'd ever get to show her how important she was to him.

After all, when his parents had died, leaving him orphaned at the tender age of ten, she'd taken him in. She'd been his mother, father, grandparent, confidant. His whole family. Only *she* could have filled so many roles, with personality left over for more.

Theo swallowed. A lump was firmly lodged in the back of his throat and a yawning sense of loss roared like an open cavity in his chest. But he stood tall, with shoulders back and squared, and eyes drilling a line straight ahead.

"If the family could please come forward to pay a final tribute," the priest said, gesturing to Theo.

The family. It was a word that belonged to a group. But he was the only person who stepped forward. This was it, the entire Garrison family reduced to a single person. A Manhattan legacy hanging by a thread.

Theo walked toward the priest, who stood next to a small portable table. It was piled with roses. Not red, because his grandmother hated a cliché. Not white or yellow, because those seemed too sad. But a hot pink so bright they seemed artificial. Theo took one, noting how the thorns had been carefully removed. His thumb skated over a spot of raw green where the sharp edge had been sliced off.

"Goodbye, Gram," he said as he tossed it into the open space where the casket had been lowered into the ground. The rose landed softly on the shuttered white lid. "Say hi to everyone for me."

He reached for another rose, and then another, tossing one in for each of the people who should have been by his side—his mother, father and grandfather, all taken too soon. All gone before they'd lived a full life.

Theo stepped back, thankful he'd remembered to wear a pair of sunglasses. He liked having a shield between him and the world at the best of times, but he needed it now more than ever.

When the service concluded, people came to pay their respects. His hand was pumped over and over, cheeks kissed in sweeping, perfumed grazes. Theo had spotted plenty of familiar faces today. The funeral was a who's-who of New York society—fashion designers, politicians, blue bloods—which was exactly how his extroverted, attention-loving grandmother would have wanted it.

It didn't matter that he would rather be alone to say his goodbyes. Today was about her. Letting out a long breath, he stuffed his hands into the pockets of his suit pants as he waited for the gravesite to empty.

"She was a magnificent woman," Father Ahern said, walking over and laying a comforting hand on Theo's shoulder. "Incomparable. Truly one of a kind."

"I know." He nodded.

"She used to come to my service every Sunday and sit in the front row. Nobody dared to take her spot, even if she was late." The older man chuckled and folded his hands in front of his robes. "The one time a few kids *did* sit there, she shooed them away with her purse. It was like watching someone scatter a flock of seagulls. Nobody tried again after that."

Theo smiled. He could easily picture it. She was like that—a woman who commanded others. A powerhouse, even back when women were rarely in charge. And recently, a Goliath as she battled illness until her last breath.

"You never attended with her," Father Ahern commented.

"I don't like crowds."

"Think of it as more of a community."

Theo watched the last few people trickle down to the town cars lining the road that wound through the cemetery. He caught a glimpse of the media further back, only stopped from getting closer because of the burly security guards he'd hired for the day. The vultures waited with cameras poised, cementing Theo's belief that there was one thing in the world that sold better than sex.

Grief.

"I don't really like communities, either," Theo replied.

That was putting it mildly. Barring today, he couldn't remember the last time he'd been in a room with more than three people—outside work. And it wasn't by accident.

The priest frowned. "I know losing your parents the way you did must have been hard."

"It was a long time ago." And he still woke with night terrors about it, even now, a quarter of a century later. He'd never get the image out of his head—the mangled car, blood splattered against the windows. Every news outlet had plastered it with bold headlines and people reacted with shocked faces like nobody had seen it coming.

Hollywood sweetheart and New York royalty pronounced dead at the scene.

His heart clenched. His mother and father *had* seen it coming. They'd taken preventive measures to avoid the paparazzi and their increasingly intrusive, aggressive behavior. Decoy cars, unfamiliar routes, evasive driving…right into the side of a bridge.

So yeah, Theo had a bit of a problem with the media. He also had a problem with people poking their noses into his private life. He discouraged that by keeping to himself. It wasn't personal, though. It was protection.

"It's okay to grieve," the priest said. "God gave us emotions for a reason and sadness is natural."

Before he had a chance to say anything further, Frank Ferretti appeared beside them. He was dressed in all black, which was appropriate for a funeral but also completely on-brand for the older Italian man. He'd been a longtime family friend, initially a bodyguard to Theo's mother and then a right-hand man and confidant to his grandmother.

"Ready?" Frank asked. "I've got a car waiting for you."

Theo stuck his hand out to the priest. "Thank you, Father. It was a wonderful service. You did her memory proud."

"If you change your views on community, I'd love to have you as part of ours."

Theo nodded, though he knew deep down nothing

would change. Ever since he was a child, he drew a circus wherever he went. Today was no different. Next week would be no different. It would never be different until he was the one closed inside a casket and buried six feet under.

It was easier to keep to himself.

"This way." Frank led Theo through the family plot, where his grandmother had been laid to rest with her husband and Theo's parents. They moved away from the road, cutting through a section of manicured garden and slipping into a gap in a hedge. Sunlight streamed down, warming the back of Theo's neck and shoulders. Reminding him that even on his darkest days, the world still turned.

Behind them came the annoyed cries of the media as they realized they weren't going to get their scoop. Frank and Theo hurried to the waiting car and slipped inside as a few photographers made it through the hedge behind them. Flashes went off, but they peeled away, causing Theo to white-knuckle the door handle.

Usually, his drivers were under strict instruction to *not* go fast. But these weren't usual circumstances. The car navigated the road out of Green-Wood's main entrance and soon they were leaving Brooklyn in the rearview mirror as they crossed the bridge back into Manhattan. Mercifully, it seemed as though the press hadn't kept up. Not that it stopped Theo looking over his shoulder.

He *always* looked over his shoulder.

"They only do this shit because you insist on being such a mystery," Frank muttered. "The quieter you are, the more desperate they are to get information."

"Let them be desperate. I'm not going to give them a damn thing."

Frank let out a raspy laugh. He had a voice as rough as alligator skin. "You know, I read an article about you the other day."

"Really?" Theo raised a brow. "Are they still rehashing the same old shit? Because I certainly haven't given them anything new to talk about."

"They called you the Hermit of Fifth Avenue."

"It has quite a ring to it." He glanced at Frank. "I also liked Most Mysterious Man in Manhattan. They're turning me into an urban legend."

"Don't let it go to your head."

"Never." Theo watched Manhattan roll slowly past them. There were times when this place felt like a shoebox, which would sound ridiculous to any normal person. But there was something about the way the towers reached up to the sky that reminded Theo of bars on a cage. "I'm really going to miss her."

"I know." Frank laid a heavy hand on Theo's shoulder. "Me too."

The car continued to work its way through the city, and as the Upper East Side got closer, Theo leaned his head back against the headrest. The weight of the past few weeks crushed down on him and brought a sense of exhaustion and finality that penetrated his bones.

It was over now. She was really gone.

"It won't take long to go through the final bits and pieces," Frank promised, as if sensing Theo's thoughts. "I found a few more old photos and some letters in a drawer. I thought you might want them."

"Honestly, I'm beat. I'll come by tomorrow after work to sort through the last of it."

"Sure, but you still have to pick up the dog."

Theo snapped his head toward the other man. Clearly his lack of sleep was getting to him even more than he realized. "The dog?"

"Yeah, the dog." Frank looked at him like he'd sprouted a second head and started speaking Elvish. "Camilla? You know, little torpedo of fluff with the disposition of a belligerent drunk in a bar fight. Teeth as sharp as needles. Invisible horns and devil tail…any of this ringing a bell?"

"I'm familiar," he said, shuddering. His grandmother's dog was as notorious for her bad attitude as Theo was for his privacy. "But why do I need to pick her up?"

Frank was still giving him that look. The look that said he could see Theo's lips moving but he didn't understand a word coming out of his mouth.

"Because," the older man said, stretching the word out like he was speaking to a small child. "You are now the proud owner of one pampered devil princess."

"What?" Theo blinked and shook his head. "Since when?"

"Since you signed off on all the paperwork for the estate. Remember, the lawyers went through your grandmother's will and all the donations she wanted to make and—"

"Yes, yes." Theo waved a hand. "I remember that meeting. But I *don't* remember anything about the dog."

To be fair, he'd been in such a daze that day. His grandmother had updated her will right before she passed, since Theo was adamant that a good portion of her money go to the charities she supported. He was wealthy in his own right, these days, and he didn't need more from her. But it had been hard to concentrate, the grief already freezing him before she died. It had been like trying to think through thick fog and all he really remembered was saying "yes, of course" over and over and over.

But adopting that tiny hellhound? Surely, he would have remembered *that*.

"It was under the list of heirloom possessions to remain in the family." Frank scrubbed a hand along his jaw.

"Heirloom possessions?" Theo sucked in a quick breath through his teeth. "Are you fucking kidding me? Heirlooms are things like antique watches and family photo albums and embroidered goddamn table linens. Not pets."

And definitely not *this* pet. Heirloom, his ass.

"She was on the list," Frank said stubbornly. "Do you make a habit of signing things without reading the fine print? Your grandfather would have something to say about that."

No, Theo never signed a thing without first using his eagle eye to parse the terms. But these had been unusual circumstances—he'd wanted to give his grandmother everything before she left this earth. He'd wanted to make her as happy and comfortable and appreciated in her final days as possible. He wanted to be the perfect grandson one last time. But he damn well *should* have noticed if she was trying to foist that awful animal on him, even with the mental fog.

Yet she hadn't said a word about it to Theo directly.

Which meant his sweet, yet cunning grandmother had purposefully hidden her pampered pooch in the fine print so Theo wouldn't notice. Because as much as he wanted to make her happy, there's no way he would have agreed to this. No way in hell.

Theo's life ran like clockwork, because he stuck to a very strict set of rules:

1. No interviews.
2. No surprises.
3. No relationships.
4. No exceptions.

The last point on that list was especially important. Which was going to pose a problem. A four-legged, glossy-maned, foul-tempered problem.

"I can't believe this," Theo said, shaking his head.

Frank sighed. "Let's see what happens when we get to her place, okay?"

"Fine."

By the time Theo and Frank made it into his grandmother's brownstone on the Upper East Side, Theo felt like his head was going to explode. The place was almost empty now, since an army of staff had spent the last week packing up her impressive art collection and all the antique furniture. Most items were being donated to museums or charity auctions, although some close friends had been allocated special pieces in the will. Her extensive wardrobe of couture clothing had been curated for a display at the Fashion Institute of Technology, and the jewels were going to the Metropolitan Museum of Art.

Well, all except her wedding ring. That one was tucked away in Theo's private safe along with the one worn by his mother for sentimental reasons *only*. Neither of them would ever again grace a woman's finger.

Everything else was checked and accounted for. Boxes were neatly labeled and piled into stacks depending on who would come to collect them. The office had been locked up, awaiting a final sweep by Theo to make sure all the important paperwork went to him.

Everything had been going according to plan…until now.

Theo's footsteps echoed through the mostly empty space, the sound bouncing off the high ceilings. The place looked cavernous without her. It was a shell, with no life and no light and no joy.

"You're early!" A woman emerged from the sitting room. "I wasn't expecting you back for another hour."

Theo didn't recognize her, but Frank was quick to make an introduction. "This is Marcie. She's been looking after Camilla for the last few weeks, ever since your grandmother went into hospital."

"I'm very sorry for your loss." Marcie bowed her head. "And I'm sorry that I had to insist on dropping Camilla off today. I know it's a difficult time. But I… can't do this anymore."

At that moment, as if summoned by a sound no human could hear, or perhaps by the devil himself, Camilla entered the room. The Dachshund was less than a ruler's length in height, with stumpy little legs that made her waddle with each step. Despite that, you would have thought the Queen of England had entered the room.

In fact, for a minute Theo was sure he'd heard trumpets announcing her arrival. Or was that simply warning sirens going off in his brain?

Her long champagne-colored fur was brushed and gleaming, and a pink collar sat around her neck, a silver C-shaped charm dangling from the loop at the front. On first glance, one might call her cute. Or even sweet.

But more fool anyone who assumed Camilla was some passive little lap dweller ready to cuddle and beg for belly scratches.

Oh no, this tiny beast was a dictator on four legs.

"Everything you need is in the other room," Marcie said, the pitch of her voice climbing. "I've marked off where we are in her daily routine and I've packed all her things so you can take her straight home. On that note, I really need to get going. Actually, right now."

And with that, Marcie scurried from the room as though fearful someone might try to stop her. The woman clearly had an exit plan. After the sound of the front door closing echoed through the room, Theo stared at the dog.

Camilla stared back.

"Well, then…" Frank cleared his throat. "What do you want to do? I can call a shelter and have her picked up. Or I can call around Etna's friends and see if anyone will take her."

Camilla's head swung to Frank, and Theo would swear he saw the little dog's eyes narrow in fury.

In his heart of hearts, he knew he couldn't dump the dog. Not now. His grandmother had meant the world to him, and while he would absolutely have argued the point when she was alive…that was no longer an option. Which meant he only had two choices: honor her wish, or not.

"I *know* I'm going to regret this," Theo said, with a shake of his head. "But I'll take her."

"You sure?" Frank asked with a grimace. "What does it matter now? Your grandmother won't know the difference."

"Yes, but *I* will." He sighed. "Gram obviously wanted me to have her for a reason."

Both men looked at the small, sausage-shaped dog and for a moment, no one made a move. Then Camilla marched over to Theo and tipped her face up, two beady black eyes looking right into his soul as if telepathically communicating how much she hated him. Why did Theo have the feeling that this wasn't going to end well? It wasn't until a few seconds later, when the dog trotted back into the other room, nose and tail in the air, that he realized she'd peed all over his shoe.

Don't miss Stefanie London's
The Dachshund Wears Prada,
available now!